TARAN'S WHEEL

(Incomers: Book 1)

Jim Forbes

K

A Kinord Book

Published by Kinord Books
Edinburgh
www.kinordbooks.com

ISBN: 978-0-9928080-2-0

Taran's Wheel is a work of fiction. All contemporary and some
historical characters and events are fictitious and any
resemblance they may bear to real persons, living or dead, is
purely coincidental. Other historical characters and events are
based on public domain sources and are partially fictionalised.

The cover illustration (copyright © 2014 Jim Forbes) on this
edition of *Taran's Wheel* represents in silhouette the view
looking west from Tomnaverie, the more distant hills being
Morven (front cover) and Culblean (back cover). It is based on
a photograph by the author.

To Elinor
for your love, inspiration and encouragement

IT WAS A SHAME she had to die like this. On the other hand, old ladies have to die of *something*. She was almost eighty, with heart trouble, for goodness' sake. What had she to look forward to? At least she was in her own home, surrounded by her beloved possessions.

Ah, those possessions. Just one of them was what he'd asked her for, and she refused to part with it. She'd shown him it years before. Now he wanted it, had a *right* to it, even. But no, she said, after she was gone it would belong to the next Keeper. Bollocks! It sat in a box in that locked cabinet, never seeing the light of day. He, on the other hand, had found a good home for it and stood to make himself rich in the process. Still, it was a shame ...

The body was now limp and motionless in the armchair. But he kept the pillow over her face and didn't dare take his weight off it yet. She'd struggled surprisingly long, lashing out blindly with hands and feet, before that final convulsion, since when she'd been absolutely at peace. Soon he'd be able to relax, return the pillow to the guest bed – maybe change the pillowcase if need be – and then look for the key to the cabinet.

The apartment was strangely quiet. A clock ticked somewhere. Trees outside the window waved soundlessly in the wind. Footsteps and a muffled child's voice in the long hall outside the door momentarily broke the silence, but didn't alarm him. Nobody could come in.

Five minutes passed without any movement. Keeping one hand firmly on the pillow, he checked her neck and her wrist for a pulse. He could feel nothing. Gently he removed the pillow and stood back, watching her open eyes for any sign of life. Finally, satisfied she wasn't going to rear up from the armchair, he took the pillow back to the bedroom. As it was surprisingly unsoiled, he simply fluffed it up, replaced it on the bed and put the shams on top exactly as he had found them.

In the kitchen he found a pair of rubber gloves, too small for him really, but he was able to pull them on. With a can of Pledge and a duster he methodically polished all the hard surfaces he remembered touching since he arrived. Then began the search for the cabinet key.

It took about twenty minutes to find it. Still wearing the gloves, he opened the cabinet, and saw at the back of a shelf the silver box that he knew contained the old lady's most treasured object. Reaching in, he noticed for the first time that his hand was shaking. God, it had been a stressful day, hadn't it? He controlled the tremor as best he could, but still managed to knock over a couple of ugly-looking silver goblets. No problem: after lifting out the box, he set them up again.

He allowed himself a deep breath of anticipation before opening the lid of the box to look inside.

I. THE PLEASANT VALE

1

THE WRONG DOOR

AN EVENING OF DINNER, drinks and chatter with three female friends in Boulder's best Indian restaurant was just what Delia needed, now that finals were over. It had been a hard few weeks. She could have taken exam preparation in her stride, along with getting her dissertation completed. But the break-up with Erik was so unexpected, so hurtful, it had knocked her off her customary even keel.

Erik the Jerk, she now called him. Angry though she was at his sudden coolness, she was angrier at herself for having become emotionally attached to him at such a crucial stage in her life.

'Ohmygod − I can't believe it,' one of her friends told her. 'You and Erik seemed such a perfect couple. He's a good-looking guy.'

'Yeah,' another said, 'he could've been a model. That thick hair, those nice teeth, the athletic build. Bet he looks really good naked.'

Delia knew exactly what Erik looked like naked, but wasn't going to be drawn into discussion on the matter. 'You want him, you can have him,' was all she said.

'I wish,' the third chimed in.

Each of the four young women at the table was attractive in her own way, but to any observer of the group Delia would have stood out. Though she was blessed with a fine figure and a pretty face, what drew attention was her sleek, shoulder-length hair in a dramatic shade of auburn with natural streaks that changed subtly in hue under different lights. Since the age of five, she had faced ridicule, even occasional harassment, on account of her hair colour. To taunts of 'ginger' she had responded tartly that the correct word was 'titian'. As she grew up she came to understand that such name-calling was motivated primarily by other girls' envy and pubescent boys' fantasies. She felt privileged to share a rare and attractive feature with only two percent of the American population.

Bidding her companions goodnight outside the restaurant, Delia set off walking back to her studio apartment. It was a fine evening, with bright moonlight glinting off the Flatirons, those foothills of the Rockies that rise steeply from the edge of the city. She found herself taking stock of her life. A master's degree in environmental studies from the University of Colorado at Boulder would shortly be under her belt, but she had no job lined up. A couple of utility companies had offered short internships, but these didn't excite her – and wouldn't pay the bills. And, of course, the planned drive with Erik to the Canadian Arctic in a camper van after graduation was now off.

As she reached her apartment, it occurred to her that she had a past and a present, but no clear future. It was a feeling very foreign to her. Friends said of her, 'Delia always has a plan.'

Well, now she didn't.

Checking her mailbox as she entered the building, she was surprised to find an official-looking manila envelope originally addressed to Ms Delia Cobb, 1215 Hickory Trail, Geneva, Illinois 60134, and redirected to her Boulder, Colorado address. On the top left corner of the envelope was printed:

Howard A. Levine & Associates
Attorneys at Law

with an address in Dearborn Street, Chicago.

She tossed the mail on her kitchen counter, took off her light jacket and kicked off her shoes. With a mixture of curiosity and dread she opened the envelope.

Dear Ms Cobb:

I am writing with sadness to inform you of the death of Grace Rosman on May 18 at her home in Glenview, Illinois. At her express instruction, given to me when she made her will some years ago, I cannot finalize funeral arrangements until I have contacted you and verified that you will be able to attend.

As soon as you receive this letter, please call me at the number below, so that we can set a date for the funeral. I will also be able to inform you of provisions made for your benefit in Ms Rosman's will.

Sincerely,

Howard A. Levine

Delia was stunned. The last time she had visited Grace in her Glenview apartment she had seemed in reasonable health and in good spirits, despite a series of heart problems over the last few years. They had talked on the phone several times since then, and there was no indication that anything was wrong. Just a couple of weeks ago Grace had sent her a chatty email wishing her well in her exams.

If there was one person in the world whose company Delia enjoyed above everyone else's, it was Grace. Theirs was a friendship that spanned two generations – Grace was old enough to be her grandmother – and had grown from a first chance meeting when Delia was only nine.

She had a vivid recollection of that first encounter. One Sunday, she had gone with her parents to visit Grandad Cobb in his apartment in Glenview, one of the many suburbs of Chicago making up what is known as the 'North Shore'. It was Girl Scout Cookies time, and Grandad, after signing up for the obligatory two boxes, suggested she knock on Mrs Mies's door along the hall. Mrs Mies would surely take a couple of boxes. But to a nine-year-old, all the doors along the hall looked the same. She knocked on what turned out to be the wrong door.

There was a rattling sound – a chain being unlatched. Then, as the door opened, she came face to face, not with Mrs Mies, but with an elderly lady who looked at the little red-haired girl with the cookie sign-up sheet in her hand, and instantly froze. The woman's face turned ashen as if she'd seen a ghost.

Which, in a sense, she had.

Delia was frightened by her reaction, but something made her stand her ground rather than run back to Grandad's. 'I'm sorry, little girl,' the woman said, eventually. 'I didn't mean to frighten you. You see, I don't get many visitors. And none as pretty as you. What's your name?'

'Delia. Delia Cobb.'

'Ah, you must be a relation of Tony Cobb in number 307. His granddaughter, maybe?'

'Yes. Would you like to order some Girl Scout Cookies?' Delia asked boldly.

The lady laughed. 'Of course. Why don't you come in for a few minutes? I'll call your grandfather and let him know you're here. I'm Grace Rosman, but I'd love it if you just call me Grace.'

The visit lasted much longer than a few minutes. Grace was not like other 'old' people Delia knew. Not, for instance, like Grandad. Grace was fun to be with, easy to talk to. She was interested in stuff that was important to a nine-year-old. And she had a knack for making grown-up subjects interesting. Such as what the world was like long before Delia was born.

'So, Cordelia, tell me a little about yourself,' Grace said.

'I'm nine and I have no brothers or sisters. I have a cat called Audrey. My Dad named her after a film star he likes. I live in Geneva, Illinois. And my name's Delia, not Cordelia.'

A smile flickered across the woman's face. 'I'd like your permission to call you Cordelia. It's an ancient name, a regal name. When you're older, you'll hear about another Cordelia. She's very famous. One day, you may be famous, too.'

'Are you famous? Does it frighten you when people recognise you in the street? Is that why you were so scared when you saw me standing at your door?'

Grace broke into a short laugh. 'No, I'm not famous, and that's the way I like it.' Her laughter faded to a wistful smile as she said, 'I'm going to show you something that might help you understand why I behaved so strangely when I first saw you at the door.'

She took down a framed photograph from a shelf that was cluttered with small boxes, china ornaments and other things that Delia couldn't put a name to. 'Look at this photograph, and tell me who you see.'

The photograph was of a girl who appeared to be slightly older than Delia, maybe eleven or twelve. Her hair was the same golden-red colour as Delia's, and her pale skin was freckled, especially across the bridge of her nose.

'She looks a bit like me, only bigger,' Delia said.

'Well, let me tell you, at the age of nine she looked *exactly* like you. She was my daughter Selena. When she was twenty, in 1987, she died in a boating accident. Seeing you at the door, I could have sworn for an instant you were Selena, though of course that was impossible. So maybe you'll forgive me for acting so peculiar.'

'You must have been very sad.'

'Yes, for a long time. I still get sad when I think of her – which I do, every day.'

There was a moment of silence. Delia looked around the room. Against one wall was a display cabinet on a cherrywood base with three doors. Another wall was taken up by a huge glass-fronted bookcase full of books of all sizes and colours. A big window looked out over trees and rooftops.

'Let's have some lemonade,' Grace suggested.

13

2

MEMORY IN THE ROCK

FIRST TESTAMENT OF GRACE ROSMAN,
KEEPER OF TARAN'S WHEEL

T*HE PLEASANT VALE WAS BORN in an episode of unimaginable violence. An asteroid with a mass of twenty to fifty million tons slammed into the Earth, gouging a crater where gathered a molten mixture of interplanetary and terrestrial rock. The crater was almost perfectly circular, about six miles across, at the focus of an area of devastation stretching for a hundred miles or more in all directions.*

The lake of molten rock in the crater's bowl soon solidified there. But that didn't account for all of it. At the moment of impact, balls of fiery liquid, some as small as raindrops, some as big as grapefruit, were blasted into the sky, even into the coldness of space. There they quickly froze to form a kind of glass, composed of the asteroid's exotic elements thoroughly mixed with elements native to the Earth. Glass spheres, large and small, rained back down on the land, the largest ones falling closest to the crater.

The cataclysm was no recent event, even by any geological measure of time. It was the Jurassic era, a time before the Atlantic Ocean opened up between what are now Europe and North America, a time when the land that would eventually become Great Britain was a lush subtropical forest inhabited by great reptilian herbivores and their predators.

Living things, wiped out by the asteroid, gradually returned to the crater and the surrounding land, just as plants and animals colonise the initially sterile ash deposits and lava flows from today's volcanoes. But, in the fullness of geological time, forces larger than life reshaped the topography. At times, a rise in sea level inundated the land. At other times mountains were pushed up, and rivers and glaciers carved valleys in them.

Eventually the entire crater was worn away. A great river arose in mountains to the west and flowed over the exact site of the impact. Though the crater was long gone, there was memory in the rock that had once lain deep underneath and was now at the surface. Lines of weakness caused by the impact were exploited by the erosive forces of the river, forming a circular basin, an echo of the perfect circle once sculpted by the primeval asteroid.

That basin, six miles in diameter, lies in what is now a peaceful corner of Aberdeenshire in north-east Scotland, about thirty miles west of the city of Aberdeen. It's called the Howe of Cromar, and it's the Pleasant Vale of my story.

In the last million years or so, ice ages have taken their toll on the Vale. A vast ice sheet covered higher ground to the west, sending a tongue of ice eastward down the valley where once the great river flowed. Having no respect for bends in the valley, the glacier took a short cut across the southern edge of the Vale, which became a kind of frozen backwater, gradually filling with standing ice.

There's nothing new about climate change. Around ten thousand years ago, a dramatic rise in temperature saw the end of the last ice age. The glacier retreated and the now much straighter valley was reclaimed by its river – the Dee, bypassing the circular basin of Cromar it had earlier carved.

As the standing ice in the basin slowly melted, it left a deep glacial till which developed into a richly fertile soil. Large rocks brought by the ice from higher ground remained scattered across the landscape. Depressions that are now shallow lakes *or swamps mark places where the last pockets of ice finally melted.*

The Howe of Cromar is readily visible from space. Now you know where to look, you'll find it quite easy to spot its circular outline on any satellite image of Scotland.

3
A HUGE SECRET

THE CLOSE FRIENDSHIP with Grace that began at their first meeting strengthened through the years as Delia became a young woman. Somehow Grace's insistence on calling her Cordelia didn't bother her at all. As she looked back on those years, Delia herself found it odd that she had been so accepting of the name, especially in view of the variety of redhead nicknames she had attracted at school, all of which she had hated. But Cordelia – that name with its overtones of ancient royalty and (as she eventually discovered) its frisson of Shakespearean tragedy – she rather liked. It was a private joke between her and Grace, part of the bond they shared.

Even after her grandfather died, Delia continued to visit Grace on a regular basis. By that time she was old enough to ride the trains on her own. Sometimes they would meet in downtown Chicago and go to the Field Museum, the Shedd Aquarium, the Art Institute or any of a dozen lesser-known attractions of the city. A particular favourite of Grace's was the Adler Planetarium, where she introduced Delia to the stars and the movements of the sun, moon and planets through the circle of twelve constellations forming the zodiac.

But Delia's fondest memories were of the times they spent together at Grace's home in Glenview. Every visit brought a new experience. Sometimes Grace would select a book at random from her huge collection, and tell Delia a little story about the book or read from its contents.

Grace had inherited an antiquarian book business in downtown Chicago from her father Eli Rosman, and had run it for twenty years. She had made a comfortable living and could indulge her passion for books. When she turned sixty, she decided to retire. Unable to find a buyer for the business, she simply closed it and brought home a selection of books from its extensive stock.

One year on Delia's birthday, August 19th, Grace gave her a rare early edition of Charles and Mary Lamb's *Tales from Shakespeare*. Some years later, they read some of the Bard's original work together. *King Lear* was a particular favourite. One point they discussed at length was the mindset of Lear's daughter Cordelia when, early in the play, she believes her father will see through her two sisters' insincere expressions of love and decides not to join in their flattery.

What shall Cordelia do? Love, and be silent.

'You know,' Grace said, 'the *real* Cordelia survived to become queen of the British people. One day I'll tell you much more about her.'

On other visits, Grace would introduce Delia to her collection of small objects, old and new, from cultures around the world. One that Grace particularly treasured was a small earthenware jar in the shape of a bell. 'My ancestors in Scotland, long ago, were Beaker People, so called because when they died they were buried with bell-shaped beakers like this. I feel a connection across thousands of years to those people. When I die, I want this to be buried with me, though it's just a modern replica.'

'Grace, do you have anything really old, handed down from your ancestors?'

There was silence for a moment before Grace confided, 'As a matter of fact, I do. Not from the time of the bell-shaped beakers, though still a long time ago. I'm going to share a huge secret with you, Cordelia. This will be just between us.' She left the room for a few seconds and came back with a small key, with which she opened the middle door in the cherrywood unit – the hutch, she called it – below her display cabinet. A set of four silver goblets were arranged in a line at the front of the hutch, and partially hidden behind them was an oval silver box that Grace said was a tea-caddy.

'These four cups – are they very old?' Delia asked.

'What they represent is very old, but the goblets themselves, the cups as you call them, are not. I bought them at a place called Glastonbury in England on one of my trips over there. See, bring out the one at the far left and let's look at it.'

Embossed on one side of the silver goblet was a naked bearded male figure, resting one hand on a six-spoked wheel and with the other hand releasing a lightning-bolt. This was the traditional representation of the Celtic god Taran, sometimes called Tar or Taranis. Images of Taran were always accompanied by a wheel and a bolt of lightning. The lightning symbol was easy to understand: Taran was a thunder-god, a counterpart of the Scandinavian god Thor. But the wheel was more mysterious. Some representations of Taran's wheel showed eight or more spokes, but on this goblet the wheel had exactly six, typical of the particular branch of Celtic culture developed by Grace's ancestors. Six was a magic number in that culture.

The back of the goblet bore an unmistakable representation of a bull. A symbol of masculinity to be sure, but with additional significance. 'Is he Taurus the bull, from the zodiac?' Delia asked.

'Indeed he is. Take a look at the engraving on the base of the goblet.'

Delia read the word 'SAMHAIN' and said it out loud: 'Sam Hain'.

'It's pronounced "saawan",' Grace corrected her. 'One of the four great annual festivals of the ancient Celtic peoples. It was celebrated in early November, traditionally on the night of the full moon. And the full moon at that time of year is always in which sign of the zodiac, do you suppose?'

'I'm going to guess Taurus.'

'Yes. The full moon in Taurus had great significance. It was the union of female, as represented by the moon, and male – the bull. The festival of Samhain was celebrated with fire, and with sex.' Grace saw that the girl was not in the least embarrassed, and went on: 'Samhain was regarded as a propitious time for young women to give up their virginity and for couples to conceive a child. A baby born in August, having been conceived at Samhain, was often said to be a child of Taran. You, Cordelia, have an August birthday. You are in a sense Taran's child.'

The word 'propitious' was new to Delia but she got its meaning right away.

Replacing the goblet, Grace mentioned the efforts of the early Christian church to replace what it called 'pagan' festivals with feast days in honour of saints. Samhain became the feast of All Saints, but its pre-Christian origins remain to the fore in the celebration of Hallowe'en.

'What about the other three goblets?' Delia asked. 'Do they have gods on them too?'

The second goblet from the left showed a female figure, the Celtic mother-goddess whose Scandinavian counterpart is Freya or Frida. Some Celtic peoples called her Brytha, Brigta or Bride, and considered themselves to be her direct descendants. They were proud to call themselves 'Brythonic' or 'British', after Brytha.

On the back of the second goblet was a lioness and engraved on the base was the word *'IMBOLC'*. Imbolc was a festival of music and a celebration of home and hearth. It was observed in February, when the full moon was in Leo. To those who worshipped Brytha, Leo was always a she-lion. Early Christians borrowed Brytha's name and repackaged her as a saint – St Bride or St Bridget – with a feast day on the first or, more commonly, the second of February.

'Groundhog day,' Delia said.

'Yes,' Grace nodded, 'or, in Britain, Candlemas.'

Picking up the third goblet, Grace pointed out the embossed image of the sun-god Bel on the front and an eagle on the back. The base was engraved *'BELTANE'*. She explained that the constellation we call Scorpio was known by some ancient peoples as the eagle. Britain had no scorpions, and people there tended to name the constellations for more familiar animals or things.

The figure of Bel had tree branches in place of arms, reaching up to a sun symbol. According to Grace, the 'Green Man' or 'Jack-in-the-Green' featured in spring festivals still observed in many towns and villages in England was an incarnation of Bel. In the pre-Christian tradition, Beltane marked the new growing season with a celebration involving dance and nakedness. Men and women had their entire bodies painted. Beltane has persisted as the Mayday holiday and, in Germanic cultures, as Walpurgis night.

The fourth and final goblet bore an image of the god Luath, sometimes known as Lugus or Lugh, and, on the opposite side, a pitcher or water-carrier. The word engraved on the base was *'LUNASA'*. This was the festival of Luath, observed when the full moon lay in Aquarius, an August occurrence. A festival of plenty, it was celebrated with an abundance of food and drink. After the coming of Christianity Lunasa became Lammas, but few people celebrate it any more.

Interested though she was in the goblets and what they stood for, Delia was growing ever more curious about the tea-caddy behind. 'And what about the silver box? What's in there?'

Handing it to her, Grace suggested, 'Why don't you open it and see for yourself?'

Inside, nestled in styrofoam packing material, was a solid glass sphere, about the size of a baseball. Delia carefully removed it from the box. It reminded her of the 'crystal ball' she had once used as a prop in a school play.

A late afternoon sun was shining through the large window. When Delia held the object up to the light, refraction produced a curious effect. The circumference was more brightly illuminated than the rest of the sphere, except for six bluish rays of light that emanated from the centre.

'It's beautiful,' Delia said. 'What is it?'

'What does the pattern of light remind you of?'

'I dunno. A Trivial Pursuit board?'

Grace laughed. 'If I told you it was really old, from a time long before there was Trivial Pursuit, what do you think people would have imagined as they looked at the bright circle and six rays?'

'A wheel?'

'Exactly. This ball has a name, in a language that was spoken long ago in the north-east of Scotland. It's the *Drogan Taranish*.'

'Drogue and tarnish? What does that mean?'

'*Drogan* is a wheel. *Drogan Taranish* means "Taran's wheel".'

Delia held the *Drogan* for five or ten minutes, turning it slowly in her hands and observing how the six bluish rays rotated, just like spokes of a wheel.

'That glass sphere, Cordelia, has great cultural significance, and it's steeped in mythology. It has been handed down through many generations, and I am its present Keeper. If Selena had lived, she would have become the Keeper of Taran's wheel. Before I get too old, I will have to find the next Keeper.'

Grace's eyes moistened, and she fell silent for a minute. Delia continued to hold the glass ball up to the light, marvelling at the bluish glow of its six 'spokes'. At length, Grace said, 'Remember the number six, because it's an amazing number that I'll tell you about another day.'

4

OTHER PEOPLE'S WASH

A S THE ICE DISAPPEARED *from the Pleasant Vale, vegetation re-established. People began to arrive from the south, following the plants they gathered and animals they hunted into new territory.*

Initially nomadic, the group of hunting-gathering people who discovered the richness of plant and animal life in the Vale soon settled there. With only crude stone tools at their disposal, any cultivation of the soil was minimal; instead they continued to subsist on the fruits and beasts of the forest that clothed the land. Like their contemporaries in other parts of Britain, they left their mark on the landscape by the building of stone circles, though these were more modest than the great circles and avenues of Stonehenge, Callanish or Stenness. Their task was made easier by an abundant local supply of large boulders left as erratics by the melting of the ice.

Particularly large rocks were needed for a portion of each circle that faces the south-west. Here, a horizontal stone (archaeologists call it a 'recumbent') is flanked by two tall upright stones. Nobody knows exactly how the recumbent was used by the stone-age circle builders. Some have suggested that it formed a kind of altar on which sacrifices could be offered to their gods; others that it provided a frame for observing the movement of the sun, moon and stars.

The circle builders were small in stature. This alone would probably not have greatly handicapped them in an encounter with taller, stronger incomers. But a little under four thousand years ago, their fertile basin was invaded by a new race of people who not only were taller and stronger, but possessed a new technology that totally outclassed the stone tools and weapons of the circle builders. That technology was the making and working of bronze.

The incomers who brought the bronze age to the Howe of Cromar were Beaker People. Their arrival coincided with a change in the climate, which became cooler and wetter. Trees died in the forests that the hunting-gathering circle builders had relied on for their food and shelter. The hardier Beaker People further accelerated deforestation in the lower parts of Cromar, using their bronze tools to clear the land and work the fertile soil.

Mark Twain wrote in his 1897 book Following the Equator:

All the territorial possessions of all the political establishments in the earth consist of pilferings from other people's wash. No tribe, however insignificant, and no nation, however mighty, occupies a foot of land that was not stolen.

There is no doubt the Beaker People stole the land they occupied from the neolithic circle builders – the Little Folk, as they called them. But, like tribes around the world that have believed in a Promised Land and driven others from it, the Beaker People believed they had a god-given right, in their case a right guaranteed by their great thunder-god, to the circular basin of Cromar.

He, after all, had made the circular basin, the Pleasant Vale as it came to be called in the Beaker People's language. And it was for them he had made it. The Little Folk who went before worshipped strange gods and spirits and knew nothing of the thunder-god. Clearly, the Pleasant Vale had not been made for the Little Folk. They were merely temporary occupants until the Beaker People arrived to claim it.

24

Tall, heavy-boned and muscular people live in and around the Howe of Cromar to this day. Their hardiness and no-nonsense work ethic quite possibly derive, just like their physical appearance, from their Beaker ancestors.

Like most cultures, the people of the Pleasant Vale had a creation myth that passed from one generation to the next. The thunder-god, so their myth went, stood on a hilltop at Samhain, just before dawn. Turning his back on the brightening sky where soon the sun would rise, he watched the full moon go down, then unleashed a huge thunderbolt, directed at the place where the land had just swallowed the moon. When the smoke and dust had cleared, he saw that he had created a beautiful circular vale that would be a homeland for his chosen people.

The Beaker tribe who settled in the Howe of Cromar built three great stone cairns. One was on the hilltop some distance from the Howe where they believed the god had stood when he launched his thunderbolt. Another marked the very centre of the Howe, the point where they believed the thunderbolt had struck. That point is on the summit of a low ridge now known as Drummy. And a third lay at the rim of the Howe, on the flank of a hill called Craig Dhu, where according to tradition the first Beaker People entered their new homeland.

The earliest Beaker settlement in Cromar was around the great central cairn on Drummy. Traces of huts and animal enclosures can still be seen there. But spirits of the Little Folk haunted the place, so the Beaker tribe moved to a new location a short distance away on the other side of running water, which they believed the spirits were unable to cross. That became the cultural centre of the Pleasant Vale. It was their Eden.

On a still night, they would look from the safety of their Eden towards the marshy land across the stream, and know that the spirits were abroad. They could see their eerie, fleeting glimmer. The land across the stream became known as the Ghost Meadow. Older children told younger ones gruesome tales of the Little Folk and their ghosts, just to frighten them.

5
MORE THAN A FEELING

IN HOWARD LEVINE'S OFFICE in the Chicago Loop, the attorney filled Delia in on the details. Grace had been alone on the afternoon of Sunday May 18th when she died of a heart attack; her cleaning girl had found her dead in her living room the next morning. A memorial service would be held on the 27th ('That's tomorrow,' Levine reaffirmed) at the Northbrook Hilton, followed by cremation of the body.

'Cremation?' Delia queried. 'Didn't Grace specify burial? She always had the idea of being buried with a bell-shaped beaker in the manner of her ancestors.'

'She expressed no preference in her will,' Levine responded. 'And I've been in touch with her closest relatives, who are coming in from England. Her cousin, Mrs Woods, assured me that Ms Rosman would have chosen cremation. In any case, everything is arranged.'

Grace rarely spoke of her English relatives, and seemed not to care much for them. Delia recalled mention of Loretta Woods, her husband and four sons, only one of whom ever visited. She remembered his name because it was a little unusual. Cato. He travelled to the U.S. on business sometimes and, when in the Chicago area, would drop in, usually unannounced. She had seen his photograph but had never met him.

'Well,' Delia said, 'I suppose the beaker could be interred with Grace's ashes.' She felt uncomfortable that Levine was taking too much account of the cousin's advice, but decided to leave it at that.

'Yes, that could be arranged, I'm sure. Now, Ms Cobb, turning to the subject of the will, you'll be pleased to know that Ms Rosman's entire estate, except for a small bequest to her cleaning maid, goes to you. It will all have to go through probate, of course, but I see no reason why you can't use Ms Rosman's apartment in the meantime. Here are the keys.'

Within the hour, Delia was at Grace's door. She steeled herself as she turned the key in the lock, but as soon as she entered the apartment, tears came to her eyes. The full reality of Grace's death hit her for the first time. That she would inherit essentially all of Grace's worldly possessions was totally unexpected, but brought her little comfort at that moment.

She began to look around the apartment. It was very tidy. The carpets had been recently vacuumed and there was a faint smell of furniture wax. There was no milk or other perishable food in the refrigerator, but the freezer was well stocked. A few dollars and some loose change lay on the kitchen counter, on top of some items of mail that had been awaiting Grace's attention.

In the living room a reclining chair faced the window, as always. Grace had loved to sit in that chair. The young Delia, on her frequent visits, would pull up alongside her, and the two of them would talk for hours about every subject under the sun. A more formal rectangular arrangement of sofa, loveseat and armchair occupied the centre of the room, but the only time Grace ever sat there was when entertaining company. Delia wasn't 'company' in that sense. She had always been welcome to share Grace's private space by the window.

The wall of books, the displays of ornaments and other knick-knacks – all seemed as Delia remembered. The cherrywood hutch, where Grace had kept Taran's wheel in its silver box, had always been securely locked and the key hidden in another room – even Delia had never found out where. But she was surprised to notice a key in the lock.

She opened the door of the hutch. There was the set of four silver goblets with their symbols of the four ancient Celtic festivals and their associated gods. And behind them, the oval silver tea-caddy. Carefully she lifted it out. Even before she opened it she knew from its weight that it was empty.

At first she did not feel unduly concerned that the *Drogan* was not in its place. Perhaps Grace had put it with other valuables in a safe deposit box at the bank, or hidden it somewhere in the apartment. She surely wouldn't have sold it or given it away. Unless, of course, she had identified the next Keeper of Taran's wheel and passed it on. Though if she had, wouldn't she have mentioned it? Setting the empty box back in its place, Delia noticed that the goblets in front weren't perfectly aligned the way Grace had always liked them to be. She straightened them up.

But something gave her an uneasy feeling. It was not just the key in the lock of the hutch, nor the silver box being empty, nor the unequal spacing of the goblets which should stand like soldiers on parade, guarding the box behind them.

Grace had always arranged the silver goblets in a particular order. Taran, then Brytha, then Bel, then Luath. This was the order of the annual festivals honouring each of these four gods in turn – Samhain in November, Imbolc in February, Beltane in May, Lunasa in August. A few years earlier, Delia had once polished them and replaced them in the wrong sequence, and Grace had made it very clear that they had to be repositioned correctly.

Yet the Brytha and Bel goblets had swapped position. Someone other than Grace had moved them. The someone, no doubt, who had found the hutch key and left it in the lock, and might now be in possession of Taran's wheel.

As she pondered this disturbing thought, she heard the apartment door open. A young woman with long black hair came in. Suddenly seeing Delia gave her a start.

'Lupita! Hi ... I'm Delia. Remember me? I met you once when I was visiting Grace. Maybe a year ago?'

28

'Yes ... now I remember. I'm so sad Grace has passed away.'

Lupita had done cleaning and other housework for Grace over several years. They got on so well together that Lupita's twice-weekly visit became almost like a social occasion. Grace would practise her Spanish with her, learning to speak the language with Mexican idiom and intonation.

Delia explained that she was to inherit the apartment, though at that moment she had no plans to live there. She told Lupita she would like her to continue coming in, maybe once a week. 'The place is very fresh. You must have done some cleaning after they took the body away.'

Lupita burst into tears. 'Yes,' she sobbed, 'I did it yesterday. And I did the laundry too. You know, her bed linen and so on. I just came back to iron and put it away.'

'That was very thoughtful of you. And I know you did some dusting and polishing. I smelled the furniture polish when I came in.'

'Yes. It was a job Grace must have started before she ... before she became ill. She had done some of the surfaces, but not everywhere. The door handles too. It was a job she usually left for me. Anyway, I finished it for her.'

Delia gave Lupita a hug. After a moment's silence, the young Mexican said, 'You know, I'm the one who found her ... dead.'

'Yes, I heard. It must have been such a shock for you.'

'At first I thought she was having a nap. But when I tried to wake her ...' Lupita's voice trailed away.

'Was she there in her favourite chair by the window?'

'No, over on that armchair.' Lupita pointed to the formal seating area.

Now Delia had *more* than a feeling. Someone must have been here with Grace, maybe shortly before she died ... or maybe even at the moment of her death. If Grace was in the formal seating area, it meant she had company.

'Lupita, do you know if anyone called on Grace that day?'

'I saw no one.'

'When you found her, was there any sign that she'd had company? Maybe coffee cups on the table or on the kitchen counter? Or a little gift someone brought?'

'Why do you ask these things? You think someone came here and killed her?' Lupita became distressed again. She crossed herself.

'I don't know what to think, Lupita. All I know is, Grace wouldn't have been sitting over there unless she had a visitor.' Delia paused. 'How about the hutch? Did you do any cleaning inside there?'

'Oh no. Grace always did that herself. I never got to touch it. When I was dusting yesterday, I saw the key was in the lock, and I thought that was strange. But I didn't look inside.'

Delia suddenly had another thought. When Grace was alone in the house, she always fastened the security chain on the inside of the apartment door. Lupita found her body, yet how had she been able to get in?

'Usually I knock, and she takes the chain off to let me in. But last Monday, she didn't come to the door when I knocked. I guessed she was out and the chain would be off, so I used my key. As soon as I came in, I saw Grace in the armchair.'

It was all starting to make sense, in a way Delia didn't like. Maybe Grace had a visitor, somebody she allowed into her apartment, somebody she knew. Somebody who left her dead in that armchair. Somebody, it occurred to her, who may have taken the trouble to do some polishing of door handles and other surfaces to avoid leaving fingerprints.

As Lupita began ironing in one of the bedrooms, Delia called Glenview police. Within minutes, Sergeant Nolan arrived. He was sceptical about the evidence of the out-of-order goblets and the location of the body. However, he agreed it was curious that the safety chain had been unfastened at the time of Grace's death.

'I'll have forensic over to take a look in the next day or two,' he said, writing a few lines in his notebook. 'It's best if you vacate the apartment.' He then had a few words with Lupita before taking his leave.

'Sergeant Nolan,' Delia called out as he made for the door, 'another thing. The funeral is set for tomorrow. The body is to be cremated.'

'I don't think so,' Nolan said. 'We'll have to put a hold on that.'

Howard Levine was not surprised to receive Delia's call, having already heard from the police. 'I suggest,' he said, 'we go ahead with the memorial service at the Northbrook Hilton. People are already on their way from England. The cremation can wait.'

Lupita left without finishing the ironing, as Sergeant Nolan had requested. Delia took one more look around before locking up the apartment, then checked into the Hampton Inn at Old Orchard. Later, she received a call from Nolan. 'Can you come to police headquarters on East Lake Avenue? We'd like a DNA sample.'

'Surely I'm not a suspect?'

'We have no suspects at this time. But your DNA will be in the deceased's home. The cleaning girl's too. And of course Ms Rosman's own DNA. We need to see if there's evidence of someone else visiting around the time of her death. It may be too late, especially as such a thorough job was done of cleaning the apartment after the body was removed.'

'I'll be there in half an hour,' Delia promised.

6

YEARS WITH NO SUMMER

THE BEAKER PEOPLE in the north-east were made up of many local tribes. The tribe who farmed the Pleasant Vale and hunted in its woods and surrounding hills were envied by their neighbours, most of whom had to deal with poorer, stonier soil and less vigorous grass for their animals. Attacks on the Vale from all sides were common; bands of men would descend from the hills to steal sheep and cattle, and often women. The people of the Vale soon found that being constantly on the defensive wasn't enough. They formed small armies to invade neighbouring lands and subdue the tribes living there, even voluntarily sharing their relative wealth as the price of peace.

So it was that the settlement at the heart of the Pleasant Vale became the cultural and trading hub not just of the Vale but, over time, of a much larger region. The local chieftain who had his seat of power in the Vale eventually ruled over the whole of that region, and acquired the status of a king. His main preoccupation remained defence of his realm. He raised armies to fight off aggressors and sometimes to indulge in unprovoked attacks.

His subjects believed in a variety of gods, among whom the thunder-god was pre-eminent. In the sphere of religion, a tradition seems to have taken hold for women to play the leading role, although in every other aspect of life they were generally subservient. As in many societies of the time, women *could be traded like cattle. A way they could escape that fate was to join the priesthood, where they would enjoy a certain rank and command respect.*

Archaeologists have dated the arrival of the Beaker People in north-east Scotland to around 1850 BC. Between six and seven centuries later, they faced their first great crisis. That crisis became known in later times as the Years With No Summer.

It was not unknown for prolonged cool weather to destroy a summer, leading to crop failure and a hungry winter. Normally, however, the following year would make up for it, or, if not, the year after that. It was an article of faith that over any three-year stretch, at least one summer would be bountiful. But the Years With No Summer did not follow that pattern. Over a period of no less than eighteen years, unrelenting cold weather caused devastating famine, disease and death.

The eighteen-year cold snap isn't mere legend, like the Biblical flood or the lost land of Atlantis. It turns out there was, in fact, just such a period of prolonged cold. Lake sediments and growth rings of trees preserved in peat-bogs not only confirm it, but allow it to be precisely dated.

It began in 1189 BC.

We even know what caused it. Eruption of Hekla, the largest volcano in Iceland, sent immense clouds of ash into the upper atmosphere. The ash spewed by its neighbour Eyjafjallajökull in 2010, that so disrupted European aviation, was nothing by comparison. As Hekla's ash clouds spread south and east over the British Isles, they became so dense that they blocked the heat and light of the sun. Effects were felt throughout western Europe and as far away as Egypt, where crop failures may have been responsible for the unusually short reign of one of the pharaohs of the time, Setnakhte, the predecessor of Ramses III.

By the end of the Years With No Summer, the population of the now not-so-Pleasant Vale and its surrounding lands was

33

almost wiped out. In a fateful twist, boys succumbed to famine and its related diseases more than girls. The survivors when finally warm weather returned were overwhelmingly female. The task of rebuilding Beaker society fell to women, in particular the priesthood. And rebuild it they did, in a very unusual way that may have lessons for religious and political leaders today, more than three thousand years on.

7
CATO

ABOUT THIRTY PEOPLE attended the memorial service at the Northbrook Hilton. Delia recognized some, including Lupita, there with her husband, and a number of Grace's neighbours: Mrs Mies, the Okafors, Eddie the Geek (as Grace and Delia had secretly named him) and Walter, who didn't know Grace very well, but could never resist a good funeral. Catholic himself, he was as familiar with Lutheran, Anglican and Jewish funeral rites as with requiem mass at Our Lady of Perpetual Help. He was probably disappointed that this one was secular, with no preacher, no hymns or prayers.

A few of Grace's former business acquaintances introduced themselves to Delia. A young man of about her own age stood apart, and left immediately after the service before she had a chance to speak to him.

At the light buffet lunch, Delia joined Grace's English cousin and her son, Cato, at their table. Loretta Woods was in her mid-sixties, rail-thin with dyed black hair, pale skin and rather too much eye makeup. Cato was fortyish, with thinning dark hair, a prominent nose and sunken eyes. Unusually for such a solemn occasion, he wore a light-coloured suit, checked shirt and bowtie.

Delia introduced herself to Loretta. 'I'm so sorry for the loss of your cousin. It must have come as a shock to you, just as it was to me. Grace was a very dear friend.'

Loretta looked down her long, narrow nose and sniffed, 'I know who you are. And I gather from Mr Levine that you will

35

inherit all of poor Grace's estate. How did you trick her into that?'

Delia was taken aback but kept her cool. 'There was no trick, Mrs Woods. Until yesterday, I had no idea ...'

Interrupting, Loretta said, 'I suppose it was your doing to postpone the cremation.'

'Well, not exactly, though Grace always did talk about wishing a burial, in the tradition of her British ancestors.'

'What can you possibly know about her British ancestors? They are my ancestors, too. And I know for a fact that Grace's wish was to be cremated.'

There was no point in further conversation with this woman. Excusing herself from the table, Delia went to circulate before people began to leave. A little later she found Cato by her side, fiddling with his bowtie.

'Ms Cobb, please allow me to apologise for my mother's unwarranted rudeness,' he said, a little stiffly. Then, apparently drawing himself up for his excessive formality, he continued with a smile, 'We're all upset, and that can make us say hurtful things we don't really mean. I know you were close to Grace. So was I. She wasn't really my aunt, but to me she was always "Auntie" Grace.'

Delia softened a little in the face of his disarming manner and Hugh Grant diction. 'It's perfectly okay,' she said. 'I quite understand.'

'I hope we can be friends. Look, here's my business card. You can call or email me any time ... you know, if you're having problems disposing of Auntie Grace's things, or if I can help you in any way. I live in London but I'm often in the States on business.'

She looked at the card. *DaSilva Rare Treasures*, it read. *Carl Thomas Woods, President*.

'Cato's from Carl Thomas?'

'Yes. My father's name is Carl, and I became Cato to avoid confusion. It was better than being Young Carl, or Carl Junior.'

'And why DaSilva?'

'It's the Portuguese equivalent of Woods. I do a lot of business in Rio. Uncut gemstones, that kind of thing. Down there the dealers like Portuguese-sounding names. So DaSilva is better for business than Woods. Er ... Delia, I wonder if I could have your email address, so that we can keep in touch?'

As he was writing it down, Loretta, from the other side of the room, peremptorily signalled that it was time to go, and he politely took his leave. Shortly afterwards Sergeant Nolan walked in and made for the picked-over remains of the buffet. Between mouthfuls of chicken and cold pasta, he told Delia he'd been talking to some of the mourners as they left. 'What do you make of Cato Woods?' he asked.

'Well, of Grace's few relatives, he seems to have been closest to her. This is the first time I've met him, but he seems very nice.' She paused for a moment, then added, 'Can't say the same for his mother, I'm afraid.'

8

WOMEN OF THE PRIESTHOOD

*I*N THE AFTERMATH *of the Years With No Summer, it helped that monogamy had never been the norm in Beaker society; with so few surviving males it became a necessary fact of life – a duty, almost – to father numerous children with different mothers. Those mothers became fastidious in appending the father's name as a patronymic to the name of his son or daughter. As the boy or girl grew up, this would guard against a sexual relationship developing unwittingly with a half-sibling.*

Even with the sharing of men, it was often hard for young women to find a suitable mate within the confines of the Pleasant Vale, and it became customary for female groups to travel to neighbouring valleys, ostensibly for purposes of trade. They were no doubt welcome visitors for what they had to offer; when they came home they brought more than the products of barter. Those trips over the hills added depth to the local gene pool.

It took about a century after the Years With No Summer for the population of the Pleasant Vale and its surrounding region to return to its former size, and for men once again to be about equal in number to women. During that time, the women of the priesthood were very much in charge, and they established a political system designed to keep things that way. The system worked so well that it lasted, in one form or another, for almost two thousand years.

Members of the priesthood were, according to legend, demigoddesses. At the apex of influence was a high priestess.

Yet this was not exactly a female-dominated society. The women of the priesthood were not Amazons, nor did the high priestess rule as a queen. To all outward appearances, power was vested in a king, who ruled from his base in the Pleasant Vale, just as his predecessors had done before the Years With No Summer.

What was different now was the manner of royal succession. The crown (or whatever symbols of monarchy were used in those ancient times) did not pass from father to son. Instead, succession was matrilineal. When a king died or was deposed, his successor, always male, was chosen from descendants of the king's mother, maternal grandmother or even great-grandmother, through the female line. Most commonly, the succeeding king would be a brother, or a son or grandson of a sister or maternal aunt, of his predecessor.

There was no concept of legitimacy or illegitimacy of offspring. Family relationships tended to be complex and fluid, and the royal succession was often unclear. Commonly several claimants arose, in which case the high priestess would, in the name of the great thunder-god, select and anoint a young man as successor to the king. Because this was a frequent occurrence, it placed great power in the hands of the high priestess. Sometimes she would be able to nominate one of her own sons as successor, further tightening her grip on power.

Succession in the priesthood itself was a more rigidly controlled affair. The rank of high priestess passed from mother to daughter, sometimes skipping a generation or sidestepping to a niece or more distant relative, but never going outside the family or relying on inheritance through a male ancestor.

It was a society, therefore, that was ordered largely by women. And it stayed that way, for a reason: education.

The priesthood was responsible for educating children and young adults in matters of religion, astronomy, agriculture, food preparation, medicine and decorative arts. Such education was universally available – for females only. The mysteries of *the gods and the heavens, sunshine and rain, heat and cold, the growth of plants, sickness and health, human and animal reproduction, remained a closed book to the male half of the population. Boys and young men received training in the hunting, fishing and martial arts; their one opportunity for a more aesthetic pursuit was in making music. Their teachers were men appointed by the king.*

The education of young women led to substantial improvements in agriculture and hence in nutrition. Among the benefits to the Beaker population were reduced infant mortality and increased longevity. Through improved breeding and care of livestock, meat and milk came to form a greater part of the diet; meanwhile new vegetable crops were introduced, giving what would nowadays be recognised as a more balanced diet, all year round. They included kale, leeks, beans and skirret. (Skirret is a root vegetable that has since fallen out of favour because of its inedible woody core.) Green leafy plants such as nettles, dandelions and sorrel, fruits including raspberries, brambles, blueberries and rose-hips, and edible fungi were gathered from the wild in season and further supplemented the diet. An important aspect of the educational curriculum for young women was distinguishing edible from inedible or poisonous plants. Medicinal plants seem to have been a more specialised subject, knowledge of which was reserved for members of the priesthood themselves.

So the bountiful period following the Years With No Summer heralded a huge transformation in Beaker society in and around the Pleasant Vale. A little over six centuries later, another transformation was about to occur. A new race of people, the Celts, had migrated from central Europe and were expanding northwards through Great Britain, bringing with them a groundbreaking new technology. Just as the Beaker People had introduced bronze, the Celts brought a new metal and ways of working it. The iron age had arrived.

9
FIND A REPO

THE GLENVIEW FORENSIC TEAM had access to Grace's apartment for a few days, during which they removed some items for more detailed examination, but by the end of the week Delia had moved in. Sergeant Nolan arrived at the door.

'Just a couple of questions, Ms Cobb,' he said. 'You told me that whoever could have been here around the time of Ms Rosman's death might have handled this silver box. Why would it have been of special interest, do you think?'

'It once contained a keepsake that Grace was very attached to. An ancient glass ball. Did you find fingerprints?'

'Only yours, Ms Cobb. This glass ball – was it a high-value item?'

'I don't know if it had monetary value, but it was significant historically. The kind of thing that should maybe have been in a museum someplace.'

'Ms Rosman's attorney gave us a list of the itemised valuables that she had insured. Here it is. No glass ball mentioned.'

Delia pondered for a moment, and scanned the inventory to see if the *Drogan Taranish* might have been listed under some other description. Nothing caught her eye. 'I suppose it would have been difficult to put a dollar value on it for insurance,' she said. 'Or maybe it's not listed because she gave it to someone.' Grace's words came into her mind: *Before I get too old, I will have to find the next Keeper.*

'Does this mean anything to you?' Nolan asked, turning the tea-caddy over. There, on the bottom, was a label bearing capital letters in pencil:

F I N D A R E P O

Delia had missed the label when she had last taken the box out of the hutch – she hadn't thought to look on the underside. 'No,' she said, 'I don't know what *"Find a repo"* means.'

After Nolan left, she set to work cleaning and polishing the silver items before putting them back where they belonged. She was careful to replace the goblets in their correct, Grace-sanctioned, order. Her mind played with the strange words *'Find a repo'*. Grace had written those words, intending them as some kind of message.

As a child she had been introduced to word-puzzles by Grace, who was particularly keen on anagrams. Could this be one? 'Actually,' Grace had once confided, 'my own name is an anagram.' Try as she might, Delia could never get her to reveal the solution to that particular puzzle.

Sometimes she would devise treasure-hunt games, giving little Delia a card bearing a clue to some object. As often as not, the search led to more clues, by which Delia eventually recovered her reward – a candy bar, maybe, or a little book. In time, she had begun setting puzzles of her own for Grace.

Recalling one that had been a favourite of Grace's, she took Shakespeare from the bookcase and opened it at *King Lear*. There, at Act I Scene I, where Cordelia ponders:

What shall Cordelia do?

was a scrap of paper on which was written in a childish hand:

0 & b S h h

– a clue of Delia's own devising, encrypting the words that come next in the play:

Love, and be silent.

42

Delia was amused that the little scrap was still there, after all these years. At the age of twelve, she was quite proud to have come up with the initial zero of the puzzle, a reference to 'love' as in a tennis score. Grace must have been amused by it, to have preserved the piece of paper.

Replacing Shakespeare in the bookcase, her attention was drawn to the volume next to it, an 1839 edition of *Grace Darling* by G.W.M. Reynolds. Grace had recounted the tale of her namesake during one of Delia's early visits. She recalled the part where the young girl and her father, a lighthouse keeper on the Farne Islands off the coast of north-east England, rowed through a stormy sea to rescue thirteen shipwreck survivors. Opening the book, Delia read the title of Chapter 1:

THE READER IS AT ONCE INTRODUCED TO A CHARACTER
THAT WILL OCCUPY A CONSPICUOUS PART IN THE PAGES OF
THIS WORK; AND THE CHARACTER HIMSELF IS ALSO
INTRODUCED TO SOMETHING REMARKABLE

Well, she thought, *there's* a snappy title to draw the reader in!

As she leafed idly through the book, to her surprise an envelope fell out. It was blank and unsealed. Inside was a colour photograph of a teenage girl who was so like Delia that for an instant she thought it was herself. Then, looking at the back of the photograph, she read:

Selena Rosman, 1967–87.

Also in the envelope was a folded document that turned out to be a copy of Selena's birth certificate, with the names of her mother and father – Grace Rosman and Arthur Johnson.

Although Grace had often talked about Selena, she had never mentioned who Selena's father was. Now at least Delia knew his name, though there were probably ten thousand Arthur Johnsons in the United States.

10

GIFTS OF THE IRONWORKERS

B Y ABOUT 550 BC, when the ironworkers were settling in and around the Pleasant Vale, their race was already a dominant force in most of the rest of Britain and Ireland. They spoke a Celtic language they had brought from continental Europe, but which over time had diverged from their ancestral tongue to become Brythonic or British. Medieval and modern Welsh, in turn, evolved from iron age Brythonic, as did other, now extinct, variants including Cornish and Cumbric. In Ireland, the language of the Celtic settlers diverged in a different way and ultimately became Irish Gaelic.

In what is now north-east Scotland, the Celts didn't supplant the Beaker population, but coexisted and interbred with them. Remarkably, they appear to have adapted to the local political and cultural system, with its female priesthood and matrilineal succession, and in doing so strengthened it. The technology of ironworking was only one of their lasting contributions.

Among other gifts of the ironworkers was their language. Whereas in other parts of the British Isles virtually all traces of pre-Celtic tongues were wiped out, here the incomers' language insinuated itself into local speech, resulting in a kind of creole. Similarities to the Brythonic spoken elsewhere in Great Britain were good for trade and exchange of ideas, but differences helped foster what might nowadays be called a national identity.

Yet another gift brought by the ironworkers in the sixth century BC was the pantheon of Celtic gods and goddesses. Among these deities was Taranis, who became Taran to the people of the Vale. Hitherto a minor god to the Celts, here he was promoted to the highest station among all the gods, as the new incarnation of the thunder-god that had been venerated by the Beaker People for centuries.

Elsewhere, Taranis was believed to be violent and vengeful, demanding constant appeasement including the ritual sacrifice of post-pubescent virgins – giving girls the strongest incentive to surrender their virginity as soon as they reached puberty. His counterpart Taran in the corner of Britain centred on the Pleasant Vale was more benign, as befitted the creator of the people's homeland. Yet he was no less masculine, as attested by his heavenly manifestation as Taurus – in the local language, Tarwe – the bull. And though sexual initiation remained a priority for young women, it was an act not of fear but of joy, part of the annual Samhain celebration in Taran's honour.

The Celts also brought a mother-goddess, Brigta, in honour of whom they called themselves 'British' and the land they occupied 'Britain'. To the people of the Vale she became Brytha. It was not long before the high priestess began claiming direct descent from the mother-goddess, taking the ceremonial name Merefrith, which meant 'daughter of Brytha'. And the all-female priesthood came to be known collectively as the Merch Nyr, *the meaning of which is lost in antiquity (though the* 'merch' *part seems to have something to do with daughters).*

Brytha symbolised many aspects of motherhood, including pregnancy. Her annual festival in February, three months after Samhain, was known as Imbolc, which can be translated literally as 'in milk'. Often nowadays interpreted as the time when ewes begin to lactate, in the community of the Vale it was celebrated as the time when a human pregnancy initiated at Samhain began to 'show', and a good time for the mother- and father-to-be to marry, if they chose to do so. It's possible the word 'bride' – a modification of Brigta or Brytha – derives from the ancient practice of Imbolc weddings.

Brytha was also the hearth-goddess, another role having a clear link to motherhood. And with the importance of ironworking, it's not surprising that her domain extended from the domestic hearth to the forge. To this day, blacksmiths have special affection for the forge-goddess Brytha, though more commonly for her Christian reinvention, Saint Bridget. And in another throwback to the iron age, blacksmiths, at least in Scotland, were until quite recently empowered to conduct marriage ceremonies uniting 'brides' with their grooms.

As a mark of the importance of Brytha in the pantheon, and perhaps of the dominant role played by women, kings frequently took, or were accorded, the name Bridei, a masculine form of the mother-goddess's name. Bridei was later latinised to Brutus by Roman writers, and remains in use today in forms such as Bruce, Bryce, Brady, Brodie and MacBride.

Other gods introduced by the Celts included Bel and Lugus, the latter becoming Luath to the people of the Pleasant Vale. The festivals of Beltane in May, honouring Bel, and Lunasa in August, glorifying Luath, together with Samhain in November and Imbolc in February, came to mark the four cardinal points of the Celtic year. Bel probably took the place of an earlier sun-god worshipped by the Beaker People. He had influence over health and illness, and was often called upon for medical advice. Luath was a patron of the arts, particularly music, and was also believed to protect travellers and traders.

But Taran – the powerful though generous creator of the Pleasant Vale, not the malevolent, insatiable Taranis of other Celtic lands, nor the warlike but occasionally slow-witted Thor of Scandinavian peoples – was the greatest of the male gods. The settlement in the heart of the Vale, the Eden of the Beaker People with its stream of running water protecting it from spirits of the Little Folk in the nearby Ghost Meadow, came to be known as Tar-lan, which means 'Taran's Garden'. A present-

46

day village occupies the site and still has the same name, only with a D added to the end: Tarland.

The people themselves, with their glorious mix of Beaker and Celtic heritage, called themselves Tarachsel, which means Taran's kin. It was a name that stuck. Seven hundred years after the coming of the Celts, the Roman-Egyptian geographer Ptolemy, referring to the people of this corner of Britain in his great work Geographia, latinised their name as Taexali. The name they gave their land was Ce (probably pronounced like 'Kay'), which may simply have meant 'Here'.

In Taran's Garden there was a barrow or great mound of earth, surrounded by a trench. In all likelihood it had originally been a burial-place for an important person, perhaps a chieftain or king, in pre-Celtic or even pre-Beaker times. At some point during the iron age, a wooden structure was erected on top of the barrow. This was where the Tarachsel king held court. It would not be considered palatial by any modern observer, but it was in a sense the royal palace and political centre of the kingdom of Ce. It was called the Kyaar. The trench around it may have been filled with water, forming a moat.

The Kyaar was an early forerunner of a type of defensive structure called a motte, which came into vogue many centuries later. Numerous examples of mottes from around the twelfth century AD can be seen just outside the Howe of Cromar; of these the Peel of Lumphanan to the east and the Doune of Invernochty to the north-west are particularly well preserved. Ironically the Kyaar at Tarland was destroyed long before these later mottes were built, and can hardly have been the model for them.

One of the symbols associated with Taran, the six-spoked wheel, had many layers of meaning for the Tarachsel. In one interpretation, the rim of the wheel represents the ring of hills surrounding the Pleasant Vale, and its spokes signify six roads radiating from the Kyaar across the hills to six provinces.

Taran's wheel may thus have been a kind of map, one of the earliest 'bird's-eye' representations of a territory known anywhere in the world.

11

A PUZZLE FROM BEYOND THE GRAVE

F INDING SELENA'S BIRTH CERTIFICATE temporarily distracted Delia from the *'Find a repo'* puzzle. But that evening she sat down with a pencil and paper and began constructing anagrams. At first fixated on the Farne Islands of the Grace Darling story, she came up with *'Farne I-Pod'* but quickly ruled that out. Likewise *'Pain for Ed'*, *'Pad of Erin'*, *'Period fan'* and *'No ref paid'*.

It didn't take her too long to crack it. *'Find a repo'* really meant:

OPEN FRIDA

She remembered, many years before, hearing from Grace that the Celtic goddess Brigta or Brytha had a Norse equivalent, Frida. She went straight to the hutch and brought out the Brytha goblet, with its depiction of the goddess on one side, a she-lion on the other and the word *'IMBOLC'* on the base. Nothing about the goblet could be 'opened'. If this was what she was supposed to find, it made no sense.

But *'Open Frida'* would make a lot more sense if it referred to a book. Delia crossed the room to the bookcase. There in a prominent position was *Frida*, Hayden Herrera's biography of the great Mexican painter Frida Kahlo. With a tingle of excitement, she opened it at the title page.

There, stuck loosely to the page, was a yellow Post-It note with a brief message in Grace's unmistakable handwriting.

Good guess, Cordelia.

But it's not an anagram this time. Did you think this was The Da Vinci Code?

Love, G.

Not knowing whether to laugh or cry, Delia did both at the same time. Grace had sent her a puzzle from beyond the grave, and now she was having a joke at Delia's expense. So maddening, so endearing, so ... so Grace!

She thought about *'Find a repo'* off and on for a few days. One of the apartments in Grace's condominium development was under a repossession order, but she was sure *'repo'* had nothing to do with that.

One day she received an unexpected email.

Hi Delia!

I've come across some old photos of Auntie Grace and thought you might like to have them. I've scanned them – see attached.

Best, Cato Woods.

She downloaded the pictures to her tablet computer. They showed Grace as a young woman, one of them with Selena as a baby. The photos were charming and Delia emailed Cato to thank him for his thoughtfulness.

That evening she was flicking absent-mindedly through the television channels, hoping against the odds to find something she could be bothered to watch. She happened to pause on the History Channel, at a re-run of an old documentary about the excavation of Pompeii. The narrator began talking about graffiti found on the walls, which had lain buried under the ash of Vesuvius since the eruption of 79 AD. Delia sat bolt upright when the narrator, with a chalk on blackboard, reproduced one of those graffiti: a famous Latin word-square.

```
S A T O R
A R E P O
T E N E T
O P E R A
R O T A S
```

AREPO! There it was! Not *'a repo'* as Delia had assumed. The narrator gave the English translation as:

Arepo, sower of seed, carefully holds the wheels.

He went on to point out that the words could be read down as well as across – something Delia had noticed the moment the word-square appeared on the screen. The 'sator square' was thought by some to be an early Christian code, a way of writing *PATERNOSTER* (*'Our Father'*) under the noses of Roman nonbelievers, despite the extreme improbability of a Christian community in Pompeii as early as 79 AD.

Delia was already thinking, not about what the graffitisti of Pompeii had in mind, but what Grace could possibly have meant by her *'Find Arepo'* message. Could *Arepo*, the sower of seed, be Arthur Johnson, the father of Grace's only daughter? And could the 'wheels' that he 'carefully holds' include Taran's wheel?

If so, how was Delia going to find him among the thousands of Arthur Johnsons in the United States and others elsewhere? There had to be another clue somewhere here in the apartment.

12

AETH AND THE KINGFISHER

*I*T WAS A TIME *of peace and plenty for the* Tarachsel. *Integration of the indigenous Beaker People with the immigrant Celts was followed by several centuries during which the* Merch Nyr, *the women of the priesthood, perfected their understanding of the world and the heavens, and passed it on to their female disciples.*

Young men continued to be denied such understanding, but their important role in society, to defend the kingdom and its provinces against threats of encroachment by neighbouring tribes, required no knowledge of 'feminine' subjects. Indeed, it would have been an insult to their manhood to educate them like women. As it happened, defence of the realm became a little easier during this period, for the climate of the more northerly parts of the British Isles had once again turned cooler and wetter, so that local tribes had less interest in attacking each other than in raiding what they perceived as richer lands to the south.

But the people of the Pleasant Vale and its six surrounding provinces remained prosperous by the standards of the day, adapting their systems of food provision to the changed climate. It probably helped that in their society individuals were not 'owners' of property such as land or livestock. The Merch Nyr *instead emphasised what we would now call partnership or custodianship in all aspects of life.*

Agriculture (almost exclusively women's work) and hunting (which, together with ironworking and the making of tools and weapons, was the primary occupation of men in peacetime) were conducted in a non-destructive, non-exploitative way. Cattle, sheep, pigs and chickens kept around homesteads were a community resource. Likewise, wild animals including boar, deer, hares and fowl were open to hunting by all. Fish in rivers, streams and lakes were another important source of food, but the Vale was remote from the ocean and seafood was an expensive commodity obtainable only by trade with coastal tribes. Brushwood from the still extensive woodlands satisfied the needs of the hearth and forge; when trees were felled for building material the forests were allowed to regenerate.

The concept of partnership extended to the institution of marriage. Whereas Celtic men elsewhere enslaved their women, treating them as little more than brood-mares and indentured labourers, Tarachsel *men and women entered into union voluntarily, and were free to dissolve their marriages by mutual consent and with little fuss.*

Keeping this social system intact required constant engagement by the Merch Nyr, *with the high priestess Merefrith at their head. The king, though more than a mere figurehead, deferred to them in matters of religion and society. No coded laws existed, but justice was administered by Merefrith. Near Taran's Garden, on a low rise now called Tomnaverie, a stone circle that predated even the Beaker People was from time to time pressed into service as a kind of courtroom for the airing of grievances, the righting of wrongs and the punishment of offenders.*

It was probably during this time that the legend of Aeth and the kingfisher arose.

As I have told you, the River Dee, following the course of an ice age glacier, cuts across the southern edge of the Howe of Cromar. You can see on a map that at one point the river takes

53

a sharp turn southward, forming what the Tarachsel called a cambus, a river-bend where erosion by the flowing water has created a cliff-like bank. Behind a low hill above the cambus there was once a small settlement where a boy by the name of Aeth lived with his mother.

Aeth's home was typical of the time. A circular foundation of stones bore the weight of a conical wooden frame supporting layers of turf piled one on top of another. A gap in the turf wall served as a doorway, which could be closed against the elements by covering it with an animal hide. Smoke from the central fire escaped through a hole in the roof.

One sunny day, so the story goes, Aeth went fishing. As he stood on a shingle bank at the river's edge, his attention was suddenly diverted by a kingfisher with iridescent blue wings that darted in front of him, skimming the water, to alight in a nest-hole in the cliff above the cambus. He was curious to see something glinting in the sunlight by the nest-hole, and climbed up to investigate.

What he found was the strangest object he had ever seen. It was a perfectly round ball, a little broader than his hand. Although as heavy as a rock of the same size, it wasn't like any rock he knew. Smooth and hard as a river pebble, it was clear, like ice. He washed it in the river and held it up to the sun, which shone right through it.

What's more, the ball had six shafts of blue, just like the colour of the kingfisher's wings, radiating from somewhere in the middle to the surface, which itself formed a kingfisher-blue circle in the sunshine.

Forgetting all about fishing, he hurried home with his find and showed it to his mother. She sent him straight to the Merch Nyr compound at Davan, a short distance away. On his way there, a sudden rainstorm struck, with lightning flashing all around. When he arrived, he was soaked. The surface of the strange ball was wet, making the circle and shafts of blue inside visible even though the sun wasn't shining.

Merefrith invited him into her hut to dry off from the rain. He gave her the ball and breathlessly told her how a kingfisher had led him to find it.

'It's a sign from the gods,' Merefrith told him. 'What you have found is the Drogan Taranish, *Taran's wheel. It's perfectly round, like the full moon – a sign of our good mother Brytha. Yet within it is the wheel of the great thunder-god. The story it tells is of their union. It is also the story of our people.'*

Aeth was afraid he had unwittingly stolen something sacred, and the thunder-god was angry with him. 'Did Taran send the storm to punish me?' he asked.

Merefrith smiled. 'No. See, the rain has gone off and the sun is coming out again. Let's go outside.'

The brilliant kingfisher-blue lines inside the ball glowed in the sunshine. Merefrith turned the ball in her hands and saw the six rays turning like a wheel. 'Aeth,' she said, 'Taran wanted you to find this. He sent his daughter down from the sky to lead you to it.'

Aeth looked puzzled.

'Of course, you're a boy. You don't learn about these things. But I'll explain if you like.' Seeing Aeth nod enthusiastically, Merefrith went on: 'You know the tight little cluster of six stars riding on the shoulder of Tarwe *the bull? We call them Taran's daughters. The brightest of them is Taran's oldest daughter. When she comes down to earth she takes the form of a kingfisher. It was she who brought you to the* Drogan Taranish.'

Merefrith lifted the Drogan *to her lips and kissed its smooth surface. 'This will be an object of great devotion for the rest of time. I, and every Merefrith who follows me, shall be the Keeper of Taran's wheel. And you, Aeth, will forever be remembered as its finder. You will be famous, and kings will bear your name.'*

At least one king, living much later, did have the name Aeth. He, no less than his namesake, played a very important part in the history of the Drogan Taranish, *as we'll see.*

13
TROJAN RAT

IN A PRET À MANGER sandwich bar around the corner from his London office, Cato Woods was enjoying a prosciutto and salad baguette with American coffee, while skim-reading the *Financial Times*. Two men entered, one tall and muscular with a full head of wavy black hair, and the other of medium height, wiry and with pointed teeth. They took seats at the bar counter on either side of him, the taller one elbowing an old man out of the way.

Cato looked up from his paper in surprise, immediately recognizing the pair he had first met a few months earlier. In his mind he replayed in fast-frame the events leading up to that encounter.

The 'rare treasures' business was getting riskier by the day, due to excessive media attention on blood diamonds and poached rhino horn. He had devised a scheme to make one last big profit before getting out of the business for good. His 'Auntie' Grace was in possession of a remarkable glass sphere that was not merely rare but, he believed, unique. If he could find a buyer for it, he would give her a fraction of the proceeds but keep the lion's share for himself.

On an anonymous website he had described the object, inviting offers. Shortly afterwards he had been contacted by a collector of pre-Christian relics, an American pastor who declined to provide his name but told Cato he would send an agent to negotiate for the glass sphere. In due course not one but two of the collector's agents turned up at Cato's London premises and, after much haggling, agreed a price of fourteen million pounds. He had been ecstatic: all that had remained to secure this tidy sum was to prise the article out of Grace's possession. He hadn't thought through exactly how he would accomplish this, but, well, Grace was an old lady and he *had* been a very attentive 'nephew'. He'd been expected to deliver by the end of May; however, the timeline had slipped. It was now the last week of June.

Though he had met the two agents and spoken by phone with them on several occasions, they had never revealed their names. He knew them only as Z and J. Now here they were again in London, and he was less than happy to see them.

He made up his mind to take an assertive stance. Okay, so he hadn't been able to deliver the goods yet, but he wasn't going to eat shit. 'What the hell are you doing here?' he demanded, drawing back from his place at the sandwich bar so that he could see both of them at once. Then, addressing the smaller man: 'J, you said in Chicago you never wanted to cross the Atlantic again. Too *high-falutin* over here for your taste – wasn't that the expression you used?' A ghost of a sneer played briefly on Cato's lips as he spoke.

J said nothing. As if expecting the bigger man to do all the talking, he looked with raised eyebrows at Z, who said to Cato in a Texas drawl, 'Please don't upset J.'

In his mind Cato was mapping the shortest route to the door. 'You haven't answered my question, Z. What brings you to London?'

Ignoring his question for a second time, Z asked laconically, 'Any progress?'

'Look, as I told you before, the girl got everything. The glass ball is hidden somewhere, and she either knows or will figure out where it is. She will lead me to it. Once it's in my hands, it's yours as we agreed.'

The man with pointed teeth could stay silent no longer. 'She's in Chicago, you're in fucking London,' he snorted. 'Doesn't look to me like you're close on her tail.'

'For Christ's sake, J,' Cato protested, 'it's just a few days since you put the bug in that photo, and I sent it on to her as soon as I got it.'

'Rat,' J corrected him. 'It's a Trojan Rat, not a bug.'

Right, Cato remembered. R-A-T, a remote access tool, slipped into an apparent gift, just like the original Trojan horse. Once installed on Delia Cobb's computer, every character entered, every link clicked on would be recorded, packaged and sent across the internet to J and Z.

'So far,' J went on, 'you know what's come in? Fuck all. You sure you sent her the photo?'

'Of course. I sent a few. She thanked me, so I know she received them.' Cato furrowed his brow. 'What if the girl has spyware protection on her computer? Won't that catch the Rat?'

It was Z who spoke. 'Not *this* Rat. Isn't that right, J?'

J gave another of his snorts. 'Dead right. This one was developed during the Bush-Cheney administration for domestic surveillance after nine-eleven. The CIA strong-armed the major security software companies – Norton, McAfee and suchlike – into leaving it alone. It was probably never actually deployed. But it's been kept updated, and we were able to get our hands on it. The Pastor has contacts at all levels of government.' He paused, then added wistfully, 'At least he did back in the Bush years.'

Z glared at J as if reproaching him for bringing up the Pastor, and immediately took over the conversation. 'What worries us, Woods, is if you get all the intelligence from the Rat but still screw up and let the girl, and the glass ball, get away. I still think we should go after her on our own. To be honest, I don't see what we need you for. But we're under instructions to do it this way.'

'Yeah, and what the Pastor says goes,' J said. Looking Cato straight in the eye, he warned, 'Just don't let us down, okay? The Pastor's a man of God, but patient he ain't.'

Observing Z flinch at J's repeated mention of the Pastor, Cato sensed a crack in their armour, an opening for renegotiation. 'You know, this operation could get costly. I can't guarantee the original price. I agreed fourteen million before. Now I'm thinking it's more like twenty. I already had to arrange a "heart attack" for my aunt. That was not foreseen.'

J spoke up: 'You're upsetting me, asshole. I don't like to be upset.'

Z calmed him down. 'It's Mr Woods' idea of a joke. The price has gone down, not up. It's now five, tops.'

It was Cato's turn to flush up with anger. Z noticed and twisted the knife in the wound. 'Before you think pounds, I mean dollars.'

'Five million dollars? That's ridiculous,' Cato said, loudly. Other diners looked up from their sandwiches and wraps. In a quieter voice, he continued, 'Maybe I should talk directly to this Pastor of yours, whoever he is. The piece he's interested in, it's not just a rare historical or archaeological treasure, though on that account alone it's worth a lot more than five million.'

Z broke into Cato's pitch. 'Hey, the Pastor don't conduct his own negotiations. Certainly not with the likes of you.'

'Look,' Cato said, struggling to sound reasonable in the face of such hostility, 'I have customers who collect this kind of thing. They'd pay twice that or more. No, the ball is worth much more than five million. It's a geological wonder. A tektite, glass formed by an ancient meteorite impact. The best example is moldavite, a translucent greenish glass found scattered in parts of the Czech Republic. But pieces of moldavite are mostly small and irregularly shaped. Nothing has ever been found, anywhere in the world, that even comes close to the size or perfect shape of the ball. And this one refracts light in a unique way, producing strange internal patterns. I can't say for sure, but I think that's to do with some partial recrystallisation of the glass while it was cooling. Y'see, a massive tektite like this ...'

'Tektite, shmektite,' Z broke in. 'Spare us the fucking lecture. We know what business you're in. We know every fucking pimple on the ass of your business. Stolen rough diamonds. *Blood* diamonds: that deal you did with the supermodel who needed to dispose of an unwanted gift – we have it well documented. And then there's the other stuff. Poached ivory and rhino horn, some of it hacked off museum specimens. Dinosaur bones from protected sites. Yep, nice businesses, all of them. Fine mark-up. But we're only interested in your fucking tektite. And its price took a nosedive when you murdered your poor Aunt Grace.'

Cato was speechless.

Z went on, 'See, Woods, the police have kinda gone off the heart attack theory. And we have evidence they might be interested in. Like, who was the passenger we brought into Chicago Executive Airport that day, and brought out later the same day? And who was it accompanied us to Glenview in our rented limo? There we were, on legitimate church business, doing you a favour. You told us you wanted to visit your poor sick aunt. Out of human charity, how could we refuse? But of course we don't *have* to share that evidence with anyone. So I think you understand why the price went down?'

Without another word, Z and J got up and left. Cato sat looking at his prosciutto and salad baguette. Somehow he'd completely lost his appetite.

14
WHAT GOES AROUND, COMES AROUND

T HE MERCH NYR *TAUGHT that Taran's six-spoked wheel had a deep symbolism. It was a reminder that six wheels (nowadays we would call them cycles) governed the universe of the people who called themselves* Tarachsel, *Taran's kin.*

The first three were the wheels of the sun (defining a day), moon (a month) and earth (a year). Next came the wheel of water and the wheel of life. But in the education of young women their teachers spent most time explaining the sixth wheel – the wheel of vairtach.

Vairtach *was a fundamental concept in* Tarachsel *philosophy, translating as truth or justice. The idea of justice as a 'wheel' resonates even today when we say, 'What goes around, comes around.'*

An eternal afterlife was not a feature of Tarachsel *belief. They no longer buried their most respected dead with things they might need beyond the grave, as their Beaker ancestors had done. Good deeds had to be rewarded, and bad deeds punished, in* this *life, otherwise the wheel of* vairtach *would be incomplete. Sometimes the gods, unbid, provided the necessary reward or punishment. But often the* Merch Nyr *had to intercede to ensure the gods knew what was going on.*

The stone circle at Tomnaverie was a most appropriate location for a court of justice, the ring of stones providing a reminder of the wheel of vairtach. Prominent in the administration of justice was the much-venerated Drogan Taranish, *the miraculous object found by Aeth and brought to the first Keeper. A verdict reached or a sentence passed in the absence of the* Drogan *would not have had the full force of law.*

When a person was close to death, a member of the priesthood would, through the power of the Drogan, *call on Taran or one of his subordinate gods to complete the wheel of* vairtach *for that person. For a dying king, it would surely be Taran himself who would intercede.*

Sudden, unexpected or violent deaths presented more of a problem. Fortunately, it was taught, life did not end at the precise moment of death, but some time afterward. (How long afterward is something we don't know; perhaps even the Merch Nyr *were vague on this point.) The spirit of the recently departed remained accessible to the magic of the* Drogan. *So a good life cut short could still be rewarded, and a wicked life punished. For this to happen, the* Drogan *had to be brought to the place of death, for even if the body had been removed from that place the spirit was believed to stay close by.*

The Drogan *also occupied an important place in ceremonial events at the king's seat of power, the* Kyaar. *Coronation of a new king, the naming of a successor, royal marriage: at these and other events the* Drogan *was the focus of rituals seeking the approval of Taran or Brytha.*

Another ceremony to which the Drogan *was central was the annual blessing of the winter food store. The store had to last for six moons, the length of time from Samhain (November) until Beltane (May). On Samhain's eve, the* Drogan *was placed in one of the many underground storehouses scattered around the countryside and left overnight, watched over by one or more members of the priesthood and perhaps an armed guard.*

In time, the original Drogan Taranish *came to be too sacred for use in everyday rituals, and was brought out only for great occasions such as the death of a king or high priestess, or when a large number were killed in battle. Stone balls about the same size as the* Drogan *were fashioned for normal use. Lacking the transparency of the original, these had features carved on their surface as a substitute for the six internal 'spokes' of the* Drogan. *Typically the surface features took the form of regularly spaced knobs, with varying degrees of ornamentation. Most commonly there were – of course – six knobs.*

About four hundred of these stone balls have been found, including one that was dug up in 2000 at Tarland, in a garden by the village square. A particularly beautiful example was discovered just seven miles away near Towie in 1860. Some have been found in association with pre-Celtic or even pre-Beaker remains, and this has led many authorities to doubt an origin as late as the Celtic era that heralded the iron age. Indeed, the National Museum of Scotland in Edinburgh, where the Towie ball is prominently displayed, dates it to around 2500 BC. However, it's been suggested that carving the intricate patterns seen, for example, on the Towie ball would have required hard iron rather than the softer bronze tools of earlier times. This is consistent with the stone balls having been made and used in the Celtic era as 'stand-ins' for the precious original Drogan Taranish.

Like many 'pagan' symbols, the six-spoked wheel was eventually appropriated by early Christians. With slight modification, it became the chi rho, *a monogram of the first two letters of 'Christ' in the Greek alphabet, enclosed in a circle, which can be seen in church carvings and decorations all over Europe. A faint echo can even be seen in* Vitruvian Man, *the iconic pen-and-ink figure created around 1487 by Leonardo da Vinci. And a wheel with six spokes has been the familiar logo of Rotary clubs worldwide since 1923.*

But I'm getting ahead of myself. To the Tarachsel *over two thousand years ago Taran's wheel had many layers of symbolism, as I've explained, none more pervasive in their culture than its representation of the number six.*

15

THE SQUARE HOLDS WHAT YOU SEEK

DELIA GOOGLED *'AREPO'*. Many leads took her to the sator square, which didn't advance her quest at all. But one caught her attention. It was a reference to *The Zen of Magic Squares*, a book by Clifford Pickover. Hadn't she seen that in Grace's bookcase?

Sure enough, there it was.

Pickover referred to the famous word-square as the 'templar square'. On page 23 the now familiar

```
S A T O R
A R E P O
T E N E T
O P E R A
R O T A S
```

was rendered in all its glory. Beside it was a yellow Post-It note, just like the one Delia had found in *Frida*. On this one, again in Grace's hand, was a number-square:

```
6 1 2
9 4 7
3 8 5
```

and a succinct message:

The square holds what you seek.

But this wasn't a real number-square, in which each row and each column should add up to the same total. Delia remembered from puzzle-time with Grace that in a number-square using the digits 1 to 9, rows and columns all added to 15. That wasn't the case here.

At first she wondered if the numbers could be telephone dialling codes, 612 being the area code for Minneapolis where Erik came from (funny, she hadn't thought about him for days). She soon gave up on this line of inquiry. Likewise, she soon abandoned the idea that the nine digits could be someone's Social Security number: 612-94-7385.

Her interest in number puzzles had been piqued when she was in middle school. With 666 for her locker number, the other kids had taunted her. They said she was the devil.

'Superstitious nonsense' had been Grace's verdict. 'You should take pride in having such a number. Six, 66 and 666 make a unique series. Take 6 first. It's a magic number, as I've told you before. Do you know that 6 is the only number that's both the sum and the product of three smaller numbers: one, two and three? It's the lowest perfect number, being the sum of all its factors including one. Six underlies the symmetrical beauty of a lily, a honeycomb, a snowflake. And it's the number of faces on a cube, edges on a tetrahedron and corners on an octahedron.'

(A few years later, in high school, Delia studied the three-dimensional geometry of the Platonic solids and was disappointed that her teacher failed to highlight the remarkable recurrence of the number 6 or its double, 12, in their construction. She was also quick to notice that every atom of carbon, the element on which all life was based, had exactly 6 electrons, 6 protons and 6 neutrons. Later still, as a college student, she grappled with the so-called Standard Model of particle physics, dealing with the most fundamental units of matter. Somehow it came as no surprise to her to learn that the universe was constructed ultimately of just six types of quark and six types of lepton. The 'answer to the ultimate question of life, the universe and everything' may have been 42 according to Douglas Adams in *The Hitchhiker's Guide to the Galaxy*, but in Delia's mind the true answer was 6.)

'Now,' Grace had continued, '6 is the mid-point of the series from one to eleven. And if we add up all the numbers in that series, what do we get? Sixty-six. There's always been a bit of mystique about that number. The famous "mother road" from Chicago to Los Angeles mightn't have been such an icon of twentieth-century culture if it had been anything other than Route 66. And people seem to think there's something special about a book with 66 chapters. Perhaps the most famous piece of fantasy literature ever published, Tolkien's *The Lord of the Rings*, has 66 chapters, grouped into 6 "books". The Old Testament book of Isaiah is sometimes called "the Bible in miniature" because it has the same number of chapters – 66 – as there are books in the whole Bible.

'But your locker 666: now that's a truly unique number with its own magic. Don't believe me? Think about squares. If you make a square with 6 rows and 6 columns, how many boxes or cells does that square have altogether?'

'Thirty-six,' Delia had answered without hesitation, though not seeing quite where this was going.

'Now I want you to give each box a number from 1 to 36. And when you've done that, add up all the numbers in all the boxes. Can you do that?'

'Yes, if I get to use a calculator.'

As Delia neared the end of the addition sum, she turned to Grace and grinned. 'The answer's going to be 666, isn't it?'

And so it was.

'Now, while you have the calculator out, let's try another exercise. You know what a prime number is, don't you, Cordelia?'

'Yes, it's a number that can't be divided exactly by any other number except one. Like two, three, five and seven.'

'Right, now think about squares again. What's the square of two?'

'Four.'

'And what's the square of three?'

'Nine.'

'What I want you to do this time, is square all the prime numbers up to seventeen, then add the squared numbers together.'

This was a more laborious calculation but Delia soon completed it. Once again the answer was 666.

'It's such an interesting number, isn't it, Cordelia? It's hard to imagine why the early Christians hated it so much that they called it "the number of the beast". Maybe it was anti-Taran propaganda. The god Taran, associated as he was with a horned animal, the bull, was already depicted by Christians as the devil. And 6 was Taran's magic number, as you know.'

Grace had gone on to explain that there was some special significance in 6 times 6 times 6, according to the mythology of her ancestors. Something about the moon. But Delia couldn't now remember what that was.

In any case, here she was about fourteen years later, faced with one of Grace's number puzzles, a square that happened to have 6 in the top left corner. She played around with the numbers every way she could think of, but could make no sense of them. Then she thought, what if this *isn't* a number puzzle, but a word puzzle in disguise? Could it be an acrostic where each number represents a letter?

First she tried using the first nine letters of the alphabet. She drew the number-square, then a word-square beside it where A replaced 1, B 2, C 3 and so on. It looked like this:

```
6 1 2    F A B
9 4 7    I D G
3 8 5    C H E
```

That didn't seem to work, either across or down. She tried again, this time using the first nine letters of the sator square, S A T O R A R E P. Now she was getting somewhere:

```
6  1  2     A  S  A
9  4  7     P  O  R
3  8  5     T  E  R
```

The solution spelled a name: ASA PORTER.

But who was he, and if *the square holds what you seek*, why would you seek Asa Porter?

It was time to get back on Google.

16

MOONDANCE

THE TARACHSEL *USED a lunar calendar. A moon, or month, was the period of twenty-nine and a half days from one full moon to the next, sometimes rounded up to thirty days. This was the basic unit of time. People's ages, lengths of reigns of kings and so on were typically recorded in moons.*

The magic number six entered into the computation of time, as it did into almost every other aspect of the Tarachsel *world. Six moons made a season, whether a summer season from Beltane to Samhain, or a winter season from Samhain around to Beltane again. Samhain and Beltane, and the intervening festivals of Imbolc and Lunasa, were celebrated at full moon.*

Six seasons made three years, a triennium. This was a period that had astronomical significance. Obviously, a year didn't correspond to an exact number of moons, so the procession of festivals based on moons quickly got out of phase with the wheel of the earth that governed the length of the year. But the astronomers of the Merch Nyr *noticed that the cycles of moon and earth were approximately resynchronised every three years. A special celebration of the harmony of moon and earth was held at Beltane one year in three, when an 'extra' moon was inserted into the calendar.*

Six of these three-year periods made a moondance. I'm using the word 'moondance' as it has been handed down to me; it's probably a translation of a long-lost word in the Tarachsel *language, and it's rather appropriate. The* Merch Nyr *observed that in the course of a month, the moon executes an interesting dance in the sky, sometimes higher, at other times lower against the background of stars. The range from high to low reaches a minimum (now known as a 'minor standstill') every eighteen and a half years, a period of just over six triennia. Nowadays moonwatchers who gather at sites such as Stonehenge in England or Chimney Rock in Colorado pay more attention to 'major standstills', the times when, midway between minor standstills, the moon's wander from high to low in the sky is at its most extreme. But for the* Tarachsel, *the minor standstill was apparently the more important marker of time. For them it was the end of one moondance and the beginning of the next.*

It seems the Merch Nyr *were quite tolerant of approximation in their ordering of the universe. They accepted that six triennia did not exactly add up to the eighteen-and-a-half-year length of a moondance, and that the cycles of moon and earth were not exactly harmonised every three years. The number of moons in a season, seasons in a triennium or triennia in a moondance was, in each case, close enough to six to give confidence that six was a truly magic number.*

The high priestess Merefrith, Keeper of Taran's wheel, had a term of office that was tied to the moondance. She would be inducted at one minor standstill and serve until the next. A Keeper could serve two, rarely three successive moondances. If she died during her term of office, her successor would serve until the next minor standstill, when she might be inducted for the next full moondance.

Multiples of six were also used to define still longer time periods. Six moondances – about one hundred and eleven years – were deemed the maximum human lifespan permitted by the gods, though only a tiny number of people ever came close to living so long. And six of those long periods were, according to legend, the span of time from one major change in direction — what the Tarachsel *called a* cambus, *literally a river-bend like the one where Aeth encountered the kingfisher — to the next.*

A cambus *could therefore be expected every 666 years or so (that famous 'number of the beast', 36 moondances each of about eighteen and a half years). Again this was accepted as an approximate, not a precise, measure of time.*

The first cambus *took the form of the Years With No Summer that began in 1189 BC, following which women replaced men as the dominant cultural and political force. The second* cambus, *in the sixth century BC, was marked by the coming of the Celts with their new language, new gods and new metal. A* cambus *was a time of great peril, a cusp of history when everything could be lost. Emerging from a* cambus, *people could find their world changed, maybe for better but just as likely for worse. The* Tarachsel *believed that* cambus *number six would be the end of the world, but that was so far in the future it was no cause for worry.*

Just over two thousand years ago, the Merch Nyr *began preaching that the next* cambus, *number three, would come soon. The* Tarachsel *people braced themselves, not just because the women of the* Merch Nyr *had calculated the timing but because they could see what form it was going to take. Other Celtic peoples were already experiencing it, according to traders and other visitors from the south.*

The Romans were coming.

17

A BUSY DAY FOR THE PROFESSOR

WHO IS, OR WAS, Asa Porter? Google had an answer, though not one that seemed relevant to the search for Taran's wheel.

Colonel Asa Porter was one of the founders of the town of Haverhill, New Hampshire. In the Revolutionary War he sided with the British, for which he was much disliked and derided by his compatriots. He was known for mistreating his slaves. One contemporary story concerns his come-uppance at the hands of a young black girl who had many times been on the receiving end of his horse-whip.

The colonel, a smallish man, had unwisely tied one end of a rope around the girl and the other around himself, to prevent her escape while he laid his whip on her. Being taller and more powerful than the colonel, she was able to drag him to the bank of the Connecticut River, which bordered his property. Afraid she was about to drown him, he cried pathetically for help, and was saved only by the mercy of one of his neighbours who might have been quite happy to see him get a good soaking.

On a whim, Delia decided to go to New Hampshire. It was a very tentative lead, but it was all she had.

She flew to Burlington, Vermont, then drove in a rental car to the little town of Haverhill, just over the Connecticut River that forms the New Hampshire state line. There, on Court Street, she spotted the small library and was lucky to find it open. She told the librarian she was doing research on slavery during the Revolutionary War, and wondered if the library might have any material on Asa Porter.

'As it happens,' the librarian said, 'there was an article about the Porter family in the library newsletter two or three years ago. Let me see if I can find it for you. We had it on our website for a while but I think we just have a paper copy now.'

She rummaged in a file cabinet by her desk and eventually produced the relevant newsletter. 'See, I'll make a photocopy for you. No charge, since you're doing research.' Delia reckoned she might be the library's only customer for the day and the librarian was probably only too pleased to take some time to help her.

Quickly perusing the photocopied article, she immediately knew she was on the right track. The author of the article was none other than Arthur A. Johnson.

'The author, is he a local man?' she asked the librarian.

'Yes, he's lived here for quite a number of years now. He's a retired professor of something or other.'

'I'd love to interview him,' Delia said.

'Well, now, that could be difficult. I heard Professor Johnson has Alzheimer's. Very sad, especially for such an intelligent man – know what I mean? He recently moved into a home.'

'Which home would that be?' Delia inquired.

The librarian started to answer, then stopped. 'I'm not really at liberty to say. You know, you being a stranger and all.'

'Not a problem,' Delia said. 'You've been very helpful.' She figured there couldn't be very many residential care homes in the immediate vicinity of Haverhill. She would check on the internet and try each one in turn, though she was disheartened to learn that Arthur Johnson had dementia and might not be able to answer her questions.

The very first facility she visited was the Autumn Leaves Care Home, not five miles from Haverhill. 'I'm here to visit Mr Johnson,' she said to the receptionist.

'Art or Cornelius?'

'I should have said Art Johnson.'

'No,' the receptionist countered, 'you shoulda said "the Professor". He's in Room 125. I need you to sign in.'

While Delia was signing the visitor's book, the receptionist carried on speaking. 'It's been a busy day for the Professor. Doesn't usually get so many visitors. He had two this morning, former students of his, they said. Nice gentlemen, both from Texas or someplace down that-a-way, judging by their accent. Very courteous, both of 'em.'

The monologue continued, and Delia stole a glance at their names – Z. Thake and J. Bazilevich.

'Now,' the receptionist continued, 'his grandson's there with him. Fine young man, he is. Comes every week. Drives all the way from Ithaca, New York just to see his grandpa. Name's Quinton. Unusual name, dontcha think?'

Delia had already noticed the signature 'Quin Johnson' in the book. As she proceeded along the hallway, the receptionist shouted directions. 'Take a left by the table with the flowers on it. Yep, that's it. It'll be the fourth door on your right.'

The door of Room 125 was lying open. An old man sat with his back to the window, facing the door. As Delia entered, his face lit up.

'Selena! What a wonderful surprise!'

'This isn't Selena, Grampa,' the young man said gently. 'It's Miss Cobb.'

Arthur Johnson's face crumpled in disappointment. Delia was first heartbroken that his joy at seeing someone he thought he knew had been so quickly dashed. And then she was surprised that the young man knew who she was.

'I'm Quin,' the young man said, extending his hand. 'I saw you at Grace's memorial service, but we didn't get a chance to talk.'

'Yes,' she said, recalling the young stranger at the Northbrook Hilton who didn't stay for the buffet. 'I remember your face. I'm Delia.'

They looked at each other for a moment, saying nothing. Quin broke the silence. 'But it was my grandfather you came to see. Grampa, Delia's from Chicago. She's a friend of Grace's.'

Delia attempted conversation with the old man, but he quickly became confused and agitated. Quin saved the situation. 'It's time for your nap, Grampa. We'll leave you now. I'll be back tomorrow.' He kissed the old man on the temple.

As they walked out, Delia said, 'Quin, I'm so sorry I distressed him.'

'Not at all,' Quin replied. 'Did you see the radiant smile on his face when you walked in? I haven't seen him smile like that for ages. I wish I hadn't been so quick to correct him when he called you Selena.'

They went to a local coffee-shop.

'So you knew all about Grace,' Delia said.

'Yes – and all about Selena too. I've seen photographs. You *are* very like her.'

'I know. I can see it myself.'

'How did you know you'd find my grandfather here in New Hampshire?' Quin asked.

'I didn't,' Delia replied truthfully. 'I found his name on Selena's birth certificate, but that's all I knew. It was only after following a trail of clues left by Grace that I decided on a hunch to come to Haverhill. It wasn't hard to find him in such a tiny town. So Quin, what do *you* know of Grace's relationship with your grandfather all those years ago?'

He told her Grace and Arthur had been college friends in the early sixties. Just buddies, no romance. A year or two after graduating, Grace contacted Arthur with an interesting proposition. She'd decided to have a baby, and she wanted him to be the father. There would be no strings. Grace would bring up the baby. Arthur could visit whenever he liked but would have no financial obligation. It was just his DNA she wanted for her child.

75

Arthur was between girlfriends at that moment, and after giving it some consideration he agreed. Grace was a good friend and, truth to tell, he was flattered at being asked to father her child.

'Grampa once told me they went about it the old-fashioned way. But he didn't go into details about how long it took, how many attempts, any of that. Or whether he enjoyed the experience.'

They grinned, amused both at Grace's unconventional approach to parenthood and at Arthur's willingness to comply.

Arthur had seen Selena many times as she was growing up. Though by that time he was married with a son and another daughter, he loved her as a father should. He was devastated when she died in the boating accident on Lake Michigan. His son, Quin's father, had a disastrous marriage. Quin was only four when his mother walked out to start a new life with her boss. His grandparents, Arthur and Cora, brought up the boy from that point on. Cora died when Quin was fifteen, not long after Arthur's retirement and the family's move from New York City to Haverhill.

'Who were the two men who visited your grandfather this morning?' Delia asked. 'Thake and Bazilevich, I think their names were.'

'I have no idea. I asked Grampa, but he had no recollection of having had visitors.'

The conversation came round to themselves. Quin, it turned out, was finishing up a Ph.D. in applied linguistics at Cornell University. He was researching the Indo-European roots of Celtic languages, taking a neo-Darwinian approach. Changing the subject, he said, 'You haven't told me why you came looking for my grandfather.'

Delia paused for a moment before answering. Then, what the heck, she thought. 'I believe Grace was murdered.'

Quin looked shocked. 'Murdered? How?'

'Well, the police are investigating. The cause of death initially given was cardiac arrest – she'd had heart problems for years – but there's to be a new autopsy. I think she was killed for a very precious, very old article in her possession. Have you heard, by any chance, of the *Drogan*?'

His face was blank. She explained briefly about the glass ball and its wheel symbolism.

'*Drogan*,' he said. 'It sounds very like an old proto-Celtic word for a wheel. The same Indo-European root that gives *rota* in Latin gives *drogo* in proto-Celtic.'

'What's proto-Celtic?'

'It's a theoretical reconstruction of a language that is presumed, over time, to have given rise to a variety of Celtic languages spoken in western Europe. Only Welsh, Breton and Gaelic – the Irish and Scottish forms – survive, all of them endangered. Proto-Celtic is a best guess as to the language spoken by the first Celtic settlers in Great Britain and Ireland. Anyway, did Grace's killer get the *Drogan*?'

'I don't think so,' Delia said. 'At least I hope not. Grace left some clues that suggest she may have given it to your grandfather for safe keeping.' She told him about the trail of clues leading from *Arepo* the sower of seed via Asa Porter to Arthur Johnson.

'I'm staying at Grampa's house for a couple of days. Why don't you come over? We can take a look for the *Drogan* together, if you think it could be there.'

18

THEY CALL IT PEACE

NEWS OF THE INVASION in 55 BC and subsequent battles between the Roman legions and British warriors filtered north. It was little more than rumour by the time it arrived in the Pleasant Vale. But confirmation was to come from a very distinguished source.

The southern half of the island we now call Great Britain was a patchwork of Celtic tribal kingdoms that had formed a grand alliance in a futile effort to resist the invaders. The northern half was made up of a number of statelets that were not part of this alliance, including the Cumbric-speaking lands of Rheged (Cumbria), Ystrad Clud (Strathclyde) and Gododdin (Northumbria and Lothian) as well as the Tarachsel domain still farther north. All of these peoples, north and south, worshipped the mother-goddess Brigta or Brytha and considered themselves 'British'. But only the Tarachsel placed the thunder-god Taran on at least an equal footing with Brytha.

The southern alliance had a succession of nominal 'supreme rulers' who styled themselves kings and queens of Britain, though their writ didn't extend to the northern kingdoms. It was none other than a queen of Britain who brought the definitive account of the Roman conquest to the people of the Pleasant Vale. According to Tarachsel tradition, that queen was Creiddylad, better known nowadays as Cordelia.

Queen Cordelia was the daughter of Llyr, much later immortalised by Shakespeare as King Lear. In my reading I have turned up two versions of the chronology of mythical and semi-mythical British kings and queens, one of which places Cordelia in the eighth century BC. The other makes her a much later monarch, in the first century BC. I believe that for her story to have survived, even in garbled form, down to Shakespeare's time, the later date is much more likely.

And it's consistent with tradition, as passed down by Keepers of Taran's wheel, that Cordelia was a contemporary of Julius Caesar in the first century BC. Indeed, more than just a contemporary, as I'll explain. David Hughes, in The British Chronicles, *gives an account of Cordelia's reign that, though not accepted by all historians, is in general agreement with* Tarachsel *tradition.*

We can imagine horsemen arriving in one of the southernmost provinces of Tarachsel *territory, announcing: 'We come in peace from the great kingdom of Britain. We are the advance guard of our noble Queen Cordelia, who wishes to greet your king. She has been granted safe passage through the lands of* Rheged *and* Ystrad Clud, *and now requests the protection of the* Tarachsel *people as she continues her journey to your royal court.'*

A messenger at once brought the news, first to Merefrith the high priestess and then to the king, Bridei, in his palace at the Kyaar *in Taran's Garden. Bridei, a little suspicious, conferred with Merefrith, who saw no threat. 'Let us welcome the British queen,' she said, 'with all the hospitality we can muster.'*

Cordelia's visit was eagerly anticipated for several weeks. When she arrived at Taran's Garden with her entourage, a huge feast was laid on in her honour. Merefrith called upon the gods to bless the British and Tarachsel *peoples and secure everlasting peace between them. The* Drogan Taranish *was laid ceremonially before the royal guest, who accorded it all due reverence. She presented her hosts with gifts made of the finest gold from Gaul, where as a younger woman she had been consort to the king.*

Cordelia spoke in a tongue that was strange to the Tarachsel. It was a pure Celtic language akin to modern Welsh. Some words were familiar to her hosts although spoken with a strange inflection; others had to be translated by an interpreter.

After the official festivities, the queen and Merefrith had a more informal meeting, attended by just a few confidants on each side and, of course, the interpreter. Cordelia told Merefrith she had long known of, and admired, the Tarachsel system of governance. 'I have so much to learn from you,' she said. 'You enjoy peace, and still you remain strong. Your rulers are always kings, never queens, but they take counsel from the women of the priesthood, and especially, Merefrith, from yourself. Yet you place the god Taran above all others, even over our beloved mother-goddess Brigta – Brytha as you call her. And your most precious jewel is what you call Taran's wheel, the Drogan Taranish.'

Merefrith recounted the foundation myth of the Tarachsel. 'Taran the giant stood at a place we call Taran's Crossing. A great cairn marks the spot. There he loosed a thunderbolt that carved this beautiful vale and gathered its rocks all around to make the circle of hills you see in all directions. Can you blame us for giving worship to such a bountiful god?

'Still, what you say – that we place Taran above Brytha – is not quite true. Consider the Drogan, which you saw yesterday. It was a daughter of Taran, in the guise of a kingfisher, who long ago led a boy called Aeth to that most sacred object. The wheel of Taran is in the Drogan, but it is embraced within the orb of Brytha, just as the rule of our king is governed by the wise counsel of the Merch Nyr.'

It was Cordelia's turn to speak. 'I am a woman and rule my kingdom. But men dictate to me what I can and cannot do.

And my realm is in danger of falling apart. The husbands of my two sisters would seize my crown and split the kingdom of Britain in two. I remain queen, and Britain remains whole, only through a pact with the invaders.'

'The invaders?' Merefrith queried. 'We have heard of the armies of Rome that landed on your shores, and their commander Julius Caesar. You have an alliance with him?'

The queen's response was unexpected. 'An alliance indeed. I have submitted to marriage with Gaius Julius Caesar, and for my faithfulness and obedience to him he protects my kingdom. I have borne his daughter, Cesair.'

Merefrith could see that the queen was happy to have a daughter but that the marriage was no more than a political expediency. She probed a little. 'Your husband, is he a good man?'

'What can I say? He is a Roman. Romans are not like the British people. Though they think themselves civilised, they are cruel and barbaric. And I have come in all friendship to warn you that the Romans will not stop where they are. They will push northward. Soon they will be here. Remember my words, Merefrith. They make a wasteland and they call it peace.'

'But we have peace. And here in this northern land we have little to offer them, little to interest them.'

'Nevertheless, they will come,' were Cordelia's final words on the subject.

19

THE PASTOR

THE KINGDOM OF MEN was a megachurch like an aircraft hangar surrounded by a huge parking lot, in the rolling green countryside about fifteen miles north of Topeka, Kansas. Inside, a vast open space could accommodate six thousand worshippers, many of whom attended twice a week to hear the word of God transmitted by their beloved preacher, whom they knew simply as 'the Pastor'. Some drove from as far afield as Kansas City or Wichita. Thousands more tuned in to watch the services live on television.

Mainstream Christians find 'The Kingdom of Men' an odd name for a church, even an unconventional one like this. Nebuchadnezzar's dream as recounted in the book of Daniel signals, among other things, that the kingdom of men is subordinate to the Most High. Churches are supposed not to glorify mere earthly kingdoms.

But to the Pastor's congregation, the meaning was clear. They believed, deep in their hearts they *knew*, that in the Second Coming the world will once again be ruled by men, with women as their most prized possessions, at the same time obedient servants and childbearers. And twice a week, the pews were packed with the faithful, all eager for reinforcement of the message that the Kingdom of Men is at hand.

It came as no surprise to the Pastor that his message of male supremacy was lapped up by the women as well as the men of his congregation. He had studied the phenomenon of 'willing subservience' and knew exactly how to nurture it. If *burqa*-clad women in Afghanistan could be trained as suicide bombers to further Taliban goals of denying them the most basic human rights; if the wives and daughters of polygamous patriarchs in the desert south-west of the U.S. could defend to the death their own enslavement – why shouldn't thousands, and eventually millions, of women be persuaded to welcome the Pastor's promise of a world controlled exclusively by men? One of the great things about women was their inherent stupidity. Fortunately education, at least the kind available in the schools of Kansas, hadn't completely destroyed that. But just to be on the safe side, in the new world order girls would not have the benefit of education.

He ran his church like the money-making operation it was. The business had been acquired at a knock-down price from a more conventional evangelist who had been caught once too often with a hooker or rent-boy and had sunk into alcoholism. By his eloquence and the clarity of his message the Pastor had built the congregation up from the few hundred he inherited to the thousands who now filled his coffers as well as his pews. A tall man of fifty who looked at least ten years younger, he had the evenly bronzed skin that only the most exclusive tanning spa could impart and a blondness and luxuriance of hair that could hardly be natural.

On a particular Sunday in July, he blessed his congregation at the end of the service and went to his office at the rear of the building. There, in the air-conditioned comfort of his inner sanctum, he sat down behind his large desk, put up his feet and lit a cigarette. After a few minutes he pressed a button on his desktop. A buzzer sounded.

Ezekiel Thackeray came in, closely followed by his sidekick Jayden Bayliss. They stood stiffly in front of the Pastor's desk until motioned to sit.

'Well,' the Pastor said, 'I hope you have some progress to report.'

'We do indeed, Most Reverend,' Thackeray affirmed. 'The Trojan Rat was deployed as planned. Mr Bayliss took care of that. And after a few days we began to receive intelligence. The Cobb girl did an online search for persons named Arthur Johnson and Asa Porter, then booked a flight to Burlington, Vermont and a hotel in Woodsville, New Hampshire. Mr Bayliss and I flew to New Hampshire, just ahead of the girl, and located Arthur Johnson in a retirement home.'

'And Asa Porter, did you locate him too?'

'He's been dead two hundred years, Most Reverend. But he was part of the trail that led us to Johnson, who, it turns out, still owns a house, now unoccupied but full of stuff. We were able to gain access to his house and conduct a thorough search.'

Bayliss had been itching to speak up. '*Very* thorough,' he said, nodding sagely.

The Pastor glared at Bayliss, then Thackeray. 'If your accomplice wishes to talk to me, he needs to learn the correct form of address.'

'Yes, Most Reverend.'

'I don't need to hear details, but did you find the glass ball?'

Thackeray shifted uncomfortably in his seat. 'Not yet, Most Reverend. But it was unlikely we would find it at Johnson's house. As you have consistently said, we need to work through Cato Woods. We can get the girl any time, but as long as she is still looking for the glass ball herself it won't do any good to approach her directly.'

'Agreed. And where is Woods at this moment?'

'He's still in London, Most Reverend.'

'London? Does he think he'll find the object there?'

Bayliss took up the narrative. 'We went to London, paid him a visit. He knows exactly what our expectations are. He still imagines he'll get rich off this deal, but he can think again.'

The Pastor glared at him again.

'Most Reverend,' Bayliss completed his sentence.

'Let him think he has a big payoff coming,' the Pastor said. 'I know his type. Greed is a bigger motivator than fear for him.'

He didn't say another word, but his two visitors knew the meeting was over. The moment they left the room, the Pastor lit another cigarette, picked up the telephone and punched in a number. His call rolled to voicemail.

'This is the Pastor. Stand by for another contract,' was the message he left.

20

THE FARMER AND THE SWORD

A HUNDRED YEARS PASSED *from the time Queen Cordelia came to the Pleasant Vale. Her visit, much talked about among succeeding generations of the* Tarachsel *people, took on a mythical quality, and was no doubt progressively embellished in the telling.*

Solidarity was strengthened among the hitherto fragmented Tarachsel *kingdoms and provinces as they prepared for Roman attack. The kingdom of Ce, with Taran's Garden as its centre of power, became dominant over other lands such as* Fortriu *to the north and west and* Cait *beyond,* Circinn *to the south and* Fib *still farther south. Defensive hillforts were built; but still the Romans didn't come, despite Cordelia's insistent prophecy. True, word made its way north of the gradual conquest of southern Britain, and occasional sightings of Roman scouting parties were reported in the* Tarachsel *borderlands. Yet, though the people of Lothian (the* Votadini *as their name was rendered in Latin) submitted to the armies of Rome, no effort was made to conquer or subdue the* Tarachsel.

All that changed under Gnaeus Julius Agricola, who became governor of Britain in the year 77 of the current era. Ambitious for political status back in Rome, he was dissatisfied that only a portion of Britain had been brought under Roman rule. It was possible that the northern, still barbarian, part was much bigger than the southern, pacified, part, and that his predecessors had therefore conquered only a tiny fraction of Britain. Agricola didn't know at that time, though he may have suspected, that Britain was an island; in any case there was a vast terra incognita in the north which could make him a triumphal hero in the streets of Rome. His campaigns in Britain were recorded by the historian Tacitus, who happened to be his son-in-law, and might therefore have been a not entirely unbiased reporter.

Agricola assembled a relatively small group of legionnaires from the ninth legion, garrisoned at that time in Eboracum (York), and a much larger force of Celtic conscripts from Britain and Belgium. The Celts were a rabble, but were fearless fighters and, most importantly, expendable. Agricola marched his force north, establishing marching camps at intervals along the way. He met his first serious resistance in the Forth valley, where his camp was attacked at night by a huge band of warriors. He succeeded in putting them to flight, but the experience unnerved him somewhat and he resolved to keep his legionnaires out of harm's way as far as possible. The conscripts would henceforward form the front line and bear the brunt of any attack by the savage natives. Tacitus puts it quite plainly: this was 'a disposition which would render the victory signally glorious, if it were obtained without the expense of Roman blood.'

By the autumn of 84, Agricola's expeditionary force had penetrated deep into Tarachsel territory, pausing somewhere between the Rivers Dee and Don. Roman camps by both rivers may date from this campaign.

A long and difficult supply line was by now necessary. Ships laden with supplies anchored off the east coast and delivered their cargo to stores along the shoreline, but these stores were constantly depleted by enemy raids. Agricola ensured his legionnaires ate well, but lacked the resources to keep his vast army of conscripts in peak fighting condition.

By capture and forceful interrogation of local people,

Agricola would have learned that the political centre of the Tarachsel *lay only a day's march west of his camp. There, in a fertile valley surrounded by a ring of hills, the natives accumulated considerable stores of food for the winter. These stores were in purpose-built underground chambers – souterrains or earth-houses as they are now called. Several of these earth-houses can still be found in the Howe of Cromar. One is by the roadside at Culsh, less than two miles from Tarland on the Aberdeen road. Others, less well preserved, are near Migvie and Braes of Cromar in the west of the Howe.*

It was October and the stores would be at their fullest. We can imagine the Celtic conscripts being told: 'If you wish to eat, you need to invade that valley, deal with any opposition you face, and take what you want from those earth-houses. Leave them empty if you like. It will be your battle, but we Romans will wait in the rear and give support if needed.'

As I previously mentioned, six roads radiated from the Pleasant Vale in ancient times. You might think these would take low ground. But narrow passes are danger-points for ambush, and in those days the roads, such as they were, tended to cross higher ground. Approaching from the east, as Agricola's forces would have done, there were two routes into Cromar. One of these followed the Dee valley to a point west of Aboyne, then crossed the shoulder of Craig Dhu near the great cairn erected there almost two thousand years earlier, to enter Cromar from the south. The other passed near the present-day village of Lumphanan and climbed the south flank of Craiglich, descending into Cromar due east of Tarland.

Hill-forts or defensive earthworks that had been built to guard the south-western approaches to the Vale, one on Mulloch and one on Knockargety, were useless in the face of an attack from the east. Fortunately, however, the Tarachsel *had good intelligence and were prepared for Agricola's arrival, massing fighters on the slopes of both Craig Dhu and Craiglich. Though Tacitus describes the scene at only one hill, which he calls* Mons Graupius, *he does clarify that the natives were massed on the 'tops of hills'* (summa collium) *before descending to the fray.*

The general leading the native forces was a controversial figure among his compatriots. His skill in swordsmanship was undisputed, but according to the Keepers' tales he had a reputation as a self-important loudmouth, given to foolish errors of judgment. Only his nickname has survived: Calgacus, from kalga *which in the* Tarachsel *language could mean a sword or a penis. So to his admirers, and no doubt to himself, he was 'the Sword' and to his detractors 'the Prick'.*

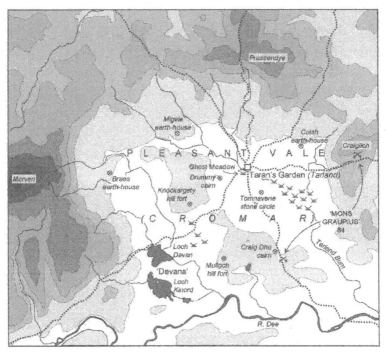

This map identifies the battlefields of Craiglich and Craig Dhu. You'll notice the six ancient roads radiating from Taran's Garden as they would have been around the year 84. See how the battlefields are close to two of these ancient roadways.

Tacitus described the outcome as a rout of the Caledonii *(according to Ptolemy the name of a different highland people living far to the west). With obvious hyperbole, he wrote that the native forces were thirty thousand strong, of whom ten thousand were killed in the battle for the loss of only three hundred and sixty of Agricola's 'auxiliaries' – his Celtic conscripts. The* Tarachsel *left no written record, but the total losses on both sides were probably around two thousand.*

Despite heavy casualties, Calgacus's warriors were able to hold off the invaders until nightfall. Under cover of darkness, many of Agricola's conscripts may have defected to the Tarachsel, *deducing they had a better chance of a square meal if aligned with Calgacus's men than if they returned to camp empty-handed.*

The Keepers tell that on the morning after the battle, Agricola surveyed the Pleasant Vale from the great cairn on Craig Dhu. There he received an emissary from Calgacus, who proposed a meeting to discuss terms of peace. Agricola agreed, perhaps reckoning that his conscript army was so depleted – by defection if not by death on the battlefield – that taking the land by force no longer seemed such a simple task. The meeting would take place in two days' time at one of the Tarachsel's *most sacred places, the stone circle at Tomnaverie.*

At the peace conference, Calgacus was unbowed. Through an interpreter (probably from Agricola's Celtic ranks), he gave a rambling speech puffing up his own skills as a military leader. He concluded his speech by saying of the Romans:

They make a wasteland and they call it peace.

His words were the ones spoken by Queen Cordelia a hundred years earlier.

It was then Agricola's turn for a bit of puffery. 'This great victory for Rome will be famous all over the world,' he intoned, 'and will be spoken of as long as men fight wars.'

Calgacus replied, 'This was no victory for Rome. We are not defeated. Your men are hiding like frightened deer in the woods. The true story of this battle will be told to our children and grandchildren. The great name of Calgacus the Sword will not be forgotten.'

'You will tell it your way,' Agricola said, 'and we will tell it ours. Let history be the judge.'

Calgacus was unprepared for this attempt at consensus, and continued for a few minutes to make empty boasts. Agricola listened patiently, then, when the opportunity presented itself, took charge of the conversation.

'You Caledonii are a proud and brave people. In these respects you are more like Romans than the other peoples of Britain. And in another way you are like us. You worship the great thunder-god, whom you call Taran and we call Jupiter – the father of the gods. Your cousins in the south worship lesser gods, and are lesser people as a result.'

Agricola then proposed an exchange of gifts to cement what he called a bond of respect between them. They would meet again for this purpose in a few days, at a location midway between the Pleasant Vale and the Roman camp.

While these meetings were going on, the women of the Vale had other work to do. For days they laboured on the battlefields of Craiglich and Craig Dhu, burying the dead where they lay. Over each body, they made a small cairn of stones gathered from the hillside. They made no distinction between the bodies of Tarachsel warriors, recognisable by their body paint, and those of Agricola's Celtic conscripts. All were buried with the same reverence; all were given equal cairns.

It was a task the women had performed many times, and they thought they were hardened to it. But they were not prepared for what they found on the two battlefields. Most of the dead conscripts on the Roman side were very young – many of them mere children. Agricola's strategy had been to dispatch a first attacking wave of ten- to sixteen-year-old boys to soak up Tarachsel *arrows before sending in more experienced fighters to engage in close combat with swords and axes.* Queen Cordelia's words of a century before seemed to echo across the blood-soaked hillsides:

Romans are not like the British people. Though they think themselves civilised, they are cruel and barbaric.

With the gruesome job completed, the women brought the Drogan Taranish *to the field of cairns on the slope of Craiglich, and placed it under the stones of one of the cairns, where they guarded it overnight. The next night they did the same thing on Craig Dhu. The power of the* Drogan *would ensure that the wheel of* vairtach *would be completed for all those men cut down in – or before – their prime.*

The cairns the women built, almost two thousand of them, are still there, both on the north slope of Craiglich and on the east slope of Craig Dhu, by the ancient roads leading into Cromar. They have been known about for a very long time – you can read a 1919 account by Alexander Ogston on the internet – but until now they haven't been associated with the battle of Mons Graupius. *Ogston claims that these cairn-fields are 'the largest prehistoric cemeteries in Great Britain', though others have suggested they are merely evidence of iron age or earlier field clearance.*

And here's another interesting thing. The hill that's called Craiglich on maps isn't generally known by that name to the people of Cromar. They call it Ladle-lick – a curious name, don't you think? It's said to be a corruption of Tarachsel *words meaning 'hill of graves'.*

Tacitus's name 'Mons Graupius' for the battlefield gave rise, via a fifteenth century misspelling, to the modern name 'Grampian Mountains', applied sometimes to the entire highland area east of a line from Inverness to Oban, and sometimes in a more limited sense to the Mounth – the range of hills forming the southern boundary of the Dee valley.

The precise location of the second meeting of Agricola and Calgacus is a matter of pure conjecture. One theory places it at a stone circle in a place called Ordie Gordon, a location about thirteen miles east of Tarland that will crop up again in our story.

Agricola brought a large earthenware jar to the second meeting. 'I am a soldier and politician,' he said, 'but I was raised to be a farmer, and at heart that is what I remain. Even my name means "farmer" in Latin. In this jar are seeds. They are my gift to your people. Plant them and tend them carefully. Every seed you harvest next year, plant again. Don't be tempted to eat them or feed them to your animals yet. Let them multiply for three years. Then you will have enough for your whole valley.'

Calgacus put his hand into the jar and drew out a handful of seeds. At first he was highly suspicious. 'What unnatural grain is this?' he asked.

Agricola called it by its Latin name, avena. The interpreter translated it as 'oat'.

'Oat,' Calgacus said dismissively, 'is a barren, useless husk. It grows in our fields but sheds its seed before it can be harvested.'

'This oat is different,' Agricola told him. 'It holds on to its seed. You can harvest it just like barley.'

To the uneducated Calgacus, the new grain seemed to defy nature. This was not, like barley and rye, a creation of the gods but a man-made perversion. He was as deeply mistrustful of it as any latter-day campaigner against genetically modified crops. 'By what infernal magic did you make this?' he demanded to know.

'No magic. Just good farming, good breeding. Go on, taste it.'

Calgacus at first demurred. One of his lieutenants, more attuned than Calgacus to the potential for offending the Roman by rejecting the gift, approached and whispered something in his ear. After a few moments, Calgacus cautiously took a couple of grains, crushed them between his teeth and moved them around his mouth so that he could taste them with different parts of his tongue. 'These grains are plump and rich,' he announced at length. Then, after a short pause: 'We accept your gift.'

Now it was Calgacus's turn. He produced a small sack, out of which, to the horror of his men, he drew a glass ball, the Drogan Taranish. He laid it before Agricola. 'Within this sphere,' Calgacus said, 'you will see the wheel of Taran. It was a gift from Taran, your Jupiter, to my people. Now it is yours.'

Calgacus held the Drogan up to catch the sunlight and display to full effect the iridescent blue rays forming Taran's wheel. Agricola took it in his hands, turning it over and over, obviously fascinated by the object.

After a few more speeches, the meeting of the Farmer and the Sword was over. Agricola rode off triumphantly with his prize.

The battle with the Romans under Agricola was a major turning point for the Tarachsel. It was the third cambus they had long anticipated. For many, it was a disaster. Added to the loss of life, surrender of Taran's wheel was more than they could bear. What could Calgacus have been thinking of? What a Prick! Now there were much worse things he was being called.

What they did not appreciate was that his gift of the Drogan Taranish to Agricola was fully supported by Merefrith the high priestess. Indeed it was Merefrith who had mooted the idea to Calgacus, an idea that he had at first resisted.

'We are at the third cambus,' she had told him. 'When we reach the sixth and final cambus the world will end. That means we're exactly in the middle. When you were a young boy, did you ever make a seesaw by placing a board over a round log? Do you remember finding the balancing point on the board, the point where the board could sit on the log without *touching the ground at either end? That's where we are, at the balancing point. Taran's wheel can buy us peace and freedom from the Romans. It's a treasure we can give up only once. If not now, when?'*

The sacrifice, it turned out, resulted in the Tarachsel *emerging relatively unscathed from the third great crisis in their history. The food stores in the earth-houses were safe. True, there were now some extra mouths to feed, as the population of the Pleasant Vale was swollen by hundreds of defectors from Agricola's army. But many of the new inhabitants of the Vale were accomplished huntsmen, and more than paid for their keep.*

The strange new oat grain that had been presented to Calgacus by Agricola was sown in a few fields near Taran's Garden. As the Farmer had advised, the entire harvest from these fields was saved for next year's crop, and this continued for three years. The grain was found to be perfectly suited to the climate and soil, not only of the Vale but of most of the Tarachsel *lands all around. And it provided better nourishment for the people and for their horses and chickens than anything that had gone before.*

Oats, known only as a useless weed before the third cambus, *became the staple grain of northern Britain, and remained so until the twentieth century. A better gift in exchange for the* Drogan Taranish *can scarcely be imagined.*

And what became of Agricola after his brush with the Tarachsel? *He attempted no more battles with them, but he did stake a symbolic claim to the whole of Great Britain by sailing his fleet around the north, proving that Britain was indeed an island. Less than one year after the battle of* Mons Graupius, *officially recorded as a glorious victory over the barbarian* Caledonii, *he was unexpectedly recalled to Rome by the emperor Domitian. He does not appear to have returned a great hero, as he hoped. Tacitus, his son-in-law and biographer, put as shiny a gloss as he could on the recall, but* it's clear that Agricola had somehow lost the emperor's confidence and he retired to his farm, taking no further part in affairs of state.

Subsequent governors of Britain made no attempt to conquer the Tarachsel. Instead, defensive walls were built defining the northern limit of the Roman empire. First, Hadrian's wall was started about forty years after Mons Graupius; later the more northerly Antonine wall was built close to the Tarachsel borderlands but was abandoned within twenty years. Incidentally, it was during the Romans' brief exposure to the indigenous people north of the Antonine wall that Ptolemy began to use the name Taexali for those people, a closer approximation to 'Tarachsel' than Tacitus's Caledonii. However, it is the name 'Caledonia' that has survived as a romantic or poetic synonym for Scotland.

What happened to the Drogan after its acquisition by Agricola is unknown. Certainly Tacitus gave no clue in his writings. Agricola is known to have been addicted to dice games, and it's possible that, after his return to Rome, he lost the Drogan in a wager.

END OF FIRST TESTAMENT OF GRACE ROSMAN,
KEEPER OF TARAN'S WHEEL

21

BACK IN BLACK

T HE MOMENT THEY WALKED UP to Arthur Johnson's house, they knew something was amiss. The door jamb was splintered and parts of the lock hardware were lying on the doorstep. They returned to Delia's car, where Quin called the police to report an apparent burglary.

Two uniformed officers were first to enter. A few minutes later, once they were satisfied there was no one inside, Delia and Quin were allowed in, but were warned not to touch anything.

Arthur's living room had been ransacked. Furniture had been knocked over, the television lying face-down on the floor. His old-fashioned audio system had been pulled from its shelf and was now dangling precariously by its speaker cables. Hundreds of CDs were strewn on the floor, some out of their cases.

'Grampa had an amazing range of music, mostly on CD,' Quin explained. 'He would be more distraught to see it scattered on the floor like this, than about any other damage or loss. It's a good thing he's not here.'

Having accompanied one of the officers on a tour of the house, to identify what might have been taken, Quin declared nothing of significant monetary value appeared to be missing. Even his laptop computer was undisturbed. Apparently they had been most interested in the music collection, though it seemed unlikely they would go to the trouble of a burglary just for a few CDs.

It was no longer an option for Quin to spend the night at his grandfather's house as planned. The police wanted to dust for fingerprints. Delia was uncomfortably reminded of having had to vacate Grace's apartment in Illinois just a few weeks earlier.

Once a local carpenter had patched up and secured the front door, she said to Quin, 'I've a reservation at Nootka Lodge in Woodsville. Why don't we head over there and see if they have another room available for tonight?'

Next day, they embarked on tidying up. Quin began collecting the CDs from the floor, matching with their cases the ones that were lying loose. 'Grampa had all his music arranged alphabetically, by composer or performer,' he said. 'With this much stuff, it's the only way he would've been able to find a particular recording.'

Delia paused in her task of gathering up pieces of a broken vase to look up at Quin with his armful of compact discs. What came into her mind at that moment was:

Arepo, sower of seed, carefully holds the wheels.

Those discs were 'wheels' of a kind, she thought. Leaving what she was doing, she joined Quin among the wreckage of Arthur Johnson's music library.

The collection had been eclectic in the extreme. A cappella to zydeco, medieval to twenty-first century, every conceivable genre seemed to be represented. 'A little light on hip-hop,' Quin ventured. 'But look at this – Debussy, Dizzy, Dylan. Grampa had wide-ranging tastes in music. Here's Sinatra cheek by jowl with Simple Minds.'

'Wide-ranging for sure,' Delia agreed. 'Quin, I wonder if what *you're* looking *at* and what *I'm* looking *for* are somehow connected?' She told him about *Arepo* the sower of seed, carefully holding the 'wheels'.

She began sifting through the CDs still on the floor and those Quin had stacked on the dining table. The Van Morrison album *Moondance* rang a bell with her; hadn't Grace once used that word when explaining the movements of the moon in the sky? She set it to one side, for later examination. Then she happened to notice that the highest of the shelves remained undisturbed. Among the very first items in Arthur's alphabetical array was the AC/DC album *Back in Black*.

Whether it was her affection for *All Night Long*, one of her favourite hard rock classics that she knew was on that album, or some other motivation, she stood on a chair and reached for the CD. As soon as she held the unopened case in her hand, she knew she had found what she was looking for.

The cover was minimalist. Pure black, with the simple words *'Back in Black'* across the middle, and above them, the Australian band's famous logo with, between 'AC' and 'DC', its jagged lightning-bolt signifying electricity.

A lightning-bolt. One of the ancient symbols of Taran.

Opening the case, Delia saw that the disc inside was not the AC/DC album promised on the cover. Virtually the entire non-playing surface was occupied by an image of a wheel with six spokes. When the disc was tilted, the wheel image disappeared and a lightning-bolt spanning the full diameter of the disc became visible. Clever, Delia thought. A hologram. Tilting it back to reveal the wheel, she caught something she hadn't noticed earlier. Around the rim of the wheel, in a non-contrasting colour, was a series of twelve letters, six at the ends of the spokes alternating with six others.

It took her a few moments to make sense of them. If she began at eleven o'clock and read anticlockwise, all the way to twelve o'clock, they spelled out a name:

E D D I E   S C H E R I N

First Asa Porter, now Eddie Scherin. Asa brought her to New Hampshire. Where would Eddie lead? She showed the disc to Quin.

'What are we waiting for?' he asked. 'Let's play it.' He popped it into the drive of his laptop and, after a few seconds, an image appeared on the screen identical to the wheel on the label, but without the letters.

'Is that it?' Delia wondered. Then a voice spoke from Quin's computer. It was unmistakable. Grace's voice.

> *Cordelia, if everything has gone according to plan, you are the one listening to this recording. Arthur, if you're there, thank you for being my* Arepo.
>
> *The* Drogan *is safe. It's back in a place it's been before. Cordelia, I have been unable to trace a blood relative through the female line to whom I can entrust it. I want you to retrieve it, and become its Keeper. It's vitally important that it doesn't fall into the wrong hands. That happened once, as you'll learn, and a thousand years passed before it came back. So I hope you'll understand and forgive me if I don't make it too easy to find.*
>
> *By naming a successor who is not a blood relative, I'm breaking a chain that extends all the way back to the Beaker People. I hope that nonetheless you'll be willing to accept the responsibility I'm passing on to you. As Keeper, you will be custodian not only of Taran's wheel but the entire* Tarachsel *tradition.*

Delia hit the pause button. 'Great,' she said, with heavy irony. 'I'm to be the Keeper of something I've no idea where to find and of a tradition I know almost nothing about.'

'I'm sure Grace has a lot more to say on both subjects,' Quin said, touching 'play'.

> *Oh, by the way, Cordelia, did you like the label design for the CD? As you can imagine, that kind of thing is way beyond me, but my good friend Eddie did it for me. Remember, we used to call him Eddie the Geek? A little unkind of us maybe, but rather accurate. He has all kinds of graphics software. I described the*

wheel and lightning-bolt for him, and he reproduced them well. The hologram was his idea. I was happy for him to add his signature to a nice piece of artwork.

'I think I met this Eddie at Grace's memorial,' Quin said.

'Yes, you probably did. He was certainly there. You know the funny thing? Until now, I never knew his second name was Scherin.'

All that remained of the recording was a 'Goodbye' from Grace. Then a caption appeared at the bottom of the screen:

Click on the hub of the wheel.

The six-spoked wheel design still occupied the computer screen. Quin clicked on the appointed spot, which caused a box to appear, together with another caption:

Enter your password in the box.

'Uh-oh,' was his reaction.

'She's addressed this to me,' Delia said, 'so she expects me to know the password. I've a pretty good idea what it is.'

He motioned her to type the password, and looked away. She entered her childhood acrostic for *'Love, and be silent'*, the words spoken by Shakespeare's Cordelia in *King Lear*. The six characters

O & b S h h

followed by the 'enter' key brought up a document that began:

FIRST TESTAMENT OF GRACE ROSMAN,
KEEPER OF TARAN'S WHEEL

The Pleasant Vale was born in an episode of unimaginable violence. An asteroid with a mass of twenty to fifty million tons slammed into the Earth, gouging a crater where gathered a molten mixture of interplanetary and terrestrial rock.

Together they read this *First Testament*, all forty-two pages of it, transfixed by the unfolding history of what Grace referred to as the 'Pleasant Vale', a location in Scotland now called the Howe of Cromar. The story began in the impossibly distant past, the Jurassic era, and continued up to the coming of the Romans, around two thousand years ago.

It was followed by a brief epilogue.

What you have read is, in part, a story passed down by the daughters of Brytha, the Keepers of Taran's wheel, by word of mouth from generation to generation. Other parts have been filled in by archaeological research, mostly the work of my good friend Megan who calls the Pleasant Vale home. And a few parts I admit I've made up, including the bit about the asteroid impact. No geologist I've talked to will say there's any evidence for such an event other than the almost perfectly circular shape of the Howe of Cromar, though none will say it's impossible.

It's Megan who came up with the name Tarachsel *for the people who called their homeland Ce, the people Ptolemy named* Taexali. *And it's Megan whose research has identified the hills overlooking Cromar as possibly the place where the battle of* Mons Graupius *was fought between the Farmer and the Sword. The book she's writing will set out her evidence.*

By the time you're reading this, Megan's book will probably have been published, and you'll have a lot more information to go on. In any case, when you go to the Pleasant Vale, as you must in order to learn the rest of the story and find the Drogan Taranish, *you'll surely meet her.*

When you get there, enter your password in the box below, to reveal what I call my Second Testament.

Why wait, Delia thought. She had the password. Quin turned away again as she typed the six-character *'Love, and be silent'* acrostic. A message appeared:

Password failed

and the screen went dark. She returned to Grace's epilogue, located the box and entered her password again. The result was the same. They looked at each other, speechless.

'Looks like I'm going to need another password,' Delia said. 'I'm going to have to go to Scotland, to this Howe of Cromar, and pay a visit to Grace's friend Megan. I bet she has it.'

As she spoke, Quin's computer screen lit up again, with these words:

A hex or riddle I propose –
On great ones' graves no garden grows.

22

AN ALMOST PERFECT CIRCLE

DELIA SPENT THE REMAINDER of the day helping Quin with the clean-up at Arthur Johnson's house. In the late afternoon he went to Autumn Leaves to spend a little more time with his grandfather and she returned to Nootka Lodge.

She couldn't wait to get on her computer. Quin had copied Grace's CD to the cloud, where she was able to access it from her tablet. Flash Earth was her next stop. Zooming in on a satellite image of north-east Scotland, her eye was immediately drawn to an almost perfect circle, a basin of green lowland surrounded by a ring of darker hills. The basin was about six miles in diameter, maybe a little more, with a river cutting across its southern edge. It was exactly as Grace had described it, precisely where she had located it on her little map of Scotland, and Delia knew she was looking at the Pleasant Vale. On her screen she brought up a map overlay and saw that the river was the Dee and the circular basin was the Howe of Cromar, just as Grace had said. Near its centre was the village of Tarland, Taran's Garden of old.

Without a moment's delay, she began making travel plans. By the time Quin knocked on her hotel room door at seven o'clock she had already booked a round-trip flight from Chicago to London, an onward flight from London to Aberdeen, a rental car at Aberdeen and a room at the Hilton Craigendarroch resort in Ballater, just eleven miles from Tarland.

When she told him what she had found, where she was going and when (in just over one week's time, at the beginning of August, for two weeks), he greeted her news with a strange mixture of elation and disappointment.

'What's wrong, Quin? D'you think I'm going too fast?'

'I'm just as excited as you are, Delia, really I am. It's just ...' He struggled to find the words. 'I wish I could go with you.'

'I'd love it if you would. Why don't you?'

'I have an interview for a job at the University of Chicago in the middle of August.'

'A job interview? In Chicago? That's great. But you could go to Scotland with me for the first week, then come back for the interview, couldn't you?'

It was settled. They booked flights for him before heading out for dinner.

Over the meal the conversation was entirely around the upcoming trip. Quin said, 'Grace's derivation of the name Tarland from words meaning Taran's Garden could be spot-on. There's an old Celtic word *lan* that originally meant an enclosure, for example a sheep-fold or a churchyard. Or a garden, for that matter. *Tar* could clearly refer to Taran, as in *Tar-achsel*, Taran's kin. It's quite consistent with the meaning of *lan* that *Tar-lan* could be Taran's Garden. In modern Welsh, *llan* has come to mean a church.'

After dinner they returned to their hotel and spent the rest of the evening over a bottle of wine. Quin felt compelled to gently clarify one aspect of their travel plan. Would they share a room at Craigendarroch? It would be an expensive trip otherwise. Delia pretended the thought hadn't crossed her mind. After a suitable pause, she said she was okay with that, if he was.

Eight days later, Delia sat in Terminal 5 of London's Heathrow airport, having arranged to meet Quin there before flying on up to Aberdeen. She turned on her tablet computer to look at the maps and satellite views she had downloaded of Cromar, the Pleasant Vale of Grace's story. She had studied them so many times she felt she already knew the area intimately. Quin had told her that *cro* was a Gaelic word meaning a round enclosure, hence a circle. *Cro-Mar* was the circle of Mar, Mar being an old name for the large tract of Aberdeenshire drained by the Dee and the upper reaches of the Don. On one of her maps, she had superimposed a circle tracing the ring of hills around Cromar, and drawn two lines, one north-south, the other east-west, each bisecting the circle. The lines were like cross-hairs of a telescopic sight. Where they crossed, right at the mid-point of the circle, the map showed, in an antique font, 'Blue Cairn'.

This had to be the great cairn built by the Beaker People marking the centre of the Vale. It was on the crest of the low ridge of Drummy, exactly as Grace had said. Near the Blue Cairn the map showed 'Hut Circles', evidence of ancient settlement. On Craig Dhu in the south of Cromar, Delia's map indicated another Blue Cairn, which had to be the one the Beaker People built to mark where they had first entered the Pleasant Vale.

Just about a mile north-east of the Blue Cairn of Drummy was the village of Tarland, and to the south of the village was the low hill called Tomnaverie, on which was marked 'Stone Circle', presumably one of those erected by the 'Little Folk' before they were displaced by the Beaker incomers.

Quin had suggested that the *-verie* part of Tomnaverie could have come from a Celtic or even earlier Indo-European word for truth or justice – almost certainly the same root that gave Grace's word *vairtach*, the sixth cycle represented by Taran's wheel. (Going into much more linguistic detail than Delia needed at that moment, he had also traced the modern English words 'very', 'verity' and 'verify' through Latin, and 'fair' in the sense of just or equitable, to the same root.) *Tom* was a knoll or low hill in Gaelic, so *tom-na-verie* meant knoll of truth or justice. According to Grace, the stone circle on Tomnaverie was the place where justice was administered in ancient times by the high priestess Merefrith.

It was Quin whose research found the 'ghost meadow' across the running water from Taran's Garden. 'Remember, Delia, how the Beaker People saw faint flashes of light on the marshy ground across the running water, and believed these were spirits of the Little Folk? The running water is the Tarland Burn. The village of Tarland, or Taran's Garden, is on the north side of the burn. On the south side is a patch of land called Dalvokie. It's from the Gaelic *dail-bhocain*, which literally means "ghost's meadow".'

One place mentioned by Grace as being in the Pleasant Vale, indeed in Taran's Garden itself, didn't appear on any map, and hadn't so far been found in any internet search by either Delia or Quin. That was the *Kyaar*, an earthen mound or barrow surrounded by a moat, providing a defensive site for the king's residence. Quin thought the word could be related to the Welsh *caer*, a castle or fortification. Perhaps they would find the *Kyaar* when they got there.

But it would be more important to find Megan, whose surname Grace had so frustratingly omitted to mention. Megan the historian or archaeologist. Megan who was writing a book, maybe had the book published by now, that told of the remarkable culture of the early inhabitants of the Pleasant Vale, up to their fateful encounter with the Romans at *Mons Graupius*.

Did Megan know about the *Drogan Taranish*? Had it really been given away to the Roman governor Agricola? If so, how could it have been in Grace's possession and now be *'back in a place it's been before'*? Might Megan be in on the secret of its hiding place?

Already elated at having arrived in Britain with the prospect of beginning the search for Megan and the *Drogan*, Delia was further cheered by the sight of Quin coming towards her across the waiting area of Terminal 5. They embraced like old friends, then kissed like lovers.

'I've missed you,' he said. She felt the same way, although it was little more than a week since they had parted in New

Hampshire, and only a day and a half longer than that since they had first met.

'I've downloaded Grace's documents from the cloud,' Delia told him. 'Have you the original CD?'

'Yes, it's here in my computer case.'

'Great. You've probably read Grace's *First Testament* as often as I have, and know it backwards.'

'I've read it only once, Delia, with you. I don't have the password. Only you know it, and it should probably stay that way. After all, Grace intended her writings for your eyes, no one else's.'

'Well ... okay, if you're more comfortable not knowing the password. But I'd like you to work together with me on this *"hex or riddle"* stuff.'

'*A hex or riddle I propose – on great ones' graves no garden grows,*' Quin recited. 'That I remember. I guess decoding the riddle is our first task.'

'Right. I can see it's a riddle, but I wonder why Grace calls it a "hex". A hex is an evil spell, isn't it? A curse.'

'Well, I suppose the hex is that no garden will grow, no vegetation will thrive, on the graves of the people Grace calls *"great ones"*. It seems to me we should begin our search in cemeteries. Maybe those two-thousand-year-old cairn-fields she mentioned.'

23
GREAT ONES' GRAVES

LESS THAN FOUR HOURS LATER, having flown to Aberdeen and driven thirty miles in their little blue rental car, they entered Cromar, the Pleasant Vale, for the first time.

The north-east portal to Cromar presents a spectacular vista. To reach the viewpoint, the road from Aberdeen winds through a pass known as the Slack between two of the hills forming the rim of the circular basin. Below the road is a deep ravine, carved by rushing melt-water from a glacier that, until about ten thousand years ago, filled the basin.

Emerging from the Slack, Delia pulled into a layby. Though she had already downloaded a number of maps from the internet, she had bought two paper ones – Ordnance Survey Landranger sheets 37 and 44 – in the airport bookshop. They spread the maps out so that they could get their bearings.

It was little wonder that the view from the Slack had been one of Queen Victoria's favourite scenes in all her realm. Away to the south-west the distant pale grey mass of Lochnagar etched its jagged profile against the sky. That mountain was on the royal estate, and Victoria might well have stood on this spot, picturing her beloved Balmoral Castle nestled at the foot of the mountain, about twenty miles from here. To the left of Lochnagar, a series of less distant hills culminated in the conical peak of Mount Keen. And to its right an even closer and darker mountain formed a brooding sentinel on the western flank of Cromar. That was Morven.

Below Delia and Quin lay the circular basin itself. A patchwork of dark green woodlands, bright green pastures and pale-green-going-on-straw-yellow fields of ripening grain. A Pleasant Vale indeed. Tarland was down there somewhere, though they couldn't pick it out.

Three more miles took them into the village that Monday afternoon. They parked in the Square, where locals shopped while visitors like themselves took a leisurely look around.

Tarland Square, they observed, was no more square in shape than Times Square in New York. Well, maybe a little – at least it had four sides, though not of equal length. The north side curved gently so that the Square was wider at its west than at its east end. The north, west and south sides were framed by mostly two-storey buildings, but the very short east side was different. Here a raised embankment led to a stone wall with an iron gate. Behind the wall was a ruined church and its churchyard.

'That should be our first port of call,' Quin said. Surely there would be some *great ones' graves* here that would provide an answer to Grace's *hex or riddle*.

The embankment was supported by a retaining wall rising five or six feet from street level, broken by a flight of stone steps leading up to the churchyard gate. Set into the retaining wall was a red granite slab bearing the inscription:

THE
FRANCIS DONALDSON
BOIG
FOUNTAIN

and the date 1919. 'Boig' was an alternative spelling of the farm name Bog, where Francis Donaldson, who bequeathed money for the fountain, had farmed at the turn of the twentieth century. The fountain itself had long since ceased to flow, and many of its metal fittings, including the lion's head that had once delivered water through its 'mouth', were missing. To the right of it was a stone horse-trough filled with flowers. The fountain and trough would in times past have been a welcome sight for thirsty travellers and their horses.

On the embankment, against the churchyard wall, was a grey granite stone commemorating the local fiddler Peter Milne. Inscribed on the stone were the words:

Riches denied, thy boon was purer joys,
What wealth could never give nor take away.

They came from a sonnet by Scotland's eighteenth-century bard Robert Burns. Later, when they read the whole poem, it was clear that these were its two best lines. The rest seemed pretentious and unmemorable. 'I guess even great poets have their off-days,' was Quin's comment.

Before going into the churchyard they explored the Square. At the west end was the village war memorial, a grey granite monolith surmounted by a kilted soldier carved in the same stone. Above the list of local young men who had died in the 1939–1945 war, and below the much longer list of men of the parish who had given their lives in the 1914–1918 war, was the inscription:

Their names liveth for evermore.

'That's beautiful,' Delia said. 'So simple and poetic.'

Quin disagreed. 'It's a travesty,' he said. 'You might have thought they would have done these brave servicemen the honour of getting the grammar right.'

'Huh?'

'*Liveth* is the third person singular form of the verb. You can't use it with a plural noun like "names". It's faux biblical. Somebody trying to be clever and coming off ignorant.'

His reaction to what seemed such a trivial matter amused her. 'Well, I like it,' she said, less out of conviction than a desire to yank his chain.

Days later, Quin was still so annoyed by the grammatical error that he checked the inscription out on the web. It turned out to be a misquote from Ecclesiasticus, one of the apocryphal books of the Bible, in Chapter 44 beginning *'Let us now praise famous men'*. In the King James version, the correct rendering of Verse 14 is *'Their bodies are buried in peace, but their name liveth for evermore'*. Clearly the singular *'name'* in that context means reputation, not what a person is called. The same quotation is found on war memorials all over Great Britain – it was apparently selected by Rudyard Kipling – and on most of those the quotation is rendered correctly. But not on this one.

The village hall, with its foundation stone dated 1951 and its carved stone lintel reading 'MacRobert Memorial Hall', stood precisely in the middle of the south side of the Square, and two hotels anchored the north side, the Commercial at the west end and the Aberdeen Arms at the east end. Above the door of the latter was a coat of arms (belonging to the Earls of Aberdeen, who once owned much of the land in Cromar) with the motto *Fortuna sequatur*. 'Let fortune follow,' Quin translated from the Latin. 'I suppose that could be our motto too.'

They went up the steps leading to the churchyard gate and entered. A man, fiftyish and sparely built, was mowing grass around the gravestones. As Delia and Quin came in he stopped his mower and took off his cap to wipe sweat from his brow.

'Aye aye,' he said. *'Wid it be a partickler steen ye're sikkin?'*

The young couple looked at each other with a puzzled expression on their faces. Realising they didn't understand him, the man switched effortlessly into the kind of polite English he would use when talking to his doctor or minister. 'Sorry, you're not from around here, I suppose?'

'You guessed right,' Delia replied, with a smile.

'American, are you? Welcome to Tarland. What I said was, are you looking for any stone in particular?'

'Not really. Maybe any stones of famous people.'

'Famous? Not many famous people lived in Tarland. And any that did, went away. They wouldn't be buried here.'

Not a promising start if they were looking for *great ones' graves*. 'Where would we find the oldest stones?'

They were directed to a corner of the churchyard. 'There's some stones there going back to 1750, maybe a wee bit before that. If there's anything I can help you with, just let me know. My name's Ewen. I'll be here for a while yet.'

Delia and Quin introduced themselves, then headed to the corner where the oldest headstones could be found. Ewen watched them with an amused expression for a minute or two, then started up his mower again.

With no clear idea of what they were looking for, it didn't help that most of the stones were so badly worn they were almost impossible to read. After about twenty minutes, Delia found herself in front of one, trying to decipher its eroded inscription, when suddenly she got goosebumps and felt a tingling at the nape of her neck. 'Quin!' she yelled. 'Come here!'

At the top of the stone was a symbol that might have been a representation of a flower or rosette, but to Delia was unmistakable. It was a circle with six rays running from the centre to the rim. Taran's wheel.

They laboured for fifteen minutes or more, trying to read the words below the wheel. Delia took pictures from various angles, hoping the words would appear clearer in a photograph than on the stone itself. Eventually, this is what they could make out:

AGNES CROMAR
died 23rd May 1874
aged 69 years
A Y E
REMEMBERED

Delia was almost dancing with excitement. Quin wondered, not very seriously, if such behaviour was appropriate in a place of graves.

'Don't you see, Quin? Agnes Cromar. Grace Rosman. Grace always said her own name was an anagram. Finally I know what it's an anagram *of*.'

'Yes, I see. That's clever.'

'Cromar is the modern name of the Pleasant Vale. It's also the family name of this Agnes. I wonder what Grace's connection to Agnes Cromar was?'

'I don't know what the connection was,' Quin said, 'but something else has just occurred to me. Isn't *Agnes* the solution to Grace's *hex or riddle*? Look.'

He took a pen and paper from his pocket and scribbled in block letters:

ON GREAT ONES' GRAVES NO GARDEN GROWS

He then underlined a selection of letters that spelled 'Agnes':

ON GRE<u>A</u>T ONES' <u>G</u>RAVES <u>N</u>O GARD<u>E</u>N GROW<u>S</u>

'Every sixth letter,' he said. 'Taran's magic number, six. And a little play on the word *hex* by Grace. Are we a team, or what?'

So *Agnes*, they were sure, was the password that would open Grace's *Second Testament*.

They hugged. Suddenly aware that Ewen had stopped his mowing and was looking in their direction, they took a few more photographs and left, waving to him as they exited the gate.

24

AYE REMEMBERED

THE SHORT DRIVE from Tarland to Ballater was beautiful. After skirting the shore of Loch Davan, they crossed the Muir of Dinnet, part of the Cairngorms National Park. The Muir was a tapestry of purple (heather just coming into full bloom), green (the vivid green of birch foliage sometimes flecked with the darker hue of Scots pine) and blue (the still water of Loch Kinord reflecting the sky). At Cambus o' May they left Cromar, joining the Deeside road that followed the north bank of the River Dee up to Ballater.

'Cambus o' May,' Delia said. 'Didn't Grace say that a *cambus* was a river-bend? Could this be the *cambus* where Aeth followed the kingfisher to its nest and found the *Drogan*?'

'Could be,' Quin agreed. '*Cambus* does mean river-bend in Gaelic. I believe the ancient proto-Celtic word is something like *kamb*. It's the same root that gives the names Cameron – crooked nose – and Campbell – twisted mouth. But I hadn't heard before of *cambus* in the sense of a life-changing crisis, like the Years With No Summer that Grace talks about, or the arrival of the iron age Celts. Actually, it's a pretty good metaphor.'

Soon they were checking in at the Craigendarroch resort. Tired and hungry, they decided, rather than go out for dinner, to eat in the hotel restaurant after freshening up. Not too tired and hungry, however, to get on Delia's tablet computer right away and try using the *'Agnes'* password to access Grace's *Second Testament*.

It didn't work. They tried it again, with and without 'Cromar'. They tried upper case, lower case, every variation they could think of. Still no success.

From Delia's camera they uploaded the photographs they had taken of the stone.

'Could it be the numbers?' Quin wondered aloud. Agnes Cromar's death on 23rd May 1874 at age 69 gave a set of digits 23-5-1874-69, or perhaps 23-05-1874-69, in which no digit was repeated. But no logical permutation would unlock the *Second Testament*.

Next morning, Quin awoke at half-past seven and found himself alone. Minutes later, the key turned in the lock. 'I've been for a swim,' Delia said, jauntily. 'The pool's really nice. And today, after breakfast, we're going to Aberdeen.'

He rubbed his eyes. 'Aberdeen? But we've just come from there.'

'That was the airport. Today we're going to the city.'

'Why?'

Answering his question with one of her own, she asked, 'What was it Grace said about the formation of the circular valley?'

'Taran created it with a thunderbolt.'

'No, not the *Tarachsel* legend. How did she say it really originated?'

'By an asteroid impact. But she also said in her epilogue that she made the whole asteroid thing up.'

'Exactly. Why would she spin such a tale unless it was some kind of clue? Let's turn on the computer and read that story again.'

Quin began reading aloud from the screen.

'No,' Delia prompted him, 'move on to the bit after the impact. What happens next?'

> *Eventually the entire crater was worn away. A great river arose in mountains to the west and flowed over the exact site of the impact. Though the crater was*

long gone, there was memory in the rock that had once lain deep underneath and was now at the surface.

'That's it,' Delia asserted. '*Memory in the rock.* Isn't that an echo of the epitaph on Agnes Cromar's stone – *aye remembered?*'

'I suppose so. But you still haven't told me why we're going to Aberdeen.'

'To buy rubbing wax. There's memory in that stone of Agnes's. We're going to try to uncover it.'

Later that morning, they were in Union Street, Aberdeen's main thoroughfare. Passing a charity shop, Delia stopped abruptly. There in the window was a glass sphere, a little larger than a tennis ball, on a metal stand. They went in.

'Do you get many like these?' Delia asked an assistant.

'Yes, we get them all the time. We have three others back here. They're Caithness glass.'

'It's pretty. Is it old?'

'Well, they're not making these any more. The company went out of business a few years ago. This one's probably from the 1980s.' She left them to serve another customer.

'Quin,' Delia said in a quiet voice, 'you never saw the *Drogan.* But it's about this size, maybe slightly bigger. See the swirl of blue glass inside? Imagine, instead of that swirl, six radiating spokes of kingfisher blue. That's what we came to Scotland to find.'

Exiting the charity shop, they found a school supply store where they purchased some wax and suitable paper for making stone rubbings, together with some other bits and pieces including a small fine brush and some masking tape.

Back at Agnes Cromar's stone in the Tarland churchyard, Delia brushed loose dust from the lettering. 'It's funny,' Quin observed, 'how the letters of the word *"aye"* seem to be spread out. In fact, it almost looks as if there had been brackets around the letter Y.'

117

Delia affixed a sheet of paper with masking tape to the stone, covering the words *'AYE REMEMBERED'*, and began rubbing lightly with the wax. As the markings on the stone appeared on the paper, she said, 'These aren't brackets, Quin. It's a C before the Y, and a D or maybe an O after the Y.'

The rubbing took form before their eyes. The word they had originally thought was *'AYE'* now looked like this:

A CYD E

or perhaps like this:

A CYO E

There was no one else around, but Quin spoke in a whisper when he suddenly said, '*Alcyone!* In Greek mythology, Alcyone was turned into a kingfisher.'

Delia, also *sotto voce*, added, 'The kingfisher that led Aeth to the *Drogan*.'

Alcyone, she knew, was also the name of the brightest of the Pleiades star cluster in the constellation of Taurus the bull, commonly known in the modern world as the 'seven sisters'. To the *Tarachsel*, according to Grace, these same stars were the six daughters of Taran. Interestingly, most people with good eyesight on a clear night can count only six, not seven, naked-eye stars in the cluster.

So perhaps *'Alcyone remembered'* could be interpreted as meaning that Agnes considered herself a daughter of Taran. Or it could be a reference to the legend of Aeth and the kingfisher. Either way, Agnes had almost certainly been a Keeper of Taran's wheel, and Grace was possibly her direct descendant.

And it turned out *Alcyone* was the password that unlocked Grace's *Second Testament*.

II. THE *SEELY HOWE*

25

THEY WITHSTOOD THE MIGHT OF ROME

SECOND TESTAMENT OF GRACE ROSMAN,
KEEPER OF TARAN'S WHEEL

ABOUT SEVENTY YEARS *after* Mons Graupius, *Ptolemy wrote that the* Taexali *(his rendering of 'Tarachsel') had an important settlement at* Devana. *Some historians have placed it near the mouth of the River Dee, in other words at present-day Aberdeen.*

Megan is among those equating Devana *with* Davan, *one of the lochs occupying depressions left by remnants of the glacier that, during the last ice age, filled the Howe of Cromar. There are actually two lochs,* Davan *and* Kinord, *in the south-western quadrant of the Howe, separated by a tapering isthmus of land.*

Remains of iron age settlement are abundant at Davan, *particularly on the north shore and scattered over the isthmus on the south side of the loch. Megan's research identifies these remains, particularly those near the present-day farms of Old and New Kinord on the isthmus, as Ptolemy's* Devana. *According to traditional tales passed down by my ancestors, the high priestess Merefrith and senior members of her priesthood, the* Merch Nyr, *dwelt by a loch. The Davan remains may mark the site of their power base, and thus the main religious and cultural centre of the* Tarachsel, *at least during Roman times.*

Around the year 300, the first references are found in Roman writings to the Picti, *meaning 'painted ones', based no doubt on the habit the* Tarachsel *warriors had of adorning themselves with body paint. I have to say that I find the term 'Picts' for my ancestors to be somewhat offensive, just as today's Native Americans might with good reason be offended if we call their ancestors 'Redskins'. But even the most authoritative historians refer to the 'Picts', to 'Pictish' language and culture, and to 'Pictland' as the territory these people once occupied.*

Their kingdom reached its zenith of power during the fourth and fifth centuries. Although the religious centre probably remained with the Merch Nyr *at Davan, the royal court migrated to various locations throughout the northern half of what is now Scotland. The* Kyaar *at Tarland retained only ceremonial function. By the fifth century the kingdom had become an alliance of northern Picts, with their centre of political and military power near Inverness, and southern Picts, centred on a royal court at Scone near present-day Perth.*

The southern Picts were more exposed to outside influences. The most momentous of these, from the fourth century on, was a new religion that began to replace the old 'pagan' Celtic gods and goddesses with a very different set of beliefs. That religion was Christianity. Some of the most beautiful Pictish stone carvings date from this period, many having a curious mixture of Christian and pagan symbolism.

The northern Picts, by contrast, held strongly to their traditional faith, nurtured as always by the Merch Nyr. *And the continuing power of the* Merch Nyr *is seen from the fact that during the fifth century the march of Christianity was for a time rolled back even among the southern Picts.*

But Christians continued to maintain isolated cells of monks in various places throughout Pictland. One of these cells was located at Banchory, on the north bank of the Dee about eighteen miles east of Tarland. Interestingly, the fifth-century founder of the Banchory cell assumed the name of the Picts' most powerful god, Taran, lengthening it slightly to Taranan, nowadays rendered Ternan. Though it may seem to us a curious strategy, it probably did help Ternan to promote Christian teachings among his Pictish neighbours. 'Saint' Ternan, as he came to be called, has been referred to by later writers as the 'Bishop of Pictland', in recognition of his early efforts to spread Christianity among the Picts, though his attempts appear to have met with limited success beyond the immediate surroundings of his Banchory cell.

A holy man with greater impact on Pictish life came along about a century later. Like Ternan, he assumed the name of a major Celtic deity, in his case Luoc, a corruption of Lugus or Luath. (Even if, as some writers have suggested, the name he took was that of the gospel writer Luke, its similarity to 'Luath' may have helped insinuate him into the hearts and minds of the Picts.) He cultivated an aura of familiarity as a 'man of the people', encouraging his followers to call him Mo-Luoc ('my Luoc'), and is nowadays usually referred to as 'Saint' Moluag.

Born in Ireland, Moluag was a member of the Gaelic-speaking Celtic people who adopted the Latin name 'Scoti' and who had established a province named Dalriada covering parts of northern Ireland and what is now Argyll in western Scotland. Around 562 he made a historic visit to King Bridei of the Picts, and obtained his permission to spread Christianity throughout Pictland. Shortly afterwards, he converted the king himself to the new religion.

It was probably not a hard sell. We can imagine Moluag's pitch.

'Your majesty, up to now the actions of Pictish kings have been dictated by women. This is an abomination before God. It is men, not women, who have dominion over the beasts of the forest, the fish of the water and the birds of the air. How can it make sense for women to have dominion over men? The right of kings to rule their subjects is a divine right, coming directly from God. If you throw off the shackles of the priestesses, who

do only the devil's work, and embrace the only true God, you will have great rewards and your people will love you. Even your womenfolk will come to love you, once they understand and accept that their lower station is ordained by God. You need no longer seek the counsel of women, but rule by the power of the wisdom God has vested in you.'

The new religion took hold, despite the best efforts of the Merch Nyr *to thwart it. In the century after Moluag's mission, conversion of Pictland to the Christian religion of the* Scoti *became unstoppable. The source of power and influence for the* Merch Nyr *was cut from under them.*

By the latter part of the seventh century, if the Merch Nyr *were still counting, the people of the Pleasant Vale encountered the fourth* cambus. *A stalwart of the new religion was a man by the name of Woloch or Wallach, who is said to have founded the church at Logiemar (later part of the combined parish of Logie Coldstone) north of Loch Davan. 'Saint Woloch's stone', a standing stone by the old churchyard of Logiemar, is probably a remnant of a much more ancient stone circle that has nothing to do with Woloch.*

Another holy man of around the same time, Nathalan, was born in Tullich just outside the Vale. It was probably at his instigation that the Kyaar, *the ancient centre of royal power at Taran's Garden, was ordered to be flattened. By forced local labour the mound of earth that had stood for two thousand years or more was shovelled into the surrounding moat. A wooden church was built on the site, dedicated to Saint Moluag. Nathalan, still venerated as a saint by the Catholic Church, is also credited with founding the church at Coull, in the south-east of Cromar.*

In one respect the Christianity brought to the Pleasant Vale by Woloch and Nathalan was probably no different from the old religion: it relied heavily on tales of miracles that defy rational analysis. Some tales were so tall they were most likely devised to test the limits of credulity of the faithful. An example is the story of Nathalan's key, still occasionally heard in and around the Vale.

Nathalan, it was said, cultivated fields at Tullich to support himself and his small cell of followers. One year, his harvest was destroyed by a storm, provoking him to protest to God. In remorse for this sin against the Almighty, he had the local blacksmith fashion an iron clamp with a lock and key, with which he locked his right hand to his leg. Then (presumably with his left hand) he threw the key into the River Dee. Years later, on a pilgrimage to Rome, he bought a fish and, while preparing it for his supper, found the key in its belly. Judging his penance to be over, he freed his right hand.

Righteous zeal accompanying religious reformation or conversion has fostered officially-sanctioned vandalism all over the world for millennia, and continues today. So it was at the time of the fourth cambus. In the name of Christianity, images of Taran on carved stones were ruthlessly defaced and destroyed throughout Pictland. Megan believes that Nathalan and Woloch were the prime sponsors of this episode of vandalism in Cromar, which may have included the smashing of a beautiful carved stone, a mere fragment of which remains at Corrachree, close to the great cairn of Drummy. It is ironic that the only images of Taran to have survived are in other parts of the Celtic world, where he was but a minor god.

To confound the desecration of sacred stones by Christian fanatics, Pictish carvers began using obscure symbolism to continue paying homage to the ancient gods. Two symbols widely used during this period were the 'double disc' and 'Z-rod'. These continue to baffle archaeologists today, but Megan theorises that they represent Brytha and Taran respectively. It is not too difficult to see the double disc as Brytha's breasts. The Z-rod takes a little more imagination, but could be a stylised lightning-bolt, one of the ancient symbols of Taran; alternatively, it may be a coded reference to the constellation Taurus (a celestial manifestation of Taran), in which the *familiar V-shape of the Hyades is linked back to the Pleiades (Taran's daughters) as a back-to-front Z. It's even possible that the Z-rod represents the magic number six, derived from zeta, the sixth letter of the Greek alphabet, or by fusion of the Roman numeral VI. Often the Z-rod is superimposed on the double disc, symbolising, like the* Drogan Taranish *itself, the union of Taran and Brytha. It looks something like this:*

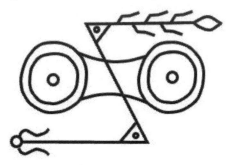

Examples of these symbols can be seen at the beautifully restored Migvie Church about three miles from Tarland. The Tomachar stone inside the building prominently displays a variety of 'pagan' symbols, as does the Migvie stone just outside, at the entrance to the churchyard. On this stone, the double disc and Z-rod, in defiant homage to the ancient gods, nestle in the upper-left quadrant of a Christian cross.

It was not only visual representations of Taran that were outlawed; mere mention of the thunder-god's name was forbidden. The name Tar-lan, Taran's Garden, could no longer be uttered in public. Churchmen proposed changing the name to something like Kilmoluach ('Moluag's church'). However, in a rearguard action, the Merch Nyr were able to persuade the local population to modify the place-name to Tarwelan, which essentially meant 'bull-pen', but the change in pronunciation was slight. The new name retained a subtle link to the ancient thunder-god; after all, Tarwe the bull was Taran's heavenly manifestation. The allusion was apparently lost on the churchmen, who found Tarwelan acceptable.

A change the Merch Nyr *were unable to prevent was the moving of the summer festival from Lunasa, in early August, to Moluag's feast day on June 25th. However, abolition of Brytha's festival, Imbolc, celebrated on February 1st or 2nd, would have proved too great a cultural shock, given the reverence in which ordinary people still held their mother-goddess. The early church cannily promulgated a feast day for 'Saint Bridget' on the same date. Almost certainly, there was never such a person as Saint Bridget; she appears to have been an invention to provide continuity for the February festival.*

Any influence the Merch Nyr *still had in the community was further diminished when they were driven from their homes at Davan, which were then burned. Some of the women embraced the new religion, some pretended to embrace it but went on practising their old ways in secret, and a few continued to worship Taran and Brytha openly and take nothing to do with the church. These few were denounced by churchmen as witches and sorcerers and lived in constant danger of being arrested and put to death.*

Soon the ancient Pictish tongue, the Tarachsel *language that had survived for at least twelve hundred years since the coming of the ironworkers, was outlawed. Only Gaelic, the language brought by the* Scoti *from Ireland, was permitted to be spoken. And as the Pictish language had never been written down, it died with the last speaker. Traces of it remained only in a few place-names. Even the name the* Tarachsel *called their own land was lost; the Irish interlopers called Pictland* Alba, *a name that in modern Gaelic refers to all of Scotland.*

Thus the religion, the language, indeed the entire culture of a people was ruthlessly destroyed. The fourth cambus *was more devastating for the people of the Pleasant Vale than any of the first three. As Megan has written:*

> They withstood the might of Rome, but lost their nation to a handful of Irish missionaries.

26

QUITE A SCANDAL

'GRACE CLEARLY INTENDED you to seek out Megan,' Quin said. 'Let's go to Tarland again today and see if we can find her. It's a tiny place. How difficult can it be?'

Having just started on the *Second Testament*, Delia would have liked to read on. Instead, having reached the point where the ancient culture of the Picts was destroyed by Christian zealots, the 'fourth *cambus*' as Grace called it, she closed down her computer.

Tarland Square was almost deserted that Wednesday morning. The silence was broken only by some hammering and scraping sounds coming from the direction of the churchyard. Curious, they climbed the short flight of steps to the gate, and saw a familiar figure.

Ewen had a large granite headstone leaning precariously against two stout wooden posts. In his hands he held a heavy iron wrecking bar – a 'pinch' he called it. A wheelbarrow filled with rounded river pebbles sat close by.

'Just one of my many jobs,' he explained. 'The gravestones subside over time. They start to lean and get dangerous. If one of these big ones fell on somebody it could kill them.'

'So you're laying a new foundation,' Quin observed.

'Aye, exactly. A bed of river rocks' (Ewen nodded his head towards the wheelbarrow) 'and a spot of cement. This stone will be good for another fifty years, at least.'

Quin needed more explanation. 'Why wouldn't the stones be given a good foundation in the first place?'

Ewen smiled, a little indulgently, Delia thought. But he was only too pleased to explain the intricacies of the job in hand and to show his local knowledge. 'Well, the problem here, y'see, is there's no bottom to the ground. That's good for grave-digging because you can dig as deep as you like. You can get four or five coffins in the same lair, stacked on top of one another. It took a long time to fill this little graveyard, with the depth of the soil here. But sometime in the 1960s it was just about full up and a new burial ground was started at the parish church. Up yonder,' he pointed, 'overlooking the golf course. The ground there has a bottom, but here, no. And without a bottom you can't lay a proper foundation for a heavy headstone. So the stones all sink here, especially the big ones. Even outside the wall there, a few years ago I had to put in a new foundation for the Peter Milne monument – you've maybe noticed it, the fiddler's stone.'

'Yes, we saw it.'

'And see the old kirk?' Ewen gestured in the direction of the ruined church. 'I'm surprised it hasn't fallen down by now. It was built in 1762 – the date's on the wall there. But, with the foundation being so poor, the walls began to bow and by the time it was a hundred years old the roof was ready to fall in. A stone building should last a lot longer than that. A new kirk was built up the road. It opened in 1870, I believe. Still in use.'

Quin and Delia looked at each other, but said nothing. All this talk of 'no bottom' and subsiding stones and church walls made sense. They had just been reading Grace's account of the flattening of the *Kyaar* to build a church dedicated to Saint Moluag, and were sure they were standing on the remains of an ancient earthwork. No wonder the ground was unstable.

'Do you ever dig up any old artefacts when you're working around these stones?' Delia asked.

Ewen smiled again, apparently amused by a word Delia had used. 'Artefacts, no,' he said. 'Just a lot of old bones.'

Delia changed the subject. 'Do you know anyone here in Cromar with the name Megan? We'd like to make contact with her but we don't know her second name.'

There was a lengthy pause before he responded. 'Well, the only Megan I know is Megan Minty. A schoolteacher. Interested in local history. She was writing a book at one time. Would that be the one you're looking for?'

'Yes, that's her for sure.'

'Well now, it'll be difficult for you to contact her.'

'Why's that?'

'To cut a long story short, she vanished.'

Delia wasn't going to allow Ewen to cut this particular long story short. *Vanished?* People don't just vanish.

Pressed for more detail, he began to tell the story. 'Megan taught at Tarland school. She was my daughter Lesley's teacher in primary seven. Oh, she was a great Mrs Minty, by Lesley's way of it. The kids all loved her. She used to take them out for walks and tell them about local history.

'Married with two young boys, she was. But about four years ago there was quite a scandal: she took up with another man. A visiting art teacher from Aboyne. Jack Ward was his name.

'They managed to keep the affair quiet, and nobody suspected for a while. Then one day – it must have been in the school holidays – she took the train to London. Told her husband she'd a meeting with somebody about her book, but that had been just a pretence. Ward went with her on the train. They stayed one night in a hotel down there, then checked out and never came back. The police tried to trace them, but they couldn't be found anywhere. It was a big story in the papers. Most folk think they ran away together to set up a new life abroad.'

'That's amazing,' Delia said. 'Being so well liked, with so much interest in the history of the area as to be writing a book, it seems strange to throw it all away.'

'Well, that's what everybody in Tarland said at the time. But wait, I haven't finished the story. Megan's husband – he was an engineer on oil rigs in the North Sea – took it real bad. Moved the two boys to Aberdeen to live with his mother, then went off to a new job. In Azerbaijan, would you believe. Before he left, though, his house at Praisewell was gutted by fire. It looked like it was started deliberately. Folk say he set the fire himself, just for spite, but the police couldn't pin it on him. The place was completely destroyed.'

'Praisewell, did you say? Where's that?'

'Up the hill off the Aberdeen road, about a mile and a half out of the village. It's probably not marked on your map. If you can find the Pett, it's near there. There's a new house at Praisewell now. New people, nothing to do with the Mintys. Nice house, very modern. I gave them a hand to put up a garden dyke using stones from the old house.'

Megan's disappearance without trace was a blow. Delia and Quin had to hope that the key to finding Taran's wheel would lie somewhere in Grace's *First* and *Second Testaments*. They must read on.

27
DARK AGES

THE DARK AGES of southern Britain followed the collapse of the Roman empire. Never part of that empire, Pictland had its own dark ages following the crushing of the Merch Nyr, who up until then had been the custodians of all useful knowledge and wisdom. The arts of agriculture, medicine and astronomy were largely lost as the women skilled in them were forbidden to teach. In the new regime men of the church provided all schooling, which only boys were deemed fit to receive.

And what did boys learn at the feet of their teachers? Rote memorisation of scripture, which, as in today's madrasahs, left little time for anything else. The teaching of fighting skills was left to military men.

Presumably the effects of this revolution in education were not foreseen at the time, although to our modern minds they would have been entirely predictable. Agricultural productivity declined drastically, and famine and disease became commonplace. This led to more frequent tribal wars within Pictland, as well as battles between the Picts and their neighbours for control of territory.

By the ninth century, the Irish Scoti or 'Scots' whose Gaelic culture had been imposed on Pictland found that unity of language and religion did not necessarily make for good relations between the neighbouring peoples. Constant warfare between them denied to both any prosperity they might *otherwise have enjoyed, and it seems the Scots generally came off worse than the Picts. Hostilities finally ended when Cinaed mac Ailpin (Kenneth MacAlpin) became the first ruler of a unified kingdom of Picts and Scots. It has long been held that Kenneth was a Scot who succeeded to the Pictish throne, but recent research indicates he was himself a Pict – and this is consistent with the name he gave his expanded realm: Alba, the old Gaelic name for the land of the Picts.*

Kenneth gave himself the nickname Ferbasach, *meaning 'the bold' or 'conqueror', an honorific name that had been bestowed on a number of ancient* Tarachsel *kings who had ruled from the* Kyaar *at Taran's Garden. (The family name Forbes, still common in Cromar, is probably derived from* Ferbasach.*) Strangely, the old Pictish system of matrilineal succession had survived the changes brought by the Irish missionaries, and for several generations after Kenneth MacAlpin the kings of Alba continued to be selected from the maternal line.*

Life in the Howe of Cromar, the ancient heartland of Pictish culture, was marked by brutal poverty during all of this period. The Howe, once so central to the affairs of the Picts, became a forgotten backwater. It no longer lived up to its old name, the Pleasant Vale. Its population dwindled. In the churches of the Howe, at Tarland, Coull, Migvie, Logiemar and Coldstone, priests continued to rail against 'pagan' practices. New stone carvings were commissioned, bearing Christian symbolism to reinforce the total defeat of the old religion. One of these was the Kinord stone provocatively erected on the site of the old Merch Nyr *settlement of Davan. It can still be seen nearby, though not in the precise location where it originally stood. An undeniably beautiful (and remarkably well preserved) example of late Pictish art, it was probably intended as a sharp rebuke to any women who still hankered after their lost power-base there.*

But remnants of the Merch Nyr *continued to meet at hallowed places without attracting too much attention. Their ways, reviled by the church as 'satanic', were nonetheless tolerated by local people, who came to them for advice in matters of illness, whether human or animal, and problems with their crops. Though the* Drogan Taranish *had long ago been lost, its memory was kept alive by frequent retelling of traditional stories, and the women of the* Merch Nyr *continued in secret to select from their number a high priestess who was styled Keeper of Taran's wheel.*

Major political developments in the tenth and eleventh centuries had little effect on the day-to-day life of Cromar. Far to the south, the lands of Lothian and Strathclyde were annexed in 1018 by Mael Coluim mac Cineada (Malcolm MacKenneth), king of Alba. Thus did the more-or-less unified nation now known as 'Scotland' – perversely in view of the relatively minor contribution of the Scoti – *come into existence.*

In due course the Lothian stronghold of Edinburgh established itself as Scotland's capital. Though now more remote from the centre of power, Cromar was once again to play a part in the affairs of the nation.

28

THE ENGINEER

AMONG THE MILLIONS of transatlantic phone calls made one day in early August were two that would have given Delia and Quin cause for concern.

The first of these calls was to Cato Woods from Zeke Thackeray, whom he knew only as 'Z'. It was late afternoon in London when the call came, as Cato was trying to close a deal with a diplomat from Qatar seeking to convert some illicit cash into rough diamonds – but his customer was driving a hard bargain. When he saw who was calling, he had to interrupt the negotiation, whereupon the client left without a word.

Irked at losing the sale, Cato struggled not to sound brusque with the caller. 'Hello, Z,' he said.

'Get your ass up to Scotland,' Thackeray told him.

'Scotland?'

Thackeray gave him precise details of Delia's arrival time in Aberdeen, her rental car reservation, and her booking at the Hilton Craigendarroch in Ballater. *Two* flights had been booked, one for herself, departing from Chicago O'Hare, and one for Quinton Johnson, departing from Newark. And she'd visited some internet websites relating to a place called Tarland.

'Tarland, yes I know it, as it happens,' Cato said. 'A flyspeck in the middle of nowhere. If that's where the tektite is, it won't be hard to find. I'll stay close on her tail. Who did you say the other ticket is for?'

'Quinton Johnson. D'you know him?'

'No, doesn't ring a bell. Anyway, Z, I've thought a little more about the price. I'd be willing to come down to ten million.'

Thackeray gave no indication he heard this. 'Just don't screw up,' were his final words before the line went dead.

The second call was from a mobile phone somewhere in Great Britain to the Pastor's office in the Kingdom of Men church outside Topeka, Kansas. The Pastor heard street noises on the phone before a voice spoke.

'The Engineer returning your call.' There was no 'Most Reverend' deference from this caller.

The Pastor, like the Engineer, had no small talk. 'I've a situation over there that may need your intervention. Usual terms. Can you take it on?'

'Will it be like the last job? A disappearance? Not sure I could do one like that now, not for the same money, anyway. See, over here there's CCTV on just about every street corner. Much harder now to stay out of range. Back then, it was more straightforward.'

'It *may* come to that. A disappearance, I mean. Like the one you took care of a few years ago. And if it becomes necessary, rest assured the money will not be an issue.

'Here's the situation. I've placed an order for a trinket that may be somewhere in Scotland. There's a dealer in London by the name of Cato Woods who's promised to secure it for me. A couple of American kids are already after it. If they find it, Woods is supposed to get it from them however he can. But he might find it himself. In any case, I don't trust him. Not one bit.'

'So, Pastor, who is it you want to disappear once this trinket of yours is found? Woods? The American kids? All of the above?'

'All I want right now is for you to keep a close eye on the Americans – Delia Cobb, female, twenty-two to twenty-four, and Quinton Johnson, male, age unknown – and, just as important, on Cato Woods, male, thirty-eight to forty-two.

Don't scare them off. Let them find the thing, then do whatever it takes to gain possession, without, of course, leaving a trail.'

'We both know the surest way of avoiding a trail. Is that what you want?'

There was a lit cigarette in an ashtray on the Pastor's desk. He picked it up and took a long, deep draw. At length, he replied to the Engineer's question. 'Do what you have to do. I don't need details, just a successful outcome.'

'So, where will I find the target individuals this time?'

'Same place as before.'

'Shit. Not that Tarland dump? What in God's name is it about that hole? There must be a link to the last job, am I right?'

The Pastor didn't answer directly. 'The woman you ... the woman who disappeared. Megan Minty.'

'I remember. What about her?'

'Adulterous whore. She was writing a book that was gravely insulting to all God-fearing people.'

'I know all about the fucking book, Pastor. You asked me to make sure no copy of the manuscript would survive. And that's what I did. Whether she had it on paper, on disc, on a computer hard drive, I can assure you nothing – I mean *nothing* – survived that blaze.'

'Better make doubly sure. If the American kids get their hands on it we could be back to square one.'

'So they want Minty's manuscript? I tell you, it's gone.'

'No, that's not what they're after. But if they happen to find a copy in the course of their search, it will be doubly important to arrange an effective disappearance.'

'Not sure I follow you, Pastor, but I don't need to know *why* you want this job done. In fact I don't give a shit, so long as the money's good. Here's my fee. As last time, plus fifty percent, for each of the two Americans. For Cato Woods, the same rate applies. Half now, half on completion.'

'If a disappearance was on the agenda, your proposed fee would be reasonable. But it mightn't be necessary, in which case your costs – and risks – will be lower. So here's the deal. Fifty thousand dollars up front, with a bonus of another fifty when you deliver the goods. Extra services will be paid for, on top, at the rate you quote, but only if they become necessary *and* the primary objective is met. The first fifty thousand will be in your account in Belize by tomorrow. You'll be kept informed of your targets' movements by my aide Ezekiel Thackeray. Expect a call from him within the next forty-eight hours. You won't hear from me again on this.'

The Engineer tersely accepted the Pastor's offer and terminated the call. Finding himself outside a pub, he went in and ordered a pint and a chaser. At the bar he swallowed the scotch, straight with no ice, then found a table in a quiet corner to drink his beer and contemplate the new contract he had just landed.

Meanwhile the Pastor lit another cigarette and, leaning back in his chair, put his feet up on his desk and let his mind wander back to his last dealings with the Engineer, four years earlier. What a stroke of luck it had been that Megan Minty sent her manuscript, unsolicited, to the London office of New Frontier Press! She obviously had no idea of NFP's Christian credentials and links to American fundamentalist churches. It would have astonished her to find her writing was sent for review to a panel of dedicated Christians across the U.S. – a panel that happened to include one of the Pastor's faithful flock.

As soon as he'd learned of that blasphemous work and its incendiary message that women were capable of taking political control – worse still, that a society run by an all-female elite could prosper – the Pastor had resolved to ensure it would never see the light of day. He'd arranged for an NFP functionary to call the author, find out which other publishers had received a copy of her manuscript (none had yet – another stroke of luck, no, let's put it down to divine intervention) and offer her an exclusive deal, subject to total confidentiality. It had then been a simple, though expensive, matter to call in the Engineer. And he had done a superb job.

Yet it now seemed the 'disappearance' of Megan Minty and the destruction of her work hadn't been the complete solution he had hoped for. He'd recently learned of a mysterious glass sphere that a small-time English shyster by the name of Cato Woods claimed he could procure for an interested collector or investor. The description and supposed provenance of the object rang a disturbing bell in the Pastor's mind. Minty had written of just such a glass sphere that was a potent talisman of the ancient matriarchal society whose history she had uncovered. He had to have it.

And he would, with Zeke Thackeray, a trusted servant of the Kingdom of Men, on the case. Jayden Bayliss he was less sure of, but Thackeray would keep him in line. Furthermore, just to make doubly sure, he now had the Engineer deployed again.

29
THE LAST PICTISH KING

*I*N THE EARLY YEARS *of the unified kingdom of Scotland, it was not uncommon to have more than one claimant to the throne.   No longer was a high priestess available to adjudicate among claimants; questions of succession were therefore usually settled by force of arms.*

A typical struggle of the time was one between Donnchadh and Aeth, cousins who, as grandsons of Malcolm MacKenneth, each had a plausible claim to the throne.   Aeth, bearing the proud name of the legendary finder of Taran's wheel, reinforced his claim by assuming the princely title Mael, thus he styled himself Mael Aeth, a name which he later modified slightly to Mael Bheatha, meaning 'prince of life'.   This has come down to us, under William Shakespeare's influence, as Macbeth.   The real Macbeth, as I'll explain, was a very different person from the vicious usurper of Shakespeare's play.

Donnchadh or Duncan, contrary to the play, was the younger of the two cousins.   He became king in 1034, at first without serious opposition.   He turned out to be a weak and deceitful monarch, and was soon highly unpopular.   Having launched an ill-conceived attack on England in which his army was roundly defeated, he marched the remnants of his force north to the old Pictish province of Fortriu or Moray.   Macbeth, as mormaer (grand chieftain) of Moray, ran the province as a quasi-independent kingdom, and was none too pleased at Duncan's arrival, uninvited, in his territory.   Without too much difficulty he persuaded the king's own men to turn traitor. Duncan was killed at Pitgaveny near Elgin in 1040, permitting accession of the much more highly-regarded Macbeth to the throne of Scotland.

Macbeth's claim to the throne followed the old-fashioned matrilineal logic of the Picts, descended as he was from royalty on his mother's side. His queen Gruoch, Shakespeare's 'Lady Macbeth', also had royal blood. Previously married to another cousin of Macbeth's, she had a son Lulach who became Macbeth's stepson. In a further nod to ancient Pictish ways, the new king named Lulach as his successor. It is with good reason that Macbeth has sometimes been called 'the last Pictish king'.

Gruoch was not only of royal descent, but came also from a line of high priestesses of the old religion. Legend has it that she herself was a Keeper of Taran's wheel (not literally, of course, the Drogan having been bartered for peace by Calgacus almost a thousand years earlier). I believe she was the only Keeper in the entire history of my people to become queen.

One thing Shakespeare got right was that Macbeth took counsel from his queen, though in the play he is portrayed as indecisive and she as insidious and manipulating. In fact, it was one of the cornerstones of his success as king that he had high regard for and acted upon her advice. Through her, he also had access to the ancient wisdom of what remained of the female priesthood. The 'witches scene' that opens Macbeth may derive from a folk-memory of meetings with women of the Merch Nyr. One of the secret meeting places was in a hollow in the hills of Cromar, a desolate spot now called Satan's Howe.

Throughout his life, Macbeth had a particular affection for Cromar, and was a frequent visitor. He recognised the ancient significance of the Pleasant Vale in the history of his kingdom, and began building a castle there, wishing perhaps to return the Vale to something of its former glory. The location for his castle was not Tarland, where Tarachsel kings had once held court, but close to Devana (Davan), where according to tradition the Merch Nyr *had their base and their seat of learning. The particular spot he chose was an island in Loch Kinord.*

Macbeth's reign was an oasis of relative peace and stability in a turbulent period of Scotland's history. So well did he govern, and so strong was his people's support, that in 1050 he was confident enough to make an extended journey away from his kingdom. In the course of that journey he made a pilgrimage to Rome, where he gave generously to the poor of that city and was praised as a great benefactor by Pope Leo IX.

It may seem odd that a king on such good terms with upholders of a 'pagan' religion, indeed having the high priestess of that religion as his queen, should be pious enough to visit the pope in Rome. But the pilgrimage was less an expression of piety than an astute political move, and was probably Gruoch's idea. It cemented his good standing with the leaders of the church at home, helping them overlook the questionable background of his queen and his tolerance for what they saw as witchcraft.

Some time after his return, the redoubtable Gruoch died. Macbeth's hold on his kingdom began to weaken, as factions loyal to the sons of Duncan began plotting his overthrow, abetted by the duplicitous Edward the Confessor, king of England, and Thor Finn, the Norse Earl of Orkney. Macbeth continued to make regular visits to Cromar, where he knew he was among friends. On one of those visits, made as usual with little fanfare, he inspected building work on his castle in Loch Kinord and arranged to meet in secret with the Merch Nyr, *probably at Satan's Howe.*

'I bring you a gift,' he told them. 'It was presented to me by His Holiness the Pope in recognition of my generosity to the poor people of Rome.'

The women could not believe their eyes when he produced the gift from a leather pouch. It was the Drogan Taranish. *They wept with joy at the return of their sacred object to its rightful home.*

'It is said that this beautiful glass sphere has been in the possession of popes since the time of Emperor Constantine,' the king told them. 'Now it is back where it belongs.'

It isn't known who succeeded Gruoch as Keeper of Taran's wheel – perhaps a niece. In any case, she was the first Keeper for almost a thousand years to have the Drogan literally in her possession. She made a prophecy that the return of Taran's wheel would herald a period of great prosperity and a return to old Pictish ways – if not to the old religion.

It was not to be.

Mael Coluim (Malcolm) and Domnall Ban (Donald the Fair), the sons of Duncan, raised an army in 1057 to try to wrest the kingdom from Macbeth. Wounded in battle, the king made for Cromar where he knew he could safely hide while he recovered. Unfortunately, as he entered his beloved Howe, he was intercepted by Malcolm's men between Coull and Aboyne. After a short but gory battle – the stream that runs by the site is still known as the Bloody Burn – he fled north-eastward. On the Perk Hill about a mile from Lumphanan and eight miles from Tarland, his enemies caught up with him again. This time there was no escape. The king's lifeless body was placed in a shallow grave by an ancient cairn close to where he fell.

According to Keeper tradition, that night women came over the hill from Cromar and, under cover of darkness, disinterred the king's remains. The body of one of Malcolm's cavalrymen who had died in the fighting was dressed in the king's regalia and buried in his place. Macbeth's body was brought to the great cairn of Drummy where it was reburied with due solemnity according to Pictish custom.

In various accounts, you will read that a body, believed to be Macbeth's, was taken from Lumphanan to Iona, a small island off the west coast of Scotland revered as the cradle of Scottish Christianity. In fact the body taken to Iona was that of an unknown horseman. Doubtless he rests in peace.

30
A WORK OF ART

THE ENGINEER CHECKED INTO A nondescript hotel in the west end of Aberdeen. It was a fine summer's evening and, though he had no love for the area, he decided to take a drive to Tarland to reacquaint himself with the place. It was four years since he'd visited, on his previous contract for the Pastor.

He recalled it with satisfaction. Truly a job well done. His six-figure fee had been well deserved. The Minty woman had been lured to London under the impression that she would meet with an executive of New Frontier Press to discuss publication of her book. Matters were slightly complicated when she showed up at the appointed place with a male companion. It meant two people had to be disposed of, not just one. He had called the Pastor, who authorised him to complete the task, and paid a premium for the additional disappearance.

The way he handled the contract was, he had to admit to himself, a work of art. Posing as an NFP staffer, he had picked up his two targets at their hotel and taken them to the Towpath, a canalside pub and restaurant near Windsor, for dinner. In one sense the place was quiet – it had few customers – but it lay directly under the flight-path of jets taking off from Heathrow airport, just a few miles to the east.

Over the meal, accompanied by the restaurant's most expensive wine, he had outlined to Minty details of her meeting the following day with a senior NFP executive, where they'd get down to the nitty-gritty of a publication contract. Afterwards, out in the car-park, which was unlit and empty except for his own car, he had dispatched both his guests in the space of five seconds with a couple of precision gunshots through the skull while a particularly noisy jet roared above.

After tying plastic bags over their heads to contain the blood, he had bundled the two bodies into the back of his car and driven to a disused gravel pit flooded with water to a depth of forty feet. There he had weighted the corpses and slid them into the water, where they quickly sank to the bottom, joining at least seven bodies from other contracts he had successfully completed.

With his victims' keycard he had entered their hotel room next morning to perform an onscreen checkout, then gather up their belongings, including Megan's laptop computer, several discs and thumb-drives, and a complete paper manuscript, all of which he had destroyed. As it was likely she had left copies of the manuscript at home, he had made a trip north to Tarland about a week later to tie up that particular loose end.

Now he was headed back there. It would be amusing to see the place again, four years after the fire.

Shortly after passing the sign for the earth-house at Culsh, he turned right up a narrow farm road leading into the hills on the north side of the Howe of Cromar. His destination was Praisewell, the cottage where Megan Minty had lived with her husband and two young children.

He found a brand-new home in the later stages of construction on the site. There was no trace of the original cottage – its stone walls had apparently been demolished and used to build a very attractive garden wall around the new dwelling. He stopped his car a little short of the house, and walked the rest of the way. The front door was open, and he saw a young couple busy laying floor tiles in the hallway. 'I'm sorry to disturb you,' the Engineer called. 'I can see you're busy. Beautiful home you're building. And what a view!' He turned away from them as if to admire the scenery, appearing lost in contemplation for a few moments.

'What brings you here?' the young man asked, as the couple walked down the footpath to meet the visitor.

'My grandparents farmed near here,' the Engineer replied. 'The Pett, I think the place was called. I thought it was up this road. Maybe I read my map wrong.'

'No, no, you're not wrong. You passed the Pett on your way up here. You just came a little too far, that's all. This is Praisewell.'

The Engineer feigned interest in the name as if he was hearing it for the first time.

'We didn't choose the name,' the young man said. 'There was an old cottage on this site called Praisewell. Don't know how it got that name, but we kinda liked it, so we're going to keep it.' The couple looked at each other and grinned.

'So did you knock down the old cottage?'

'Well, what was left of it. It was just a shell. It burned down a few years ago.'

'Oh, it's tragic when someone loses a home like that,' the Engineer said. 'But of course one person's loss is another's opportunity, isn't it? You know, some friends of mine bought a burned-out homesite a year or two ago. In Somerset, it was. When they were clearing the site, they found all kinds of stuff that had survived the fire. Papers, photos, that kind of thing. They sent the stuff they found to the previous owners. Bad enough having a fire destroy your home, but at least insurance pays for that. It's all the personal stuff you lose that's the worst thing.'

The Engineer was pulling strings and he pulled the right one.

'Well, nothing like that survived *this* fire, I can tell you,' the young woman said. 'We've heard that by the time the firemen arrived the whole place was burnt to cinders. The sheds at the back, too. They said it must have been an incredibly hot fire, not to leave *some* bits and pieces.'

'I suppose. Well, I'll let you get on. Nice talking to you.'

The couple went back towards the house. After a few paces, the young woman stopped, turned around and said, 'Sorry, what did you say your name was?'

But the Engineer was already walking back to his car and made no reply.

31
BIG-HEAD

MACBETH'S STEPSON AND HEIR *Lulach reigned as King of Scots for less than a year before Malcolm's henchmen caught up with him at Essie, about fifteen miles north of Cromar, and killed him. The local people were resolutely anti-Malcolm for the murder of Macbeth, and the death of his rightful heir further strengthened their hatred. An ancient standing stone at Kildrummy is to this day called Lulach's stone. Another one at Whitehouse, likewise not far from the Howe of Cromar, is known locally as 'Luath's stone' but is believed to be another memorial to King Lulach rather than to the Celtic god Luath or Lugus.*

The death of Lulach left no barrier to the ascent of Malcolm to the throne of Scotland as Malcolm III. In more recent times he has become known as Canmore ('Big-Head'), though this has probably arisen through confusion with his great grandson Malcolm IV, whose skull was enlarged and deformed, probably as a result of Paget's disease. In spite of the confusion, I'll refer to Malcolm III as 'Canmore' because the nickname is appropriate. Lulach's son Mael Snechtai ('snow prince') made several attempts to provoke a rising against Canmore but little came of them.

Canmore may have been blissfully ignorant of the depth of feeling against him in Cromar, but more likely he chose arrogantly to defy it. He made a show of completing the castle in Loch Kinord that Macbeth had left unfinished, but it is not clear he ever risked staying there. He began a campaign of propaganda against the Macbeth dynasty, perhaps out of fear that it would somehow reassert itself. It may have been this that led eventually to the dim view of Macbeth taken by the historical sources on which Shakespeare later relied. And it was probably Canmore who first referred to Macbeth's short-lived successor as 'Lulach the Fatuous'.

Though his reign was a relatively long one, Canmore would be little remembered but for his good fortune in matrimony. His first wife, Ingibiorg, was the widow of the Earl of Orkney who had supported him in overthrowing the Macbeth dynasty. That marriage may have been unpopular with many of his subjects but it bought a period of peace with the usually warlike Norsemen who still ruled the northern mainland of Scotland as well as the northern and western isles.

His second wife, Margaret, came from a branch of the English royal family that had been exiled to Hungary. The people of Scotland, regardless of what they felt about their king, took Queen Margaret to their hearts. She was credited with many good deeds and with great Christian piety, for which she was later canonised.

Canmore was greatly impressed by the Norman dynasty that, during his reign in 1066, was founded across the border in England by William the Conqueror. Pretentiously he decreed that, as in England, the language of the royal court should henceforward be Norman French. Nobles and other sycophants vied with each other to display their fluency. Gaelic, however, continued to be the medium of communication among ordinary people throughout most of Scotland.

Queen Margaret, by contrast, adopted the Germanic language spoken by the Angles in Lothian, a northern variant of Anglo-Saxon that is the parent of the modern Scots tongue.

Treachery and duplicitousness were among Canmore's hallmarks. Having ensured that no legitimate successor from the house of Macbeth could reign again, he set about disinheriting his own brother Donald who had loyally supported him in winning the throne. In a break with Pictish tradition, he replaced Donald with his own son Edward in the line of succession. However, the king and his heir were both killed in battle against the English at Alnwick in 1093, and the throne came to Donald after all.

The saintly Queen Margaret died just a few days after Canmore and Edward. The outpouring of grief for her was far greater than for the king and his heir. She was, in a way, the Diana of her time – adored all the more for the shortcomings of her husband.

Following Canmore, Scotland was ruled by a succession of mostly forgettable kings. Some of them were king in name only, the real power in the land being devolved to provincial chieftains. One of these was the mormaer (or earl) of Mar, who ruled over the area still known as the province of Mar, with the Howe of Cromar at its centre. His original seat was at Migvie Castle in the north-western part of the Howe or, when a more defensive location was needed, at the Doune of Invernochty, an artificial mound or motte in Strathdon surmounted by a fortified keep. Later, he moved to more palatial quarters at Kildrummy Castle, about eight miles north of Cromar.

The line of eleventh-to-thirteenth century kings came to an end with the death of Alexander III and accession of Margaret the 'Maid of Norway', who died in 1290 at the age of seven without ever setting foot in her kingdom. Her demise left the throne vacant and ripe for plucking by the notorious Edward I of England. At one point he installed a puppet king, John Balliol, but for most of the period from 1290 to 1306 power in Scotland nominally lay with a series of Guardians of the Realm. Some Guardians were pro-English; others were more nationalist, favouring a return to full independence. The most famous of the nationalists were William Wallace ('Braveheart') and, at least latterly, a nobleman of Norman extraction, Robert de Brus, better known as Bruce.

Most of the lands in the north-east of Scotland, including Cromar, were by this time held by nobles whose affiliation was with the pro-English faction and who were therefore opposed to Wallace and Bruce. Their strongholds in Cromar were the castles of Migvie, formerly the seat of the mormaer of Mar, in the north-west and Coull in the south-east. Between them was the village known as Tarwelan (Tarland), but this had greatly declined in importance, records of the time giving greater prominence to Kincraigie, an estate about a mile to the east of the village.

Coull Castle had been established by the Durward family, who were hereditary 'door-wards' of Scotland, an honorary title bestowed by an earlier king. Descendants of the mormaers of Mar, the Durwards owned extensive tracts of that ancient province, including the lands of Coull and Kincraigie. The castle occupied a defensive site near where the Tarland Burn leaves the broad valley of Cromar and enters the narrow defile between the hills of Balnagowan and Mortlich.

The Durwards were so closely identified with Coull that a legend grew up in Cromar that when a Durward died, the bell of Coull kirk would toll of its own accord. The most powerful scion of the family was Alan Durward, who for a brief period had effectively ruled Scotland while the king of the time, Alexander III, was still a child. When Alan died he left three daughters and no sons. Daughters being mere women who couldn't inherit property, the lands of Coull and Kincraigie, including the castle, passed to the Scottish crown.

In due course they were granted to the earldom of Fife. Thus begins the story of one of the most remarkable people ever to emerge from Cromar – the tale of Isobel of Coull.

32

COMMON CAUSE

'SO, ZEKE, IS EVERYTHING in place?' Jayden Bayliss asked.

'Believe so,' Ezekiel Thackeray replied. 'Woods is on his way north, and expects to be at Tarland by tomorrow. He knows Cobb and Johnson are staying at the Hilton Whatchacallit and he'll be able to keep track of them from there. And the Engineer has already revisited the Minty place and confirmed it's clean. For the next few days he'll have his eye on Cobb and Johnson *and* on Woods.'

'Didn't you say he was a bit trigger-happy, that Engineer? Any risk he'll kill 'em all without getting his hands on the glass ball?'

The two men were in an otherwise deserted chicken shack in a forlorn part of downtown Topeka, for a face-to-face update on progress of Operation Curveball, as they'd come to call the Pastor's latest obsession. Each day they would meet in a different greasy fast-food establishment.

While thinking for a moment about the concern Bayliss had raised, Thackeray stuffed some fried chicken in his mouth and took a big gulp of Diet Dr Pepper to wash it down. 'Not much danger of that, I'd say. I don't know exactly how the deal's structured, but I'm sure as hell he won't get his money if he doesn't deliver the ball.'

'What if Woods gets the goddam ball? Does he get paid too?'

Thackeray laughed, spattering chicken fragments over the table. 'What do *you* think?'

'No, I guess we've enough on Woods to avoid having to pay him a brown fucking cent. His payment will be to stay outta jail. *If* the Engineer doesn't pop him first.'

'You got it. So, Jay, what's the latest intelligence from the Rat?'

Bayliss grunted. 'Not too much in the last twenty-four hours. The girl's been spending most of her computer time reading some stupid document. She uses a tablet the Rat doesn't work too well with – it's really designed for laptops – but it can still record and transmit what text she enters and what links she follows. Unfortunately it can't tell us what she's seeing on her screen. So we can't figure out much about the document. But we do know the password she uses to open it. A-L-C-Y-O-N-E, whatever the hell that means. It would be good if we could get our hands on that tablet. Could the Engineer get it for us, d'ya think?'

'Of course he could, but that's not really his line of business, and we need her for a while yet. What web searches has she done since yesterday?'

'She was looking on Google Books for something called *The British Chronicles* by – let me check my notes – David Hughes. Took a look at it myself. Boring as hell. A litany of ancient kings and queens. She also accessed some Wikipedia pages. Here's a list for you.'

Thackeray scanned the list Bayliss handed him. Agricola. Calgacus. *Mons Graupius*. Tacitus. Oats.

'*Oats?*' Thackeray said aloud. 'What the fuck's that to do with anything?'

'Beats the shit out of me,' Bayliss conceded. 'But I suppose we can learn something about this document of hers by seeing what it prompts her to look for on the web. Oh, there's one other thing she looked at. Downloaded it, in fact. It's a dry-as-dust paper, a hundred years old, called *"The Cairns in Cromar, Aberdeenshire"* by Sir Alexander Ogston. Here, I made a copy for you.'

'Gee, can't wait to get my teeth into that.'

The two men were silent for a few minutes while they finished their meal. Then Bayliss opened a new topic of conversation.

'Ever wonder, Zeke, what's so important about this glass ball? I mean, why the Pastor is so desperate to get his hands on it?'

'Yeah, I sometimes wonder, but it's not our place to question him. He has a good reason, whatever the hell it is. That's enough for me.'

Bayliss lowered his voice, although there were no other diners to overhear him. 'I know more about the Pastor than I'm supposed to,' he said.

That got Thackeray's attention. 'What d'ya mean?'

'Like I said, I know a lot. I put a Rat in his computer too.'

Zeke stared at him in amazement. 'You did *what*? Are you crazy? If he finds out, even suspects, you're dead fucking meat. Me too – I was the one who vouched for you, got you into this project.' He was beginning to have second thoughts about Jayden Bayliss. The man's total lack of a moral compass fitted him well for doing the Pastor's dirty work, but now it could be a liability.

'So, d'ya wanna hear what he's up to?'

Thackeray needed a little more time to consider the implications, and made no reply. Bayliss took his silence as a 'yes'.

'It's big. He's working on an alliance with other religious groups who want to curb the influence of women in society, in politics, in business.'

'Well, big fucking deal, that's no surprise,' Thackeray observed. 'The Kingdom of Men Church stands for a new male-dominated society. That's what it's all about. It's natural the Pastor would make common cause with other churches that have a similar mission.'

'It's not just other churches,' Bayliss said. 'It's all kinds of fundamentalists – Christian, Jewish, Islamic. Christ, he's even got a contact in the fucking Taliban in Pakistan. I got to wondering, why does he have such a hatred of women?'

'He doesn't *hate* them, any more than he hates animals. He just believes in the teaching of scripture about the dominion of men over all other creatures.'

'Yeah, yeah. So do we all. But he's never seen with female company. Even I go out with a woman sometimes. But him? I used to wonder if he was gay. You know how he rails against homos in his sermons? I've heard that kind of stuff before from preachers who've turned out to like boys, know what I mean?'

'What if he *is* gay?' Thackeray said. 'Long as he keeps it to himself, he can do what he likes.'

'He ain't gay,' Bayliss declared. 'You should see the porn sites he visits. *Very* hetero. Really hard-core, a lot of it. He especially likes the violent stuff. Often with knives, always with women. There's a ton of gay porn sites on the web, but he never goes there.'

Thackeray suddenly found himself worrying that he himself was likewise under Bayliss's surveillance. 'And what about the surfing *I* do?' he asked.

Bayliss assumed an air of shocked surprise. 'Aw, Zeke! You don't think I've set the Rat on *you*?'

'If the Pastor's on your list, fuck, I don't know what to think.'

'Naw,' Bayliss said, soothingly. 'We're buddies. I wouldn't. But if you like, I can show you how to check your computer for the Rat. He has a paw-print, if you know how to find it.'

Thackeray's concern for his own internet privacy gave way to renewed disquiet over Bayliss's invasion of the Pastor's computer.

'Keep all this to yourself, okay?' Thackeray warned him. 'Especially the "common cause" agenda. If it became known that the Pastor has friends in the Taliban, he would come under suspicion. The whole church would. You and me included.'

33
ISOBEL OF COULL

D UNCAN MACDUFF, EARL OF FIFE became regent of
Scotland for the infant Maid of Norway. His wife
Joanna lived at Coull Castle with their daughter Isabel
or Isabella. (Following Megan's practice, I use the more
common Scottish spelling 'Isobel'.) A local woman by the name
of Margaret Baird was lady's maid to the countess.

Unknown to the Macduffs, Margaret Baird was a Keeper
of Taran's wheel. It's because of this that the story of Isobel of
Coull has been preserved in such detail; but I must warn you
that the story as passed down by the Keepers is not always in
perfect agreement with official history. You will have to make
up your own mind as to where the truth most probably lies.

As members of the Scottish nobility, the Macduffs spoke
French, not deigning to use the Gaelic language of their lower-
born neighbours. Margaret accompanied Joanna everywhere
and learned to speak French fluently. To Isobel, Margaret was
more of a mother than Joanna herself; and Margaret loved
Isobel like a child of her own.

Duncan was deeply in debt. Some time after his
assassination in 1288, Joanna was obliged to travel to
Edinburgh on matters relating to the deceased earl's debts.
Margaret accompanied her, as always, but first (so Keeper
tradition says) hid the Drogan Taranish under a flagstone in the
kitchen floor at Coull Castle. Although Joanna had been
promised safe passage, she and Margaret were kidnapped

near the village of Plean, between Stirling and Falkirk, by a roguish baron, Herbert de Morham. For his crimes de Morham later became an object of scorn, acquiring the nickname 'Cockybendy', meaning a small, bumptious man. According to most accounts, he held his hostages at Castlerankine, about four miles away; but a local tradition holds that their prison was on a site at Plean later occupied by a fortified tower, still referred to as 'Cockybendy's Castle'.

Perhaps unaware of the fragility of Joanna's financial affairs, de Morham demanded that she marry him. Joanna steadfastly refused his advances. Eventually, with Margaret's aid, she was able to escape, but not before Cockybendy had stolen all the jewels and fine clothes she had been relying on to pay off her husband's debts. He didn't enjoy the fruits of his crimes for long; he was put to death in London in 1306.

De Morham's much more illustrious father Thomas, a hero of the Scottish resistance along with Wallace and Bruce, was for much of this time incarcerated in the Tower of London and had been unable to control his son's criminal behaviour. He was eventually released in 1314 following defeat of the English by Bruce at Bannockburn, coincidentally only a few miles from Cockybendy's Castle.

But back to the fraught journey of Joanna and Margaret to Edinburgh. Finally arriving there, Joanna was obliged to sell the lands of Coull and Kincraigie to discharge the debt. It meant that Margaret Baird was unable to return to Coull to retrieve the Drogan from its hiding place under the kitchen floor.

In an earlier effort to stabilise the family's finances, Isobel had entered into an arranged marriage while still in her teens to the much older John Comyn or Cumming, Earl of Buchan. This grieved Margaret, who knew that the marriage was loveless, that Buchan treated Isobel with cruelty and neglect, and that he openly had affairs with many mistresses. When Joanna sold her home at Coull, Margaret went to Ellon, north of Aberdeen, to become lady's maid to the young Countess of Buchan. This reunion with Margaret was of great comfort to the unhappy Isobel.

The Comyn family were staunchly pro-English, supporting the puppet king John ('Toom Tabard' as he was called by his opponents, meaning 'empty cloak') and continuation of Scotland's status as a vassal dominion under the English sovereign, Edward I ('Longshanks'). When Buchan's cousin 'the Red' Comyn was murdered by Robert the Bruce or his supporters in a Dumfries church, Buchan became even more vociferous in his support of the English cause.

His young wife Isobel of Coull, however, secretly supported Bruce's goal of returning Scotland to full independence, and finally 'came out' to perform his coronation as Robert I, King of Scots at Scone in March 1306. This was like painting a target on her own back. Chief among the enemies she made was her own husband. For her protection she remained close to Robert; some have speculated that during that time she and the king secretly became lovers. Whether Robert's queen, Elizabeth, knew of any such affair isn't known, but the two women appear to have remained friends.

A few months after the coronation, Robert was defeated in battle at Methven by pro-English forces, and, fearing for the safety of the women in his life, he sent Queen Elizabeth, Isobel, his sisters Christina and Mary, and daughter Marjorie north to Kildrummy Castle. Their lady's maids, including Margaret Baird, accompanied them.

Disastrously, they were betrayed by the pro-English faction that remained entrenched in that part of Scotland, and were captured. Isobel's husband was probably instrumental in the betrayal. Edward Longshanks gave express instructions as to their 'punishment'. Queen Elizabeth was imprisoned in England. Christina was consigned to a nunnery. But Longshanks devised a singularly cruel fate for Isobel, Mary and the nine-year-old Marjorie. Each was to be locked in a cage that would be suspended in the open air from a castle wall, 'as a spectacle and eternal reproach to travellers'. Isobel's cage was in Berwick, Mary's in Roxburgh, and for maximum exposure the little girl was to be exhibited at the Tower of London.

The king's advisers may have persuaded him that displaying a nine-year-old royal princess, caged like an animal, was not likely to endear him to his people; he relented and instead sent her into solitary confinement in Yorkshire, which she endured for eight long years. On her release after the Scots' victory at Bannockburn in 1314, Marjorie was given in marriage to a High Steward of Scotland and died in childbirth at the age of nineteen. Her short, tragic life changed the face of Scottish, and eventually English, history: the son she bore lived to become the first in a long line of monarchs of the Stuart dynasty.

As for Isobel and Mary, both survived in their cages, summer and winter, for four years. During their imprisonment, Longshanks died, to be succeeded by his son Edward II. The new king of England, effeminate and ineffectual, gradually became a laughing-stock among his subjects. Soon Isobel's warders, in awe of her resilience and fortitude, released her – to the waiting arms of her ever loving, ever faithful Margaret Baird. Mary was similarly freed around the same time.

During Isobel's ordeal in Berwick, Robert the Bruce took steps to purge north-east Scotland of its pro-English element. In a concerted harrying campaign in 1308, one of his prime targets was the seat of Isobel's husband the Earl of Buchan at Ellon; indeed he destroyed the whole town. In Cromar, the castles of Migvie and Coull were sacked and reduced to rubble. The estate of Kincraigie, having some of the most fertile and productive land in Cromar, was spared but taken by Bruce as a crown possession. The inhabitants of the small settlement, the site of which is at the present-day farm of Oldtown of Kincraigie, became tenants of the king.

Tragically Isobel of Coull, having survived four years' imprisonment in a cage hung from the wall of Berwick Castle, and still a young woman, took a fever and died around the time of Bannockburn in 1314. Bruce rewarded Margaret Baird's faithful service to Isobel by giving her life rent of a home and land at Kincraigie.

And what of the Drogan Taranish, *hidden in Coull Castle all those years before? Margaret enlisted the help of some women of the* Merch Nyr *still living in Cromar. With their bare hands they worked for weeks, digging down through the heaps of stones until they reached the flagstone floor. Eventually they lifted the slab under which Margaret had concealed the* Drogan.

Glory be to Taran, it was still there.

34
DELIA'S LIST

B
Y THE TIME Delia and Quin had got up to the time of Macbeth in Grace's *Second Testament*, they realised it was a highly revisionist history. Now having reached the fourteenth century story of Isobel of Coull, they wondered how much of what they were reading was simply made up. Grace had already indicated that her *First Testament* was based partly on oral tradition as passed down through generations of Keepers, partly on Megan's research and partly invented.

'It doesn't really matter whether it's true or not,' Delia suggested. 'Grace wrote all this to keep the tradition alive. I'm her chosen successor as Keeper, but only by default. Most of the stories we've been reading are entirely new to me; if she hadn't set it all down it would have been lost forever. And she had another reason.'

'Namely?'

'To provide clues to the location of Taran's wheel, of course.'

'You know,' Quin said, 'Grace's version of things is maybe not so revisionist as we're thinking. I've been reading some Scottish history on the web. *Mons Graupius* probably wasn't the great Roman victory Tacitus made it out to be. Agricola didn't return to Rome a hero as he expected. As for Macbeth, it's pretty well settled that Shakespeare's king bears little resemblance to the real man. And the story of the lady in the cage – referred to by Grace as "Isobel of Coull" – has a long pedigree.'

'Maybe,' Delia conceded, 'but look at the way she presents the coming of Christianity to the Picts. She's very negative about the whole thing, which I don't have a problem with. But isn't it a bit over the top? That an entire culture was destroyed? A language spoken for a thousand years obliterated? A political system destabilised? Economic ruin? Women condemned to a life of subjugation?'

'Over the top, perhaps for most writers. But for Grace? I don't know. From everything my grandfather told me about Grace, and what I've learned from you so far, it all seems very much in character.'

'True, Grace professed no religion. She believed all the world's great religions were devices, very effective devices, she maintained, to perpetuate male supremacy. She saw the rise of fundamentalism as a dangerous but natural response of organized religion to the advances in women's rights that have been chipping away at male domination, especially in the West.'

'And what do *you* believe, Delia?' Quin asked, in a mischievous tone of voice.

She didn't rise to the bait. 'I believe we should focus on the job in hand.'

They were sitting on a sofa in their room at Craigendarroch. She spread out her Ordnance Survey maps on the low table. 'We should compile a list of all the places in or near Cromar mentioned by Grace in her *First* and *Second Testaments*,' she proposed. 'I'm sure the *Drogan*, or – knowing Grace – a further clue to its location, is hidden at one of them. She said something in her spoken introduction about returning it to its origin. What was it exactly, again, that she said?'

Quin replayed Grace's voice message.

The Drogan *is safe. It's back in a place it's been before.*

'Problem is, she's mentioned dozens of places,' he protested. 'And we haven't even read all the way to the end yet. There could be a lot more.'

'Well, it doesn't look like we're going to have Megan to help us narrow down the search. Let's drive up to Praisewell anyway and see what's there, though from what Ewen said there was nothing left after the fire.'

Skim-reading Grace's *First Testament*, telling the story of the Pleasant Vale from Jurassic times up to the aftermath of *Mons Graupius*, went fast. The first few chapters of the *Second Testament*, continuing up to the fourteenth century, took longer and provided more items for the list. Delia tapped the place-names into her computer, adding notes. She used a few abbreviations: 'PV' for 'Pleasant Vale' and 'MN' for *Merch Nyr*.

By the time they got up to the battle of Bannockburn in 1314, she'd reached number twenty.

POSSIBLE HIDING PLACES

1. *1st large cairn – Taran's Crossing (location not yet known) – here T. unleashed thunderbolt creating PV – but Drogan never here?*
2. *2nd large cairn – on Craig Dhu, S. rim of PV (also here: one of Mons Graupius battlegrounds & many burial cairns)*
3. *3rd large cairn – 'Blue Cairn' of Drummy – dead centre of PV – Macbeth's reburial site*
4. *Tarland village – was Taran's Garden (many possible hiding places here)*
5. *'ghost meadow' – Dalvokie – no connection with Drogan?*
6. *Kyaar – destroyed – now site of old church & churchyard in Turland (search again at Agnes Cromar's stone?)*
7. *Tomnaverie stone circle*
8. *cambus (riverbend) where Aeth found Drogan – somewhere on R. Dee – Cambus o' May?*
9. *Aeth's home – settlement behind hill above cambus*

10. *MN village – Devana/Davan (also Pictish carved stone at Kinord)*
11. *Agricola's camp (location not yet known) – unlikely, though he did return there with Drogan*
12. *Culsh earth-house – Drogan used in blessing of foodstores*
13. *Craiglich (Ladle-lick), E. rim of PV – the other Mons Graupius battleground & burial cairns*
14. *Ordie Gordon (location not yet known but midway between PV and Roman camp) – Agricola & Calgacus exchanged gifts here*
15. *Migvie church – Pictish carved stones – was Drogan ever here?*
16. *Satan's Howe – poss. where Macbeth returned Drogan to MN*
17. *Bloody Burn – battle between Malcolm & Macbeth – no mention of Drogan here*
18. *site of Macbeth's killing near Lumphanan*
19. *Coull Castle – Drogan hidden under flagstone*
20. *Kincraigie (now Oldtown of K.) – Margaret Baird's final home*

'Why do you think Agricola's camp is an unlikely hiding place?' Quin asked.

'Well, for a start Grace doesn't say where it is, except that it's a day's march away from the Pleasant Vale.'

'But you're not saying "unlikely" for other places outside the Vale, for example Taran's Crossing and Ordie Gordon, wherever *they* are – Grace doesn't say – and Lumphanan.'

'I dunno. It seems to me those have a stronger connection to Taran or the *Drogan*. Ordie Gordon is where Calgacus gave away the *Drogan*, and Lumphanan, or near there, is where Macbeth died. Remember, the *Merch Nyr* used to bring the *Drogan* to a place of death, especially a king's death, to ensure *vairtach* for the deceased.'

'Yes, *vairtach*, the wheel of justice,' Quin agreed. 'They believed the dead person's spirit hung around for a short time. I guess when Macbeth's body was moved, the spirit didn't necessarily travel with it. So it makes sense to think the *Merch Nyr* would have brought the *Drogan* to Lumphanan.'

Delia's eyes lit on number 13. 'Grace says the local name for Craiglich is Ladle-lick. It's such a curious name, I wonder if there's a clue hidden in it somehow? I'm going to ask Ewen if that's what *he* calls the hill, next time we see him.'

'I was thinking about Ladle-lick too. According to Grace, it means "hill of graves".'

'You're going to say it means nothing of the sort.'

'No, I think she's exactly right. I don't know what her source is for the Pictish language, but in proto-Celtic *letri* is a word fragment meaning a hill or a slope, and *leg* is a bed, or by extension a resting-place or a grave. And *letri-leg*, "hill of graves", could easily have morphed into Ladle-lick over two thousand years.'

'Look on the map, Quin.' Delia pointed to Craiglich on one of the maps spread out on the table. 'The east face of the hill is named Leadlich here. Maybe the mapmakers found the name "Ladle-lick" a bit too fanciful.'

'Maybe. Incidentally, Grace said the meaning of *"Merch Nyr"* was unknown, though she thought *merch* signified daughter. Well, she's right. *Merch* or *verch*, same word. *Creiddylad verch Llyr* in Welsh is Cordelia the daughter of Lear. *Nyr* could come from proto-Celtic *nero*, meaning hero. So *Merch Nyr* could mean something like "daughter-heroes" – not a far cry from demigoddesses, which is what they believed themselves to be ... why are you grinning like that?'

Delia's grin turned into a laugh. 'I love it when you get into linguistic analysis.'

The next task was to prioritise. Some spots seemed more likely than others. The Blue Cairn of Drummy, for example. The stone circle at Tomnaverie, for sure. They began to plan an itinerary, beginning with the most promising locations.

It was an exciting moment. They would begin the hunt for the *Drogan* in earnest first thing next morning.

35
THE FIFTH *CAMBUS*

THE WARS OF INDEPENDENCE dragged on. Bannockburn was an important victory for Scotland, but there remained throughout the country, and especially among the nobility of the north-east, a stubborn body of pro-English sentiment. Bruce's harrying of the nobles had weakened their grip, but some families, notably the Strathbogie family who had extensive lands in the area, continued to favour the English. A decisive battle was the only way the future of Scotland would be set on a path to resolution, one way or the other. That battle was fought in Cromar in 1335, six years after Bruce's death.

David Strathbogie, Earl of Atholl supported the English king's plan to install another Balliol on the throne of Scotland in place of David II, the young son of Robert the Bruce. Strathbogie laid siege to Kildrummy Castle, hoping the fall of this nationalist stronghold would swing the whole of north-east Scotland behind the English cause. Resident in the castle at the time was Bruce's sister Christina, now released from her English nunnery and married to Sir Andrew Murray, regent for the eleven-year-old King David. Hearing of the siege, Murray raised an army and marched north from Edinburgh with the intention of relieving the blockade. On the evening of November 29th, 1335, he camped by the east shore of Loch Davan, en route to Kildrummy about twelve miles away.

Learning of Murray's approach, Strathbogie led a detachment south to Cromar to intercept him. He and his men camped on the west shore of Loch Davan, by the old road that runs from Tarland to Tullich. The opposing camps were within earshot of one another across the still, cold waters of the loch.

Murray adopted a tactical ruse that was to prove decisive. Leaving behind a small detachment of men, he led the bulk of his forces around the loch to a position within striking range of the Strathbogie camp. Those remaining in camp burned fires and made loud noise for much of the night, thus Strathbogie's men were caught totally off-guard by Murray's early morning attack. In the ensuing battle on the lower slopes of Culblean, Strathbogie never regained the initiative.

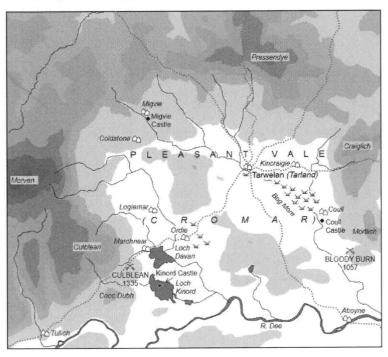

This map of fourteenth-century Cromar shows the location of the Culblean battlefield; also indicated is the site of Macbeth's skirmish with Malcolm almost three centuries earlier at the Bloody Burn.

The fighting on Culblean was fierce but was quickly over, a crushing victory for Murray and the Scottish cause – appropriately enough on the feast day of Andrew, Scotland's patron saint, November 30th. The battle proved to be a turning-point as significant in its way as Bannockburn more than twenty years earlier, and with more permanent effect. The Pleasant Vale had yet again played a pivotal role in the history of the Scottish nation.

Now, you can read accounts of the battle in history books and you will find it happened more or less as I have described it. But what you won't find in the history books is that close by Strathbogie's camp and the Culblean battlefield was a tiny settlement where lived some women of the Merch Nyr, a vestige of the nearby township recorded by Ptolemy as Devana. A dwelling at the precise location of that township is still called Marchnear. Following the old practice, the women would certainly have buried the dead on the battlefield that was right there on their doorstep, and brought the Drogan to the burial sites.

Did the battle of Culblean in 1335 mark the fifth cambus? *The timing is about right, just a little short of 666 years from the fourth* cambus, *when Pictish culture and language had been destroyed in favour of Gaelic. But though Culblean had lasting political impact, its effect on the lives of ordinary people in Cromar was slight. Now their overlords were unequivocally Scottish, no longer beholden to England; but being ruled from Edinburgh rather than London made little difference.*

I prefer to think that the fifth cambus *was something that happened over a longer period, beginning around the time of Culblean and continuing for eighty or ninety years. Important though its outcome was, the battle of 1335 didn't usher a time of peace to north-east Scotland. There was something new to fight about: the creeping of lowland ways into what had hitherto been regarded a highland region. And the touchstone of this conflict was language. For highlanders spoke Gaelic, as* they had since it was forced on them in the eighth century, while lowlanders spoke Inglis – originally the language of the Angles of Lothian.

Migration from the south, together with a recognition that Inglis *was the language of Scottish government and commerce, made the gradual decline of Gaelic in north-east Scotland unstoppable. The battle of Harlaw, fought in 1411 on a field near Inverurie, was a particularly bloody encounter between supporters of the rival tongues that cemented the supremacy of the* Inglis *language.*

After Harlaw, the Howe of Cromar found itself on the very western edge of Inglis-speaking Scotland. Glen Gairn just over the hill of Culblean held fast to Gaelic. Inglis *speakers regarded their language as the true national tongue, calling it 'Scots' (as they do to this day) while referring deprecatingly to the Gaelic language of the highlands as 'Erse'. Though 'Erse' meant 'Irish', in the pronunciation of the word it was no different from the Scots word for the backside or rectum.*

So the Gaelic language imposed by the fourth cambus was consigned to history by the fifth. In Cromar it survives only in place-names – Morven, 'big mountain'; Culsh, 'woods'; Dalvokie, 'ghost meadow'; Drummy, 'low ridge'. A few place-names in Cromar are survivors of the ancient Pictish or Tarachsel language; they include Tarland, 'Taran's Garden', Ladle-lick, 'hill of graves', Pett, a farming settlement. By the late fifteenth century, the church's objection to Tar-lan as commemorating a pagan god had been long forgotten, and the name of the village had reverted from Tarwelan ('bull-pen') to its original form. The final D of 'Tarland' was added more recently, but in local speech has never been pronounced.

36

PRAISEWELL

ON THURSDAY MORNING, Delia and Quin awoke strangely refreshed. Any jet lag they had felt since arriving in Great Britain on Monday had dissipated.

After breakfast, their first destination was Praisewell. Even though Megan Minty was long gone from there, perhaps they would find *some* clue to the mystery of her disappearance, *some* way to access whatever information she had gathered, perhaps a copy of the book itself or a manuscript. Maybe – who knew? – even a clue to the location of the hidden *Drogan Taranish*.

The rough track leading past the Pett and Praisewell was one of the six ancient roads radiating from Tarland to what Grace had described as 'six provinces' of the *Tarachsel*. This one, known as the *Lang Ley*, took a course over the shoulder of Pittenderich, one of the hills on the north rim of the Howe of Cromar, towards Bennachie and the great plain of Buchan beyond. At the summit of the *Lang Ley*, by the appropriately-named croft of Hillhead, there had once been a neolithic stone circle, larger than Tomnaverie and even more spectacularly sited. Its historic stones were casually looted for a twentieth-century roadside wall.

Bennachie was a landmark Delia and Quin had noticed on their drive from Aberdeen airport to Tarland the day they arrived: a hill with a series of peaks, the most easterly of which resembled nothing so much as a female breast. The hill had been sacred to the *Tarachsel*, a site of pilgrimage to their goddess

Brytha. Quin noted that the very name 'Bennachie' was probably derived from Gaelic words meaning 'mountain of the breast'. Some historians have thought Bennachie to be the most likely site of the battle between Agricola and Calgacus, the Farmer and the Sword, at *Mons Graupius*; many alternative locations have also been proposed. Grace had alluded to the 'impressive amount of evidence' marshalled by Megan for the battle having been fought at none of these places but right here in Cromar, on two of the other ancient roadways radiating from Tarland.

From the *Lang Ley*, they gazed at the view around them. To the north-west, rising directly from where they stood, was the densely wooded Pittenderich and behind it, though hidden from view, the higher summit of Pressendye. To the east was the Long Hill and, visible as a gap between it and Craiglich, the Slack where they had first entered the Howe of Cromar, just a few days before. South of Craiglich was the round dome of Mortlich; between Mortlich and Balnagowan Hill they could make out the narrow valley through which the Tarland Burn escapes from the Howe to join the River Dee near Aboyne.

From their elevated viewpoint they could see beyond Balnagowan to the range of hills south of the Dee. Since Pictish times that great east-west ridge had been known as the Mounth and had presented a natural hazard to travellers, not to mention invading armies. A landmark of the Mounth, away to the south-east, was Clochnaben with its rocky outcrop forming a carbuncle on its side. Due south was Mount Keen, and in the south-west the Mounth culminated in the now-familiar craggy profile of Lochnagar.

Somewhere lay Taran's Crossing, the place where according to legend the thunder-god unleashed the bolt of lightning that created the Howe of Cromar, the 'Pleasant Vale' as it was named by its early inhabitants. Consulting their map, Quin pointed to a place called Corsedarder.

'It's a crossing point, for sure,' he said, 'on a low ridge between Cromar and those distant hills. It could be Taran's.

Corse can mean a cross or crossing place, and I suppose *Darder* could be a corruption of "Taran". It lies in that direction, beyond Mortlich.' He pointed towards the south-east.

'What's that?' Delia asked, pointing to some indistinct lettering on the map.

'It's another Blue Cairn. Just like the one on Drummy. I bet this is the one the Beaker People built to mark where their thunder-god stood to create the Pleasant Vale.' Another mystery was solved. They knew where to find Taran's Crossing. A modern road ran close by the ancient cairn.

They drove the remaining half-mile or so up to Praisewell. 'Presumably,' Delia remarked, 'the people who named this place took their religion seriously.'

'Not necessarily,' Quin said. 'Praisewell could be derived from Gaelic. Something like *preas a'bhealaich*, meaning "thicket of the pass".'

A young man emerged from the newly built house. 'I'm sorry to trouble you,' Delia said, 'but we're trying to trace the people who lived in the house that was here before.'

'You mean the Mintys, I suppose?'

'Yes, Megan Minty, her husband and her two boys. We know their house burned. We were wondering if you might have any contact information.'

'You're American?'

Noting the suspicion in his voice, Delia laughed in an effort to break the ice. 'It's that obvious, huh? Thing is, Megan and I had a mutual friend Grace who died recently in the States. I wanted to let Megan know she had passed away.'

Still a little distrustful, he nonetheless told them what he knew, which matched what they had heard from Ewen. 'We bought the land through a firm of solicitors. We had no direct dealings with Mr Minty.'

'Did you by any chance find anything in the ruins? Anything belonging to the family?'

The young man's eyes narrowed slightly. 'You're the second person coming here this week asking the same question.'

Delia and Quin turned to each other, a look of astonishment on their faces.

'The other guy was maybe from the press or something. The "Minty mystery" is still fresh round here. There's occasionally a wee story in the paper with some new speculation as to what really happened.'

'Did you know Megan was writing a book?' Delia asked.

'So I've heard. The history of Cromar, something like that?'

'I believe so. It seems it never got published.'

He laughed. 'It might have had local interest, but would hardly have made the best-seller list. Have you checked on the internet or Kindle? You might find it there.'

'Maybe I need to take another look. Anyway, the man who was here earlier, what was he like?'

'Fiftyish, medium height, close-cropped hair. Very fair – looked Scandinavian, but he was definitely English. Drove a silver BMW. It was just the day before yesterday.'

'Did he tell you his name?'

''Fraid not.'

'Thanks anyway,' Delia said. 'I hope you don't mind if we take a look around for a few minutes.'

'Be my guest,' the young man said, and went back into his house.

37
JAMIE THE HOORMAISTER

MARCHNEAR, THE PLACE BY Loch Davan where Strathbogie's men camped the night before their defeat in 1335, was to figure again in the annals of the Keepers, almost two hundred years later. The King of Scots during the 1530s was James V, a handsome young man with red hair and a prodigious sexual appetite. Before and during his two marriages, he had mistresses all over Scotland. Nine of his illegitimate children are known to historians; undoubtedly there were many more. Among his less respectful subjects he was popularly known as 'Jamie the Hoormaister'.

At that time Marchnear had an inn that catered to the needs of travellers on the road from Tarland to Tullich on upper Deeside. While the nominal tenant of the property lay in his sickbed, his daughter ran the business with great efficiency. A good-looking woman in her twenties, Peggy Walker was one of the king's conquests, and also a Keeper of Taran's wheel.

When resident at Kildrummy Castle, James made fairly frequent visits to Cromar, almost always calling at the inn at Marchnear. One hot summer day he turned up, dusty and sweaty from his ride, and immediately proposed accompanying Peggy to her chamber.

'I have an even better idea,' she said coquettishly. 'I know a quiet spot under the trees by the loch. Together we can lie there and listen to the sounds of the forest.' She led him down to a small cove on the shore of Loch Davan, where she threw off *all her clothes and ran into the water. 'Come on in, Jamie,' she called to him. 'You'll love it.'*

Within minutes, the king was cavorting naked with Peggy Walker in the cooling freshness of Loch Davan. At one point she swam to the shore, and he made to follow her.

'No, stay there, I'm coming right back.'

She gathered some chickweed by the water's edge, formed it into a ball and wrapped it in a muslin cloth, then rejoined him in the loch. Gently, she sponged every part of his body. The soap-like natural cleansers in the chickweed oozed out as she worked. 'Now, your majesty,' she said, 'I am ready to submit to you, as your loyal subject.'

Cold and wet, they joined hands and ran to retrieve their clothes. With the king's cloak spread on the grass beside a large boulder, Peggy lay down and saucily pulled him towards her.

Back at the inn the king demanded food and wine. Later, on his horse and ready to depart, he said, 'I would not insult you with payment for the pleasure you have afforded me. But, in gratitude for the food, wine and most of all the excellent bath, you will find reward in the long grass by the rock where we lay today.' With that, he was gone.

Exactly as he had promised, a silk pouch awaited her, containing as much money as her inn would normally make in a year of business. That boulder is still known to local people as the Siller Steen – *literally the 'money stone'.*

Unknown to the king, Peggy bore his child, a daughter named Ellen. Any bastard son of the king born of a noblewoman would be in line for a government or, more usually, church sinecure, but Ellen had no such claim.

James V's travels among his subjects, often disguising himself as a gentleman farmer, have been well documented. Stories abound of his encounters with ordinary people in many parts of Scotland, often with suspiciously close similarities. Sir Walter Scott recounted one of them in his Tales of a Grandfather. *It could be therefore that the following account from Cromar is derivative. (Some versions feature James IV, but his son James V is a better fit.) This legend is attached to another named stone – like the* Siller Steen, *one of the erratic boulders deposited on the land during the ice age.*

As the king rode from Kildrummy to Cromar, we are told, he was waylaid by a band of ruffians on the Birk Hill intent on robbery. He broke free and made fast for Migvie, the nearest settlement, where he called at the home of a landowner or 'laird' in the area. The local blacksmith, a man by the name of Reid, happened to be there paring the hooves of the laird's horse. Breathlessly explaining his narrow escape, the king asked the laird and the smith if they knew who his assailants might be or where they came from.

Concerned and curious, Reid volunteered to ride up to the Birk Hill to see for himself. The king lent him his horse and his cloak. When the smith reached the scene of the attack, the robbers mistook him for the same traveller they had set upon earlier, and killed him on the spot. The horse galloped riderless back to Migvie and the alarm was raised. The smith's body, still wearing the royal cloak, was found by a large stone that to this day is known as the Gow Steen *('blacksmith stone').*

The king, in sorrow for the blacksmith's loss of life on his account, visited Reid's widow at Smiddyhill. He promised her as much land as she could run over in a day. Off the poor woman set at a brisk pace, eventually covering, so it's said, nine acres. Those nine acres and the farm of Smiddyhill remained in the Reid family for over four hundred years.

If there's any truth in the story, it's likely the king stayed the night at Migvie and the next day made the short ride to Marchnear for his customary assignation with Peggy Walker. Aghast at the death of Reid the blacksmith, a popular man throughout Cromar, she probably brought Taran's wheel to the Gow Steen *to ensure* vairtach *for his spirit.*

38

MYRTLE

NOTHING AT PRAISEWELL provided any kind of clue. Resigned to Megan and her book being lost forever, Delia and Quin set off for the Blue Cairn of Drummy. According to myth, it was the point of impact of the bolt of lightning loosed by the giant thunder-god. And according to Grace's retelling of the story, it was the true burial place of Macbeth, the much-loved king who brought Taran's wheel back from its thousand-year exile in Rome. What better place to hide it?

The road to the top of Drummy being rough and potholed, they decided to walk most of the way. At the summit of the ridge, a footpath led along its crest towards the cairn. Dense bracken up to their waists crowded in on the footpath, which became difficult to follow in places.

Despite having been a hallowed spot for the *Tarachsel* and the Beaker People before them, the cairn was something of a disappointment. Over centuries stones had been scavenged from it to make field enclosures – the *dry-steen dykes* so prevalent in this part of Scotland. But the size of its base hinted that this had once been an impressive pile. Its paltry remains were covered in blue-grey lichens. Delia remarked that these extremely slow-growing organisms – actually a symbiotic association of fungi and algae – were sensitive to atmospheric pollution and acid rain. Their abundance here, she said, was a sign of clean air.

They circled the cairn, then clambered over it looking for any hint of the *Drogan*. Nearby were other stones arranged in small rings, marking foundations of bronze age huts. But there was no indication of the hiding place they so desperately sought.

After a dull start it had turned sunny and the air felt pleasantly warm. They sat down to eat a snack. A lark, so high above them that it was a mere speck in the sky, delighted them with its trilling refrain.

'This has to be one of the best moments in my life,' Quin announced.

Delia leaned over and kissed him. 'Why do you say that?'

'To be in such a heavenly place with you, makes me incredibly happy. I wish this day could last forever.'

'Me too.'

Reality intruded on the tender interlude. They had work to do, and time was short.

Next on their list was Tomnaverie, the hilltop stone circle that predated even the coming of the Beaker People. Just a mile from the village of Tarland, on the road to Aboyne, the circle was accessible by a well-maintained footpath from a small roadside car-park. One car was there when they arrived. They walked up the gentle slope, to find a petite woman in her early forties flitting among the stones of the circle.

Four, maybe five thousand years of history lent an undeniable atmosphere to the place. The circle was dominated by two large uprights, one on either side of a massive horizontal stone – the 'recumbent' as it was termed. Located in the south-west quadrant, the uprights perfectly framed the distant peaks of Lochnagar when viewed from the opposite rim of the circle.

'Hello,' Delia called out. 'Beautiful day!'

The woman came towards them, smiling. 'Yes. Don't you love it here?' She introduced herself as Myrtle, revealing that she lived 'in the forest' with her partner Joyce. 'I come round a lot to make sure things are in good shape. Most visitors show respect and don't create a mess, but some – especially bus parties – are more careless and leave a trail of Coke cans, crisp packets, orange peel, that kind of thing. We do our best to keep it tidy.'

'You said "we". Are there "Friends of Tomnaverie"? Do you belong to a group that looks after this wonderful place?'

'Well, not exactly. We're a religious group. We meet here and at other megalithic sites in the area. Historic Scotland has given us permission to hold our rituals at Tomnaverie, but if there was ever any damage or vandalism we'd be blamed for it, and be banned. So we don't take any chances.'

Myrtle's group practised a neopagan or druidical religion derived from pre-Christian Celtic beliefs. 'We call ourselves the Grove of the Mayflower. Our most sacred rituals are held in the month of May.'

'At Beltane?'

'You know about the Celtic festivals, do you?'

Could the group represent some latter-day incarnation of the *Merch Nyr*, still holding on to fragments of the old beliefs that Christianity supplanted thirteen centuries ago? Might Grace have contacted them? Might they hold some clue to where the *Drogan* might be? Might they even have it in their possession?

Delia's mind was racing as she replied, 'I know a little bit, yes, but only from reading online. I find it quite interesting. There are four ancient festivals – Beltane, Lunasa, Samhain and Imbolc, isn't that right? – but I'm sure my understanding is very rudimentary compared to yours.'

Myrtle smiled. 'I'm impressed that you pronounced "Samhain" correctly. Most people get it wrong.'

'Lunasa – that's just past, isn't it? Did you celebrate it here?'

'Actually, the Grove of the Mayflower waits till the 9th of August to observe Lunasa. That's the day after tomorrow. It will begin a countdown to the next Beltane, exactly nine moons away. Samhain will be on November 5th – six moons from Beltane, and Imbolc on February 2nd – just three moons from

Beltane, which we always celebrate on May 1st, as our ancestors did long ago.'

'Was that the pre-eminent festival for your ancestors?' Delia asked, testing for some corroboration of Grace's belief that Samhain, with its focus on Taran, was more important.

Myrtle's response was not encouraging. 'As far as we can tell, yes. There are two places not far from here whose names are thought to derive from the ancient Mayday celebration of Beltane. One is Cambus o' May.'

'I know where that is – it's on the way to Ballater.'

'That's right. The other's on the road to Strathdon, just over the Birk Hill. It's called Boultenstone. There was once a standing stone there, originally known as the Beltane stone, but it was destroyed over a hundred years ago. One day we'd like to erect a new one there and consecrate it with a Mayday ceremony.'

'I hope you do.' Still wondering if the Mayflowers were a latter-day vestige of the *Merch Nyr*, Delia said, 'I suppose your group has roots here in Cromar?'

'As a matter of fact, no. We're all incomers. I'm originally from the south of Scotland, and our leader – First Druid is his title – is English. What unites us is our faith in the old religion.'

'Well, with Lunasa coming up, I'd better let you get on with your preparations.'

'I think I'm done,' Myrtle said. Then her face brightened. 'Would you like to join us on Saturday? We welcome guests who respect our creed, even if they don't agree with it. Once we had a minister of the kirk.'

'We'd love to come,' Delia said, eagerly.

'Great! Meet us in the car-park at eleven forty-five. Our service starts at the stroke of midnight. This is a special year, because all four festivals will coincide with a full moon. Hopefully this weekend the sky will be clear and her rays will shine on us. At midnight she'll be exactly over Craig Dhu.' Myrtle pointed to the southern skyline.

'We know about Craig Dhu. There are ancient cairns up there we're planning to visit.'

'Are there?' Myrtle seemed genuinely not to know about the Blue Cairn of Craig Dhu and the field of smaller cairns nearby. 'You've really been doing your homework.'

'Just a hobby. Anyway, you were saying this was just one of the sites where you hold your meetings.'

'It's probably our favourite. We'll be coming back to Tomnaverie for all the festivals of this cycle. One or two members of the Grove are worried about Lunasa this year because it falls on the same day as the Tarland Show. There'll be a big dance in the showground marquee and they think we might be disturbed by a bit of noise and traffic. But I'm sure nobody will bother us up here.'

'Is Taran among the gods you honour in your rites?' Delia asked. 'I believe he was sacred to the ancient people of this region, wasn't he?'

'Yes. We will honour Taran at Samhain, when the full moon is in Taurus the bull.'

'Have you by any chance heard of Taran's wheel?'

'Of course,' Myrtle replied. 'That and the thunderbolt are symbols of Taran.'

'What about an actual wheel-like object, venerated by the ancients?'

'I think you're talking about the legendary *Drogan Taranish*, a crystal ball with magical powers,' Myrtle said, quite matter-of-factly. 'I'm surprised you've heard of it, since there's not much about it in books or on the internet.'

'Long ago, an old lady told me a tale of it.'

'That's what it is, I'm sure. A tale.'

With that, Myrtle took her leave and set off down the footpath. Delia joined Quin by the recumbent stone. Just a few feet beyond was a fence, on the other side of which was a vertical precipice dropping down twenty feet or so to a disused quarry.

'I can't imagine Taran's wheel being hidden somewhere in the stone circle,' he said. 'Too many people come here. There have even been archaeological excavations. Grace wouldn't have put the *Drogan* where it might be discovered accidentally.'

'No, you're right,' Delia agreed. 'Maybe we've seen all there is to see here. But I've a feeling Myrtle knows more about the *Drogan* than she's letting on. We should learn more at the Lunasa gathering on Saturday.'

'Uh-huh. But while we're here, I'd just like to take a look on the other side of this fence. There might be hidey-holes down there.'

The quarry had been worked right up to the edge of the circle. The buildings in Tarland Square had been constructed, at least partly, with granite from Tomnaverie. Whether by good fortune or by design, extraction of stone had stopped just in time to save the ancient circle.

Clambering about on the rocks, they found no crevice where the *Drogan* might be hidden. In any case, it was unlikely that an old lady with a heart condition would have climbed on a quarry face like this. It was time to move on.

39
A MEETING OF SISTERS

W**HEN ELLEN WALKER WAS** old enough to understand, her mother broke it to her that she was a daughter of the King of Scots, though without any of the privileges that would go with being a royal princess. Peggy warned her against ever revealing her father's identity – there was nothing to be gained; on the contrary it was information that in the wrong hands could put her in mortal danger.

Ellen grew into a beautiful young woman, with flame-red hair that was her father's legacy. Though her beauty attracted many admiring glances, she resisted all attempts to woo her.

From an early age her mother had schooled her in the ancient wisdom of the Merch Nyr and the tales of her ancestors. In due course Ellen became Keeper of Taran's wheel in her own right.

Long before that, while Ellen was still a child, the king died in 1542 at the age of just thirty. In a state of depression after a disastrous battle against the English, he hid himself away in Falkland Palace in Fife where he succumbed to a fever. Given his history of promiscuity it's likely syphilis was a contributory cause of death. The crown passed to his (legitimate) daughter – who was six days old at the time. The infant became Mary, Queen of Scots. Like her half-sister Ellen Walker, she grew into a tall, strikingly beautiful young woman with red hair.

Among the lesser-known of many battles of Mary's reign was Corrichie, fought in 1562 when she was twenty. On one side was James Stewart, her half-brother and one of her closest advisers at that time. She had recently conferred on him the title of Earl of Moray.

On the other side was the previous holder of that title, George Gordon, Earl of Huntly. A Scottish hero, he had defeated an English army twenty years earlier, but he was vain and sorely piqued at having had to renounce one of his two earldoms in favour of a bastard half-brother of the queen. Outlawed by the queen when he gave orders for her to be denied entry to Inverness Castle, he was keen to do battle in spite of ill-health related to obesity.

Being a superstitious man, he is said to have consulted a band of witches as to how he would fare against Moray. Those so-called 'witches' may have been women of the Merch Nyr whom he met in Cromar. If so, they would almost certainly have included the Keeper of Taran's wheel herself, Ellen Walker. They told him that the night after the battle he would lie without a wound on his body.

Taking encouragement from this ambiguous prophecy, Huntly marched his small army towards Aberdeen, laying up near the foot of the Hill of Fare. Historians have placed his camp by the Loch of Skene, but tales of the Keepers have him resting his troops, perhaps on the previous night, at the place now known as Ordie Gordon, thirteen miles from Tarland. A small settlement close by is to this day called Campfield. This name is supposedly derived from the Gaelic for 'bent wood', but it may have more to do with the location of Huntly's camp field.

I've previously mentioned Ordie Gordon as the possible site where, many centuries earlier, Calgacus handed over the Drogan Taranish to the Roman commander Agricola. The location is notable too for an ancient stone circle just like the one at Tomnaverie, and a very large erratic boulder known as the Bishop Steen where, according to legend, Ternan the fifth-century 'Bishop of Pictland' preached Christianity to the heathen natives just a few miles from his base at Banchory.

185

The opposing sides met in battle in a valley called Corrichie on the south slope of the Hill of Fare. Moray won the day for the queen. Huntly was out-manoeuvred and captured unharmed, but suffered a stroke and died on the battlefield. That night he was brought to Aberdeen, where he lay 'without a wound on his body' as prophesied. In a macabre twist, his corpse was taken to Edinburgh to stand trial for treason.

A day or two after the battle, Ellen Walker and some of the Merch Nyr *travelled from Cromar to the Corrichie battlefield on a cart pulled by two horses, to search for wounded survivors and bury the dead. While they were there, the queen arrived with a small group of cavalrymen to survey the scene of Moray's victory. She found a vantage point in a small defile between rocky outcrops overlooking the battlefield, a formation that has become known as the Queen's Chair. There, Mary observed Ellen and her companions checking bodies for signs of life, tending to the living and burying the dead, without regard to which side they had fought on.*

The queen happened to catch two of her cavalrymen whispering to each other. 'What is the secret that you share?' she demanded to know. 'Pray tell your queen.'

Blushing, one of them admitted they had their eye on a particular woman toiling below. 'That young woman with red hair is so like you, Ma'am. But for her poor attire and your regal bearing, you could almost be sisters.'

'Sisters, eh?' Mary said. 'In that case, bring her to me.'

Ellen was brought before the Queen of Scots, who remained mounted on her steed. Never having been taught how to curtsy, Ellen executed a clumsy attempt that she hoped would be suitably respectful. The queen had the advantage of status and, on her horse, height. Ellen, on the other hand, had the strange advantage of being the only one who knew that she and the lady to whom she had just curtsied shared the same father.

'What is your name?' Mary asked.

'Ellen Walker, your majesty.'

'Ellen Walker, my cavalrymen tell me we look alike, you and I. They say we are like sisters.' Ellen knew the queen had spent most of her young life in France, yet her strongly French-accented speech came as a surprise. 'You are indeed tall, like me,' Mary continued, 'and your hair is as red as mine. You may even be prettier. But of course we cannot be sisters, can we?'

'It would be hard to imagine how that could be, your majesty.'

'Indeed. Ellen Walker, you and your companions are doing good work. I thank you and wish you well.'

The queen motioned to her cavalrymen, then turned her horse around and rode off. Ellen resumed her labours. It had been the briefest of encounters, a meeting of sisters, of whom one went on to a famously tumultuous life of tragedy and abuse, and the other returned to obscurity as an innkeeper's daughter.

It was already becoming dark when the women left Corrichie. A bright moon illuminated their homeward way. Not far into their journey, at the place now called Campfield, one of their horses lost a shoe. There was a smithy there, which though closed up for the night had a visible glow of fire from the forge. They roused the blacksmith, and were able to persuade him to replace the shoe that had come off.

When the job was completed, the women had no money to pay the smith. He looked in the cart and saw a couple of wounded warriors. 'I know who you are and what you have done today,' he said, 'and I seek no payment. Godspeed.'

Ellen said, 'You are a good man. Thank you. For this favour, you and every smith who follows you in this place shall be free to hang a horseshoe upside-down on your door; instead of bringing bad luck, this will bring good fortune to you and your family.'

So he did, and Ellen's blessing came to pass.

40
BONANZA

THACKERAY AND BAYLISS held their Thursday lunchtime rendezvous at Long John Silver's on Fairlawn Road. Few places in the United States are further from the sea than Topeka, Kansas, but nonetheless Thackeray ordered himself what passed for seafood – a deep-fried lump of reconstituted white fish, served with french fries. He downed it while waiting for his Operation Curveball co-conspirator to arrive.

When Bayliss appeared he was visibly excited.

'You have some good news, Jay?' Thackeray said.

'How do you know?'

'Let's just say you wouldn't make a great living at poker.'

'We've struck a bonanza,' Bayliss told him, in a stage-whisper loud enough to attract the attention of a group of women three tables away.

'Okay, keep it down, willya? Let's have it.'

'It just came in. I thought of calling you, but you know you start to shit yourself when we talk too much on the phone. The girl listed twenty places where the glass ball could be hidden. Twenty! While she was connected to the web.'

'And?'

'What she's transmitted to us, courtesy of the Trojan Rat, is like a roadmap. Here, I printed it for you. Also sent it to your email address half an hour ago. Like I said, a fucking roadmap.'

Thackeray took the sheet of paper, folded it and stuck it in his back pocket. 'This is good,' he said. 'I'll forward it to our friend Cato and to the Engineer. I'll also mention it to the Pastor this afternoon. He'll be pleased with your work.'

By nine o'clock British time that Thursday evening, Cato was settling into his hotel room in Tarland. He had stayed at the Commercial once before, on a business trip. That time he had met with a client offering some rare pearls, the product of several nights' illegal fishing for freshwater mussels in one of the few Scottish rivers where these were still to be found. Also for sale was a clutch of osprey eggs stolen from under the noses of the Scottish Wildlife Trust, which he had declined – not worth the risk for all they would fetch in London. Having paid the young man two hundred pounds for the pearls, he promptly sold them for two thousand. Not a great return for such a long journey.

This time, he thought, the profit would be well worth the trip. A vision of ten million pounds (or was it dollars? – no, he would hold out for pounds) danced before his eyes.

What brought the payoff significantly closer was Delia's list, now in his hands. Had he known of the existence of the Engineer, also in possession of that same list and only a few miles away at that moment, Cato would have had reason to feel less confident.

41
KATE FERRIES

WHILE MARY, QUEEN OF SCOTS was spending her childhood and teenage years at the French court, reformation of the church in Scotland was occurring under the leadership of the firebrand preacher John Knox. When her husband King Francis II – a boy of sixteen who hadn't yet entered puberty or consummated their marriage – died of an ear infection in 1560, Mary lost her French royal status and returned to Scotland to assume power as monarch in her own right.

As a result of her upbringing, she was devout and unyielding in her Catholic faith, constantly at odds with Knox and with those elements of the Scottish nobility that had embraced his new Protestant church. The same Earl of Moray who won the day for the queen at Corrichie eventually saw the way the wind was blowing and threw his lot in with the Protestant establishment, becoming one of Mary's most bitter enemies.

Mary made a series of disastrous choices in affairs of the heart. In 1565 she married her half-cousin Henry Stuart, Lord Darnley, a Catholic like herself. Scarcely could she have chosen a more arrogant, self-aggrandising, dissolute apology for a man. She became pregnant despite his numerous liaisons with other women, but her friendship with her Italian secretary David Rizzio aroused such jealousy that Darnley accused him of fathering her unborn child. In March 1566, with a group of henchmen he stabbed Rizzio to death in her presence and buried him while his body was still warm. Mary's son James was born in Edinburgh Castle in June of the same year.

In February 1567, it was Darnley's turn to die violently, following a gunpowder explosion in an Edinburgh abbey where he was recuperating from syphilis. Suspicion fell on James Hepburn, Earl of Bothwell, a member of the Protestant nobility who was rumoured to be in an illicit relationship with the queen. However, Bothwell was cleared in a show trial, and in May 1567 he married her, having divorced his first wife twelve days earlier.

Their union strengthened suspicions that Mary had been complicit in Darnley's murder. Among those clamouring most loudly for her arrest were Moray and Knox. Shortly after her marriage to Bothwell she was seized and imprisoned in a castle on an island in Loch Leven. A month later she miscarried twins. On July 24th, 1567 she was forced to abdicate the Scottish throne in favour of her infant son, who became King James VI.

James was raised a Protestant. During all the years he was growing up he showed no interest in the wellbeing of Mary his mother, and as a young man made only a token protest when she was sentenced to death by an English court and led to the executioner's block in 1587.

The handsome looks of his mother and his grandfather James V were not visited on James VI. Having remarkably spindly legs – in Scotland they were described as 'spurtles', the thin wooden rods traditionally used for stirring porridge – he insisted on being mounted on horseback for meetings with foreign dignitaries and for most of his official portraits. His jaws were so narrow that he had difficulty eating. He did possess one of his grandfather's attributes: an appetite for sex with numerous partners, though in the case of James VI the appetite favoured males. His initiation was at the age of about fifteen, by the almost forty-year-old Esme Stuart, Earl of Lennox, who had become James's favourite courtier.

All his life, the king harboured a deep contempt for the female sex, though he did take a queen and fathered numerous children. His misogyny may have resulted from having a mother suspected of conspiracy to murder his father, compounded by the strong influence of Knox, a notorious woman-hater. Whatever the reason, it made itself felt in Cromar in 1597, where it led to the tragic fate of Kate Ferries.

Thirty years earlier, in the year James VI became king as a one-year-old boy, sixteen-year-old Kate was in the employ of a farmer in the parish of Coldstone, under the shadow of Morven. This farmer was married with grown sons, an elder of the kirk at Coldstone and a highly respected man of the parish. As was common at the time, he and his sons regarded young female workers on the farm as legitimate playthings.

Kate became pregnant – whether by the farmer or one of his sons is unclear – and when her condition became apparent she was summarily dismissed. She went to live with an aunt who had a herbal garden at Braes of Cromar and was highly regarded locally as a healer. There Kate gave birth to and raised her son, all the while learning the healing arts.

In due course her aunt, herself a member of the Merch Nyr, inducted Kate into the ancient priesthood. Together with other members including Ellen Walker, high priestess and Keeper of Taran's wheel, Kate and her aunt would go to Satan's Howe for secret midnight meetings to worship and make offerings to Taran and Brytha, just as their ancestors had done for centuries. As Ellen's closest relative on the maternal side, Kate became Keeper when Ellen died.

Once her son was seventeen, Kate finally told him he had been fathered by the 'goodman' (tenant farmer) at the place where she had worked as a young girl, or by one of his sons. Being hot-headed as teenage boys can be, he went straight to the goodman and confronted him.

'I am your son or grandson,' he announced, 'and I am here to claim my birthright. Give me money so that I can leave

Cromar and make my way in the world. Otherwise, I will tell everyone what you have done. You will be shamed.'

The farmer was scornful. 'Who will believe your word against mine? I am the goodman of this fine farm and an elder of the kirk. You are just a silly laddie.'

The boy left empty-handed, but returned under cover of darkness and stole a calf. When he arrived home at the Braes, Kate was horrified. 'You must return it at once,' she said. 'No son of mine shall spill his blood for a calf.'

Unfortunately, when the boy took the calf back to the farm, one of the farmer's sons caught him and tied him to a tree. Sheriff's men were summoned from Aberdeen and the seventeen-year-old was taken away to be tried for cattle theft, a crime punishable by hanging. After a summary trial in Aberdeen he was led to the gallows, where his last words were: 'My mother said my blood should not be drawn for what I have done.'

In an effort to overcome her grief and feelings of guilt for letting her son fall into the clutches of the law, Kate began to practise her religion openly. Word spread that she was a witch. Though witches were denounced routinely from pulpits every Sunday, the people of Cromar were generally tolerant. They were especially willing to overlook Kate's strange behaviour because of her healing powers, which were much in demand.

She continued to administer herbal medicines to the sick of Cromar for some time, tending especially to women's needs. Tireless in her mission to make life more bearable for her 'patients', she would undertake long treks to find specific herbs that didn't grow in her garden.

She had a particular belief in the power of elf-shot (lady's mantle). Though the common elf-shot could help relieve vaginal itching and discharge, menstrual pain and the like, and was supposed to enhance feminine beauty, she had a particular belief in a variety that grew on the mountain-tops. She planted this mountain elf-shot in her herb garden, but it lacked the potency of plants harvested from the wild. She would therefore climb to the summit of Morven, coming back each time with a large sackful of the herb.

On the lower slopes she would also gather the tart fruits of averins (cloudberries), which she believed effective in treating urinary infections. Leaves of the same plant could be used to prepare a tea for pregnant women to shorten and ease the pain of labour. She would venture even further afield to find the rare moonwort – she knew a hillside where it grew in Glen Nochty, more than ten miles away – that could help the healing of tissues ruptured during childbirth.

Sometimes the best way to improve or safeguard a woman's health was to reduce her husband's libido, which also had the benefit of curbing his extramarital urges. Administering an anaphrodisiac herb to a man had to be done by stealth; Kate was adept at training a wife how to pop something in her husband's porridge or ale. An infusion of red clover was the 'something' most favoured by Kate for this purpose. Farmers knew well that feeding hay rich in red clover to a bull risked lowering his interest in cows; Kate merely extrapolated this knowledge, centuries before scientists found that red clover is rich in oestrogens.

Indeed, her understanding of medicine was surprisingly sophisticated. She was familiar with the placebo effect, if not by that name. To maximise the healing power of a herbal medicine, the patient had to have faith that it would work. Sometimes it helped if the patient believed in supernatural influence; knowing that Kate practised 'witchcraft' led many women to have implicit trust in her healing talent. They would sometimes request that Kate leave them an amulet along with the medicine. For this purpose, Kate made little clay tablets with runic inscriptions that she baked in her oven. These she presented to her more superstitious patients to wear as pendants during their course of herbal treatment.

It was in 1597 that James VI, in a frenzy of righteous misogyny, declared all-out war on witchcraft. Men of good *standing in Scottish churches were enrolled to seek out witches and turn them over for appropriate punishment. The king ensured no stone was left unturned by publishing a witch-hunting primer,* Daemonologie. *He took delight in promoting the most painful and protracted deaths for those found guilty, and many pious churchmen were only too eager to prove their obedience to his wishes.*

Thus it was that Kate Ferries was hauled that very year before an assembly of elders in Coldstone kirk. I can hardly do better justice to the proceedings of that assembly than reproduce the official transcript, as found in John Michie's 1896 History of Logie Coldstone. *Michie was a local minister writing three centuries after the 'trial' of Kate Ferries, yet in words that expressed little more sympathy for her plight than had been exhibited by the elders of Coldstone whom she faced in 1597.*

I'll update the spelling and language of the transcript, and interject some commentary where needed.

At the Kirk of Coldstone, the tenth of April 1597. In presence of Patrick Forbes of Pitellachie, John Forbes of Mill of Melgum, Arthur Skene of Tulloch, Alexander Forbes of Daach, George Forbes and Alexander Forbes of Melgum, William Forbes of Kinaldie, Thomas Emslie of Little Groddie, William Reid of Coldstone and John Tun of Ballamore, all elders of the parish of Coldstone; ...

One of these elders now sitting in judgment was almost certainly Kate's former employer and father or grandfather of her son, whom he had handed over to be hanged for stealing a calf. Most of the places listed as their homes are still in existence. You'll find Daach spelt 'Davoch' on the map, but I'm using an old spelling because that's how it's still pronounced.

It's no surprise that six of the ten elders had the name Forbes. It was the most common family name in Cromar at that time. As you'll see, two other Forbeses are mentioned later in the transcript.

... charged by John Coutts, messenger-at-arms in the name of our Sovereign Lord James VI, by a commission given to the sheriffs of Aberdeen to make indictment against all persons suspected of witchcraft; in obedience whereof we have convened at the Kirk of Coldstone for trial of Katherine Ferries, accused by the above-named elders.

1. You being in James Lakies's house eight years ago using the Devil's sorceries, a man called Alexander Welsh came into the house upon whom you cast your sorcery and he died.

Then, as now, the practice of medicine was not always successful. Sometimes the patient died despite the best efforts of the healer.

2. Your own son confessed, at his death in Aberdeen, that you had promised him, by information of the Devil, that his blood should never be drawn, and this he confessed before he was hanged.

3. You fell out with your son, and said that this would be the best day of his life.

I suppose this means the day he was to hang. Even if true, it's hard to see how this is evidence of witchcraft.

4. You cast upon Robert Fyfe's wife such devilry that he held you for two days until you freed her of it.

5. George Richie being sick, you came to look at him and promised his mother that you would take away his sickness, whereupon you laid it upon his sister and she died.

6. You and Elspeth Forbes, the goodwife of Bog, being in the house of Bog, you gave her a tablet that made

devilry and sorcery, and told her to keep that tablet and hang it around her daughters' necks at all times, until they were married. Then you gave her a ring, and she has the ring and the tablet hanging together still.

7. The same Elspeth Forbes then, from a distance of six miles, bewitched the oxen of William Forbes of Shiel while ploughing, and three of them died in that year.

The charges against Kate therefore included 'witchcraft' conducted at second hand by Elspeth Forbes of Bog, a farm near Tarland. Elspeth seems to have been engaged in some kind of long-distance vendetta against William Forbes of Shiel (now called Deskryshiel).

The next item in the rap sheet introduces two other presumed 'witches', known as Spaldairg and Trachak, who were allegedly put up to their 'crimes' by Elspeth Forbes. So Kate was charged at third hand for their supposed misdeeds.

8. Spaldairg confessed at her hanging that she and Trachak received payment of a hundred merks from Elspeth Forbes to make witchcraft and destroy William Forbes's corn every year.

A merk is an old Scottish coin worth two-thirds of a pound Scots. A hundred merks would have been equivalent to just over five pounds in English money, a substantial sum in those days. It seems Elspeth Forbes was a lady of means, to have such funds at her disposal.

9. The same Elspeth Forbes of Bog received a belt from Spaldairg, who told her that if the belt ever wore away grown men would cry, that there was a spirit in the belt that spoke, and that anyone putting the belt around him would be taken by the Devil.

10. Elspeth Forbes caused her own husband to bring sorcery out of Cloak between his shoulders, where the

mark remained as long as he lived and eventually was the death of him. The mark was red and continually broke out, turning black before he died, causing him to cry out for it to be soothed with cream to stop the burning.

That Kate Ferries should face charges relating to payment of money by Elspeth Forbes to Spaldairg, to a belt given by Spaldairg to Elspeth, or to a 'mark' allegedly laid by Elspeth upon her husband, was typical of the standard of justice in the witchcraft trials so diligently pursued by the Scottish Kirk in the name of King James.

Kate had no opportunity to contest the highly questionable charges. The accusations were sufficient to convict her. She was taken to Aberdeen where she was tied to a stake and publicly burned to death. She was just one of a procession of 'witches' who met the same fate that year.

Some of them were convicted on even more dubious accusations. Women who looked 'different' were often assumed to be witches. In the frenzy of the 1590s, any abnormal or disfiguring feature might have been enough to send a woman to the stake. There's no record that Kate possessed any such feature, but it's possible the case against Spaldairg and Trachak was founded on aspects of their appearance. 'Spaldairg' may have been a corruption of a Gaelic nickname referring to a red birthmark; 'Trachak' could be how speakers of Scots might have misheard the Gaelic word for Snowy; my guess is that Trachak might have been albino. Why Spaldairg was hanged – a merciful end by comparison with burning – isn't known.

The place where Kate and many others met their cruel fate is now a traffic roundabout at the east end of what is ironically called Justice Street, just off the Castlegate, the old market square in the centre of Aberdeen. The local citizenry were encouraged to turn out to witness the spectacle; men, women and children would circle the blazing fire hurling insults at the latest victim of their king's pious witch-hunt. Saturday evening was a good time for a witch-burning, when the work week had ended and people were in the mood for some free entertainment. Next morning they would all be in their pews thanking their gracious God for his tender mercies.

Later, the place appointed for the burning of witches in Aberdeen was moved from Justice Street to the Broad Hill about half a mile away, so that the good citizens of the town would no longer have their sleep disturbed by the victims' screams and the acrid smell of burnt human flesh.

The judicial murder (for that is what it was) of Kate Ferries left the women of Cromar with no recourse to medicine. No one dared provide herbal treatments for fear of suffering the same fate. It would take three hundred years or more before decent medical care would again be available, and then only to those who could afford the physician's fees.

Six years after issuing the order for extermination of witches, James VI of Scotland ascended the throne of England as James I, the first monarch to rule the entire island of Great Britain. He immediately left Edinburgh for London and, for the remainder of his reign, set foot in Scotland no more than once. His move to London seems to have provided cover for ending any pretence of marital relations with his queen. For some reason he did not pursue 'witches' in his new realm with anything like the vigour he showed in his native land.

The supreme irony of this nasty little king is his most famous legacy: the English language translation of the Bible that he commissioned. Next time you open the King James Bible at the obsequious dedication 'To the most high and mighty Prince', *perhaps you will spare a thought for Kate Ferries.*

42
PREJUDICE

MIGHT THE *DROGAN TARANISH* appear as part of Saturday's Lunasa observance at Tomnaverie? If it did, Delia's search was over, almost as soon as it had begun. It would mean that Grace had identified the Grove of the Mayflower as some kind of successor to the *Merch Nyr* and entrusted the precious *Drogan* to its adherents. Even if it didn't show up on Saturday, it might still be in the Mayflowers' possession. They honoured Taran at Samhain; maybe the *Drogan* would only be pressed into service then, in three months' time.

Clearly, the search of places on Delia's list had to continue. Having written off Drummy and Tomnaverie on Thursday morning, she and Quin devoted the early afternoon to the earth-house at Culsh, the restored church at Migvie with its Pictish sculptured stones, and the supposed location of the 'ghost meadow' at Dalvokie. They found nothing.

Later they headed for Corsedarder, which they had convinced themselves was the site of Taran's Crossing. They took the road over the bridge at Aboyne, turned left and continued in the direction of the Cairn o' Mount. At the point where the road crossed the low ridge between the Dee and Feugh valleys stood an impressive war memorial and, close by, a stone erected in 2000 to celebrate the millennium. Opposite was a small standing slab of granite that had been broken and roughly repaired with iron bands. According to local folklore, it marked the place where a Pictish king called Dardanus, from whom Corsedarder supposedly got its name, had been felled in battle, though no such king has ever been recorded. Quin and Delia remained sure of their theory that Corsedarder was *Taran's* Crossing.

In the woods on the south side of the road they came across the cairn supposedly marking where Taran stood when he created the Pleasant Vale with his lightning-bolt. Once upon a time it would have provided a fine vista of the hills surrounding the Howe of Cromar, away to the north-west, but now thick forest blocked the view. Similar in size and construction to the one on Drummy, this cairn likewise offered no apparent hiding place for the *Drogan*.

Tired and hungry, they were ready to call it a day. They set off for Ballater along the south side of the Dee with Delia at the wheel while Quin followed their route on the Ordnance Survey map. Between the Aboyne and Dinnet bridges the road ran closely alongside the water. Anglers were out in force casting their lures in the river.

'Can you pull up here for a minute?' Quin suggested. 'I've a feeling the *cambus* featured in the story of Aeth and the kingfisher isn't Cambus o' May, as we'd thought. I think it's over there.' He pointed across the river, towards the north.

Delia stopped the car and squinted at the map. About half a mile away, by the main road on the other side of the river, was the Mill of Dinnet, where the Dee took a turn of more than ninety degrees to the south, bringing it close to where they sat. On his laptop computer, Quin pulled up the kingfisher legend and read aloud:

You can see on a map that at one point the river takes a sharp turn southward, forming what the Tarachsel *called a* cambus, *a river-bend where erosion by the flowing water has created a cliff-like bank. Behind a low hill above the* cambus *there was once a small settlement where a boy by the name of Aeth lived with his mother.*

'See, Delia, over there the river does turn *southward*, which it doesn't at Cambus o' May. And look, there's a low hill as described in the story. Tomachallich, it's called. Cock Hill. Behind it are remains of a Pictish settlement at Knockenzie.'

After dinner Delia updated her list, putting a check-mark against the places they'd already visited. She amended numbers 8 and 9 to read:

8. *bend in river (cambus) where Aeth found Drogan*
   – prob. by Mill of Dinnet
9. *Aeth's village – prob. Knockenzie*

That same evening, they read more of Grace's *Second Testament*, bringing them up to the end of the sixteenth century and the tragic story of Kate Ferries.

'I have to say,' Quin observed, 'that Grace lets her prejudice against religion – in particular against the Christian church – colour her telling of Kate's story. I mean, she blames John Knox for King James's alleged hatred of women. James, who commissioned a translation of the Bible that produced some of the finest prose and poetry ever written in English, was, according to Grace, a "nasty little king". And she makes a bit of a meal of Kate's accusers being pious men of the church.'

'She calls it like she sees it,' Delia countered angrily. 'And I see it the same way. Are you going to defend witch-hunting? Was the torture and killing of these poor women justified in the name of God and Christ?'

'Of course not. No need to pop your eyes at me like that. I was just making an observation, that's all. I didn't say I disagreed with Grace's point of view.'

'But you do.'

'To be honest, I don't have enough background in the history of that time to have an opinion one way or the other. But *if* it happened as Grace described, then I'd have to agree that James *was* a "nasty little king" *and* that there was a pervasive nastiness in the church of the time that made elders in places like Coldstone so diligent in executing his orders.'

'Well, that's okay then,' Delia said, keen to have the last word on the subject. 'Because I believe it *did* happen just as Grace described.'

Quin wasn't quite ready to concede. 'Belief can be a dangerous thing,' he said. 'It can easily turn into prejudice. And prejudice can turn into fear and hate. Wasn't it belief in witchcraft, however misguided, that led the men of Coldstone to dispatch poor Kate to her awful death? Wasn't it prejudice that condemned as witches women like Spaldairg and Trachak, for no greater crime than looking "different"?'

She could see he had a point, but rather than agree Delia seized on his last remark. 'So you're comfortable with Grace's suggestion that these women's nicknames relate to abnormality or disfigurement?'

'In the case of Spaldairg, absolutely. *Spailc dearg* literally means "red blotch". I'm less convinced that "Trachak" comes from *sneachdach,* the Gaelic for "snowy". That's maybe a bit of a leap. Though to be fair to Grace, she did say it was just her "guess" that Trachak had been an albino.'

The mention of albinism somehow triggered in Delia's brain a memory of Robert Langdon's nemesis in Dan Brown's bestseller *The Da Vinci Code.* And that, in turn, reminded her of Grace's teasing little note from beyond the grave when she thought *'Open Frida'* was the solution to the *'Find a repo'* puzzle:

> Good guess, Cordelia. But it's not an anagram this
> time. Did you think this was <u>The Da Vinci Code</u>?

A half-formed thought played at the periphery of her consciousness. There was *something* about that note of Grace's she hadn't picked up on before. And she wasn't getting it, even now. What could it be?

The thought passed. She glanced at her watch. 'Look at the time, Quin.' She began tapping on her computer. By eleven o'clock her list of twenty had grown to twenty-seven:

21. *Culblean (battlefield) – close to Marchnear (see 22)*
22. *Marchnear by Loch Davan – Peggy Walker's inn, Siller Steen (money stone) nearby*
23. *Gow Steen (blacksmith stone) on Birk Hill – Drogan taken to site of blacksmith's death?*
24. *Corrichie (battlefield on Hill of Fare), esp. Queen's Chair where Ellen Walker met Mary, Q of Scots*
25. *Braes of Cromar – Kate Ferries's herb garden*
26. *Coldstone church – Kate's trial for witchcraft – Drogan never there?*
27. *traffic roundabout at Justice St, Aberdeen – Kate burned as witch – Drogan brought here to ensure vairtach for Kate?*

'So where's it to be tomorrow?' Quin asked as she turned off her computer. 'Aeth's village at Knockenzie and the *cambus* where he found the *Drogan*?'

'Maybe,' Delia replied, 'but first I'd like to see Coull Castle.'

'I'm *cool* with that.'

43
HIS NAME WAS ENOUGH

PERSECUTION OF PRACTITIONERS *of the ancient healing arts as 'witches' drove what remained of the* Merch Nyr *into hiding. Instead of going underground, they hid in plain sight. They kept alive the old legends and stories of their predecessors, but it was too dangerous to continue the practice of herbal healing.*

By 1597, when Kate Ferries was so callously sent from Coldstone kirk to her terrible death, she had already identified her successor as Keeper of Taran's wheel. Having no daughter of her own, she had prepared a more distant relative for the role. The herb garden that had been lovingly tended by Kate and her aunt became overgrown with weeds and most of the precious herbs died out.

The new Keeper married a man by the name of Begg, who came to live at the Braes. She and her husband integrated themselves into society, even attending church every Sunday. When in 1618 the parishes of Coldstone and Logiemar were united, the Beggs took an active part in establishing a new kirk by the Logie Burn, a short distance from their home. (The small village that grew up there was known as Newkirk for many years; today it's called Logie Coldstone.)

Begg was a hard worker with a good head for business. He came up with a new use for the old herb garden: the cultivation of plants that yielded dyes for the woollen mills that were springing up around the countryside. The Begg family harvested the plants, boiled them to extract their dyes, and sold the resulting products to mills in Cromar and beyond. Business boomed and the Beggs became well-to-do by local standards.

During all this time, Mrs Begg kept her role as Keeper of Taran's wheel a closely guarded secret. Her husband must surely have known, but had seen no harm in it. Her oldest daughter Annie was groomed to succeed as Keeper, which she did in 1643. By that time she was married with twin daughters.

The relative prosperity of the Beggs came at a time of great lawlessness. The reformation did not bring peace to Scotland; instead the country was riven by fighting over what seem now to be minor, arcane issues of religious observance. A flashpoint was the question of which prayer-book should be used in the Kirk. A presbyterian group known as the Covenanters, opposing King Charles I and the Scottish bishops, had the upper hand by the early 1640s.

In much of Scotland, the fighting was only ostensibly over religious doctrine. This was used to legitimise warfare between clans competing for land and resources, at a time of weak central government. In Cromar, for example, much of the land was owned by two feuding sets of clans, the Irvines and Gordons on one side and the Forbeses on the other. The Irvines and Gordons were ardently royalist and became a target for Covenanter forces, who sacked the Irvine family seat at Drum near Aberdeen in 1640.

Four years later, a particularly vicious Covenanter regiment drawn from the Campbell clan of Argyll was deputised to 'cleanse' the lands of the Irvines and their allies in and around Cromar. This was a euphemism for wholesale burning of homes and crops, butchering of livestock, and theft of any valuable possessions. It was said that 'not a four-footed beast' survived. Tenants were ruthlessly driven from their homes in this orgy of destruction, whether they had royalist sympathies or not. Resistance was pointless, and usually fatal. The 1644 'cleansing' of the Howe left its inhabitants destitute.

Of several low points in Cromar's history, this was probably the lowest.

The following year another Covenanter army, this one consisting of two thousand foot-soldiers and over two hundred cavalrymen under the command of William Baillie, marched into Cromar, plundering and destroying all before them. A brief respite followed, as Baillie's army was routed by royalist forces at the battle of Alford, a few miles to the north. But by 1647 the Covenanters were victorious, and their troops returned to Cromar to finish the task of demolishing royalist strongholds, including the island castle in Loch Kinord built by Macbeth six hundred years earlier.

Still Cromar was plagued by lawlessness. Some local lairds came up with a plan to bring greater peace and stability to their Howe. They would hire a gang to police the roads, especially those crossing the hills, where enemies as well as common thieves and rustlers would be intercepted. As a reward and incentive, the gang would be allowed to retain a portion of any stolen goods and livestock they recovered.

The plan backfired badly. The gang the lairds hired was led by a tough highlander called Patrick MacGregor, a giant of a man with red hair that earned him the nickname Gilderoy. Like his more famous, and later, kinsman Rob Roy MacGregor, Gilderoy was a known brigand and cattle-thief. Throughout the troubles of the 1640s the MacGregor gang had exploited the fog of war to steal whatever they could from the hard-pressed population. Now the fog was clearing, they had a new source of income, sanctioned by the very people whose lands and homes they had plundered.

Gilderoy quickly turned his commission into a protection racket, extracting a toll from innocent travellers for safe passage; soon afterwards he and his men reprised their favoured source of income: cattle rustling, supplemented by highway robbery. He became the scourge of Cromar, basing his operation in what was then a dense forest on the slopes of Culblean.

The fear and distrust of highlanders engendered by the Campbell 'cleansers' in what was still the western frontier of lowland ways was further aggravated by the MacGregors' depredations, giving rise to a kind of xenophobic prejudice against the entire Gaelic-speaking population that persisted for centuries. Tales of the caterans, as the highland thieves and freebooters were called, are still heard in Cromar. One such tale relates to John Thom's wedding.

Thom was a popular man in the Howe; on the occasion of his marriage friends and neighbours flocked to the celebrations which went on for days. The MacGregors, on hearing of the festivities, descended from Culblean to steal the cattle and plunder the homesteads of the absent wedding-guests. In revenge, the people of Cromar set fire to the forest of Culblean in an effort to deny the caterans their hiding-place. The tale is sometimes told in rhyme, reversing the sequence of events:

> Culblean was burnt, Cromar was harry't –
> Dowie's the day Jock Tam was marry't.

Returning to the Begg family of the Braes, Annie had been wooed by, and in 1638 had married, George Crichton, the operator of a 'waulk mill' at Tarland with whom the Beggs did business. The mill fell on hard times following the 'cleansing' of 1644 but ambition drove George to work long hours to get the enterprise back on its feet.

Waulking, or fulling as it is called outside Scotland, is a process for thickening woollen cloth to give it greater body and resistance to shrinking. Traditionally, cloth was stretched or 'tented' between hooks – literally 'tenterhooks' – and people, usually women, had to walk (waulk in Scots) on the stretched fabric. By the seventeenth century, the work of 'waulking' was more commonly done by a mechanical contraption called a waulk mill involving hammers driven by a water-wheel. The place where George Crichton had his business at Tarland is called Waulkmill to this day.

Annie Crichton became a pillar of the (now reformed) church in Tarland. She held regular meetings of her 'kirk ladies' at Waulkmill. Few members of the congregation other than Annie's 'ladies' suspected that these meetings were a cover for the Merch Nyr.

Not all the Merch Nyr had the social standing to be convincing in the role of 'kirk ladies'. One who didn't was Molly Watt, an elderly woman who worked a tiny croft called Ballachbuie, close to an ancient Pictish settlement – hut circles can still be seen there. Though no trace of her dwelling remains, you can drink from her water supply: a cool, limpid spring known as the Lazy Well. Only half a mile away, just over the crest of a hill, is Satan's Howe. You'll recall that Satan's Howe had been a gathering place for the Merch Nyr, for 'witches' as the church would call them, at least since the time of Macbeth.

Molly spent a lot of time at Satan's Howe, communing with the ancient gods. To avert suspicion, she cut peats and stacked them there to dry, always returning over the hill to her croft with a blanket on her back filled with dry peats for the fire. Sadly, one day she collapsed and died on the top of the hill. It's said that her ghost haunts the place. You'll see it marked on the map as Molly Watt's Hill.

I keep sidetracking myself from Annie Crichton's story. Of Annie's twin daughters, Jeanie, the first born, was pretty and bright. The other, Barbara or Babie, had a more difficult delivery. She was as pretty as her sister, but was what would nowadays be called developmentally challenged. At age seventeen, Babie announced one day that she had a 'lad'.

Annie was not too concerned at first. Babie had had a succession of imaginary friends, some of them boys. 'Aye, Babie,' she said, 'and does he have a name, this lad of yours?'

'His name's Hamish MacBain.'

'Hamish, eh? A hielanman, is he?'

'I don't know. He talks funny. Uses a lot of words I don't understand.'

Annie began to have an uncomfortable feeling. Hielanmen had been bad news since the hated Campbells had laid waste to Cromar in the 'cleansing' of 1644; now it was another gang of highlanders led by Gilderoy MacGregor that was terrorising the Howe. She asked Babie, 'What does he work at?'

'He works on the Tullich road.'

Exactly what Annie didn't want to hear: the Tullich road – MacGregor's main centre of operations. She and George had to tell their daughter in no uncertain terms that she must never see this Hamish MacBain again, that he was a common criminal and could offer her no kind of life. He would probably hang on the end of a rope within the year.

There were tears and remonstrations, but Babie agreed to give up her 'lad'. Soon it became obvious she was pregnant, and in due course she gave birth to a daughter at Waulkmill. Most people were understanding and sympathetic – they had no idea who the father was, probably a local boy, and Babie was a 'simple soul'. The baby was named Catriona, a Gaelic form of 'Katherine', as a subtle tribute to the long-departed Kate Ferries.

All the while, Annie kept Taran's wheel safe. She had a hiding place for it in an ancient stone circle that stood close to Waulkmill. (Unlike Tomnaverie, hardly any of its stones remain.) One day in 1658, she was horrified to find it missing. She confronted her daughters; eventually Babie admitted tearfully that she'd been seeing Hamish again and had told him all about Taran's wheel. Annie was sick that she'd lost the precious Drogan Taranish her forebears had kept safe ever since Macbeth had brought it back from Rome. She stood in the stone circle at Waulkmill in a thunderstorm, crying out to Taran to forgive her and begging him to help return it to her care.

Not long afterwards, Gilderoy and his gang were caught in a sting. Word was passed around of an expected delivery of gold and silver to a castle in the area – it may have been Craigievar, about ten miles north-east of Tarland – and, as expected, Gilderoy arrived on the scene with a dozen of his men. A much larger force of armed men assembled by the laird set upon the would-be thieves and took them into custody in a dungeon of the castle.

Among the few that escaped was Hamish MacBain. Having nowhere to hide, he turned up the following night at Waulkmill, begging to be taken in. He immediately admitted to having stolen the 'glass ball' as he called it, offering to return it if the Crichtons would hide him for a few days.

Annie and George argued about what should be done. George was in favour of turning the young gangster in to the authorities. Annie wanted the Drogan *back at any price, and eventually won George round by reminding him that Hamish was the father of their beautiful granddaughter.*

'We'll have to be quick,' Hamish said. 'The soldiers will torture Gilderoy and his men until they learn where the booty is hidden. Then you'll never get the ball back.'

He gave precise directions. Fulfilling the Crichtons' side of the bargain, George led him to a tiny chamber under the mill machinery where he would have to stay until it was safe to leave.

Early next morning, Annie and Jeanie set off on the Tullich road on a pair of ponies. They passed Marchnear and started up the long slow climb on the slopes of Culblean, where the battle for Scottish independence had been fought more than three hundred years earlier. At a point where the road forded a burn, they turned left and followed the burn down a valley that rapidly got deeper and narrower as they descended. Soon they found themselves in a deep ravine, at the head of a waterfall. Looking down, they saw the water cascading into a huge round cavern. Except that it wasn't a cavern – a narrow cleft between cliffs to right and left brought daylight from above.

Jeanie and her mother tethered the ponies and scrambled down the slippery rocks. At the bottom, just as Hamish had described it, was an entrance to a dark cave, over which the waterfall formed a kind of curtain.

'Somehow we have to get in there,' Annie said. 'Maybe if we dam the burn above the waterfall we can halt the flow long enough to get in and out.'

Even as she was saying this, Jeanie boldly stepped through the cascading water and disappeared into the cave. Shouting to be heard above the noise of the rushing water, she told her mother there was just enough light to see some wooden chests and what looked like cowhide bags.

'Can you see the crevice that Hamish described?'

'No,' Jeanie shouted, 'but I'm feeling around the walls. The cave is small. If there's a crevice here I should find it.'

Then there was silence. Annie's concern grew as minutes passed. 'Jeanie! Jeanie!' she cried.

The waterfall parted and Jeanie emerged, drenched but triumphant. She held the Drogan in her outstretched hand.

'Praise be to Taran,' Annie whispered. 'Let's get out of here.'

On their way back to Tarland, it started raining. Before they reached Marchnear they met a group of sheriff's officers on horseback, with several of Gilderoy's men shuffling along behind in shackles, soaked and shivering. The officers demanded to know where Annie and Jeanie had been, and where they were going.

'We're on our way home from Tullich,' Annie lied. 'We were visiting my sick uncle. Poor man, he's not got long to live. We're from Tarland, we're wet through, and with your leave we'd like to get home before we catch our death of cold.'

'Be on your way,' they were told.

The cavernous gorge they entered that day to retrieve Taran's wheel is now a popular tourist attraction. The Vat, it's called. The Burn o' Vat provides the water that falls over the mouth of the cave. You can go see it for yourself, but if you *decide to go through the waterfall into the cave, I suggest you have some dry clothes to change into.*

Gilderoy MacGregor was summarily tried in Edinburgh. His activities in Cromar were almost irrelevant to the case for the prosecution. A law still on the books from the time of James VI made it a capital offence just to have the name MacGregor. For his hanging in 1658, an extra tall scaffold had to be constructed because of his great height. He pleaded for mercy to the end, but his name was enough to hang him.

Tragedy struck the Crichton family in 1664, when twin sisters Jeanie and Babie succumbed to tuberculosis. They died within days of each other at the age of twenty-four, outlived by their parents. In 1681, Babie's daughter Catriona MacBain succeeded Annie Crichton as Keeper and went to live at Daach, on the old road to Strathdon that runs by Ballachbuie and the Lazy Well, passing close to Satan's Howe. Catriona may have cut peats there and, like Molly Watt, communed with Taran and Brytha.

44
A HEAP OF STONES

ELIA'S INTEREST IN COULL CASTLE had been piqued by an old (1923) article she'd found on the internet. Written by W. Douglas Simpson, it detailed what was known of the castle's history, including the travails of Joanna, Countess of Fife and her daughter Isobel. It was in general agreement with Grace's account, except that no mention was made of Margaret Baird or the hiding and recovery of the *Drogan Taranish*.

Friday August 8th brought a change in the weather. It was heavily overcast, though still dry, and distinctly chilly. Over breakfast Delia reread the Simpson article on the web, before she and Quin set off for Coull. By the time they arrived a light drizzle was falling. As they walked along a rutted farm track towards the ruins of the castle they called 'Good morning!' to a farm worker hammering fence-posts into the ground. He raised his arm in acknowledgement and continued with his task.

That same grey overcast morning, Cato was enjoying coffee and toast in the Commercial Hotel dining room, by a window overlooking the Tarland Square. Leafing through the morning paper, his mind was not on the day's news but on Delia's list. It was great to have it in his possession, but with so many locations to choose from, where should he start? More to the point, where was *she* likely to start?

As if in answer, he felt his mobile phone vibrate in his pocket. It was a text message from Bayliss.

> More places added
> Will email update
> Coull castle (#19) today
> Get there asap

Without finishing his toast he returned to his room where, consulting his map, he noted the castle remains only about two miles away. Throwing on a waterproof jacket, he set off immediately. By Coull Church, a quarter-mile from the castle, a small blue car was already parked. He reversed into an inconspicuous gap beside a farm steading, where he watched and waited. The drizzle turned to rain.

What had been an impressive building in the late thirteenth century was now nothing but a heap of stones, overgrown with grass and bushes. Remains of a fortified wall adjacent to the Tarland Burn were still discernable, but otherwise it was hard to make out the shape of the castle as it had once been. Delia had secretly entertained hope of finding a flagstone floor – the floor under which Margaret Baird had hidden Taran's wheel – but if such a thing still existed it was buried under many feet of rubble.

Just when they were ready to move on, Quin drew her attention to an elongated stone lying half hidden in long grass. It looked like a lintel that would once have surmounted a doorway or window. They pulled aside the grass to get a better look. The stone glistened with the rain. Exactly in the middle a faint but unmistakable letter D had been chiselled into its surface.

'D for Durward,' Delia announced. 'The family who built the castle.'

'Right,' Quin added, 'the Durward for whom the bell tolls of its own accord.'

'Could this be the sign we're looking for? D is also for *Drogan*.'

'Sure is,' Quin said. 'D'you think Grace hid the *Drogan* for you to find under this stone? To you, the letter D has special meaning. To anyone else, it's D for Durward.'

'There's one way to find out.'

Hard though they tried, the stone was much too heavy to move with their bare hands.

'We need a wrecking bar, something like the one Ewen was working with the other day. A pinch, he called it. Bet that guy over there has one.' Quin gestured in the direction of the fence builder, at that moment driving his tractor off the field.

'Yeah, but I saw a little hardware store in Ballater,' Delia said. 'Let's go buy what we need there. While we're at it, I wouldn't mind going to the hotel for some warmer clothes.'

Pulling up beside Cato's car, the tractor driver leaned out of his cab. *'Are ye gaan t'be here for a while?'* he shouted over the din of the engine.

Unsure of exactly what was said but grasping its meaning, Cato asked, 'Am I in your way?'

'It's aaricht the noo, but I'll need in aboot t'the steadin by half past three.'

'I'll be gone by then,' Cato assured him, understanding only his last three words. 'Just waiting to see if the rain goes off before I venture out.'

'Are ye wi the ither twa ower yonder at the castle ruins?'

'Castle? Er ... no, I didn't know there was a castle. I was going to have a look in the churchyard. Hunting for ancestors, you know. I'll check out the castle while I'm here.'

The tractorman shrugged and drove off.

A few minutes later, a young couple appeared, walking purposefully down the track, their heads bowed against the steadily worsening weather. Cato turned on his wipers for a single sweep to give him a clearer view through the rain-spattered windscreen, but with her hood up he couldn't be sure the girl was Delia. He slid down in his seat to peer below the arc of the steering wheel and saw them reach their car, where the girl pulled back her hood and shook her red hair free. Yes, that was Delia, all right. With never a glance in his direction, they drove off.

No point in tramping along there in the rain, he thought; he could easily drive all the way. On reaching the castle, he began exploring on foot. The rain got even heavier. Though his jacket kept his upper half reasonably dry, his footwear was not at all appropriate for trudging through tall wet grass.

He had gone around the entire site a couple of times, his feet growing colder and wetter with every step, before noticing a big rectangular stone with grass flattened around it. Getting closer, he saw that the stone was inscribed with the letter D.

D for Delia. What a good place to hide the tektite. Well done, Auntie Grace!

But the stone refused to budge. If *he* couldn't move it, he was pretty sure Delia and her friend would have had the same difficulty. 'Tools,' he thought. 'They're off to get tools to shift this damn thing.'

That thought immediately sparked another – the fencing gear he had seen on his way along the track. With a borrowed pinch bar and spade, he quickly prised the D stone out of its position. Underneath there were dozens of rocks of various sizes embedded in brown soil. Using the iron bar, he loosened the larger ones, and as he dug with the spade the hole filled with muddy rainwater, making it difficult to see what lay on the bottom. Having excavated to a depth of about two feet and finding nothing, he gave up. He replaced the tools where he had found them, then drove back to the Commercial Hotel for a hot shower, a change of clothes and a stiff scotch.

At the hardware shop Delia and Quin bought a crowbar that would do the job, together with a robust-looking spade. Then, passing an antiquarian bookshop, Delia couldn't resist having a look inside. The shop's musty odour transported her back to the glass-fronted bookcase in Grace's apartment. Opening the door of that bookcase had always released a smell that promised surprise discoveries among the volumes arrayed within. Her brief daydream was punctured by a voice saying: 'Can I be of any assistance, Miss?'

The speaker was a man in his early sixties, with a goatee and long grey hair tied back in a ponytail.

'Perhaps in a few minutes, but if it's okay I'd like to browse first.'

'Of course,' the man said. 'Just take your time. Not much to be outside for today, is there?'

'Look,' she said to Quin, 'here's a lot of local stuff. A whole shelf devoted to the Deeside railway – can you believe it? I didn't know there ever was a railway here.'

Overhearing her, the shopkeeper said, 'There's a lot of interest in the old Deeside line. Its terminus was here in Ballater, you know. The railway company wanted to continue on up to Braemar, but Queen Victoria feared it would disturb her solitude at Balmoral, so that section was never built. It was a sad day for Ballater when the line closed in the 1960s.'

While half-listening to this monologue, Delia's eyes alighted on a thin volume bound in a dull green cover with the title *Antiquities of Cromar* on the spine. Published in 1931, it was by 'the late Sir Alexander Ogston of Glendavan' – the same author who had written about the cairn-fields on Craiglich and Craig Dhu, which Megan Minty's researches had subsequently associated with the battle of *Mons Graupius*. The place-name 'Glendavan' added to the interest; it was next-door to Marchnear on the shore of Loch Davan where, according to Grace, the King of Scots made love to the innkeeper Peggy Walker. On impulse, she bought the book. They decided to grab some lunch in a coffee shop, while waiting for the rain to ease.

Driving the two short miles from Coull to Tarland, Cato was oblivious to a silver BMW following a discreet distance behind him. He parked behind his hotel, the hot shower and stiff scotch he'd promised himself now in imminent prospect.

The Engineer parked his BMW in the Square by the war memorial, where he waited for a few minutes before walking to the rear of the hotel. Sure that no one else was around, he forced open the tailgate of Cato's SUV. It was the work of a second.

As expected, the vehicle's alarm was triggered. The Engineer hid and waited. A car alarm was almost always ignored by the public; people generally assumed it was some kind of malfunction, not an actual break-in. After five minutes, the screeching stopped. Calmly he approached the Range Rover and climbed in through the tailgate, to search every inch of the interior. Leaving everything as he found it, he returned to his BMW.

It was one o'clock. Seven in the morning in Kansas, where Zeke Thackeray would already be up and about. He called from his mobile. There were no pleasantries.

'Woods spent an hour digging at a ruined castle this morning.'

'Yeah, and did he find what he was looking for?'

'Don't know. It's not in his car, so if he found it he has it with him. It's pissing down rain here and he got soaked. I bet he's in the shower right now. I could incapacitate him and search his room. Do you want me to do that?'

'No, just stay close to him so you know what he's up to. If he's got it, we'll be hearing from him very soon.'

The rain grew steadily heavier, and Delia and Quin gave up on the idea of returning to Coull that afternoon. The stone with the D would still be there when the rain went off – if it ever went off. They retreated to their room at Craigendarroch, where he read what was left of Grace's *Second Testament* and she immersed herself in *Antiquities of Cromar*.

There she found detailed accounts of the Pictish settlements at Knockenzie and Davan, though the writer didn't relate Davan to Ptolemy's *Devana*. The book left the impression that during the iron age, about two thousand years ago, Cromar was much more densely populated than today. It seemed that evidence of human residence and activity from that period or earlier could be found on virtually every bit of ground where it had not been erased by subsequent cultivation.

A curious feature of summer weather in that part of Scotland is that, no matter how dull and wet the day, it nearly always clears in the evening. Friday August 8th was no exception. Just after six o'clock, Delia became aware of birdsong outside the window. Looking out, she saw green wooded hills etched sharply against blue sky, where until a few minutes earlier there had been only leaden grey.

'Let's go, Quin,' she said.

In twenty minutes they were back at Coull. Carrying the spade and crowbar, they quickly found the lintel stone with its letter D. They stood looking at it in silent horror. The stone had been moved, and the ground underneath dug up.

45
GOOD TIMES AND BAD

AFTER THE EXTIRPATION *of Gilderoy MacGregor and his band of thieves, Cromar had good times and bad, just as it always had. In the latter part of the seventeenth century things were looking up for the people of the Pleasant Vale. Once again that old name was a reasonably apt description of the place. It had been translated from the ancient Beaker language, whatever that may have sounded like, through the* Tarachsel *or Pictish language to Gaelic and finally, with the firm establishment of Scots as the language of Cromar, from Gaelic to Scots. It was now the* Seely Howe.

There are many words that resist precise translation from Scots into standard English. Scots adjectives are especially evocative – thraan, dreich, couthy, fashious, nackit *and* orra *are good examples. Seely is another of those adjectives, the meaning of which lies somewhere between 'pleasant' and 'enchanted'. A* seely-wight, *for instance, is a fairy.*

There's an old rhyme that relates to the estate of Blelack, by Logie Coldstone. Legend has it that a laird of Blelack rounded up the seely-wights *on his estate and carted them off, whereupon they put a curse on him:*

It's dool, dool to Blelack
And dool to Blelack's heir,
Who banished us from the Seely Howe
To the cold Hill of Fare.

For some, the name 'Seely Howe' refers to a small hollow in the wood of Carue, near Blelack, but I'm convinced it's an old name for the whole circular basin of Cromar. 'Dool', you'll have gathered, means 'woe'. Perhaps at the heart of the rhyme there is a faint echo of the neolithic 'Little Folk' being driven out by the Beaker immigrants when they arrived in the Seely Howe almost four thousand years ago.

The roads over the hills were now safer. Tarland became an important stop for drovers bringing cattle from the north to the great markets that had sprung up in central Scotland, most notably at Falkirk. On this map the heavier broken lines show some of the more important drove roads through Cromar in the late 1600s.

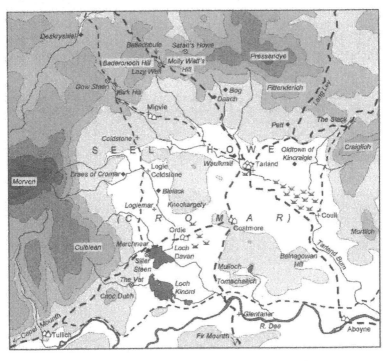

One of the busiest of these roads entered Cromar at Ballachbuie, the pass between Molly Watt's and Baderonoch

Hills, where the Lazy Well provided a welcome draught to thirsty animals and their drovers. The route then descended into Tarland, followed the Tarland Burn south-eastwards to Aboyne, and from there crossed the Mounth to the Angus glens and eventually the Scottish lowlands.

Another drove road was the Lang Ley on the eastern flank of Pittenderich, that continued south through Tarland to the little settlement of Coatmore, where it divided into two branches. One branch followed the old Tullich road to take the high pass known as the Capel Mounth to Angus; the other headed due south to cross the no less forbidding Fir Mounth.

Even in ancient times, Taran's Garden had been a hub from which six roads radiated. Now, as a drovers' stop, Tarland was once again 'on the map' (though maps of the time were few and inaccurate). Tradespeople such as blacksmiths, saddlers, soutars (shoe repairers) and merchants of all kinds set up shop. Innkeepers provided accommodation and liquid refreshment; no doubt prostitutes plied their profession. On August 3rd, 1683 Tarland was chartered by King Charles II as a burgh of barony, enabling it to set up a courthouse, levy taxes and host weekly markets and an annual fair (to be held on a Friday in July and known as the Luoch fair, after Moluag). This was a remarkable turnaround of fortune, less than forty years after the 'cleansing'.

Catriona MacBain, Keeper of Taran's wheel, therefore had good cause for celebration in her secret observance of Lunasa that year. Twenty-four years later, she observed Beltane on a truly historic day: the effective date (May 1st, 1707) of the Act of Union, which dissolved Scotland and England as sovereign nations and created the new United Kingdom of Great Britain with a single parliament in London.

The Act of Union, significant as it was nationally, was probably little noticed in Cromar. Likewise, the Jacobite rebellion of 1715 had little impact on the Seely Howe, even though it began with the raising of a standard by the Earl of Mar only twenty-seven miles away, at Braemar.

But the aftermath of the second Jacobite rebellion, which ended bloodily at Culloden near Inverness in 1746, spelled the end of the good times for Tarland and the Seely Howe. *New military roads were constructed across north-east Scotland, allowing faster movement of people and livestock, but these bypassed Cromar on both east and west. The stationing of a garrison in Tarland during the latter part of the eighteenth century further depressed the local economy by stamping out the illicit distilling of whisky.*

The kirk at Tarland (dedicated to Moluag and occupying the site of the ancient Kyaar) *needed to be rebuilt and in 1762 the first stone-built church was erected on the site. It's a reflection of the poor state of local finances by that time that the new church was shoddily built, using inferior materials. It needed constant repairs and was in use for little over a hundred years. Only its walls now stand.*

Tarland towards the end of the eighteenth century had acquired a reputation for (in the words of the local minister writing a half-century later) 'indifference, idleness, dissipation and immorality'. But the nineteenth century brought another resurgence in the fortunes of the village, coinciding with the lunar standstill of 1829, when a remarkable woman became Keeper of Taran's wheel at the tender age of twenty-four. Her name was Agnes Cromar.

46

THROUGH THE WATERFALL

D ELIA WAS SHOCKED. In the few hours between their first and second visits to Coull Castle, someone else had been there, and got the same idea she and Quin had – to look under the D stone.

The strange events of the last few days and weeks began to form a pattern. There was Grace's very suspicious death, and evidence that someone had opened her cabinet looking for the *Drogan*. There was the burglary at Arthur Johnson's house in Haverhill, the very day Delia went looking for him. There was the mysterious visitor to Praisewell, just a couple of days before them. And now this.

She and Quin were not the only ones in the hunt. Of that she was sure. Whoever else was after the *Drogan* possessed the same information, the same clues they had. Could there be another copy of Grace's CD? One that Arthur Johnson's burglar found?

But how could anyone possibly guess Delia's secret *'Love, and be silent'* password? Almost convinced that the *Drogan* had been found at Coull, she became despondent.

Saturday August 9th was a much brighter day. The rain that soaked the area on Friday had moved out over the North Sea towards Scandinavia. The morning air was cool and fresh, but a fairly warm day was forecast. They were on the road early, equipped this time to investigate any potential hiding place.

The list had now expanded from twenty-seven to thirty

possible locations:

She was reminded of Grace's words in her *Second Testament* relating how the remnants of the *Merch Nyr* had reacted to the persecution of Kate Ferries. The women hid 'in plain sight', Grace had written. Was this a hint that Taran's wheel wasn't buried under a rock or secreted in some dark chamber, but 'in plain sight' someplace? Was it staring them in the face? But if so, where?

Their first stop was at the Burn o' Vat. Whereas Annie and Jeanie Crichton had approached the gorge with its waterfall from the old road that crossed the burn higher up, Delia and Quin arrived on the newer low road that took a tortuous course through the Muir of Dinnet. Already, so early on a Saturday morning, there were several vehicles in the car-park.

They set off along the footpath that followed the course of the burn upstream to the Vat, the wet leaves of birch trees brushing against their faces. The mixed scents of pine, birch, bracken and heather raised their spirits. The valley gradually narrowed, ending in a rock wall that had a couple of openings through which the burn emerged. As they approached, a family including two small children clambered out from one of the openings. Delia and Quin went in through the same narrow gap, their feet on slippery wet rocks or in the flowing water of the burn, which was almost up to the tops of their boots.

The narrow passageway led into a round space that was just as Grace had described it. Blue sky was visible between overhanging cliffs above them. A few hardy trees clung to ledges and crevices. The floor of the Vat was flat and gravelly, evenly covered by shallow water. In front of them was the waterfall. Its roar echoed all around, and behind the white curtain of water they could make out the dark mouth of a cave. The cave that Gilderoy MacGregor had used to hide his booty; the cave where Hamish MacBain had briefly stashed the *Drogan* until Jeanie Crichton had retrieved it.

'I'm going in,' Delia announced. 'The same way Jeanie did. I'll get a soaking, but it'll be no worse than we got yesterday. And it'll be a whole lot more fun.'

Before Quin knew what was happening Delia had stripped down to her underwear and was climbing barefoot up the rocks towards the tumbling water. Left holding her boots, socks, jeans and teeshirt, he stared in amazement at her, then became aware of a pair of hikers enjoying the spectacle. In a minute she stepped confidently through the waterfall and disappeared from view. Quin turned and gave a shrug that said, 'She's crazy.'

From the closest point he could reach without getting drenched, he called at the top of his lungs, 'Are you all right in there?'

'I'm fine,' she yelled back. 'Gimme time to adjust to the darkness.'

He waited for perhaps ten minutes, doing his best to protect Delia's clothes from the spray. When she emerged dripping wet, she reported there were numerous cracks and crevices in the walls of the cave. 'Never in a million years would Grace have gone in there,' she said, wringing out her hair.

'This is too popular a place nowadays,' Quin said. 'Anything hidden here would soon be found. We had to check it out but ...'

'Are you just going to stand there or are you going to give me my dry clothes?'

In a surprisingly deft move, Delia put on her teeshirt and then removed her wet bra from underneath. Pulling on her jeans was a slightly more tricky manoeuvre on the wet rocks.

Within twenty minutes, they were back at Craigendarroch. A black Range Rover with tinted windows and a broken tailgate lock tied with a bungee cord sat in the hotel car-park. 'Not too secure, that,' Quin remarked. Her teeth still chattering, Delia made no response. A hot shower was all she could think of.

That afternoon they visited the Queen's Chair at Corrichie and, on the way back, Ordie Gordon with its stone circle. By 4 pm, they found themselves outside the village of Lumphanan, by a small grove of trees where, according to the Ordnance Survey map, 'Macbeth's Cairn' was located.

The way Grace told it, this was where Macbeth was killed and unceremoniously buried, before the women of Cromar disinterred the body and replaced it with another. The *Drogan* would have been brought here to complete the cycle of *vairtach* for a popular king. Even so, it seemed unlikely that Grace would have chosen this miserable heap of stones as its hiding place.

What if, after all, it been snatched from under their noses at Coull Castle? The D stone at Coull was the only promising clue they had so far found. As they walked back towards the road, becoming more pessimistic with every step, they saw a black SUV slow down alongside their car before speeding off.

'Isn't that the vehicle we saw at Craigendarroch this morning?' Quin asked. 'The one with the bungee cord?'

'Looks like it. Well, if somebody's tailing us, it means they haven't found the *Drogan* yet.'

They took the road back to Tarland. Being the second Saturday in August, it was the day of the annual agricultural show, now winding down. Cattle-floats, a procession of vintage tractors and a stream of people starting to make their way home were causing a traffic jam, the one occasion in the year when such a thing happened. With the official programme completed, the beer tent was overflowing with people reluctant to leave.

They decided to pay one more visit to the old churchyard. With nowhere to park in the Square – the flower show in the village hall was just as popular as the agricultural show they had just passed – they found a spot in Bridge Street. Walking back towards the churchyard, they came across the same black Range Rover yet again.

Though it was tightly parked between other vehicles, Delia

squeezed in to undo the bungee cord. On the carpeted floor of the cargo compartment, among other junk, were two rectangular metal plates. Turning one of them over, she saw it was a motor vehicle licence plate: DA51 LVA.

'DaSilva!' she breathed. 'These are Cato's personalised plates – he's replaced them with ordinary ones.' Quickly she secured the tailgate again.

The *Drogan Taranish* would indeed be a fine acquisition for DaSilva Rare Treasures. Cato had to be the one who had looked for it in Grace's cabinet. But could he have been cold-hearted enough to murder her? The burglary at Haverhill had probably been his doing, but who was the guy in the silver car snooping around Praisewell? Maybe Cato had an accomplice.

47
'IMPROVEMENTS'

B Y 1831, AGNES CROMAR, Keeper of Taran's wheel, was a behind-the-scenes moving force in the district whose name she bore. Her mother had passed on to her the ancient lore of Keepers past, and her father had instilled in her a love of books, which stood in for a formal education. She had an inquisitive nature and persuasive manner. To her great credit, she did not conform to the mid-nineteenth century ideal of feminine character: a 'person of delicate mould and womanly diffidence'.

Agnes used her relationships with people of influence to get things done, almost always receiving no credit herself. But she needed none. It was enough for her that the Seely Howe lived quietly up to its history as the cradle of Pictish culture – a history reaching back to the coming of the bronze age Beaker People and the iron age Celts. Many had sought to destroy that culture but, thanks to the Merch Nyr and the Keepers who had gone before her, it was still at least a flickering flame.

A particular relationship she cultivated was with William Gordon, who had been the local Member of Parliament since 1820. The Palace of Westminster in London, though revered throughout the English-speaking world as the 'Mother of Parliaments', was nothing like the democratic institution it is today. Absolutely no women, and only a tiny proportion of men – principally landowners and senior churchmen – could vote in those days. So an MP could be elected by just a handful *of his cronies. And most MPs, whether Whig or Tory, were drawn from the aristocracy. William Gordon was no exception. A younger brother of the 4th Earl of Aberdeen, by now a major landowner in Cromar, he was a member of the Tory party. Prior to becoming MP, he had a career in the navy, eventually rising to the rank of vice admiral.*

Agnes Cromar became a close confidante of Gordon. It was whispered that she was his mistress, a theory discounted by Megan who suggests Gordon may have been gay, or perhaps asexual. In any case, he never married. It was well known that he was a slave to superstition, and Agnes played on his gullibility.

Commerce in north-east Scotland in the early nineteenth century was hampered by poor infrastructure. Though Tarland was tiny compared to other centres of population, Agnes persuaded Gordon to support the building of a first-class road to the village from Aberdeen, as well as improved roads linking Tarland to Deeside.

The first fruit came in the form of a magnificent stone bridge over the Tarland Burn, completed in 1835. That bridge still stands, carrying traffic many times heavier than can have been dreamed of when it was built. The upstream side of the arch is decorated with masonic symbols.

The thirty-mile road from Aberdeen was opened around 1840 as a turnpike, on which travellers were required to pay tolls at six-mile intervals. Most of the toll-houses can still be seen, for example at Corse, 6 miles from Tarland, at Tornaveen, 12 miles, and at Echt, 18 miles.

Another important engineering project was completed in 1840. Up to that time, much of the flat plain to the south-east of Tarland was wetland. Earlier still, it was almost certainly a shallow lake, which gradually became silted up by inflowing streams, principally the Tarland Burn. With its wildlife, the wetland would nowadays be treasured as a conservation area, but in the nineteenth century it was regarded as a waste of space. It was known as Bog More – the big swamp. Below the bridge at Tarland, the burn simply lost itself in the tall vegetation of Bog More, re-emerging as flowing water near Coull. In 1840 a new channel was excavated for the burn, in a series of three straight lines from the Tarland bridge to the Coull Castle ruins. The resulting drainage of the wetland provided hundreds of acres of new, highly productive arable land.

Around this time many of the crude dwellings in the village of Tarland began to be replaced by more handsome stone buildings. Stone was quarried locally; Agnes must have worried about the proximity of the Tomnaverie quarry to the hallowed stone circle.

So by the early 1840s, the village was on an upswing again, for the first time in a hundred years. Tarland had no fewer than five alehouses, though the minister of neighbouring Coull noted with some satisfaction in 1842 that his parish had 'the advantage of being without a single alehouse'. Even more to the benefit of the lucky parishioners of Coull, he stressed the provision of 'a parochial library, consisting chiefly of practical religious works'.

But developments were afoot that worried Agnes: they meant the village and surrounding Howe could become vulnerable to outside forces. Good roads and bridges were fine, but there were other 'improvements' being mooted.

In 1841 William Gordon's brother Lord Aberdeen became Foreign Secretary in the British government. Prince Albert, who had come from Germany to marry Queen Victoria just a year earlier, took a strong interest in British politics and Lord Aberdeen became a favourite of his. Victoria and Albert paid a visit to Scotland in 1842. So enamoured were they that they returned on a regular basis, and soon decided to acquire a summer home in the north.

It was in 1846, according to Megan, that Lord Aberdeen proposed a 'perfect location' for a summer retreat for Victoria, Albert and their young children, on his estate in Cromar.

Albert travelled north to survey the proposed site, which lay on a south-facing slope half a mile east of the village of Tarland, with spectacular views towards Mount Keen and Lochnagar. With no existing building there, Aberdeen eagerly made the pitch that the prince could have a brand new castle built there to his specifications. The village could supply all the servants, coachmen, labourers and tradesmen that would be needed for the castle operations. And the site would be leased to Victoria and Albert at a peppercorn rent.

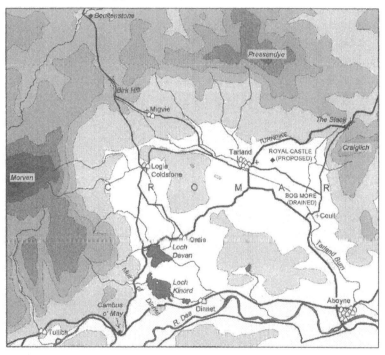

The location of the proposed royal castle is indicated on this map of Cromar as it was around 1846. (The road network shown here, building on and partially replacing the old system of drove roads, hasn't changed greatly since that time.)

William Gordon let Agnes in on the secret that the queen and her consort favoured Tarland as the location for a new summer home. The idea was anathema to Agnes, who had an ambition to see the development of the village as a commercial centre in its own right, rather than a mere adjunct to a royal castle that would be occupied one month out of twelve. Fearing the Seely Howe would lose its special identity if invaded every summer by the royal family and their hangers-on, she devised a two-pronged plan to thwart Lord Aberdeen's proposal.

First, she persuaded William that a superior location for the royal summer home would be Balmoral, about twenty miles away near the foot of Lochnagar. As it happened, the Balmoral estate was at that time leased to another of the Gordon brothers, Sir Robert, who might be persuaded to relinquish his lease in favour of Albert and Victoria.

Second, she brought her 'crystal ball' to Lord Aberdeen's site east of Tarland and, taking advantage of William's superstitious nature, consulted it on what lay in store for that location. Any great house or castle on the site, she foretold, would be the scene of debt, death and destruction. These tragedies wouldn't come immediately or all at once, but over a period of 111 years (an ancient Tarachsel measure of time: six moondances of eighteen and a half years).

William was horrified by Agnes's prophecy. He persuaded Lord Aberdeen to withdraw the proposal for a royal castle at Tarland and encouraged Sir Robert to entertain the queen and prince. The seed was planted, and in 1847, Victoria and Albert were guests of Sir Robert and fell in love with Balmoral.

Very shortly afterwards, the strangest thing happened. Sir Robert choked on a fish bone and died, leaving the lease of Balmoral vacant. Albert snapped it up. A few years later, he purchased the Balmoral estate outright and presented it as a gift to the queen.

For the rest of his life, William believed that Sir Robert's death was the result of a hex by Agnes, to deflect Prince Albert from establishing his Scottish home at Tarland. This seems only to have strengthened Agnes's influence over him.

Meanwhile, Lord Aberdeen's political fortunes were in a state of flux. The Tory party split over issues of free trade and agricultural tariffs; Lord Aberdeen sided with the anti-protectionist faction led by Sir Robert Peel and was forced to resign from the government in 1846. However, in 1852, as leader of the short-lived Peelite party, he formed a coalition government with the Whigs, becoming Prime Minister. Thus the laird of Cromar was for a time the most powerful political figure in the whole of Great Britain.

It was not to last. Britain became embroiled in a disastrous and unpopular war in Crimea, for which Lord Aberdeen as Prime Minister took the blame, and he resigned in 1855. Not for the last time, a western leader fell from grace as a result of a futile war in a distant eastern country. The Peelites and Whigs later amalgamated; out of this a new British political entity, the Liberal Party, was born.

Back in Cromar, another threat was perceived by the ever-watchful Agnes. It was the golden age of railway construction, and in 1853 a new line was opened from Aberdeen to Banchory. Surveyors and engineers were prospecting a route that would extend the line all the way to the west coast of Scotland. An east-west line through the highlands was a dream of several railway magnates. Great pine forests in the central highlands would be opened up to logging; and fast 'fish trains' were foreseen bringing catches from west coast ports such as Mallaig to the east coast fish-market of Aberdeen.

If you draw a straight line from Aberdeen to Mallaig, it runs across the high plateau of the Cairngorm Mountains, an impossible barrier for a railway. Route prospectors considered two options. The initial favourite followed the Dee valley to its upper reaches before crossing into Glen Feshie, then proceeding through upper Strathspey and Glen Spean to Fort William and onward to Glenfinnan, Arisaig and Mallaig. It was the most direct route, passing to the south of the Cairngorms, but it crossed a lengthy tract of barren, uninhabited land between Braemar and Strathspey. The Aberdeen-to-Banchory line was its first leg. An attraction of this Deeside route was the ancient Ballochbuie pine forest to the west of Balmoral. A few years of clear-felling would more than repay the railway-builders' investment – in those days there was no thought of conserving such a magnificent resource for future generations.

Construction of the Banchory line was already in progress when the railway builders had a change of heart. They began to favour the alternative option, which was to take the upper Don valley, cross to the River Avon and descend into Strathspey at Boat of Garten. From Strathspey the route west would be the same as in the first option. There were engineering challenges aplenty with this route, and furthermore it was considerably longer, curving as it did around the north of the Cairngorms. But it passed through more populated areas than the south route, and offered the prospect of branch lines to tap into the malt whisky distilleries of Strathspey that had transformed the economy of that valley following the easing of governmental control in 1823. To be sure, it wouldn't access the Ballochbuie forest, but the even larger Abernethy forest would be in its path.

The north route would bring the railway line away from its easy course alongside the River Dee. From Banchory it would climb steeply towards Lumphanan and thence to a summit between the hills of Craiglich and Mortlich. From there it would descend into Cromar and continue on over the Birk Hill into upper Donside. In 1854, Agnes intercepted the leader of a team of surveyors looking for a site to build a station at Tarland. It was to be on high ground just north of the village, by the parish poorhouse. She persuaded the surveyors to show her a map; it had the proposed course of the line marked in red ink like a knife-wound across her beloved Seely Howe.

She quickly primed William Gordon to take action. She saw that trying simply to kill the railway plan was doomed to failure, so strong was the commercial lobby for its construction.

Instead, she had William propose reversion to the south route, with vague offers of government subsidy.

But things were moving very fast. Construction of the line from Banchory to Lumphanan, including a costly viaduct at Sundayswells, had already begun and couldn't now be changed. However, William persuaded the railway company to put a right-angle turn in the line at Lumphanan to bring it back to the Dee valley at Aboyne. One of his selling points was the new royal residence at Balmoral, which would provide additional business for the railway if it took the Deeside route. The line from Banchory to Aboyne, with what now looked like a pointless detour via Lumphanan, opened in 1859.

By 1865, construction had begun on the next section of the railway, from Aboyne to Braemar. Prince Albert, with his keen commercial sense, might have been supportive, but he had died of typhoid in 1861. As things turned out, Queen Victoria vetoed the running of trains close to Balmoral; the line was therefore built only as far west as Ballater and the heralded coast-to-coast railway never materialised. Ballater station opened in October 1866; one of the first passengers to alight there was Victoria herself.

At the turn of the twentieth century, Mallaig on the west coast did become a railhead, but for a line running from Glasgow, not from Aberdeen. That railway is still in operation. By contrast, the truncated Deeside line, described by some as the railway to nowhere, was closed in the 1960s. One positive outcome of the failure of the coast-to-coast project was that both Ballochbuie and Abernethy pine forests were spared the axe, and remain havens for native highland plant and animal life to this day.

Agnes's rerouting of the railway was her last major intervention through her association with William Gordon. Perhaps he was tired of doing her bidding; in 1854, the very year he had talked the railway bosses into bypassing the Howe of Cromar, he stood down as MP, to be replaced by his nephew.

But Agnes had one remaining ambition that would have to be realised without William's help. She wanted to move Tarland's Luoch Fair from July to an August date, celebrating the ancient god Lugus or Luath. In short, she sought to recreate the old Lunasa festival, which had been outlawed by Moluag's followers more than a thousand years before.

She wouldn't propose the change by invoking ancient Pictish gods. Her suggestion, made to a group of farmers and businessmen, was to replace the annual fair with an agricultural show, and to move it later in the year to be one of the last shows of the season. That way, she said, it would become the 'show of champions', attracting from a wide area livestock that had already won prizes at other venues. After much discussion and lobbying, the idea was accepted and a date was fixed: the second Saturday of August each year. The first Tarland Show was held in 1866.

48
LUNASA

IT HAD BEEN a long day. At Burn o' Vat Delia had walked through the waterfall, and after a change of clothes she and Quin had made a partial ascent of the Hill of Fare to visit the battlefield of Corrichie and the Queen's Chair. At Macbeth's Cairn they had seen the black Range Rover; at Tarland they'd been left in no doubt it was Cato's.

And the day wasn't over, not by a long way. It was Saturday evening, when they were to join the Grove of the Mayflower for a midnight celebration of Lunasa at Tomnaverie.

Back at the hotel, Quin went for a swim; Delia had had enough cold water for one day and curled up with her computer to read more of Grace's *Second Testament*, up to the revival of Lunasa as an annual event in the form of the Tarland Show. It seemed an uncanny coincidence that she should reach that story on the very day of the show and just before attending a real Lunasa celebration in person.

At about quarter past eleven they walked out to their car. Although it was still early August, there was a chill and a distinctly autumnal smell in the calm night air. The sky was clear and a full moon accompanied them as they drove to Tomnaverie.

They were first to arrive. To the south, only the most brilliant stars were visible against the moon's glare, but in other directions the sky was peppered with stars. Only once, on a camping trip in Colorado, had Delia seen the heavens like this. There was the Big Dipper (the Plough) and the Pole Star, surprisingly high in the sky. Overhead was the 'summer triangle' of Vega, Altair and Deneb. On a moonless night the Milky Way, running through that triangle, would cleave the dark sky in two. But tonight, it was the brilliant moon that provided the spectacle. Not even the distant throb of disco music from the Tarland showground could disturb the tranquillity.

A couple of cars arrived, then a minibus. Myrtle emerged and came over to greet them. Fourteen people walked up the footpath to the Tomnaverie stone circle. The First Druid wore a full-length black robe, while the others were in everyday dress.

A flat board was laid on the grass at the centre of the stone circle and various articles were placed on it, all covered with light linen cloths. Everyone, including Delia and Quin, gathered in a ring around the makeshift altar.

On the stroke of midnight, the First Druid spoke. 'We the Grove of the Mayflower are ordained to prepare for Beltane, and to count the nine moons from now until that glorious night. Tonight is Lunasa, when we make sacrifice to Lugus, to guide us and protect us for the first three moons, from now until Samhain when we shall gather here again.'

Beside the First Druid, a man raised a drum with his left hand and began pounding it with the palm of his right, softly at first, gradually becoming louder. Eventually it ended in a deafening boom. For a few moments the assembled group made not a sound.

'Are there Outsiders in our presence? If so, let them show themselves.' Quin and Delia took a step forward, and the First Druid addressed them directly. 'We ask Lugus to look kindly on you, our guests tonight. We live in your midst, and you no longer persecute us for our beliefs and practices. For this we are thankful. Lunasa, our communion with the god Lugus, is the festival you probably know as Lammas. We do not expect you to join in our acts of praise and offering to Lugus tonight, but we ask that you respect the sanctity of our ritual. You may step back into the ring.'

Since childhood, Delia had known about Lunasa from her conversations with Grace, who had called the god Luath rather than Lugus. Thanks to the efforts of Agnes Cromar in the 1860s, Lunasa was back on the local calendar in the form of the Tarland Show. The muffled music still emanating from the showground marquee was living proof.

The drummer set up a soft rhythm in two-four time, and Myrtle stepped forward to sing a song of love at Lammas, from the pen of Robert Burns. Delia and Quin glanced at each other wordlessly, both recalling the Burns sonnet quoted on the fiddler's memorial in Tarland Square.

Myrtle let her head nod almost imperceptibly to the drummer's rhythm, then began singing, every note pitch-perfect in the still night air.

> *It was upon a Lammas night,*
> *When corn rigs are bonny, o,*
> *Beneath the moon's unclouded light*
> *I held away to Annie, o.*
> *The time flew by with tentless heed*
> *Till 'tween the late and early, o,*
> *With small persuasion she agreed*
> *To see me through the barley, o.*
>> *Corn rigs and barley rigs,*
>> *And corn rigs are bonny, o,*
>> *I'll ne'er forget the night I spent*
>> *Among the rigs wi' Annie, o.*
>
> *The sky was blue, the wind was still,*
> *The moon was shining clearly, o;*
> *I set her down with right good will*
> *Among the rigs o' barley, o.*
> *I kent her heart was aa my ain,*
> *I loved her most sincerely, o,*
> *I kissed her o'er and o'er again*
> *Among the rigs o' barley, o.*

Corn rigs and barley rigs,
And corn rigs are bonny, o,
I'll ne'er forget the night I spent
Among the rigs wi' Annie, o.

I locked her in my fond embrace,
Her heart was beating rarely, o;
My blessings on that happy place
Among the rigs o' barley, o!
And by the moon and stars so bright
That shone that night so clearly, o,
She aye shall bless that happy night
Among the rigs o' barley, o.

    Corn rigs and barley rigs,
    And corn rigs are bonny, o,
    I'll ne'er forget the night I spent
    Among the rigs wi' Annie, o.

As the rhythm of the drum faded into the night, so too did the distant music, and Tomnaverie was bathed in perfect silence under the moon and stars.

After several incantations by the First Druid, it was time to make offerings to Lugus. Removal of one of the linen cloths revealed a flat cake – the worshippers called it a bannock – in the shape of a bull. Strange, Delia thought, that a bull, the symbol of Taran, should be a centrepiece of offerings to Lugus or Luath, who Grace had always said was a lesser god. Might Taran's wheel yet appear?

'I call forth the Knifeman,' the First Druid intoned.

Quin barely suppressed a chuckle. Now the guy was channelling the Eagles! The words came unbidden to his mind:

    'Relax,' said the Knifeman,
    'We are programmed to deceive;
    You may check out any time you like,
    But you can never leave.'

The Knifeman approached the bannock with his '*steely knife*' in both hands and drove its point through the middle, skewering the bannock to the wooden board, where he left it and returned to his place in the ring. The First Druid called on Lugus to accept the offering. A few moments elapsed. Then he announced that the god had duly noted the offering but wished the faithful to eat it in fellowship. Delia and Quin hung back, but the others went to the board and helped themselves to a piece of the bull-shaped bannock. The First Druid was last to claim his share; the piece left for him included the bull's outsize testicles.

A jug of water was then unveiled. A pitcher, Delia thought, the sign of Aquarius, home to the full moon that very night. A woman came forward to pour water into paper cups and hand a cup to each participant.

Myrtle then unveiled a third object on the board. It was a bowl of fruit. 'Fruits of the forest,' she whispered to Delia and Quin as she approached them. 'Please taste.' Both sampled the offering of wild blackberries, strawberries and small round berries that neither of them recognised.

The druidical rite over, its paraphernalia were gathered up in silence and carried back to the minibus. The *Drogan Taranish*, if the Grove of the Mayflower now possessed it, had not appeared. A stream of vehicles was leaving the show dance, forming a procession along the road past the foot of Tomnaverie. Sounds of hilarity emanated from rolled-down car windows.

On the way back to Ballater, Quin confided that he had found Myrtle's song quite moving. 'I'm sure Sting was reworking that same song when he wrote *Fields of Gold*, but he left less to the imagination.'

Delia smiled and said nothing.

49
DEBT, DEATH AND DESTRUCTION

T HERE IS A POSTSCRIPT to Agnes Cromar's foretelling of *'debt, death and destruction' over a period of 111 years, should a great house or castle be built on the site that Lord Aberdeen had sought to lease to Albert and Victoria. Megan filled me in on the story last time I visited her, and I had her write it down. Here it is, in her own words.*

Not only William but the entire Gordon family were notoriously superstitious. William relayed Agnes's prophecy to his brother Lord Aberdeen, who made no further effort to develop the site. Almost sixty years passed before a country house, in the style of a French château, was built in 1903 by the 7th Earl and Countess of Aberdeen. They named it Cromar House.

Farmland stretching from the front of the house westward to the village of Tarland was converted to a fine golf course. The earl commissioned none other than Old Tom Morris, the pioneer of modern golf who was by then in his eighties, to design it. Old Tom did not see its completion; he died in 1908, the year the course opened for play. Characteristically, the earl welcomed its use by all interested residents of Cromar, prompting the formation of Tarland Golf Club, which is still going strong.

The Aberdeens were a generously philanthropic couple, much respected and admired by the people of

Cromar and beyond. The 7th earl was at different times governor of Ireland and Canada, and in 1916 he was created Marquess of Aberdeen and Temair. Large charitable gifts by the marquess and marchioness to worthy causes in both Ireland and Canada, along with a rather extravagant lifestyle, effectively bankrupted the couple. In 1918 they were forced to sell their lands in Cromar and even their beautiful new country house. Debt, as foretold by Agnes, had come to pass.

The purchasers of the Aberdeens' house and lands were Sir Alexander and Lady MacRobert, who had made their fortune in colonial India and had built their own stately home at Douneside, just north of Tarland, in 1907. They agreed, however, that the Aberdeens could continue to be tenants of Cromar House for as long as they both lived. Sir Alexander died in 1922, leaving Lady MacRobert the sole owner of the Cromar estate, which together with the Douneside lands covered about eleven square miles around Tarland.

Now only tenants, the Aberdeens continued to use Cromar House for lavish entertainment. Queen Mary, consort of King George V, was a frequent visitor when the royal family were resident at Balmoral each summer. Prized possessions were removed from sight before her arrival, as she had a habit of 'admiring' a particular object, which then had to be presented to her as a gift.

Lady Aberdeen was an early feminist. In 1931, for example, she presented to the Church of Scotland a petition signed by 336 women demanding ordination of female ministers. It eventually happened, many decades later.

On the marquess's death in 1934, Lady MacRobert arranged the removal of his widow from Cromar House; the tenancy, after all, was guaranteed only as *long as both the Aberdeens were alive. With characteristic fortitude, Lady Aberdeen entertained Queen Mary to tea on the eve of her eviction. No doubt she listened politely to the queen's tales of the lamentable behaviour of the Prince of Wales, her eldest son and heir to the throne, who after a long series of high-profile affairs, was now in the clutches of a twice-married American socialite by the name of Wallis Simpson.*

Upon her forced departure from Cromar House, Lady Aberdeen retired to her city residence (Gordon House in Aberdeen) where she reputedly held seances in the hope of communicating with her beloved husband.

Ill-fortune was soon visited on the family of Lady MacRobert, when her eldest son was killed in a flying accident. And three years later, in 1941, her two younger sons were killed in wartime action with the Royal Air Force. Cromar House was renamed Alastrean in honour of the three MacRobert boys.

In 1952, Alastrean House was burned to a shell in a devastating fire. Debt, death and now destruction, the trio of disasters supposedly seen by Agnes Cromar in a crystal ball in 1846, had all materialised within the promised timeframe of 111 years.

Those words of Megan bring me close to the end of my tale. It remains only to tell you how the Drogan Taranish *and the responsibilities of Keeper passed down from Agnes to myself.*

A few years before Agnes died in 1874, she contacted a distant relative – the daughter of a second cousin – in Edinburgh, and was able to persuade her to take on the responsibility of Keeper of Taran's wheel. The relative's name was Verity Kelso. Her husband, Leonard Kelso, was a chemist and had a small factory making medicines.

Verity's name reminds me of vairtach, *the ancient Pictish concept of truth and justice. She was my great grandmother.*

The Kelso family emigrated to America shortly after Agnes's death. Leonard set up a new pharmaceutical business there, which did well. From Verity, the Drogan *and its associated myth and history passed through my grandmother and my mother to me. I believe I'm the first to write it all down.*

I've often wondered about the real origin of the Drogan. *The story of Aeth and the kingfisher has all the hallmarks of mythology, and may have been dreamed up at any time, even quite recently. Is it possible that the* Drogan *is one of those glass spheres that rained down on the land in the aftermath of the Jurassic asteroid impact? As I've admitted, the asteroid was my invention; even if the Howe of Cromar does mark the site of an ancient impact crater, what are the chances that a three-inch glass ball would have survived the ravages of all those millions of years of mountain-building and erosion?*

At the same time, it seems unlikely that the Drogan *was a product of bronze or iron age craft. Glass beads have been found among Pictish remains at various sites in north-east Scotland, but there's no evidence the Picts themselves mastered glassmaking. Those beads are probably Roman in origin, subsequently decorated by Pictish artists. They're mostly opaque, and only about half an inch in diameter. The notion that the much larger, translucent* Drogan Taranish *could have been made by local craftsmen in pre-Roman times is not supported by any evidence I'm aware of.*

The glass ball that Macbeth brought back from Rome may not have been an object originally acquired in Pictland. It could just as easily have been a product of Italian artisans – for example in Venice – who were turning out highly sophisticated glass articles by the eleventh century.

Whatever the true nature of the Drogan, *its symbolic power is undeniable. What it represents is so much more important than what it is. I think you understand this, Cordelia, and I have therefore named you as the one to whom the precious* Drogan *and all the knowledge I have shared in these* Testaments can be entrusted.

It is possible we are at the sixth and final cambus, *the one the* Tarachsel *believed would be the end of the world. Certainly the time is at hand – almost 666 years have passed since the fifth* cambus. *In your hands, I hope the* Drogan *and all it stands for will nonetheless have a future, and so prove the* Tarachsel *wrong.*

END OF SECOND TESTAMENT OF GRACE ROSMAN,
KEEPER OF TARAN'S WHEEL

III. THE FINAL *CAMBUS*

50
THEY'RE ON TO YOU

EZEKIEL THACKERAY HAD JUST RECEIVED a call from the Engineer. Immediately, he called Cato Woods. 'Z here. They're on to you.'

'Meaning what, exactly?'

'The redhead and her boyfriend, dummy. You left your car unlocked in the street, and they were in it.'

'How do you know this, for Christ's sake?'

'Never mind, asshole. You know we have our methods. What the hell do you think you're doing, blowing your cover like that?'

'Look, I was unable to park at my hotel like I usually do. This place is dead 364 days, and once a year it wakes up and you can't move for people and traffic. Today's the day. So I parked on the street, end of.'

'Yeah, except they opened your tailgate and rummaged through whatever crap you keep in there.'

'Shit!' Cato muttered under his breath. Delia had rumbled him. But he wasn't ready to admit that to Z. 'So they got into my car. Big deal. It doesn't mean they know it's mine. Anyway, it only happened because somebody busted my tailgate lock yesterday.' As he spoke, it dawned on him that the break-in was no random event. Somebody was pursuing him, keeping an eye on him, checking whether he'd found the glass ball, reporting back to Z and J.

'And the ball? Has it turned up?'

'They're still looking, so what do *you* think?'

Z rang off. He then called the Pastor.

'Dammit, Thackeray, it's Saturday afternoon. Don't you realise I've a sermon to prepare?'

'I apologise sincerely, Most Reverend. I just need to report a small glitch in Operation Curveball.'

'Not what I want to hear. But you'd better tell me.'

'We *have* to take Cato Woods out of the operation. He's too slipshod and has blown his cover. Maybe we should turn the whole thing over to the Engineer.'

'Thackeray, you've wanted this from the start. No, I'm not ready to sacrifice Woods yet. The Engineer's a little too ready to use that gun of his. We got away with it last time, but I don't want this messed up. By the way, did I tell you I'm going to Scotland?'

'Most Reverend, I know you were invited to preach in Glasgow, but you told me the British government had banned your visit.' Thackeray was well aware of the 'named and shamed' list that included the Pastor's name.

'Fools and blasphemers, the lot of them! The Glasgow church wants an alliance with the Kingdom of Men, so they'll find a way around the ban. From what I hear, they're making progress. The government welcomed the visit to Scotland of Pope Benedict, against heavy lobbying, back in 2010 when he was still embroiled in the paedophile scandals rocking the Catholic church. They can't welcome him, and shun me.'

Thackeray mumbled agreement while thinking: *You're not the Pope, Most Reverend.*

51

PLEASE MAKE IT QUICK

ELIA AND QUIN SLEPT LATE. Meanwhile, Cato finished breakfast at the Commercial Hotel in Tarland before driving over to Ballater. Seeing Delia's car in front of the Craigendarroch, he parked among some staff vehicles to wait and watch without being observed.

Having eaten, Delia went online. First, she needed to learn some more about the history of glassmaking. She *wanted* to believe that the *Drogan Taranish* was truly ancient, that its origins were right here in Scotland before spending a thousand years in Rome. But she found no support for the possibility that such an object could have been crafted in pre-Roman Britain. Was it, after all, a natural object that could have lain undisturbed in the ground until river-bank erosion released it to the light of day? Could there be some truth in the legend of Aeth and the kingfisher? Another search yielded information on tektites, glass rocks found in the vicinity of meteorite impact craters. If the *Drogan* was a tektite, it would be by far the largest ever found, and would be unique among tektites in its transparency and internal colour pattern. No, Grace had told a nice story about an asteroid impact but, as she herself had admitted, it was pure invention. It was hard not to conclude that the *Drogan* was at most a thousand years old.

Not that that made it any less imperative to find it.

For a few minutes, her internet journey was sidetracked by references to the mysterious carved stone balls found all over

Pictland, most abundantly right here in Aberdeenshire. The symmetries displayed by these artefacts were, she read, evidence that the neolithic peoples of this region understood three-dimensional geometry two thousand years before Plato, who, around 400 BC, wrote about the five solid shapes that bear his name. Balls with four regularly spaced knobs, like the Towie ball for instance, were said to echo the symmetry of a tetrahedron, while those with six knobs, by far the commonest type, called to mind a cube with its six faces or perhaps an octahedron with its six vertices. Even the Platonic dodecahedron with twelve faces and the icosahedron with twelve vertices were supposedly represented among the Aberdeenshire finds.

Perhaps, as Grace had suggested, the carved stone balls were much more recent than the neolithic era. If they were inspired by Taran's wheel sometime in the iron age, they were roughly of Plato's vintage, not two millennia older. And perhaps their manufacture didn't require any concept of the underlying mathematics of Platonic solids.

She began checking out the best walking routes to visit the cairn-fields on Craig Dhu and Craiglich, numbers 2 and 13 on her list of possible hiding places. After visiting a number of websites, she announced to Quin, 'I'm not convinced it's worth going to the cairn-fields. Both hills are so densely wooded now, the cairns will be very difficult to find. And there are so many – about two thousand – we couldn't possibly check them all.' Instead, they planned an itinerary to Braes of Cromar, the *Gow Steen*, and the Pictish remains at Knockenzie and Kinord.

Outside, Cato was growing impatient. Too much coffee at breakfast forced him to venture into the Craigendarroch health club in search of a toilet. By the time he returned to his car, Delia and Quin had emerged and driven off.

He cursed loudly to himself. At that moment, a text message came in on his mobile phone from J.

Searching ##2 & 13 today

Perfect. He didn't need to follow them. Numbers 2 and 13 on Delia's list were the battlefield sites with burial cairns. He'd marked them on his map.

Thus it was that Cato spent most of Sunday tramping up hills and through forests without ever catching a glimpse of Delia and Quin, who were able to inspect a number of locations unobserved.

Still, Taran's wheel remained elusive.

Early next morning, Delia drove Quin to Aberdeen for his flight to London and connection to Chicago. She wished him luck with his interview and gave him her key to Grace's apartment in Glenview. His flight was already boarding when they got to the airport; all they had time for was a hurried goodbye kiss outside the terminal, and he was gone.

Another visit to the city was next on her agenda, in particular to the spot where Kate Ferries had been burned as a witch. She walked along Union Street to the Castlegate, where she found the Tolbooth Museum. Climbing the narrow spiral stairs inside she saw dank cells where, four centuries ago, witches and common criminals had awaited their fates. The tolbooth dated from the early 1600s; Kate could not have been held here in 1597 but the place of her brief imprisonment would have been no less grim.

Continuing her journey, Delia walked down Justice Street to a large traffic roundabout where five streets converge. This was Kate's place of execution. When a gap in the traffic presented itself, she dashed across to the grassy island in the middle of the roundabout. The constant clockwise circulation of cars, lorries and buses around her conjured up a vision of a jeering crowd parading around a heap of brushwood on top of which the helpless Kate was tied to a stake, waiting for the fire to be lit.

In that vision, all of a sudden she *was* Kate. Entrepreneurs had set up stalls selling rotten fruit and small parcels of fish guts for people in the crowd to throw at her. She searched for any expression of sympathy on the faces of the crowd as they wheeled around her. No, they were enjoying the event. She implored her gods, 'Make it quick. Please make it quick.' A minister in a black robe stepped out of the crowd and took the trouble to assure her that the imminent flames were but a foretaste of the eternal fire that awaited her in hell. Then, as he offered a brief prayer to *his* God, an official brought a blazing torch to the pile of brushwood below her and set it alight ...

The circulating throng of spectators became cars, lorries and buses again. As she woke with a shudder from her reverie, Delia's eyes were wet with tears.

The broken tailgate lock had to be repaired. When the mechanic asked if he'd reported the incident, Cato brushed the matter aside. The last thing he needed was any contact with the police.

It was late in the afternoon when he got back to Tarland, and he was surprised to see Delia's car in the Square. It had been embarrassing to admit to Z that his prey had eluded him the day before, though he had blamed his fool's errand to the cairn-fields on faulty intelligence received from J. This time the girl wouldn't give him the slip.

Leaving his vehicle at the back of the Commercial Hotel, he bought a newspaper and sat down on one of the seats by the fiddler's monument at the end of the Square, just outside the churchyard. From that vantage point, he would be able to watch out for Delia returning to her vehicle.

Unknown to him, she was in the churchyard chatting to Ewen, not fifty feet from where Cato sat.

On her way from Aberdeen, Delia had pondered what she had been missing. Grace's two *Testaments* were probably awash with clues, but somehow she hadn't picked up on them. The funny name 'Ladle-lick' – was that supposed to tell her something?

The hill the map called Craiglich was clearly visible from the churchyard. 'What's the name of that hill?' she asked Ewen, pointing to the east.

'Ladle-lick,' he replied.

So Grace hadn't made it up.

Delia stood watching Ewen throw stones from his wheelbarrow into a trench he'd dug at the base of a headstone. 'Remember I asked you about Megan Minty?'

His mouth formed a knowing smile. 'Yes, I mind fine. In fact I think it was me who told you her name was Minty.'

'You did. You also said your daughter Lesley had her as a teacher.'

'Ye-e-es,' he replied cautiously.

'Would Megan have been especially friendly with any of her co-workers? Other than the man she ran away with, I mean? I'm really interested in her local history research, and wonder if some of her colleagues might have been involved in any way.'

'There's been a terrible turnover of teachers at the school in the last two or three years. I don't think anybody from Mrs Minty's time is still there, other than the headmaster.'

'I'd like to talk to him.'

'You won't get him this week. It's the last week of the school holidays and he won't be back from France until Sunday, I'm sure. Goes there every summer.'

'Pity,' Delia said. 'I'm flying home to Chicago on Saturday.'

Ewen announced, 'Well, that's enough work for one day. Time for a pint at the Aberdeen Arms.'

'Can I join you? My treat.' Delia wondered if she was being too forward.

Ewen was obviously delighted to have a drinking companion. 'I've a better idea,' he said. 'Help me carry these tools to the van, save me a trip, and I'll buy the beer.'

He had parked on the Coull road, out of sight of the Square. They left the churchyard by a side gate, loaded up the van, then walked over to the Aberdeen Arms bar. And Cato never saw them, nor they him.

52

FOUL AND FAIR

ON TUESDAY MORNING, Delia resolved to visit Waulkmill, Daach and Satan's Howe. At the site marked 'Waulkmill' on the Ordnance Survey map, no remains of George Crichton's mill were evident, but a single standing stone survived of the nearby circle. It was a former hiding place for the *Drogan*, yet nothing suggested that Grace might have brought it back here.

Her next stop, Daach, turned out to be two adjacent farms, named on her OS map as East and West Davoch. The next-again farm to East Davoch was Bog or Boig, home of the notorious Elspeth Forbes for whose 'witchcraft' Kate Ferries had been put to death, and, much later, of the benefactor who provided the fountain in Tarland Square. Bog was one of those homesteads in Cromar that, from its name, would not seem to promise an easy, comfortable life. Others included Windsee ('Wind's Eye'), Coldhome and, Delia's favourite, the now abandoned Scrapehard. She searched around the farm buildings of Bog as well as the two Davochs, but drew a blank at all three.

At East Davoch, the minor public road took a sharp turn to the right, but she continued straight ahead on foot. She was now on one of the six ancient routes radiating from Tarland, which crossed out of Cromar at the Lazy Well and led to Strathdon and the highlands beyond. The weather was one moment sunny and warm, the next chilly. Short rain-showers came and went without warning.

Half-hidden among tall broom, she caught sight of a black vehicle. Without looking closer, she knew it was Cato's Range Rover. Should she turn back? Or pay no attention, let him approach if he wanted to? She was still sore at being beaten to whatever lay under the D stone at Coull, and resolved to press on. He was maybe already at Satan's Howe, looking for the *Drogan*, or maybe he was sitting there in his car, waiting for her to do the hard work. Either way, this would bring matters to a head.

Making her way up the ancient drove road, she wondered how Cato could possibly have known she'd be there that morning. At Coull, he had found the D stone *after* she and Quin had. At Macbeth's cairn, he had arrived *after* they did. He could have been following them. But now on the Lazy Well road, he was already here before her. It was most unsettling.

About a mile from East Davoch, the track forded a small stream – Ellen's Burn it was called on the map. She wondered idly if it commemorated Ellen Walker of Marchnear, Keeper of Taran's wheel and half-sister of Mary, Queen of Scots. She might well have been no stranger to this place. Striking off the track there, Delia climbed through heather, bracken and coarse tussocks of grass and rushes to the top of Molly Watt's Hill. The sun was shining. From her vantage point at the summit, she saw no sign of Cato. Below her, on the other side of the hill, lay Satan's Howe.

She began her short descent. The moment she got to the hollow, the sun went behind a cloud and an intense chill settled on the land. Within a few minutes, it was raining. Gusts of wind drove rain into her face, even under her hood, soaking her hair.

So this was where Macbeth, according to Grace's history, met with the *Merch Nyr*. The 'blasted heath' of Shakespeare's play, where three witches cackled their prophecy that Macbeth would 'be king hereafter'. A line from that famous scene in *Macbeth* suddenly came into her head:

So foul and fair a day I have not seen.

The place was indeed desolate and forbidding. And on a 'foul and fair' day like this, it was easy to understand why it would be called Satan's Howe.

It was essentially featureless. Where would you hide something here, with any hope that it would be found? Before moving on, she decided to make a little mischief.

Finding a large moss-covered boulder embedded in the peat, she flattened the vegetation around it, and pulled some heather out by the roots to reveal the base of the stone. With her trowel she dug a hole in the peat where she had uprooted the heather. Then she got to her feet, walked around the rock a couple of times, and placed her foot against it as if trying to move it. Finally, she picked up her backpack, took a couple of photographs, gave a shrug and walked away.

On her way back to East Davoch, Delia was amused to see that the Range Rover was still parked among the broom bushes. Several times that evening she smiled to herself, imagining Cato fruitlessly digging around a common-or-garden boulder up there in Satan's Howe.

53

D

AROUND TEN O'CLOCK, Delia received a call. 'Hi, sweetheart.'

'Quin! Are you in Chicago?'

'I could've sent you an email, but I'm already missing the sound of your voice. Hope you don't mind me calling you so late.'

'No, it's great to hear you.' She filled him in briefly on what had transpired since he left.

'I'm at Grace's apartment,' Quin reported. 'Everything here is fine. Lupita's doing a good job. I've some information for you.'

'I'm listening.'

'First, there's a letter here for you from the Glenview police. Will I open it?'

'Of course.'

There was a rustling sound. 'It's from Sergeant Nolan. He wants you to contact him.'

'I have his number. What else?'

'I ran into Eddie the Geek in the lobby. I recognised him from the funeral, and introduced myself. He said, "I'm Eddie Vos." V-O-S. I asked him if he knew an Eddie Scherin. No, he said, but Grace had once asked him to print the name "Eddie Scherin" on the label of a CD he made for her. By the way, he made only the one CD. There were no copies.'

'That's good. But Eddie *Vos*, huh?'

'I think the "Eddie Scherin" name has to be a clue, Delia. I've had the CD in my computer bag all this time. To be honest, I thought you had it. Anyway, we never took a really good look at the label before.

'You mean the AC/DC logo on the case? I've been wondering if that was supposed to represent Agnes Cromar/ Delia Cobb.'

'Hadn't thought of that. But no, I meant the label on the CD itself. The six-spoked wheel design. Have you got a pen and paper?'

'Yes.'

'Okay, draw a circle like a clock face. Now, start at eleven o'clock, and, working counterclockwise, write the letters of "Eddie Scherin" in place of the hours. Got that? Right, now think of what you've drawn as a compass rather than a clock. You'll see there's an N for "north" at the top, an E for "east" on the right and an S for "south" at the bottom. But there's no W for "west".'

'No, there's a D where you'd expect a W.'

'Exactly. D is for *Drogan* and it's in the west. I think we can forget about the D stone at Coull Castle. Coull's on the east side of the circular vale – south-east, actually. We have to look on the *other* side of Cromar – the west side.'

'Mm ... I see what you mean. But maybe D isn't for *Drogan* but Davan, or Drummy or Dalvokie. Or Daach where I was already today.' Delia's mind was racing. 'Maybe D is for "debt, death and destruction" as visited on Cromar House. Or the D of "Tarland" that's still never pronounced here.'

'Think again about the wheel. If it represents the circular vale, the *Seely Howe*, what's at the centre?'

'The Blue Cairn on Drummy – one of the first places we looked.'

'Right, and what's due *west* of the Blue Cairn?'

She pulled out her now tattered Ordnance Survey map from her backpack. 'I'm looking.'

'See, there's an east-west grid line – the 04 line – running right through the Blue Cairn. If you follow it west, it goes precisely across the summit of Morven.'

'True, but Grace scarcely mentioned Morven, did she? There's no reason to suppose the *Drogan* was ever there.'

'You're forgetting, Delia. Kate Ferries used to climb to the top of Morven to gather a medicinal herb. *Mountain elf-shot.* Kate was a Keeper of Taran's wheel. She could have carried the *Drogan* with her on her forays for herbs.'

'I suppose. Okay, I'll put Morven on my list. But you know, D could be a reference to the River Dee. Or it could be the Roman numeral D, for five hundred.'

'Yes, but five hundred what?'

Delia was looking at the map again. 'Well, exactly five hundred metres due west of the Blue Cairn is a minor road. It seems more likely than the top of a mountain, especially for a seventy-plus-year-old lady with a heart condition.'

'You should check that out. But don't ignore Morven! Wish I was there with you.'

After he rang off, Delia called Sergeant Nolan. He was surprised to hear she was in the U.K. 'Interesting that you're there,' he said. 'I wanted to talk to you about your English friend Mr Cato Woods.'

'He's no friend of mine.'

'You said he was nice.'

'That was then, this is now.'

'It turns out he was in the U.S. at the time of Ms Rosman's death. At least we know he was in New York. We haven't traced him to Illinois yet.'

'Do you think he killed Grace?'

'If we could place him in Glenview on the day Grace died, he'd be a suspect, for sure. We have DNA here that doesn't match hers, or yours, or the cleaning girl's. If we can match it to Cato Woods, we'll have quite a case against him.'

'DNA, you said. From the apartment?'

'Actually, from the deceased herself. From skin cells, not her own, under her fingernails. She scratched someone, maybe her assailant during a struggle. Our pathologist has confirmed she died as a result of cardiac arrest, but he believes it was brought on when someone tried to suffocate her with a pillow, because the autopsy showed fibres in her trachea. We found the murder weapon, a pillow with fibres exactly matching those found in the autopsy, on the guest bed in Ms Rosman's apartment.'

54

IT HAS TO BE MORVEN

ON WEDNESDAY, DELIA PARKED in the village of Dinnet – yet another 'D', she noted to herself – and took a walk eastward along the trail that had been created on the bed of the old Deeside railway. Three quarters of a mile from Dinnet was a point where the old line had squeezed between the main road and the River Dee. To her left was the low hill of Tomachallich and to her right the bend in the river – the *cambus* – where legend said Aeth, aided by a kingfisher, found the *Drogan Taranish*.

If 'D' meant Dee, this had to be the spot. Grace's words came into her head: *'It's back in a place it's been before.'* What could be more appropriate than the scene of its first appearance?

Out of habit, she looked around for any sign of Cato; satisfied he wasn't around she scrambled down the steep riverbank to the water's edge. She checked for any kind of marker – a conspicuous stone, perhaps – but saw nothing. Her high hopes for this place were dashed; yet again she had to leave empty-handed.

Quin's idea of somewhere due west of Drummy's Blue Cairn now seemed the most rational solution to Grace's puzzle substituting D for W in the points of the compass. She drove to Tarland.

A shock awaited her at the top of Drummy. The blue-grey lichen that she vividly recalled from her visit there with Quin the previous week no longer uniformly coated the ancient stones of the cairn. Many of the rocks had been turned over, some removed altogether, leaving empty hollows.

'Cato!' she muttered. He had beaten her to it. Was he already on to 'D for W'? Had he figured out the clue before Quin did? That would explain why he was nowhere to be seen today.

Yet why was he on the Lazy Well road yesterday, if he had got his hands on the *Drogan*? She began to feel a little less pessimistic.

A small rowan tree, laden with red berries, grew out from among the stones and bracken on the west side of the cairn. The rowan was long ago believed to have magical powers, giving protection against witches. Most homes, even the tiniest of cottages, in rural areas of Scotland had a rowan near the door to keep the occupants safe from witchcraft. Could this tree be the sign she was looking for? She began lifting rocks from the cairn around the rowan. Any she couldn't move would certainly have been too heavy for Grace.

After an hour or so, it became clear that she was wasting her time. Painstakingly, she replaced the stones she had moved, saving lichen-encrusted ones till last.

She unwrapped some sandwiches and sat down on the cairn to eat, facing west towards Morven. The sky was overcast, the mountain's bulk dark and ominous. She had one more 'easy' place to search – a point five hundred metres due west of where she sat.

Biting into an apple, she set off westward. It was mostly downhill. She glanced around the minor road that crossed her path exactly five hundred metres from the Blue Cairn, but saw nothing. Another fool's errand.

Back at Craigendarroch, after a swim and a long hot shower, she checked Google for the best route up to the summit of Morven. There were several options, the easiest of which began on the public road at the top of the Birk Hill, not far from the *Gow Steen* she'd already visited. Though not the shortest route, it began at an altitude of almost four hundred metres, and was a relatively gentle climb. She dashed off an email.

Hi Quin:

Missing you. Hope preps for your interview are going well. Best of luck tomorrow.

Got interesting news from Nolan – will fill you in when we talk. Went to the cambus near Dinnet, then the Blue Cairn at Drummy. Evidently Cato's been sniffing around since we were there last week. I did some digging, to no avail. Likewise 500 m west of the cairn.

Tomorrow, it has to be Morven. I'll park at the top of the Birk Hill – remember we were up there when we checked out the blacksmith's stone?

Love, D.

Thursday August 14th dawned dull and overcast. From her Craigendarroch window, the wooded hills she was accustomed to seeing were invisible. A damp foggy chill hung in the air. Today she dressed in layers, not knowing quite what to expect on Morven, 872 metres in height – not far short of three thousand feet.

Driving up the Birk Hill, low cloud closed in on her. At the top, she was just able to discern the gates at the west entrance to Tillypronie House. She could pull off the road there. Several tracks led into forest; she selected one that surmounted a small ridge and descended to a grassy area hidden by trees from the road. In the fog she could dimly make out rippling water with a raft of water lilies – the Witchock Loch. *Witchock*, she later learned, is a Scots word for a sand martin or bank swallow, though some writers have suggested an association with witchcraft.

Putting on her waterproof jacket, she hoisted her backpack over her shoulders. She had scarcely taken ten paces before deciding to cut her losses and return when the weather was better.

Just then she made out the headlights of an approaching vehicle. Her first thought was: Cato. But no, it was a small green Land Rover that stopped beside her. A pair of gundogs snuffled at the window behind the driver. A gamekeeper, she realised.

'Aye aye, lassie,' he said. 'Faar are ye aff till this nesty day?'

'I had planned to go up Morven,' she said, 'but I've changed my mind. I'll come back when this lot clears.' As she spoke, it hit her that tomorrow, Friday, would be her last full day before she was due to return to the States. Time was running out.

'Better ging noo, quine. Let me tell ye why. The first fine day, there'll be guns on the hill. Grouse season opened twa days syne. It widna be safe for ye.'

He sensed her disappointment. 'Theday,' he said with an air of worldly wisdom, 'if I let shooters up yonder, it widna be safe for onybody. In that fog, they'd be shootin each ither, the beaters, the loaders, the dogs. Na, if ye're determined to climm Morven, aff ye go.'

'I'm kinda scared I'll lose my way. I've GPS on my phone but still, if I can't see where I'm going ...'

'Lassie, ye winna need the GPS. It's simple. Jist tak yon gate at the ither side o' the road, follow the track and keep climmin. When ye canna climm ony farrer, ye're at the tap.'

'But coming down ...'

'Dinna worry aboot that. By then the cloud'll be aff the hill. Ye'll see fine then.'

'So the forecast's good?'

'I've trampit these hills for sixty years, man an boy. I dinna need a forecast. I've seen enough August mornins like this to ken that by one o'clock it'll be a fine sunny day.'

He rolled up his window and drove off.

Delia followed his advice. She climbed through the fog, seeing nothing but grass, heather and stones a few feet in front of her and hearing only the occasional go-back-back-back call of a grouse. By midday, she stood on a high place where the ground sloped away from her in all directions. She thought she had reached the top, but saw no marker of any kind. Checking her GPS she found she was still a few hundred metres short of the true summit.

She began walking westward, gently downhill. Soon, the ground levelled out and began ascending again. Within a few minutes, what looked like an enormous cairn loomed out of the mist. But in three paces, she found herself there, and it was actually rather small. Close by was a white pillar once used as a surveying station. Years of wind erosion on this exposed summit had gouged holes under the concrete.

Cold moisture-laden air was blowing in from the west. Feeling hungry, she sat down in the lee of the cairn and ate lunch, after which she got to her feet and turned her face cautiously into the wind. The fog was clearing and she was rewarded with a stunning view of distant mountains, some with tiny snow patches. Ben Avon, Beinn a Bhuird and the Cairngorms, with four of Britain's five highest mountains, all gleaming in sunshine. Fifteen minutes later, the last of the clouds over Morven cleared and she felt the warmth of the sun on her face. To the east, the *Seely Howe* lay below her like a map. The sudden change in the weather was just as the gamekeeper had predicted.

Now she had work to do. Carefully she inspected the cairn and the holes under the surveyors' pillar. Nothing. Another futile journey – except that she wouldn't have missed that view for the world.

The ground was scattered with small stones, around which a few hardy plants eked out a living from the shallow peaty soil. Large areas were carpeted with alpine lady's mantle, the *mountain elf-shot* that Kate Ferries had come all the way up here to gather for its medicinal properties. From her backpack Delia took out her trowel and a plastic bag, and dug up a single plant to take back for a closer look.

Retracing her steps to her car on the Birk Hill, she reckoned that by now she'd looked in all the logical places. It was inconceivable that Grace would have sent her on such a laborious and expensive wild goose chase. What was she missing? Would she figure it out before Cato?

Speak of the devil, she thought, catching sight of his car beside hers. He stood close by, on the shore of the Witchock Loch throwing stones into the water.

He swaggered over to greet her, smoking a cigar.

'Hello, Cato,' she said boldly. 'What brings you here?'

'I could ask you the same question, Delia, but then we'd both be playing silly buggers, wouldn't we? Excuse the cigar, by the way. The midges up here are vicious and this is the best way to keep them at bay.'

'Maybe I should take up smoking to see if that would keep *you* at bay. Wouldn't be so bad if you were more discreet, or if you came up with some ideas of your own about finding the *Drogan Taranish*.'

'Is that what it's called? Look, let's not beat about the bush. That funny little ball is a tektite – glass formed in a meteorite impact ...'

'I know what a tektite is.'

'Okay, but what you may not know is that this one's worth a lot of money. I've a customer who's ready to pay half a million U.S. dollars for it. Look, Delia, why don't we go halves? If you have it or find it, I'll give you two hundred and fifty thousand dollars for it. Or just tell me where it is. I'll retrieve it, same deal.'

'Cato, Grace was your mother's cousin. She was part of your family. Doesn't it matter to you what *she* would have wanted?'

'You're right. *My* family, not yours. But I know she had a soft spot for you. What I'm offering you is a win-win. Grace would have been happy to know we both benefit from finding the drogue thingy.'

'The *Drogan Taranish*,' Delia corrected him. 'Taran's wheel. You have no idea of its significance, do you?'

'Significance all comes down to price in the end. And that price is half a million. Two hundred and fifty K in your pocket, same in mine. Isn't that significant enough for you?'

Delia opened the rear door of her car and threw in her backpack. 'I'm leaving,' she said.

After taking a final draw, he crushed the butt of his cigar between thumb and forefinger and threw it on the wet turf. She made to get into the driver's seat, only to be grabbed roughly by the wrist. He opened the rear door and seized her backpack.

'You won't find it in there,' she said, rubbing her arm where he'd wrenched it.

'Where is it then?' He began rifling through the backpack and brought out the little bag with the plant she'd collected on the summit. 'What the hell's this?'

'It's alpine lady's mantle. The herb that Kate Ferries climbed to the top of Morven to find.'

'Kate *who*? – never mind.' He tipped the remaining contents on the ground. Seeing no glass ball, he thrust the empty backpack at Delia, who quickly gathered up her belongings and threw them on to the back seat.

Through the encounter, she had grown steadily more indignant but managed to keep outwardly calm. Here she was in a remote place with a man she was certain was a murderer, nobody else around to come to her help. She was determined not to show any emotion, any sign he might interpret as weakness. There was plenty she could say, but the important thing was to get away. Without another word, she dived into the driver's seat and started up the engine.

'You'll regret this, my lady!' Cato shouted, as she executed a nifty U-turn, rejoined the main road and set off down the Birk Hill. In her rear-view mirror she saw him following. About half a mile down the hill, the road forked. She held right towards Ballater. Cato swung left for Tarland.

Shaking with a mixture of anger and relief, she pulled over. As she calmed down, a thought came to her and she turned around to drive back to the Witchock Loch. From her backpack she produced a clean Ziploc bag saved from airport security. Rolling it back over her hand, she picked up the butt of Cato's

271

cigar, being careful not to let her fingers contact it. Triumphantly she fastened the bag.

She had a specimen of his DNA for Sergeant Nolan.

55

HE KNOWS *EVERYTHING*

BY THE TIME she got back to Craigendarroch, Delia was exhausted. She flopped down on the bed and fell asleep. A car horn outside woke her with a start about forty minutes later. After a shower, a towel around her body and another on her head, she sat down and absent-mindedly picked up her *Antiquities of Cromar* book, but dozed off again.

What woke her the second time she didn't know. But she was suddenly wide awake, and sat bolt upright, filled with a terrible realisation.

It was Quin!

'He knows *everything*,' she said to herself. 'Anything we learn, he passes on to Cato. They're in cahoots! My god, I've been so stupid! How could I have trusted him, knowing so little about him? Jeez, I was better off with Erik the Jerk than this!'

The more she thought about it, the more it all seemed to fit. Just yesterday, she'd emailed Quin, not only telling him she was going to Morven today, but revealing which route she would take. And who should be there, waiting for her to come down off the mountain, but Cato.

What to do now? Should she say nothing to Quin for the moment, so as not to arouse his suspicion? Or should she confront him at the first opportunity?

It was late in the evening when he called. 'That's the interview over,' he told her. 'Won't know the outcome for a couple of months, probably, but it seemed to go okay.'

She said nothing.

'Delia, are you there? I can't hear you.'

'I'm here. Glad the interview went well.'

'Is something wrong? You're very quiet. Did I waken you?'

'No, and no.'

'Did you go to Morven today? Find anything?'

Her icy façade cracked. 'Why would I tell you? Whatever I say, you're just going to pass it right along to Cato, aren't you?' She heard protest and remonstration on the other end, but ignored it. 'Why I didn't see it before, I don't know. You told him about Coull Castle, the D stone. You told him about Macbeth's cairn. You told him about the Blue Cairn on Drummy, which he promptly vandalised. Seems you told him exactly where to find me on the Birk Hill today. I had quite an interesting exchange with Cato. No doubt you already know that.'

'Delia, I ...'

'You're the only other person besides me who knows Grace's *Testaments*. How else could Cato know about all these places? How much has he offered to pay you, Quin? He'll split the proceeds of the *Drogan* with you fifty-fifty, is that it? He offered *me* that deal today. But the *Drogan* means something to me. It's nothing to you, is it? He murdered her, Quin. He murdered Grace trying to get his hands on the *Drogan*. The police are sure of it. I suppose it's okay with you if he kills *me* next.'

'Baby, believe me, I've no ...'

'Don't baby me!' She hung up on him.

After a restless night, she was in no humour to speak to him again. Finally she could no longer ignore the ringing of her phone, though it was two in the morning in Chicago. 'What do you want now?' she snarled.

'Look, Delia,' he said, 'you made a lot of accusations last night, and never gave me the chance to ...'

'Apologise? Explain?'

'No, just to tell you you're wrong. You couldn't *be* more wrong. Sure, Cato has inside information and I've no idea where he's getting it. But it's not from me. I really wanted to know if you're okay. Did he hurt or threaten you in any way, on the Birk Hill yesterday?'

Something in his tone caused a slight softening in her heart. 'He threatened me, yes. Got physically rough, but he didn't hurt me. Don't worry, I got the better of him, though he doesn't know it yet. But thank you for asking.'

Refusing to let her polite 'thank you' block any further discussion, he continued, 'I think Cato might have a copy of Grace's CD. Eddie Vos made only one, but she could easily have made a copy herself.'

'In which case, all Cato needs is the password, *Alcyone*, which you could have given him.'

'Don't you remember, Delia? *Alcyone* only opens the *Second Testament*. He can't even get to that without going through the *First Testament*. And only you know the password for that.'

It was true. She hadn't – at least knowingly – shared her secret *'Love, and be silent'* password with Quin. But he could have looked over her shoulder when she entered it.

He hadn't finished. 'And consider this: Praisewell – it only cropped up in our conversation with Ewen in the churchyard. That was Wednesday the 6th. On the 7th, the owner himself told us about the English guy who'd been snooping around two days previously, the 5th. There's no way I could have tipped off anyone before I'd even heard of the place.'

'Hmm. We don't actually know that person at Praisewell had any connection with Cato.'

Quin allowed himself a short laugh. 'You're not giving in easily, are you?'

'I'd love to know it's not you. But it just makes no sense otherwise.'

'Here's something that makes no sense. I was the one who came up with the whole idea about D replacing W on the compass. The idea that led to you going to the top of Morven. If

I was in league with Cato, wouldn't I just have let *him* in on the secret, and kept you in the dark?'

She was starting to feel better. Quin was putting up a pretty solid defence. It seemed he wasn't the 'mole' after all. Then she started to feel worse, for having mistrusted him. What if her awful accusations had turned him against her? All of a sudden, she couldn't bear the thought of that.

She had no answer to his questions. He broke the silence. 'Delia, I love you, and I would never do anything to hurt you. I'm as keen as you are to keep the *Drogan* out of Cato's hands, and wouldn't help him get it, not for a million dollars.'

'Two million, then?'

'Not for a billion. Is that enough?'

'Cato offered me a quarter million.'

'And you didn't accept. I guess that's when he threatened you?'

'Pretty much, yes. And he grabbed my backpack, to see if I'd found the *Drogan* on Morven. Of course I hadn't.'

'Maybe just as well.'

'God, I was so nasty with you last night. I wasn't thinking straight. Will you forgive me?'

'I told you. I love you. There's nothing to forgive.' There it was. Quin had uttered the four-letter word twice now.

'I love you too, Quin. And I'll be back in the States on Saturday. Will you still be in Chicago?'

'Yes, I wanted to be here when you get home. I called the Autumn Leaves and Grampa's okay, but I'll head over there next week and see him.'

After the call, she found herself repeating something he had said. Strangely, it wasn't the L-word. It was 'when you get home'. Chicago hadn't been home to Delia for a long time, yet she began to picture herself living in Grace's apartment there. And Quin was in that picture too.

56
THE TEAROOM

DESPITE THE DRAMATIC IMPROVEMENT in the weather that Delia had experienced on Morven, by Friday morning heavy rain was again sweeping the area. It was her last full day in Scotland, her quest for Taran's wheel unsuccessful. As the downpour lashed against Craigendarroch's windows, she gave up the idea of any last-minute search.

She would re-read Grace's writings, hoping to discern some pattern, some encrypted message that had eluded her up to now. A pity she didn't have the original CD to study the label – Quin had it in Chicago. From memory, she sketched on her computer screen a simplified version of Taran's wheel with the twelve letters of *'Eddie Scherin'* arranged around it, highlighting the letters at north, south, east and west

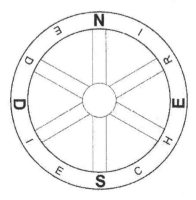

For a while she studied it, willing some new meaning to emerge. There was no denying Quin's conclusion that there had

to be some significance to the letter D taking the place of W on the 'west' side of the wheel. Unable to store the drawing in the cloud, she saved it on her memory stick under the title *'D in the west'*, together with the two *Testaments*.

Around noon, she headed into Ballater and found a tearoom. If she had noticed Cato following, she wouldn't have cared. As it was, he had spent the entire morning sitting in the Craigendarroch car-park watching and waiting; now he faced another tedious couple of hours just along the street from where she sat.

Neither he nor Delia had any reason to pay attention to a silver BMW that settled itself neatly into a parking space directly across the street from the tearoom. After ten minutes or so, the driver got out, put up an umbrella and crossed the street. Of medium height and build, he was unremarkable in appearance except for a bullet-shaped head with a thick covering of closely-cropped fair hair.

Delia concentrated on her computer screen, at a table right by a door leading to the toilets. She looked up briefly as Bullethead entered. He folded his umbrella, sat down by the window, and placed his order.

Half an hour later, there was no let-up in the weather. Worried that she might be overstaying her welcome, Delia ordered more tea and a scone. Bullethead was still there; evidently he too was just passing time waiting for the rain to go off. He avoided eye contact when she looked in his direction.

As the waitress set down Delia's fresh pot of tea, he stood up and headed for the toilet. Just as some other customers had done, he bumped against her table as he passed, and murmured an apology. Shortly after, he emerged, collected his umbrella, settled his bill and left.

Delia sat on for another hour or so. Before turning off her computer, she reached for her memory stick. But where was it? She clearly remembered laying it on the table beside her. Frantically she hunted in her bag and bent down to check the floor, but it was nowhere to be found. Had Bullethead lifted it when he passed, while she was distracted by the waitress?

But who on earth was he, and why would he steal her memory stick? Could he be the mysterious Scandinavian-looking stranger with the silver car who had called at Praisewell? An accomplice of Cato's, for sure. Even if he hadn't previously been in possession of a copy of Grace's writings, he was now. She consoled herself with the thought that the passwords for the two *Testaments* were still secure – or so she believed. But he would have the drawing she'd made earlier in the day, oh-so-helpfully titled *'D in the west'*, which she hadn't thought to password-protect.

A complex mixture of emotions flooded over her as she packed her bags that evening. Anger at her own carelessness in losing the memory stick. Disappointment at her failure to find Taran's wheel, and at leaving some avenues unexplored; in particular she wished she could have met Megan Minty's schoolmaster. Frustration at her inability to solve Grace's last – and greatest – puzzle. Satisfaction at having secured a DNA sample from Cato, which might prove him guilty of Grace's murder. And happiness that in a day's time she would be reunited with Quin.

57
EDDIE THE GEEK

QUIN WAS THERE to meet her on Saturday afternoon at Chicago O'Hare's international terminal. It was good to see him again. When they arrived at Grace's apartment, Delia was impressed that he'd bought in groceries and even had a vase of fresh flowers on the kitchen table.

He would be returning to Ithaca on Monday to take up a temporary teaching fellowship at Cornell, in the department where he'd recently completed his PhD studies. The money wasn't great but it would keep the wolf from the door. And he'd be able to visit his grandfather once a week, as before.

Monday came and Quin went. Delia – she who 'always had a plan' – had no idea what she would do next with her life. There were a couple of immediate matters to attend to. First, she had to deliver Cato's DNA specimen to Sergeant Nolan. Next, she needed to see Grace's lawyer, since her credit card bills had mounted alarmingly in the last month. She also wanted to talk to Eddie the Geek.

Nolan was pleased to receive Cato's cigar butt, but cautioned her that even if a match were found to the DNA from under Grace's fingernails, it mightn't stand up as evidence in court. There would be questions of who collected the sample, under what conditions, with what documentation, yada, yada, yada. But at least it would confirm the primary focus of the murder investigation, and it might be sufficient to begin extradition proceedings from the United Kingdom.

Howard Levine sucked some air through his teeth when Delia first requested an advance. It would be 'irregular', he told her. However, he eventually agreed she was entitled to expenses while trying to retrieve and secure one of Grace's most treasured personal possessions, and helping the Glenview police in their investigation of Grace's death. He wrote a cheque large enough to clear her debts and promised a monthly stipend until the estate was fully wound up.

She called on Eddie the Geek, who repeated what he had told Quin. Grace had asked him to put the letters of 'Eddie Scherin' − not his actual name, Eddie Vos − around the circumference of the wheel design on the CD label. She had been very particular as to how the letters were to be arranged: counterclockwise, beginning at 11 o'clock and finishing at the top.

Not the most accomplished of hosts, Eddie was clearly unused to receiving a pretty girl as an after-dinner guest. Rather than bring her into his living room, he had shown her into his 'office', a smallish bedroom filled with electronics but with only one chair. Delia had to suggest bringing in a stool from the kitchen so that they could both sit down. Flustered and deeply apologetic, Eddie overcompensated by offering drinks, snacks, an extra cushion, a coat-hanger for her jacket, ... She eventually got him settled down by agreeing to take a Coca-Cola − 'No, thank you, never mind a glass, never mind ice, I'll just drink from the can if that's okay.'

Coming to the point of her visit, she said, 'Something's been bothering me, Eddie. Is there any way somebody could be hacking into my computer, reading my emails, snooping on my internet searches, that kind of thing?'

'Unlikely if your internet security is up to date. You *do* have internet security, don't you?'

'I do, and I have the green check-mark that supposedly means my system is secure. Would you mind taking a look at my machine? I have it here with me.'

Nothing could have pleased him more. Though it was certainly interesting to have the company of such a nice-looking young lady – she *smelled* nice, too – it didn't compare with the delights of examining her computer.

'What makes you think you've been hacked, er ... Delia? Can I call you Delia?'

She saw him blush, and smiled. 'Of course you can. Well, I was in Scotland for two weeks, various places there, and someone I know kept turning up. It was as if he always knew where I would be going next. I could never figure out how he did that. It occurred to me he must have bugged my computer. I often did Google searches on places I would visit that day or the next. Or I would send an email to Quin telling him where I was going.'

'You think this creep is stalking you?'

'I'm not sure he was stalking me, exactly. But could he be spying on me through my computer?'

'Let me check a few things.' He tapped into some of the deeper recesses of her tablet, bringing up information on the screen that made no sense to her, until eventually he announced, 'I can't see anything here that would give him access. No worms, no spyware. You've got good internet security. If you'd gotten infected, you'd know about it.'

'Well, there must be another explanation.'

'You said you know this man who's been stalking – I mean following – you?'

'Yes, I do know him, but only slightly. He sent me an email once, with some photos of Grace.'

'Photos? Are they still on here?'

'Yes, I suppose so. I haven't looked at them for a while. They'll be in the album folder.'

In two seconds he was there. 'Are these the ones he sent you?'

'Yes.'

'Interesting.' He toggled back and forward from one of the photos – the one with Grace and her daughter Selena as a baby – to a window filled with numbers. He was silent for a long time.

Eventually, Delia asked, 'What's interesting, Eddie?'

'This photo should be no more than three to four hundred kilobytes. See, when I zoom in it's quite grainy. Not a lot of pixels. But it's taking up over five megabytes of storage space. There's something hidden in it, I just can't see what. When I do a security scan of the photo, it comes up clean.'

'If I delete it, I should be okay, though?'

'Not necessarily. I think it contained a Trojan Rat. If you download one of these, it's gonna reproduce itself all through your files.' He took his eyes off the screen long enough to notice her puzzled expression. 'R-A-T – remote access tool. It records everything you do on-screen and transmits it across the web. Rats are quite common. But I can't understand why your security software wouldn't have found and destroyed this one.'

'So what can I do about it?'

Eddie shrugged. 'Scrub your machine. Clean everything off it – apps, programs, docs, the lot – then rebuild it from scratch. You'll lose all your stored files, unless you backed them up somewhere before you got the Rat.'

'Can you do that for me? I'll pay you for your time, of course.'

'No, it's my hobby. Give me a couple of days and I'll get it back to you. Maybe you'd like prints of the photos before I wipe everything?'

Back in her apartment (Delia was already thinking of the place as her own) she had a horrible realisation. Many times she had accessed Grace's *Testaments* when her computer was connected to the web. Documents, passwords, lists and diagrams: Cato now had them all. She could only hope he would be no smarter than she was in decoding whatever message they held about the location of the *Drogan*.

Maybe it would be better to let him think she was still unaware of the Rat. She might even be able to use it against him. Meanwhile, she could use Grace's old desktop computer for internet access and emailing. She would get Eddie to hold off for the moment.

When he arrived at her door a couple of days later, he told her, 'I've been reading some blogs. There were rumours, back in the Bush-Cheney years after nine-eleven, of a secret information-gathering programme. Some said it was the CIA, others the NSA. The idea was to eavesdrop on suspected terrorist cells by placing a Trojan Rat in their computer systems. Supposedly, security software companies agreed to leave the Rat undetectable, in the national interest. As a conspiracy theory, that one's a little rich, even for me.' He gave a snorting laugh. 'Still, maybe that's what you have. The Bush-Cheney Rat.'

'Thank you for passing that on,' Delia said. 'I owe you one. Next time Quin's here, we'll treat you to dinner. Maybe here, maybe we'll go out somewhere.'

Eddie's limited social graces deserted him again as he said, 'Maybe.'

No sooner had he left than her phone rang. 'Ms Cobb, this is Sergeant Nolan, Glenview police. About the DNA on the cigar butt. It's a perfect match for the DNA recovered from the deceased. We have our man. Mr Carl Thomas Woods. Well, we don't exactly *have* him. But we know who he is. We'll just have to figure out how we get him over here.'

'It *had* to be him. Can he be extradited on this evidence?'

'The state's attorney's office says it will be difficult. There's a political dimension to this. Relationships between the U.S. and U.K. governments aren't quite as cordial as they used to be.'

'So are we out of luck?'

'As long as Mr Woods keeps his nose clean at home, probably yes, I'm afraid. But if he gets into any kind of trouble with the British police, we might be in with a shot.'

'What kind of trouble? A traffic ticket?'

'No, it would need to be something a little more serious than that. Anyway, Ms Cobb, I'll keep you posted. Let me know if you're going back to the U.K. any time soon.'

She had a strange feeling she *would* be returning, sooner rather than later.

58
MISINFORMATION

A T THE BEGINNING of September, Delia went to Ithaca in upstate New York to spend a few days with Quin. His tiny apartment had only just room for two in the kitchen, on the sofa, in the bed if they snuggled up close. On Friday, they drove together through Vermont to Haverhill, where they fixed up a bedroom and bathroom in his grandfather's house that they could share for the weekend.

At the Autumn Leaves retirement home, Delia noticed quite a decline in Arthur Johnson's condition since she had last seen him. With never a flash of recognition for her, he seemed to know Quin only intermittently.

On Sunday evening, as they were driving back to Ithaca, she suddenly announced, 'I'm going to Scotland again. I'll book a flight and rental car on your computer, if that's okay, to avoid alerting Cato and Bullethead.'

'And a room at Craigendarroch?'

'No, I thought I'd rent a cottage near Tarland for a week or two. I've seen a few advertised. By this time of year it shouldn't be too expensive. It'll be more difficult for Cato to find me.'

Quin looked upset.

'Don't pout, sweetheart,' she said. 'I know you won't be able to go at that time, and that you'd like to be there with me. I'd like that too. But one will be less conspicuous than two. I hope to be completely under the radar.'

By ten o'clock on Monday morning she'd reserved a flight to Aberdeen via London Heathrow departing on September 22nd, with open return, and a rental car at Aberdeen. She'd found a cottage by Loch Davan, the key to be collected from the owner at Ordie, a mile or so from the cottage.

On her own computer, she created some misinformation for Cato's benefit. She did several searches for events in Chicago during the weeks of September 22nd and 29th, and emailed Quin:

> *Looking forward so much to seeing you here at the end of the month. I've been checking what's on in Chicago, and there are some good shows coming up. Fancy a rock concert, or would you prefer something more jazzy/ bluesy? Maybe we could do both.*
>
> *Incidentally, there's to be a Seurat exhibition at the Art Institute – I've seen* Sunday at La Grande Jatte *there a dozen times but it'd be nice to see it alongside some of his less famous works.*
>
> *Hope you're having a good day. Miss you! D.*

The email was immediately picked up by Bayliss in Topeka. The Operation Curveball meetings in fast-food restaurants had become less frequent of late, but he sent a text message to Thackeray informing him that late September and early October would likely be dead periods. He in turn called Cato Woods.

'Where are you?' he asked when Cato picked up the phone.

'That you, Z? I'm back in London.'

'Those two *Testaments* I sent you. Did you find anything in the places they mention?'

'No luck so far. But don't worry, I'll find the tektite. Sooner or later, Delia Cobb will be back with some new ideas and I'll stay on her tail. How the hell did you get hold of those documents anyway?'

'We have ways.'

'Ways like you have of breaking into my car?'

Thackeray ignored that remark. 'Look, the Pastor's getting impatient. If you don't find the glass ball in the next month or so, he'll want to call off the deal altogether. If he figures it's lost, he'll lose interest. It's not so much that he wants the goddam thing, he just doesn't want anyone else to have it.'

Cato couldn't afford to let the deal slip away. He'd backed off from his original price of fourteen million, but ten million pounds would still set him up for life. He was keen to close down DaSilva Rare Treasures before the business got him into hot water. Z and J had already hinted that they knew about the blood diamonds, the poached ivory and rhino horn, the contraband fossils. If they knew, how much did the authorities know? He *had* to acquire the tektite and wring ten million pounds out of that damn Pastor for it. He might even settle for ten million dollars.

'I'm going to get it, Z, mark my words. The girl isn't going to rest until she solves the stupid puzzle of the two documents. And the moment she does, I'll be there to snatch the prize out from under her nose.'

'Well, you can forget the two weeks starting September 22nd. She's going to be staying home in Chicago entertaining her boyfriend.'

'And after that?'

'Soon as we learn anything, we'll let you know.'

Thackeray rang off, then placed a call to the Engineer.

59
TIME CAPSULE

I N THE EARLY EVENING TWILIGHT on September 23rd, Delia arrived at Ordie to pick up the key for the cottage that would be her home for the next couple of weeks. The owner, a retired farmer in his seventies, was obviously happy to have the place occupied so late in the season. Pointing to a thin crescent moon gracing the sky above Culblean, he smiled and said, 'Turn your money for luck. It's good to start something under a new moon.'

'So I've picked a good time for my short stay at Loch Davan?'

With a twinkle in his eye he declared, 'It's *aye* a good time to come to Davan. But I hope you're prepared for rain. See the way the moon's lying?' He then recited a piece of weather lore in Scots that Delia understood just well enough to get the gist.

> *The bonny meen*
> *Lies on her back,*
> *So mend yer sheen*
> *An sort yer thack.*

The cottage was clean and comfortable, with a slightly temperamental propane-fuelled boiler that supplied sufficient heat and hot water for her needs. To her surprise, she found she even had wireless internet connection. She stocked the refrigerator with groceries she'd bought in Aboyne and made herself dinner.

On the Muir of Dinnet, the bloom was off the heather and the birches had turned from green to yellow. But, contrary to her landlord's forecast, the weather stayed dry, with just a hint of frost in the morning leading to a sunny autumn day.

Her main priority on the 24th was to make contact with the headmaster at Tarland. Arriving just at the end of the school day, she found him in his study. Once she had introduced herself and told him she was interested in the history of Cromar, he was very cordial. No, he had no pressing engagements and would be glad to talk to her for a few minutes.

He raised the subject of Megan before Delia did. 'I had a teacher here a few years ago who was writing a book on the history of Cromar,' he told her. 'Megan Minty was her name.'

'Yes, I've heard of Mrs Minty. In fact, that's one reason I came to see you. I know she vanished mysteriously a few years ago, but I'm wondering if, by any chance, you had copies of her notes or manuscript.'

'Sadly, no. She did give me one chapter to proofread. It was well written, but took a most unconventional approach. She developed a theory that early Pictish society was female-dominated, at least in the spheres of religion and politics. Megan, you have to understand, was something of a feminist. Nothing wrong with that, of course. But I felt that to some extent she let her political views cloud her objectivity as a historian.'

'How so?'

The schoolmaster pressed his hands together on his desk. There was a short pause before he responded. 'She observed that Cromar is spectacularly rich in antiquities of the pre-Christian, pre-Gaelic period, and drew the conclusion that this was a politically and culturally important centre in those times. It was her contention that the ancient capital of Pictland was located right here. Well, I think the evidence is thin, but it's an interesting theory. Where she went a little off the rails, in my view, was in insisting that real power lay not with the king but with the priesthood, which was exclusively female. Cromar, she believed, was a sacred place, where the priesthood passed on their secret knowledge, their rituals, their creed, from one generation to the next.'

What Delia was hearing of Megan's beliefs was precisely in accordance with Grace's account. They had sung from the same song-sheet. Had Grace picked up the story from Megan, she wondered, or was it the other way around?

The schoolmaster kept talking. 'There was, according to Megan, a high priestess who held the real reins of power. She counselled the king in almost all matters; in Megan's words, the high priestess made the balls and the king fired them. She had a ceremonial name, which I forget.'

'Was it Merefrith?'

'That's it, yes! Have you read some of Megan's work?'

'No, that's what I'm here looking for. But I knew someone who may have been a source for some of Megan's ideas. Her name was Grace Rosman.'

The schoolmaster's eyebrows went up. 'Grace Rosman? I remember her. American like you, only much older, of course. Yes, she was here, must have been four or five years ago. You said "knew", not "know" – is she okay?'

'I'm sad to say she died earlier this year.'

'Sorry to hear that. She was a really nice lady. Seemed to love Tarland.'

Upon returning to the subject of Megan's book, the schoolmaster furrowed his brow. 'She wrote that Pictish society was what would nowadays be called "liberated", with no strong taboos about sex outside marriage. Megan's Picts had no concept of adultery or illegitimacy. Children were raised communally. It was because of the fluidity of family relationships, she wrote, that matrilineal succession evolved. And that in turn put a lot of influence in the hands of the female priesthood, especially the high priestess.'

'Did Megan mention any symbols of power?'

'Like what? Sceptre and crown?'

'Could be. Or religious talismans, jewellery, anything like that?'

'Not that I recall.'

'What about a glass ball?'

He looked blank. Delia answered her own question. 'I guess not. Anyway, back to Grace Rosman. I wonder what she got up to when she was here. Do you recall?'

'I met her just a couple of times. Megan had her come into the school at least once to talk to her class. She was a real hit with the kids. At the time they were working on a project to prepare a time capsule. The idea was to place it in the foundation of the hall, which was having some work done at the time.'

'The village hall, in the Square?'

'Yes, the MacRobert Memorial Hall.'

Delia's heart missed a beat. Could Grace, alone or in collusion with Megan, have slipped the *Drogan Taranish* into the time capsule?

'Unfortunately,' he continued, 'there was a mix-up. The foundation was sealed before the time capsule was ready. It was never put in place. And Megan's strange disappearance happened not long after that. So the project remained unfinished.'

'What happened to the time capsule?'

He got up and walked to a cabinet behind where Delia was sitting. 'It's right here, in this drawer.' He pulled a large biscuit tin out of the drawer. It had a picture of Balmoral Castle on the lid, and a blue ribbon was tied around it.

'May I open it?'

The schoolmaster nodded. Delia undid the ribbon. Inside was a collection of small objects. A mobile phone. A Barbie doll. A few ears of barley. A series of postcards with views of Cromar. A CD of fiddle music. A pressed flower of some kind. A copy of the weekly *Deeside Piper*. A label from a jar of local heather honey. But no Taran's wheel.

60

THE HUB OF TARAN'S WHEEL

OVER THE NEXT FEW DAYS, Delia revisited some of the places mentioned in Grace's *First* and *Second Testaments*, all the while keeping up an online pretence that she was with Quin in Chicago. Occasionally she would check the CTA for times of trains, the Art Institute for opening times, local movie listings and the like. She sent a couple of emails to friends from the University of Colorado asking what they were up to, and reported she was in Chicago with her new boyfriend. All at times consistent with living in the central time zone of North America.

On Monday September 29th, she went to Alastrean House, now a residential home. Here Agnes Cromar's 'crystal ball' had supposedly yielded its 'debt, death and destruction' prophecy. Next she walked to the nearby Oldtown of Kincraigie, Margaret Baird's onetime home, and explored its old walled garden. Initially puzzled by the common suffix '-town' or '-ton' in farm names, she had learned this didn't signify that there was ever a town here but merely a collection of farm buildings (*fermtoun* in Scots) that might include a few small cottages.

She climbed to the cairn-fields on Craiglich and Craig Dhu but, as she expected, found them too overgrown with trees to permit any meaningful search.

Several times she came back to Agnes's headstone in the old churchyard in Tarland, but even there she found no inspiration. Now, around five o'clock that Monday, she sat on a stone facing

Agnes's and stared at the eroded inscription, willing it to speak to her.

A voice spoke. She jumped with fright.

'*I didna mean to gie ye a fleg,*' Ewen said.

'Sorry,' Delia said. 'I was lost in my thoughts there. It's nice to see you again, Ewen. You did give me a bit of a – what did you call it? – a *fleg.*'

He laughed. 'I'm not all that surprised to see you here again. I was sure you'd be back. Isn't Quin with you?'

'Not this time. He's back to work in the States. Ewen, did you ever meet an American lady by the name of Grace Rosman?'

'That I did, about four years ago. She spent a couple of weeks here. As soon as I saw you here in the kirkyard for the first time – what was that, six weeks ago? – something about you reminded me of her. She spent a lot of time at Agnes Cromar's stone, just like you. Seems to me you've been searching for the same thing she was. Am I right?'

'What makes you think that?'

'You asked me about Megan Minty. I saw your car at Tomnaverie one day, and another day at Coull kirkyard. It all added up. Well, it's none of my business, of course, but did you find what you came for?'

Unwilling to seem evasive, Delia nonetheless could not risk giving away too much. 'Let's just say my search is over. I'm heading back to Chicago at the end of this week.'

'Are you up for a drink at the Aberdeen Arms? I'll be there in about ten minutes.'

'Great. See you there.' She resumed her contemplation of Agnes's stone. There was at least one loose end she hadn't tied up. Somewhere in the *Seely Howe*, was there still a remnant of the *Merch Nyr*?

Grace had said she'd been unable to find any trace of the ancient female priesthood. Not for the first time, Delia wondered whether Myrtle, and perhaps some of the other women of the Grove of the Mayflower, might be keeping the

Merch Nyr flame alive in the guise of their neopagan cult. Myrtle certainly knew about the *Drogan Taranish*, although she'd dismissed it as 'just a tale'. Delia wished she had thought to ask for her phone number.

Once they were seated at the bar, she asked Ewen, 'Do you happen to know a lady by the name of Myrtle? I met her at Tomnaverie one day.'

'Well, let me think,' Ewen said, turning his pint of beer on its mat and gazing into the distance. 'There's a couple of Myrtles in the village. One would be about sixty, the other maybe seventy.'

'No, this one's younger than that. She's a nurse. Lives with someone called Joyce. They're in a civil partnership.'

'Doesn't ring a bell.'

'They live "in the forest". Where would that be?'

'When folk round here talk about "the forest", it's usually the Forest of Birse. Go to Aboyne and over the Corsedarder hill. That'll take you there.'

The conversation flowed until nearly seven o'clock, when Ewen stepped back from the bar and announced he'd better be heading home.

It was a beautiful calm evening. The sun had just gone down and the sky over Morven was ablaze in reds and pinks. Climbing the few steps to the raised embankment at the east end of the Square, Delia had a superb view of the display of colours over the western horizon. Low in the south hung a half-moon, appearing steadily brighter against the darkening sky. As if making a photographic record in her mind, she took in every detail of the Square. It might be a long time before she would be here again.

Behind her was the old church and, outside the churchyard wall, the fiddler's monument with its quotation from Burns. In the rapidly fading light, she was still able to read the inscription:

> *Riches denied, thy boon was purer joys,*
> *What wealth could never give nor take away.*

It occurred to her, there at the east end of the Tarland Square, that she stood in a sense at the hub of Taran's wheel. Not at the geometric centre of the circular vale created according to legend by Taran's thunderbolt, for that centre was about a mile away, at the Blue Cairn on Drummy. But at the point of origin of the six ancient roads that radiated to provinces of the Pictish kingdom beyond the hills encircling the Howe. The point where once had stood a moated earthwork, the *Kyaar*, before its destruction by followers of the Christian missionary Moluag.

She looked once again all around her, turned her eyes towards the half-moon in the southern sky and back to the ground on which she stood. Suddenly she felt a strange shiver. At last she knew, beyond a shadow of a doubt, exactly where she would find the *Drogan Taranish*.

61

NOT A PLACE, BUT A TIME

THAT EVENING, SHE STAYED UP late. The cottage began to get chilly, the boiler having timed out an hour or two earlier. She wrapped a blanket around her as she drafted a long email to Quin, writing as if from Chicago.

Missing you terribly, though it's only yesterday you flew out. Even the weather has turned cold in Chicago since you left. Hope you find your Grampa in a better state. I'm sure he'll cheer up when he sees you.

I've some exciting news. The puzzle is solved! I'm sure of it. I just got back from grocery shopping. When I came out of Garden Fresh, straight in front of me was a half-moon, a perfect letter D in the sky! That means it's at first quarter – midway from new moon to full. Grace's 'D' isn't a letter, Quin, it's a half-moon. This is exactly the kind of clue she loved. She was fascinated by everything to do with the moon, as you know, even giving her daughter the name of the moon-goddess Selena.

Finally I know what 'D in the west' means. Up to now, we've assumed it referred to a place. We were wrong. It's not a place, but a time. When the moon at first quarter is in the west, it's midnight. Right now, it's just after 6 pm here in Illinois, just after 7 pm where you are, and just after midnight in Scotland. If we were there, and it was a clear night, we'd see the moon, a beautiful letter D, in the western sky, getting ready to set behind the hills.

So the clue is 'midnight'. And what do we know happens at midnight in the Seely Howe? Four times a year, the First Druid, the drummer, the Knifeman and all the others get together for their neopagan ritual. We joined them for Lunasa. The next meeting will be for Samhain, at midnight on November 5th.

Quin, I'm sure Grace contacted them when she was in Scotland 4–5 years ago. Remember the lady we talked to? When I raised the subject of Taran's wheel, she was kind of evasive, if you recall. Didn't she say something like 'I'm sure it's just a tale'? Anyway, Grace must have given the Drogan to them for safe-keeping. If we were to show up for their Samhain gathering at Tomnaverie, I bet we'd find them using the Drogan in their ritual. It would have had no particular relevance at Lunasa, which is why we didn't see it then; but at Samhain, when Taran takes over from Luath as their guardian god, I'm sure the Drogan will be center-stage.

I'm planning to return to Scotland in time for Samhain. Any chance you can get time off in early November? It would be great if we could both be there.

Love, D.

She had given a great deal of thought to what she would say in the email, knowing that it would be intercepted by Cato or Bullethead. Still, after clicking on 'send', she began to have fresh doubts that her plan was *too* risky. But the die was cast.

Next day, she set off in search of Myrtle, stopping *en route* at the summit of Corsedarder, where she waded through the now senescent bracken to the great cairn. There was evidence of recent disturbance of some of the stones, which she put down to Cato's search for the *Drogan*.

The Forest of Birse was a large tract of land drained by the Water of Feugh, a tributary of the Dee. Despite its name it was only partly wooded. Having no idea how she would find Myrtle's home, she hoped some discreet questions would lead her there.

Towards the Bucket Mill she came upon several cottages among trees. At one of them, bearing a sign on the gate reading 'Hawthorn Cottage', a woman was working in her garden, lifting potatoes. Delia stopped the car. 'Good morning!' she called out. 'I'm sorry to trouble you, but I'm looking for someone called Myrtle. I believe she lives around here.'

The woman turned towards the house and yelled 'Myrtle!' At a more conversational volume, she said to Delia, 'You came to the right place.'

'Then you must be Joyce. I'm Delia Cobb. Myrtle spoke to my boyfriend and me a few weeks ago at a stone circle, and invited us to join her group for their celebration of Lunasa.'

'Oh, yes,' Joyce said in a world-weary tone. 'The Grove of the Mayflower. Don't know why she gets herself involved in that, but it's harmless, I suppose. As long as she doesn't rope me in, she can do as she pleases. I let her choose the name of our house before I knew its significance. Mayflower is another name for hawthorn, as you probably know.'

'Actually, I didn't,' Delia said.

Joyce bellowed again, 'Myrtle!' even more loudly than before. Delia noticed the ample chest from which such volume was summoned.

A few seconds later, Myrtle came hurrying out of the house. When she saw Delia, she stopped in her tracks. 'It's all right, Myrtle,' Joyce said. 'Miss Cobb has told me she attended one of your meetings. Maybe you could offer her a cup of tea. And if you're making tea, I'll have a cup too.'

'I don't want to put you to any trouble,' Delia said.

'It's no trouble,' Joyce said on her partner's behalf. 'Is it, Myrtle?'

Over tea and a pancake, spread with home-made blackcurrant jam, the three women chatted until Joyce left to continue her work outside.

'Remember, the first time we met,' Delia said, 'I asked you about the *Drogan Taranish*? You knew about it, but said "it was just a tale".'

'That's right,' Myrtle said, refilling their teacups from the pot.

'So it's not something the Grove of the Mayflower might use, say, in worshipping Taran at Samhain?'

Myrtle appeared slightly uneasy. 'If we had such a thing, it might well have a place in our Samhain ritual. But ...' The sentence hung in the air, unfinished.

'Did an American lady by the name of Grace Rosman ever make contact with the Grove? Maybe about four years ago?'

'It's possible, but that was before I joined. I was inducted to the Grove only the year before last. Why are you asking? Did this lady have the *Drogan*?'

'Just wondering.' Delia sipped her tea, deep in thought. After a few seconds, she set down her teacup and said, 'I've an idea.'

Myrtle listened intently as Delia spoke, becoming first interested then enthusiastic. There was some discussion as to exactly how the upcoming Samhain observance at Tomnaverie might be structured. 'Of course, I'll have to verify all the details with the First Druid. But I'm sure he won't object. And this time, would you be willing to take a more active part in our worship?'

Delia promptly acquiesced. 'Just let me know what you'd like me to do. I won't let you down.'

The remaining few days of her stay passed quickly. She did some shopping in Aberdeen, had a couple of drinks with Ewen one evening – at her suggestion, in the Commercial Hotel bar for a change – and paid one more visit to Myrtle at Hawthorn Cottage. She hoped she'd thought of everything.

Excitement bubbled up inside her. The search for Taran's wheel was nearing its conclusion. And Cato might not know it yet, but he had a date with destiny on November 5th.

62

A CHANGE OF PLAN

THE PASTOR WAS SCEPTICAL. 'You gave me your assurance, Thackeray. You said that, with the documents retrieved by the Engineer from the girl, we would have everything we need to get our hands on the glass ball.'

Zeke Thackeray's head was bowed in shame. 'Yes, Most Reverend, I did. And I beg your forgiveness. But the situation now is different. The girl says she knows where the ball is. It's to be the centrepiece of some heathen ceremony at midnight on November 5th. We know exactly where that ceremony will take place. It will be easy for the Engineer to get hold of it.'

'How do you know this?'

'Through the Rat on the girl's computer. Jayden Bayliss obtained the intelligence just yesterday.'

The Pastor's eyes narrowed. 'How well do you know Bayliss? Can he be trusted?'

'I'm not sure I understand what you mean, Most Reverend. He's a real expert in computer surveillance.'

'Yes, and that could be a problem. Say you found out he'd put a Rat on *my* computer, would you tell me? My machine has been playing up recently. If he's spying on me, we'll dispose of him. If he's spying on me and you're in on it, we'll dispose of both of you. Are you understanding me now?'

Thackeray's face paled. He had no option but spill the beans on his accomplice. 'Actually, Most Reverend, there's reason to believe Jayden hasn't limited the Rat to the girl's computer.

From remarks he's made, I think it's possible he may have infected mine, and possibly even yours. Of course I was going to tell you, but I wanted to be sure first.'

'So what dirt has he dug up on me? The websites I visit, the contacts I have outside the Kingdom of Men?'

'He's mentioned nothing to me, Most Reverend,' Thackeray replied. There was no future in admitting he knew the Pastor's deviant tastes in pornography, or his plan for making common cause with the Taliban.

'Bayliss must be sacrificed, just in case. I leave that to you. But let's keep him around until November 5th, in case we need some further intelligence from the girl.'

'Yes, Most Reverend. And when it comes to November 5th, are we to cut Cato Woods out of the loop? Simply walk in there and recover the ball?'

'Dammit, Thackeray, you keep wanting to work around Woods. Don't you see he's our best cover? If anything goes wrong, we need him to take the fall, rather than someone who can be traced back to you or me. He can't squeal on us, can he?'

'No, Most Reverend. He knows Bayliss and me only by single initials. I'm "Z" and Bayliss is "J". We've only ever phoned him from untraceable pay-as-you-go mobiles. If he gets caught, he's on his own.'

'Bayliss I don't give a shit about. He'll soon be out of the picture. But you ...'

Thackeray felt a shiver run down his spine. If he lost the Pastor's trust, he could be just as vulnerable as Bayliss.

'Who does Woods think you work for?' the Pastor asked. 'Have you mentioned the Kingdom of Men to him?'

'Of course not, Most Reverend. All he knows is you're a private collector who wants to remain private.'

'Well, then, we're okay. Tell Woods to be at the appointed place on November 5th, ready to seize the ball. And have the Engineer call me directly. I need to alert him to a change of plan.'

63

SAMHAIN

IT WAS NOVEMBER 5TH, the Pictish Samhain, exactly six moons before Beltane. Many present-day neopagan cults celebrate the fire festival of Samhain five days earlier, on Hallowe'en, but the Grove of the Mayflower, true to ancient local tradition, would hold its ritual tonight. Each year on this same evening, a fire festival of a different kind is observed throughout Great Britain, ostensibly marking defeat of a plot led by Guy Fawkes in 1605 to blow up the English parliament with gunpowder. The pagan tone of bonfire night is unmistakable, culminating as it does in the burning of a human effigy (the 'guy').

Frost had settled in the bowl of Cromar. Snow was forecast, but so far the sky was clear, except for an icy haze that formed a halo around the bright full moon. There was little wind, just enough to spread the smell of smoke around the *Seely Howe*. By eleven thirty, commemoration of the gunpowder plot was over but for a few sporadic fireworks that briefly challenged the moon for supremacy over the night sky. Even with the car windows fully rolled up, Quin and Delia heard the delayed bangs, like distant gunfire.

It was only his second, her third, trip to Scotland, yet they felt a sense of belonging there. Incomers they might be, but wasn't everyone in this country an incomer, if you went back far enough? Even the Beaker People four millennia ago had, to paraphrase Mark Twain, 'pilfered' the land from the native circle builders.

Quin and Delia were now in the car-park at Tomnaverie, awaiting arrival of the Grove of the Mayflower. If all went according to plan, an uninvited guest would also turn up. A vehicle approached from the Aboyne direction, its headlights on full beam. They watched in silence as it passed without stopping. A few minutes later there was another, then another.

Finally, one slowed down and turned into the car-park – the same minibus Myrtle and other members of the Grove of the Mayflower had arrived in at Lunasa. A man emerged carrying what looked like a small suitcase. A couple more cars pulled in shortly afterwards.

'Okay,' Delia whispered, 'I'm off to join them. My mobile's on vibrate if you need to alert me to anything. You know what to do if I page you. Give me a kiss and wish me luck.'

She joined Myrtle and the others for the short uphill walk, the frosty air nipping at her nose and cheeks. Myrtle pointed discreetly to the man ahead of them with the suitcase. 'He's carrying it,' she whispered excitedly.

At the stone circle, a board was laid down, just as at Lunasa, but this time a circular tablecloth bearing a wheel design was spread on the board. Out of the suitcase came, first, a tripod topped with a small brass ring. This was placed, not on the tablecloth, but on the uneven surface of the recumbent stone. The tripod was moved around until a position was found for it that would keep the brass ring perfectly horizontal. Then a glass sphere was carefully brought out of a velvet bag and set on the tripod. It seemed to capture the moonlight, and emit in its place a faint bluish glow.

At precisely midnight, the ritual began. In effusive language, the First Druid instructed the company to raise their eyes to the moon in her appointed place in the heavens, the constellation of Taurus the bull. Of the V-shaped formation known as the Hyades, only the bright star Aldebaran shone through the moon's glare; a little to the right, the Pleiades –

Taran's daughters as Grace had called that star cluster – were just discernable as a fuzzy patch of light.

In the next order of business, one of the female worshippers opened a wide-necked vacuum jug. With a small ladle she carefully measured its steaming contents into clear plastic goblets. Delia was unfamiliar with traditional hot toddy, made from whisky sweetened with honey and laced with spices. The warm sensation as it slipped down her throat was more than welcome.

It was then time for another speech by the First Druid. 'Tonight,' he intoned, 'we turn our eyes, our hearts and our minds to Taran, and ask him to be our guide and protector through the cold dark months ahead.' He stepped over to the recumbent stone, picked up the glass ball with both hands, and held it aloft. It was like an iridescent bluish replica of the moon itself, glowing as if with an internal source of illumination.

'Great Taran,' he cried, 'through this ancient symbol of your might and mercy, be present with us this night! May your wheel keep turning, bringing us a new day, a new month, a new year!'

He placed the ball back on its tripod, then motioned the participants to form a circle around the board. While the attention of others was fixed on offerings to Taran, Delia kept her eye on the recumbent, where the familiar glass sphere continued in its eerie way to reflect and refract the moonlight. She felt a little shiver, a tingle of excitement at what she hoped would happen next.

Sure enough, as the First Druid droned on, a dark figure rose up out of nearby broom bushes and rushed towards the recumbent stone. One of the worshippers, seeing the movement, ran to protect the glass ball. Delia pressed the keypad of her mobile phone in her pocket, signalling Quin to call the police.

Neither of the runners reached their goal. Out of nowhere, someone shouted, 'Stop, or I shoot!' They both froze. When the dark figure started moving again, towards the ball, a shot rang out. He howled in pain, and fell to the ground.

It was not what Delia was expecting. The gunman appeared, brandishing his weapon. With his free hand, he picked up the ball and raised it above his head. It glistened in the moonlight. The wounded man staggered to his feet, screaming 'No!' But the ball was hurled against one of the upright stones flanking the recumbent. It smashed into thousands of tiny shards.

For a long second, the shooter aimed his firearm directly at Delia and stared chillingly into her face, then ran off down the footpath. Though he wore a woollen ski cap, she recognized him. It was Bullethead, who had stolen her memory stick in the tearoom three months earlier.

Myrtle had dropped to her knees beside the casualty, whose thigh was bleeding profusely. Easing off his trousers, she called, 'Somebody bring me the tablecloth!' She tore it into strips to fashion a tourniquet to staunch the flow of blood. An ambulance was called.

Alone among the company, Delia knew the victim. 'Cato,' she said as she approached him, 'we meet again.'

He grimaced and cast his eyes towards the scattered shards, then looked straight into Delia's face. 'You should've done the deal with me,' he said. 'Now, after all our effort, we have nothing but broken glass.'

Meanwhile, the Engineer reached his car, started it up and sped along the mile-long section of road known locally as the Gellan straight, his headlights turned off to avoid attracting attention. His eyes were well adjusted to the moonlight and he was by now familiar with this road. Seeing flashing blue lights in the distance, he made a fast left turn on to the road that climbed past Coull to the Slack. He would head to Aberdeen that way, rather than by Aboyne as originally planned.

In a call to Zeke Thackeray he said only, 'Mission accomplished. The glass ball is in a million pieces.'

'Well done,' Thackeray replied. 'The balance of your fee ...' *Call ended*, his handset display told him. 'Shit!' he muttered.

The Engineer joined the Tarland-to-Aberdeen road without slowing down and hurtled into the narrow pass known as the Slack. It was one thing to know the contours of the road, quite another to know its hazards at that time of year. He turned the steering wheel a few degrees to negotiate a slight bend, but his road wheels over-responded on a patch of black ice and lost all traction. At the speed he was travelling, the momentum of his silver BMW carried it off the road, crashing through a fence into the ravine below. The driver's-side airbag inflated explosively, socking him in the chest as the car came to rest against a tree, its front half a crumpled wreck.

There was silence. He was dazed and winded but alive. Tried to move but couldn't: both legs were trapped in the wreckage. Snow began to fall, drifting through the hole where the windscreen used to be. His mobile rang, sounding strangely distant. It was out there in the snow somewhere, beyond his reach.

In Topeka, Thackeray dialled the Engineer's number. Getting no reply, he left a message. 'Like I was saying, the balance of your fee will be wired immediately to your account in Belize. The Pastor will be very pleased with your work. A better outcome even than the Minty-Ward job. And I gather no one died this time.'

He had no idea how wrong he was.

64
PRICELESS?

THE OCCUPANTS OF THE TWO police cars racing towards Tarland from Aboyne failed to notice the speeding, unlit BMW. When they arrived at the Tomnaverie car-park a minute or two later, Quin was waiting for them. Four officers accompanied him up the footpath. 'Smells like snow on the way,' one of them remarked, as a cloud came over the moon and it suddenly got very dark. A chill wind was now blowing.

At the stone circle a pathetic figure with a bandaged leg sat in his underpants on the frosty grass by the recumbent, surrounded by members of the Grove of the Mayflower.

One of the officers took the lead. 'I'm Sergeant Finney, Police Scotland,' he announced. 'Who's in charge here?'

A man in a ceremonial hooded cloak stepped forward. 'Alan Hetherington, First Druid of the Grove of the Mayflower.'

'Oh aye?'

'This is a lawful assembly, Sergeant. I have the permit in my car if you need to see it. We were having a peaceful meeting when we were interrupted first by this hoodlum – I'm informed his name is Cato Woods – and then by another person, who fired a gun, grabbed one of our sacred objects, a glass ball, and smashed it to pieces.'

A constable shone his flashlight around, causing fragments of glass to glint in the turf.

'Then what happened?' Finney asked.

'The gunman ran down the hill and drove off.'

Quin broke in to say that he had seen the speeding car. Pale-coloured was the only description he could come up with; it was being driven without lights. 'It was just a minute or so before you arrived. I'm surprised you didn't meet it.'

'He must've turned on to the Coull road.' A call was immediately made to police HQ, then Finney resumed, 'Okay, we have to get some statements. There's a lot we'll need to know. But first, let's have a look at Mr Woods.'

He turned his attention to Myrtle, who was still tending to Cato's injured leg. 'I take it you're a nurse. Is he badly hurt?'

'No,' Myrtle said, 'I've fixed him up as best I can. We've already called for an ambulance.'

The sergeant then addressed Cato. 'What's your business here, sir?'

'I came to make an offer for the tektite – the glass ball,' Cato groaned. 'I have previously been in negotiation with one of the company here, but before I could say anything I was shot ...' His voice trailed away.

'Do you know the person who shot you?'

'I don't think so. I didn't get a good look at him.'

'Why would he smash the glass ball?'

'I've no idea. It's a priceless treasure. Now it's totally destroyed.'

'Priceless?'

'Could've been worth millions.'

'Millions, eh?'

Delia stepped forward. 'Sergeant Finney, my name is Delia Cobb. I'm the one he's referring to, though I was never in "negotiation" with him, as he claims. A few months ago, he offered me two hundred and fifty thousand pounds. Quarter of a million. He apparently didn't think it was worth "millions" then. I refused to do a deal with him, at any price. But as we're talking about the value of the glass ball that's lying in pieces here, I can tell you exactly what it was worth.'

'Yes?'

'Nine pounds fifty.'

Cato stared at Delia. 'Are you crazy?' was all he could say.

'No, that's what I paid for it, in a charity shop in Aberdeen.' Then, to the police sergeant, she said, 'I have the receipt. It's Caithness glass, circa 1985, I believe. I donated it to my friends, the Grove of the Mayflower. They know it's not ancient, but they have blessed it for use in their sacrament, as a symbol of the god Taran. It was in use tonight before the meeting was disrupted by Mr Woods and his partner in crime.'

'Whoever he is, he's no partner of mine,' Cato protested. 'Did you think you would double-cross me by selling me a cheap fake?'

'Whether cheap fake or real thing, Cato, it was no longer mine and it wasn't for sale. You had no intention of buying it anyway. You were here to steal it. From these nice people in the middle of their religious observance.'

The wind was growing stronger on the exposed hilltop, and the first flakes of snow had begun to fly. An ambulance arrived for the wounded Cato, who was carried down to the car-park on a stretcher, accompanied by two officers. The other two noted names and contact information for all witnesses. The First Druid told the police he would be pressing charges against Cato Woods and the man with the gun, for malicious desecration of a religious service and destruction of a sacred artefact.

Delia chimed in. '*And* I have evidence that Mr Woods has committed another crime.'

'What would that be?' Sergeant Finney asked.

'Computer hacking. The only way he could possibly have known that the glass ball he's been after would be here tonight was by hacking into my email account.'

'We'll follow up on that in the coming days.'

As Delia and Quin drove back to Ballater that night, the snow grew steadily heavier. By the time they parked at their hotel, a blizzard was blowing. Grateful to reach the comfort of their room, they took a hot shower together and slipped into bed.

65
THE WHOLE STORY

EAVY SNOWFALL IS RARE though not unknown in Scotland at the beginning of November. When it comes so early in the winter, it tends to catch public services unprepared.

Snow kept falling all day on the 6th, finally tapering off in the early hours of the following morning. Roads all over Aberdeenshire were blocked; power and telephone lines were brought down.

By midday on the 7th, the main road from Aberdeen to Ballater had reopened to traffic. A couple of visitors arrived for Delia and Quin.

'Inspector Colin McCandless, Police Scotland CID. This is PC Fiona Henderson. We'd like to ask you some questions relating to the incident at Tomnaverie near Tarland in the early hours of November 6th. In fact, what we're hoping for is the whole story.'

They sat down in the study, a cosy lounge fitted out as a library but functioning as a bar. A log fire was burning and they had the room to themselves. PC Henderson placed a recorder on the table and switched it on.

'Before we begin,' Delia said, 'have you caught the second man?'

'Not yet,' the inspector replied, 'but we will. Now, your Mr Carl Thomas Woods is an interesting fellow. Running him through our databases, we find a couple of things.' McCandless liked the sound of his own voice and had a tendency towards pomposity. He paused for effect, chewing the inside of his cheek for a few seconds. 'First, he's what we like to call a "person of interest" in some ongoing investigations relating to illegal import and trading in gemstones. You may have heard of "blood diamonds". It turns out the Metropolitan Police in London have had their eye on Mr Woods for some time. Second, and this may be of particular relevance to our discussion today, it appears he is a suspect in a murder inquiry in the United States. Informal approaches have been made by the State of Illinois with a view to extradition. Now tell me what *you* know.'

It was Delia who spoke. The inspector took copious notes, apparently not wishing to rely entirely on the recording. She began by talking about the death of her friend Grace Rosman, who owned a precious heirloom, an ancient glass sphere with supposedly mystic properties. She recounted that Grace had apparently been murdered by someone wishing to steal the heirloom, and that she understood Cato was a suspect, as confirmed by DNA evidence. Grace had previously brought the glass sphere to Scotland, leaving a lengthy coded message as to its location.

'And have you found it?' the inspector asked.

'No, I haven't,' Delia said, perfectly truthfully, without revealing that she now knew exactly where it was.

'And I understand the glass ball that was smashed by the gunman was a fake. Am I correct?'

'If by "fake" you mean it wasn't the particular glass ball brought to Scotland by Grace Rosman, then you are correct.'

Delia described how, through an email to Quin, she had lured Cato into showing up at the Samhain ceremony.

'We'll need a copy of that email. Indeed, we'll have to borrow your computer to check all files and correspondence relating to the matter under investigation.'

It made Delia nervous that the whole of Grace's *First* and *Second Testaments* could become public. However, as Cato and

Bullethead already had them, along with the necessary passwords, objection was pointless. 'Of course,' she said. 'My tablet's in my room. I'll give it to you before you leave.'

'What did you hope would happen at the druid ceremony?'

'Exactly what *did* happen, except that I didn't anticipate the shooting. I wanted to set a trap for Cato Woods that would result in his arrest. Even if the police – if you – were only to hold him briefly, I hoped you would be alerted to his "wanted for extradition" status.'

'Quite a plan, Ms Cobb,' the inspector said. Then after one of his pauses, he continued: 'Weren't you afraid he might be armed and dangerous? After all, he's a murder suspect. You might have placed, indeed you did place, not only yourself but members of the ...' (consulting his notes) '... Grove of the Mayflower in serious danger.'

Delia acknowledged that the situation had become dangerous, but there had been no reason to expect the appearance of the gunman. 'I had assumed he and Cato were working together,' she said, 'but when he shot Cato and deliberately smashed the glass ball that Cato was so desperate to obtain, that didn't make sense any longer.'

'Quite.' The inspector turned to Quin. 'Were you fully in on Ms Cobb's plan, Mr Johnson?'

'Yes. My role was to remain by the roadside and call the police as soon as I got Delia's signal. I heard the gunshot just after I made the call, but thought it was a firecracker or bottle-rocket being set off somewhere. There were quite a few that night.'

Inspector McCandless came up with many more questions, until eventually he ran out of steam and signalled PC Henderson to turn off the recorder. He then spent ten minutes summarising what he had heard, based on the notes he had taken. Before departing, he said, 'You know, your plan probably wouldn't have worked if the gunman hadn't appeared. If our uniformed officers had arrived on the scene to find nothing more than a stranger making a nuisance of himself in a druidical gathering, they would simply have sent him off with a warning, and given you both a talking-to about wasting police time. It's only because of Mr Woods's gunshot wound that the matter took on greater significance, leading to a background check.'

Delia apologised for what she admitted in retrospect was a naïve plan.

'As it turns out,' McCandless said, 'we're very glad to have Mr Woods in our custody. Extradition to face a murder charge in the U.S. may still be blocked, but we'll be throwing the book at him for a number of illegal activities in this country, if our investigations are conclusive.'

'The blood diamonds?' Delia asked.

'Exactly. And more besides. There's also the matter of invasion of computer privacy, if we find sufficient evidence. Fiona, please accompany Ms Cobb to her room and retrieve her computer.'

On the way upstairs, Delia asked PC Henderson, 'One thing that's been puzzling me – how did Cato come to Tomnaverie that night? Neither Quin nor I saw him arrive.'

'It seems he came in a black Range Rover that's now buried in snow at Scrapehard, close to Tomnaverie but on the south side, away from the main road. Presumably he approached the stone circle from that side, hoping to leave the same way.'

66

THE WHEEL OF *VAIRTACH*

SNOW LAY DEEP over the *Seely Howe* for a week, but flights out of Aberdeen were not seriously affected. Delia and Quin flew back to the U.S. via Heathrow a few days after their meeting with Inspector McCandless.

By November 15th, the weather had turned mild, and throughout Cromar the snow disappeared quickly. Only a few patches on the upper slopes of Morven remained. Later in the month, a woman was in the ravine at the Slack gathering brushwood for her fire, when she came across the wreck of a silver-coloured car, the front wrapped around the trunk of a tree and the windscreen completely detached from its frame. She could see a body slumped inside the mangled remains of the vehicle, and immediately called the police.

The Aberdeen *Press and Journal* carried the headline on its front page:

MYSTERY DEATH PLUNGE NEAR TARLAND

It reported that an unidentified man had been found dead in a silver BMW that had left the road at the Slack. The car was believed to have been travelling at high speed and probably skidded on ice. The accident appeared to have happened shortly before the snowstorms of early November, and the wreck had lain undiscovered under deep snow until it was found by a local woman.

The driver was believed to have initially survived the impact, thanks to the vehicle's airbag, but he was trapped by his legs and

315

had struggled unsuccessfully to free himself. He may have lived for a matter of days after the accident. It was not yet clear if his eventual death was due to injuries sustained or to exposure. Police had so far been unable to identify the crash victim, who had registered the car under a false identity. A handgun was found on his person.

What was not reported in the *P and J* was forensic evidence of firing of the handgun by the crash victim, and of a ballistic match between the handgun and a bullet used in the non-fatal shooting of a man at Tomnaverie in the early hours of November 6th.

Also not reported was that a mobile phone, again registered under a false identity, was found near the car. A voice message received at 12:28 am on November 6th linked the mystery man to the hitherto unsolved disappearance of schoolteachers Jack Ward and Megan Minty four years earlier. Police learned that a man answering the description of the crash victim and driving a silver BMW had called at Praisewell, the site of Megan Minty's home, in August.

On page 13 of the same *P and J* was an apparently unrelated one-paragraph story:

Controversial U.S. preacher Walden Wilkes will be permitted to make a 'pastoral visit' to Scotland, the Home Office has announced. Rev. Wilkes is the founder of the fundamentalist Kingdom of Men church in Topeka, Kansas. The Home Office decision overturns a ban imposed two years ago because of his extremist pronouncements against women's rights, in which he appeared to support a particular interpretation of Islamic Sharia law mandating death by stoning of women who commit adultery. A condition of the decision is that Wilkes must conduct no public services or meetings. He will, however, be permitted to host a men-only 'spiritual retreat' in the Scottish Borders for members of a Glasgow-based fundamentalist congregation, at their invitation.

A snippet of news that failed to make it into the Aberdeen *Press and Journal*, indeed spread no further than the *Capital-Journal* of Topeka, Kansas, told of the crash on November 8th of a small twin-engined plane on take-off from Forbes Field in Topeka. Both the pilot, Ezekiel Thackeray, and his only passenger, Jayden Bayliss, were killed. Weather conditions were good and the cause of the crash had not yet been determined.

It was not until the following spring that Quin got the news he'd been waiting for since August. The position he'd interviewed for in Chicago had finally opened up and was his if he still had interest. He accepted immediately and made arrangements to move his grandfather to a residential care facility not far from Delia's apartment. They flew together to Chicago O'Hare, where Delia met them and brought them to Glenview.

At the same airport exactly a week earlier, another passenger arrived, this one from London. He emerged from the terminal handcuffed to a police officer, who hustled him into a waiting car that drove him to 26th and California, on Chicago's south side.

Cato Woods found his accommodation in the Cook County jail, awaiting trial for murder, even less appealing than what he'd become familiar with in London. He shared a tiny cell with a serial burglar who lacked even the most basic understanding of personal hygiene. As the junior occupant Cato had the lower bunk, whose pillow rested against the side of the steel lavatory pan. A chill draught of Chicago air blew constantly over his bunk. Covering the grille was not an option; the resulting lack of ventilation made the stench of his cellmate unbearable.

Brief 'social' time with occupants of adjacent cells was spent in a cheerless room with metal tables and benches bolted to the

317

concrete floor. Meals eaten at these tables varied little from day to day, a sandwich of 'baloney' (cheap bologna sausage) between slices of dry white bread being the mainstay of the prison diet.

Showers had to be taken in full view of fellow prisoners and warders – from his experience in a London prison Cato already knew it was safer that way.

For half an hour each day, the outdoor exercise yard offered the opportunity to fill his lungs with less noxious air, but the highlight of his week was chapel. Services were non-denominational – not that it mattered to Cato, who had barely been in a church since quitting Sunday school at the age of ten. Though talking in chapel was forbidden, even while filing in and out, the level of nonverbal business transacted was astounding. During this one weekly occasion when otherwise segregated inmates came together, the ingenuity of the prison population, in particular the Latinos, focused on communication based on furtively exchanged scraps of paper. What was written on those scraps, if anything, was irrelevant; instead the way they were folded or torn constituted a 'language', one that the authorities had so far failed to decode. Cato paid not a shred of attention to the chaplain's words, but found his weekly service a welcome break from the tedium and unpleasantness of life in the Cook County jail.

Twenty-five miles away, on the sofa in Delia's Glenview apartment, she and Quin enjoyed a bottle of wine together. She looked around with satisfaction; some of the décor and furnishings were as Grace had left them, but youthful touches had crept in, with colourful cushions and fewer ornaments and knick-knacks. The formal living room set where Grace had died at the hand of Cato Woods was gone.

Cato. Now he was securely locked up, his lawyers' efforts to defeat the extradition order having failed, likewise his appeal for bail. With good reason he was deemed a 'flight risk'. As for Bullethead, he had died a slow death. The wheel of *vairtach* had been visited on both of them.

Though forensic examination of Delia's computer had revealed the Trojan Rat, it could not be linked to Cato Woods. Instead, it appeared to transmit data to an account held by Jayden Bayliss of Topeka, Kansas. A message on the dead gunman's mobile phone had been left by one Ezekiel Thackeray. The same Bayliss and Thackeray who had died together in a plane crash at Topeka just a few days after the events at Tomnaverie. *Vairtach* again.

Cato's connection to the Topeka victims would come out in the murder trial. Yet to emerge was the link to the shadowy individual known only as 'the Pastor', a target of police investigations following mention of him in Thackeray's message retrieved from the gunman's phone. Not that there was much to learn from those investigations up to now; speculation by one detective that the Reverend Walden Wilkes of the Kingdom of Men church in Topeka, at that moment hosting a retreat in the Scottish Borders, might be 'the Pastor' hadn't gained much traction. Topeka was full of crackpot fundamentalist preachers.

After the second or third glass of wine, Quin suddenly gave voice to something that had been on his mind for half a year.

'Delia, you told me last September that you knew *exactly* where the *Drogan Taranish* was hidden. Then you spun that whole yarn about the first-quarter moon in the west meaning midnight, the time when the Samhain ceremony would be held at Tomnaverie. You bought the fake *Drogan* and somehow persuaded Myrtle and the other Mayflowers to go along with your entrapment plan for Cato. In the end of the day it all worked very well. But I wonder sometimes.'

'What about?'

'The true *Drogan*. Do you *really* know where it is? Have you already found it?'

'Why would you wonder such a thing?'

'It's just that you're much less – what should I say? – *anxious* about it now. It's as if you don't care any more.'

She thought about Quin's words. He was right, she was no longer anxious. But he was wrong about her not caring. She cared deeply. The truth was, she felt Taran's wheel was safe in its hiding place, so long as only she knew where that was. One day, for sure, she would retrieve it. As Keeper, that would be her responsibility. One she took very seriously.

For it turned out that her 'anointing' by Grace was not after all in violation of the ancient law of succession, which required Taran's wheel to be passed always to a *relative* in the female line. Recently she had received surprising news from Sergeant Nolan: a full analysis of DNA samples obtained during the investigation showed that she and Grace shared a common female ancestor, probably five to ten generations back. Their mitochondrial DNA was virtually identical.

At length, Quin said, 'I believe you *did* find Taran's wheel.'

Still Delia wouldn't be drawn. She reflected on her epiphany in Tarland, the moment when at last she *knew* where the *Drogan* was hidden. Her realisation that the clue was, after all, an anagram, Grace's favourite kind of word puzzle. Once again, Grace's yellow Post-It had come into her mind:

Good guess, Cordelia. But it's not an anagram this time. Did you think this was The Da Vinci Code?

There, as she had gazed around the Tarland Square on that September evening with the half-moon in the sky, she had finally understood. Not an anagram *this time*. 'Find a repo' wasn't an anagram, but that didn't mean the ultimate clue to the location of Taran's wheel wouldn't be one. She recollected how, in that instant, she had rearranged the letters in the Burns quotation on the fiddler's monument at the end of the Square:

RICHES DENIED

to spell the name

EDDIE SCHERIN

that Grace had asked Eddie the Geek to inscribe on the CD label he made for her.

In that same moment, the multiple meaning of the clue *'What you seek is in the square'* had become clear. Grace wasn't just referring to the 'sator square', or her little number square that led via Asa Porter to Arthur Johnson in Haverhill, New Hampshire.

What she had been seeking was in the *Tarland* Square, hidden under the fiddler's monument, the granite stone with the *'Riches denied'* inscription. The hiding place, if not the *Drogan* itself, was 'in plain sight' as Grace had hinted; indeed the fiddler's stone and its inscription had been the very first thing to catch Delia's eye when she and Quin arrived in Tarland last August. How could she have missed the anagram?

Then there were other clues she had overlooked. Ewen had mentioned that he had repaired the foundation of the fiddler's stone a few years earlier. It turned out that was precisely at the time of Grace's visit. It wouldn't have been difficult for Grace to slip the *Drogan*, perhaps in a protective box, under some of the river pebbles that would form the new foundation.

Even the magic number six featured in the solution to Grace's puzzle. *'Riches denied'*, two six-letter words that had stared Delia in the face since the very start of her search for Taran's wheel.

She gave Quin's remark another moment's consideration. She loved him, and was sure he loved her. Undoubtedly they were a couple, but they had never really talked about a long-term future together. Was she ready to trust him with knowledge of where Grace had secreted Taran's wheel? Did he even need to know? Quin himself had carefully avoided learning the password to Grace's *First Testament*. Suddenly it came to her.

What shall Cordelia do? Love, and be silent.

AUTHOR'S NOTE

Other than the *Kyaar*, Praisewell and Hawthorn Cottage, which are fictitious, all places in and around the Howe of Cromar mentioned in this book are real and are given their real names. For their precise locations, readers are invited to consult Ordnance Survey Landranger (1:50,000) Sheet 37 or Explorer (1:25,000) Sheet 405.

Grace Rosman's two *Testaments* to the history of the Pleasant Vale (Cromar) and its people are, of course, fictional but most of the characters and events they feature are known from history or local legend. A few 'historical' people and events associated with them are drawn entirely from my imagination, including Aeth, Merefrith and the *Merch Nyr* of the *First Testament*, and Margaret Baird, Peggy and Ellen Walker, the Begg and Crichton families, Molly Watt, Hamish and Catriona MacBain and Agnes Cromar of the *Second Testament*. The *Testaments* sometimes deviate from generally accepted history (much of which is, in any case, a matter of conjecture) but are, I believe, not inconsistent with recorded fact. Almost 30 locations having been posited as the *Mons Graupius* battlefield of 84 AD, the novel siting of the battle in the hills of Cromar seems to me a harmless fictional device. I have also taken a few liberties in describing (through the medium of Grace Rosman) nineteenth-century plans for a royal residence and a railway in the Howe of Cromar.

The fictionalised historical account behind the contemporary story of *Taran's Wheel* is mainly a matter of adding flesh to the bare bones of known history. Interested readers are encouraged to assemble those bones from some of the sources listed in the Acknowledgements that follow, and perhaps do some fleshing out of their own.

Attempts to standardise spelling of Scots words have never caught on. I have used spellings that reflect Aberdeenshire pronunciation: for example *faar* (where), *climm* (climb), *steen* (stone) and *meen* (moon).

Jim Forbes.

ACKNOWLEDGEMENTS

Sources of historical information drawn from in writing *Taran's Wheel* include:

Alexander, W.M. (1952) *The Place-names of Aberdeenshire.* Aberdeen: Third Spalding Club.

Bittinger, J.Q. (1888) *History of Haverhill, N.H.* Haverhill.

Campbell, W. (1842) Parish of Coull. In *The New Statistical Account of Scotland,* Vol. 12, pp. 957–962.

Craig, P. (2004) Drummy Ridge archaeological trail. *Echoes of Cromar's Past* No. 10, pp. 45–47.

Farquhar, J. (1998) The Gow Stane. *Cromar History Group Newsletter* No. 5, p. 7 (reprinted in *Anither Keek at Tarland's Lang Syne*, 2004, p. 53).

Gibson, R. (2011) The battle of Culblean. *Echoes of Cromar's Past* No. 16, pp. 55–58.

Hughes, D. (2007) *The British Chronicles*, Book 1. Westminster, MD: Heritage Books.

Jamieson, J. (1808) *An Etymological Dictionary of the Scottish Language.* Edinburgh.

Maitland, W. (1793) Parish of Tarland. In *Statistical Account of Scotland,* Vol. 6, pp. 222–232.

Marchant, J. (2009) Tarland Kirk. *Echoes of Cromar's Past* No. 15, pp. 3–7.

Marren, P. (1990) *Grampian Battlefields.* Aberdeen: University Press.

Marshall, D.N. (1976) Carved stone balls. *Proceedings of the Society of Antiquaries of Scotland,* Vol. 108, pp. 40–72.

McHardy, J. (1842) Parish of Logie-Coldstone. In *The New Statistical Account of Scotland,* Vol. 12, pp. 1070–1074.

Michie, J.G. (1872) *Deeside Tales.* Aberdeen: Wyllie.

Michie, J.G. (1896) *The History of Logie-Coldstone and Braes of Cromar.* Aberdeen: Wyllie.

Milne, J. (1912) *Celtic Place-names in Aberdeenshire.* Aberdeen.

Ogston, A. (1919) The cairns in Cromar, Aberdeenshire. *Proceedings of the Society of Antiquaries of Scotland,* Vol. 53, pp. 175–179.

Ogston, A. (1931) *The Prehistoric Antiquities of the Howe of Cromar*. Aberdeen: Third Spalding Club.

Ross, S. (2002) Loch Kinord and its islands. *Cromar History Group Newsletter* No. 9, pp. 23–27.

Ross, S. (2004) The Barony of Auchtercoull. *Echoes of Cromar's Past* No. 10, pp. 21–24.

Simpson, W.D. (1923) The excavation of Coull Castle, Aberdeenshire. *Proceedings of the Society of Antiquaries of Scotland,* Vol. 58, pp. 45–99.

Simpson, W.D. (1930) The campaign and battle of Culblean, AD 1335. *Proceedings of the Society of Antiquaries of Scotland,* Vol. 64, pp. 201–211.

Simpson, W.D. (1944) *The Province of Mar*. Aberdeen: University Press.

Spalding, J. (1624–45) *The History of the Troubles and Memorable Transactions in Scotland and England,* Vol. 2. (republished 1828, Edinburgh: The Bannatyne Club.)

Tacitus (ca. 89) *Agricola*. Oxford translation.

Watson, A. & Watson, J. (1842) Parish of Tarland and Migvie. In *The New Statistical Account of Scotland,* Vol. 12, pp. 839–846.

Wyness, F. (1968) *Royal Valley: the Story of the Aberdeenshire Dee*. Aberdeen: Reid.

I would like to pay tribute to the work of the Cromar History Group in unearthing (literally, in many cases) and assembling fragments of the rich heritage of the 'Pleasant Vale'. Their annual newsletter, *Echoes of Cromar's Past*, is a mine of information; just a representative few of its articles are included in the list above.

Finally, I am deeply indebted to the team at Kinord Books for a fine editorial job on my manuscript.

Look out for the second *Incomers* novel,
Scotch and Water by Jim Forbes,
to be published by Kinord Books in 2014.

Also from Kinord Books:

A Bad Woman by Elinor Hunter

*It takes **a bad woman** to make a bad man*, the saying goes. Though Queen Victoria's affair with John Brown raises barely an eyebrow, it's a different story for her working-class subjects.

In Scotland, Bella and Isa each discover the harsh realities of loss and single parenthood. Like Victoria, the supposed moral compass of the nation, they risk their reputations to survive tragedy and retain their sanity, only their efforts are met with public censure and humiliation.

The fates of all three share uncanny parallels, yet posterity will brand one of them **a bad woman**. But then nothing is ever as it seems ...

www.kinordbooks.com

Printed in Great Britain
by Amazon